OFF WITH THEIR HEADS

ZOE HANA MIKUTA

HYPERION
Los Angeles New York

First Edition, April 2024
1 3 5 7 9 10 8 6 4 2
FAC-004510-24060
Printed in the United States of America

This book is set in Walbaum MT Pro/Monotype
Designed by Zareen Johnson
Stock image: birds 2141171219/Shutterstock

Library of Congress Cataloging-in-Publication Data
Names: Mikuta, Zoe Hana, 2000- author.
Title: Off with their heads/Zoe Hana Mikuta.
Description: First edition. • Los Angeles ; New York : Hyperion, 2024. • Audience: Ages 12-18. • Audience: Grades 7-9. • Summary: Witches and lovers Caro Rabbit and Iccadora Alice Sickle's twisted past comes to light as they are once again thrust into each other's lives and beckoned back to Wonderland, the dark, monster-filled forest where it all began.
Identifiers: LCCN 2023029414 • ISBN 9781368099066 (hardcover) • ISBN 9781368099141 (ebook)
Subjects: CYAC: Witches—Fiction. • Magic—Fiction. • Kings, queens, rulers, etc.—Fiction. • Lesbians—Fiction. • Fantasy. • LCGFT: Lesbian fiction. • Fantasy fiction. • Novels.
Classification: LCC PZ7.1.M5554 Of 2024 • DDC [E]—dc23
LC record available at https://lccn.loc.gov/2023029414

Reinforced binding

Visit www.HyperionTeens.com

Logo Applies to Text Stock Only

For the girls going stranger and stranger…

We grow. It hurts at first.

SYLVIA PLATH, "WITCH BURNING" C. OCTOBER 1961

How much can you change and get away with it, before you turn into someone else, before it's some kind of murder?

RICHARD SIKEN, *WAR OF THE FOXES*,
"PORTRAIT OF FRYDERYK IN SHIFTING LIGHT"

Well, since you're already here, dear readers, past the middle of this sentence, at its frayed end . . .

Humor a faceless narrator for a moment? Suppose, a nasty little fairy tale, and— Oh! Oh! How brave a reader is! Still directly here, again, and again . . . That deserves a treat, a comfort, a familiar start, to start it all off, and so:

ONCE UPON A TIME, in a Saint-stricken world, there were two horrible girls in love. . . .

I

ONE

THERE EXISTS AN OLD CREATION TALE that they tell in the country of Isanghan: a girl asleep in a flower field, who dreams up the world. Carousel and Iccadora always liked this guess at existence especially. Of some sickly little witch they were tucked away in, dreaming up dark things.

Dreaming up them.

Dreaming up Wonderland.

TWO

Year Zero Zero Ninety-Four, Winter Season

There Are 1006 Remaining Saints

"'LIKELY DRAWN TO THE SCENT OF MOURNING, *the Saint Dorma Ouse was seen in the southern district of the Yuhwa Ward, late at night the eighth day of the Winter season. Imprints of bare feet and fingers were discovered pressed into the mud of the river bordering the southern Wall. It should be reasonably believed the Saint has returned to Wonderland.*

"'It was reported that after scaling the cobbles of the forgery wall, the Saint tore back the shutters of the attic room (where only two of the four beds remained occupied following another rampage of saltfever) and rolling head over hips over floor, shot under the bed, where it crouched to await the arrival of the blacksmith Dak Merryweather and his wife, Rana Merryweather, both drawn hastily by the shrieks of their youngest daughter. The Saint then skittered out from beneath the bed, felled and devoured the blacksmith, the blacksmith's wife, and the littlest child, and, taking ahold of the skeletal necks of all three between its teeth, darted backward on hands and feet,

departing out the window from which it had arrived. Eyewitness account was provided by eleven-year-old Ren Merryweather, the only surviving member of the Merryweather family.

"*'It is predicted that the Saint has returned to its nest, and may be distracted for a time with either feeding or necromantic spellwork. Regardless, it is recommended that the river be avoided until such a time it is deemed—'*"

Caro rapped her knuckles on the edge of the bar, pausing the reading. She rose from her seat but stilled a moment to waver in place, then dragged her wrist to the remaining slick of liquor on her lip.

"Should I keep going, noonah?" queried the paperboy, the story wilting over his knuckles.

Caro stared, then clasped the boy as if to shake him, decided against it, and instead dropped a kiss to his brow just to startle him, and took the story from his hand and held it up to the tavern lanterns.

She couldn't read more than a lick, and was momentarily drunk enough to forget that, watching the small mouths of the candle flames breathe faintly behind the dashes of ink for a few seconds before she re-collected herself and crushed up the paper in her hands.

"Yeah, I'll take it," she said, without slurring, she was almost sure. Then she did shake the boy a little, thinking the wideness of his eyes marked disbelief. "Ya, geokjeongma, o-kay? Noonah will take it. Don't worry."

"Take *what*?"

But Caro had already released him and punted out the tavern doors, their handles bundled up in red ribbons to mark the approaching holiday—the Saints' Races. It was pouring rain. Caro ambled on the open street for a few minutes with her hood down, singing and shaking her fist violently at passersby to send them pinging out of her way, eventually kneeling in a gravel puddle to murmur sweet nothings to her chosen gods, and afterward, got up to vomit at the base of the willow tree bowing over the road. A crow, stubbornly indifferent to the downpour, cocked its head from its watching roost.

—

"Take what?" asked the paperboy again, watching the ordeal from the tavern window.

"The head," responded the barkeep.

"The head?"

"Do you know who that was, boy?"

"No, adjeossi."

"Fortunate. That there was Carousel Rabbit."

They watched as Caro gave a sharp salute to the willow tree and then strutted out of sight, chin tilted high, rain slicking her blond locks to her temples.

The paperboy winced. "Who?"

The barkeep leaned over the countertop. The paperboy leaned in, too, sensing a conspiratorial moment.

"Carousel Rabbit," said the barkeep, "takes the heads from Saints."

Then he smacked his large hand down next to the boy's shoulder, and the boy yelped, and the barkeep barked a chuckle, and neither saw the crow outside, interested in Carousel Rabbit as crows tended to be, falling from its perch and circling the road.

—

One of the skeptical ones, thought Caro distantly, as the bird finished examining her and dropped onto her shoulder. She snapped her teeth at it when the talons curled, then threw her head back and laughed.

The sound was barbed; perhaps this was why the bird tried to get away. More likely he saw the magic weeping from her back molars when she opened her mouth.

Either way, Carousel spat on him before he could lift his wings, and then he tried to lift his wings, and he fell apart.

Feathers sloughed. Sinew went slack, unraveled from bone. Caro batted the mess off her shoulder, already bored. Already thinking of Wonderland.

THREE

Year Zero Zero Eighty-Nine, Winter Season

There Are 1104 Remaining Saints

UNDER THE COVER of the gazebo, Carousel Rabbit put a hand under her girlfriend's dress and squinted out into the misted courtyard. It was before first bell and it had rained the night prior, the grass choked under gray mud sloshing against gray stone bordering the lawn. The covered gallery that connected Empathy's two buildings was abandoned, diamond alcoves sticky with frost—Icca's next cutting breath came out in a cloud against the shell of Caro's ear.

She felt a stab of triumph, biting down on the flash of the smile underneath the dip of her hood. *I am so viciously real*, Caro thought to herself, in the dramatic fashion she relished, sought after. Carousel Rabbit and Iccadora Alice Sickle—they were teeming flesh and bone and magic in their pinprick corner of existence, and that corner was fucking boring; it was *paper*, Caro rambled in her head, this world was paper and when some enormous flame came to swallow it up, Caro would burn down nice and slow.

Icca shoved Caro away, wiping her thin, sharp mouth with the back of her hand as the bells began to shriek across the courtyard. They were leaned up in the corner of the gazebo with the least amount of spiders, which was still a lot of spiders, and Icca crushed a sorry arachnid that had gone to chew on her temple under her thumb. She wiped the legs against Caro's skirt, and Caro let her, then caught Icca's wrist when she tried to pull away.

"Ya, ya, Icky. Let's ditch," said Carousel. Icca ignored her, freeing her hand and then ducking under the arm Caro planted across her path, black, silky hair brushing Caro's sleeve.

"Tecca," shot the other witch harshly, as Caro trailed her through the mud and into the gallery, and then left into the south wing. All of Icca's words, so very harsh. Caro wanted to devour each of them down until her throat split from all the barbs.

"She's usually here by now," Caro mused, and tried to run her hand around Icca's waist again. Icca batted her away as their feet moved over the black-bricked floors that shot through Our Blessed Lady of Divine Empathy Parish Academy for Young Ladies. Straggling students hurried soundlessly around them, and Caro scanned them for Tecca's dark brown curls. "Maybe she's already in class, being a good academic...."

A joke. Tecca would cut class with Caro as soon as it was suggested. It was Icca who was such a stickler for the books. Icky Sickle and her books and the way she furrowed her black brows as she read... she deserved a better place than this. She deserved some pretentious academy in some distant, glittering Ward, and Caro deserved to trail her there, trail her everywhere.... Was that all that Caro wanted from her life? She looked around the dim hall, Icca glaring at her from the middle of it. Perhaps. Maybe it was all she could hope for, what with the Saints in Wonderland Forest that would keep her in this Ward for all her life, but Caro thought that she might think, regardless of all of it: perhaps, perhaps...

Caro also thought, one, really, it was quite bold for their school to be such a pretentious mouthful while amounting to absolutely nothing, and two, that she'd rather walk into Wonderland Forest, in search of a louder life than this one, and instantly get gobbled down by a Saint than have to listen to Madam Killington again squawk about geometric runework for the next hour of her existence.

Empathy was the only girls' school in Astara and the surrounding villages clustered within the Mugunghwa Ward, so the class pool consisted of both wisteria farmers' daughters and the orphans from the conservatory just up the dirt road, the latter being, for the sake of putting it simply, from where Icca and Caro hailed. Thus, Icca and Caro hadn't been very far past the one street itself in their sixteen years, except when they visited Tecca Moore's home and her family's orchard.

There, under the sweet wisteria trees, they practiced their little, painful magics; sometimes they tried to find new gods; sometimes they talked of killing the White Queen, Delcorta October Kkul, and the Red Princess, Hattie November Kkul, and taking the throne for themselves. For they were so powerful already, certainly, certainly, the greatest witches of their age.

Caro hummed, snatching Icca's wrist again before the girl could make it around the classroom doorway. She put her lips right to Icca's ear and breathed, "Let's go smoke in the bell tower, Icky. We have much to discuss—royalty's in town, after all. It's high time for an assassination, don'tcha think?"

"Hajima. You are so *irritating*," Icca returned, which made more words than she'd usually utter by this time of day, which meant it was a good day—it was usually noon before she'd open her mouth. *To say something*, Caro added in her head, and chuckled to herself; Icca thought she was being laughed at. She snapped her body away and the words off her tongue, "And you didn't even ask Tecca."

Caro tsked, pouting. "Why are you so sour, Icky? On the *holiday*, too!"

"What holiday?" scoffed Icca bitterly, though they both knew. It'd been in the papers all week—it was that time of year for the Saints' Races again. It was the only time royalty stepped foot outside of the capital, besides for funeral processions for their bloodline, for a tour around the lesser Wards. "There's no holiday."

It would be a particularly brutal day of parties and games at the White Queen's discretion—worse, her imagination. The revelries would be taking place in a larger village on the opposite side of the Mugunghwa Ward; Astara always remained the same. Some traveled to go watch the Saints that Delcorta had brought along with her go through the trials she'd designed for the day—Caro peeked into the classroom and saw a handful of empty desks. Lucky little girls, off to watch the carnage.

Kat Pillar—that was the Saint slated for the day's festivities, according to the papers. The White Queen's caravan had probably arrived in the Ward in the wee hours of the morning—she'd be gone before the next, leaving the ground stained. Was it just a rumor, that she sometimes enjoyed selecting certain people in the crowd to race the Saints? The contenders were only supposed to be reaped from the criminal population, but everyone had heard the stories. How Delcorta would allow the contestants to live, or leave them to die, depending on her mood. How Hattie, the blank-faced Princess, would fold and unfold her hands on her hanbok skirts, never once flinching when the blood started to spray. And every year when the Saints' Races were happening and people tied white ribbons to their front doors to show their support—after all, the Queen would always slay the Saint at the end of the game, reducing the overall count—Caro and Icca and Tecca would talk of putting an end to all of it. An end to royalty. An end to all the fun. People shouldn't be scared of the Queen. They should only be scared of them.

Was it all talk? Well, well. The important thing was passing the time. . . .

Caro sulked into the classroom after Icca and deposited herself in the seat behind her, next to the window painting the hills piss yellow with its warbled glass. It seemed impossible that the light managed to claw inside at all, gray streaks cutting across the desk surfaces and scrubbing away color. Caro threw a look around the half-empty room of bored students and waited for Killington to turn to the board before leaning to hiss into the back of Icca's head, "Tec's not even here."

She was probably already up in the bell tower, feet kicked up on their usual perch, shoving back the bricks where Caro had stashed their contraband and the matchbook.

Icca tilted her chin on her hand, her soft, wide nose sloping into her knuckles as she glanced back at the empty seat at the end of the desk row. Normally it went Icca-Caro-Tecca; *Shut up and let me focus*, *Let's leave immediately and never return*, *Let's burn down the building first*, respectively.

Such was the common tone of the trio's conversations, these glorious, brutal musings. It made Caro feel wicked and grand for it, and, after the best of them, vaguely nauseous. She knew Icca felt some similar way, as after classes, when they wandered back to the orphanage with their own words and dreams stuck in their stomachs like pins, they could hardly stay for very long before they were pushing out the windows of the sleeping room—reminding the other orphans of the usual consequences should any of them squeal—climbing out, away, dashing toward Tecca's home.

One night in particular, as Caro and Icca ran back and found Tecca with her hip checked against the front gate at the border of her family's farm, awaiting them, she greeted them with her brash smile and stated firmly, "The moon is as fat and round and pale as a wedding cake, and thus I believe we should all get married. What say you, darlings?"

"I say," Caro said, snatching one of Tecca's hands, and, flashing her own rictus grin, regardless of the fact that there was never a moon to be seen past the thick of the clouds, declared, "I do, darling."

But Icca drew her skinny arms around herself and glared at them. "We've no rings."

"My, you do love to be spoiled," cooed Tecca, and both she and Caro closed around Icca. One of their hands in her black hair, one poking at her ribs; it was strange, how Caro often couldn't differentiate herself from

Tecca, but this could be because she never cared to. Icca batted out of the loops of their arms, claiming the fence post Tecca'd been leaning against with her spine.

Caro watched the shadows briefly bend toward Icca's feet, before they remembered themselves and straightened back.

"What's got you in a mood?" Caro queried, stamping her feet against the bottom post to lift herself from the ground. She watched Tecca swirl a lock of her brown hair around her forefinger as she touched the toes of her boots against Icca's.

"Yes, Alice," Tecca said, those sharp brown eyes slicing through Icca. "Or is it cold feet? You're breaking our hearts."

"Black, black hearts," chattered Caro.

Icca spat, "I don't want it just in my head."

Above them, the sky and the clouds and the rays that surely bled from the wedding-cake moon were blotted out by the quiet movement of the wisteria branches, their sticky-sweet perfume already stuck in every thread of Caro's clothes. For Tecca, it was always in her hair, too.

"What's the matter with that?" Caro asked sincerely. She scrubbed a knuckle at her temple. Weren't they in each other's heads anyway?

"Are we so easy to forget, Alice?" Tecca laughed, putting her chin on the top of Icca's head—she was by far the tallest of the three. "Worried you'll wake up and it'll all have been a dream? That's okay. Here. I thought you'd say something like this. Give me your hand. I brought a knife."

The older they grew in this nothing Ward, the more the three of them believed they would find nothing of themselves in other people, and only in each other. Because of this diagnosis, they would be doomed to rot if they were ever separated. They would wither and, without the other two as mirrors, they would forget themselves, and be ridiculous, clueless beings; they would misplace being wicked, and alive for it; their magic would dry up in their veins and be useless.

And to be known by other people! *Other* people? No, no, it would never work. Caro knew she'd just end up destroying them.

She was possessed of sharp bits, of something dark and restless she could feel sitting in her chest, primed to explode all over the world like shrapnel, if she could ever get out of this place. Icca and Tecca saw it in her; they did not flinch away, and instead were fascinated, and Caro saw it in them, too, the little jagged bombs hung up in their ribs like mistletoe, and often had the thought that if one of them went off, so must the other two, a chain reaction. So, maybe someday . . .

An affectionate narrator would be doing a grave injustice to act as if these girls did not have a hearty sadism set fast in their pretty little heads, which they hid lazily under a false guise of masochism—their affinity for the agony that came with doing their natural magic did separate them from most of the population, certainly from their peers.

In earlier years, they would even have been called Saints: a term for people who had practiced and honed their magic—even though it corroded them, even though it was painful—to fight off the swarms of fanatics during the plague raids. But Caro and Icca and Tecca had grown up in an era where Saints weren't the righteous any longer; they were the deformed, starved beasts that skittered around in the Wonderland Forest past the Wall. Hardly anyone used their natural-born abilities—the world ate at them enough as it was.

The fact that the trio did indulge in their powers ostracized them, and on this Carousel often thought—what luck! Everyone else should just stay far away and not ever think of bothering them.

—

"Miss Rabbit," came a voice like a whip from the front of the classroom, and both girls straightened in their seats. Killington was staring down Caro with flaming eyes. "Remove your hood."

"Sorry, seonsaengnim," Caro said, mumbling both apology and honorific, and dusted her cloak off her shoulders and onto the back of her seat.

She scrubbed at the blond curls on her crown and looked up at the lesson. Holy shit. She had no clue what was going on.

But it didn't really matter. The only good university was in the Petra Ward, miles outside the Mugunghwa Ward Wall. Caro could forget shucking it through Wonderland to make the entrance exams—going on foot meant Saints, or Jabberwockies, so that wasn't an option, and she'd never make enough to pay for passage on an armored caravan. Graduating—if she graduated—didn't mean anything; she was just going to end up some farmhand in some patch drying up inside the same Wall that she saw licking the landscape outside her window every night; didn't matter much that she was getting better at the bird-magic stuff every day.

Didn't matter, and so Caro didn't really care.

Icca and Tecca were stuck here, too.

With her.

Caro often mused that if she were rich—or if she were a more powerful witch, one who could do more than mess around in the orphanage basement, magic webbing her fingertips in sickly, auroral strands as she wove some shitty enchantment over the crow she'd stoned off the fence posts—she would be quite a cruel girl.

Caro tugged at her ring finger, thumbing the thin scar that encircled it. Icca and Tecca wore the same. They weren't just married. They were bound by blood, by pain.

Caro snapped her head up at the screech of a chair against the bricks.

Icca was standing, hands braced on her desk. Her fine eyes narrowed as they focused on something out the glass.

"*Iccadora Alice Sickle,*" Killington shrieked. "What do you—"

It should've irked Caro—Tecca was the only one who was allowed to call Icca *Alice* out loud—but she didn't hear the rest. She was seeing what Icca was looking at, and then Caro was standing, too. Icca took her wrist; it surprised Caro, and she was lucky for it, because she sucked in a breath before Icca stepped forward into the shadows slanting under the wire windowsill, and then they were nothing and nowhere at all.

And then they were outside. Stepping out from the dark spots strained from the foliage of the garbled willow that bowed over Empathy's gallery, and they were running up the road and toward the smoke curling from the Moores' farm.

It was raining ash and wisteria petals, which were still burning around their silken edges as they streaked the wind. Icca paused them a few dozen paces away from the mouth of the burning grove, and Caro was thinking *Not Tecca, not Tecca* as she looked into those lively, gasping flames, and then up, at the black body of a crow circling far above.

Magic welled in her eyes, the work excessively rich, hot, electric sap that webbed her eyelashes together but then it wasn't anything at all—she blinked in the bright fluid and blew the enchantment outward, and upward, and then she had snatched the crow's form as her own.

She didn't know how to fly, of course, so then she was barreling wings-over-talons toward the ignited ground, taking in everything she could before she hit the flames, and burned alive.

Carousel jerked back into her body, which had collapsed on the dirt and was being mercilessly joggled by Icca's grip. The other witch was kneeling beside Caro, her teeth clenched and stained silver from her own magic. Caro shoved her away and vomited on the ashen road. Heaving, she scraped the gummy mess of the magic from her eyes, and it stung where it met the back of her knuckles.

"I saw someone in the house," Caro rasped out of the bile between her teeth, and coughed as she sucked down smoke. "Someone moving—"

Icca wrenched Carousel to her feet. "Tecca?"

"Don't know..."

Icca squinted down the orchard lane again. Countless afternoons had been spent between the wisteria trunks, the perpetual gray light of the perpetually pathetic weather softened by the lavender canopy, Tecca Moore down in the roots enchanting the mice to eat one another as Icca and Caro watched, revulsion and fascination twined in their guts.

"I don't know if I can," moaned Caro, poisoned with her own magic—she'd brought it on too fast, sick in the excess of it. A headache pulsed in her temples in staccato flashes of fever, vision spasming. It was a hundred times worse than the worst hangover she'd ever had. *Just end me,* she prayed sloppily, as her stomach twitched around its acrid hollowness. *Refracted gods— Oh my gods justendme.* "Icca, I don't think I can—"

"Carousel Rabbit," hissed Icca, with her gloves wrapping in Caro's cloak. Her eyes singed Caro's, glittering from the burn of the air. There was a lot in that stare. A lot of afternoons leeching into cold dusks and the three of them talking about the worst kinds of things: horrible, delicious kinds of things, like Sainthood, like death.

And none of them ever said it aloud, but it was there in their clasped fingertips, the hush and awe at the laughs they shot at one another. *I can't imagine a world without you in it.*

So when we die—let's do it together.

I'll kill you if we don't go together.

Caro drew in another pinched breath, and shoved it all back. "The kitchen," she gritted out. "No fire yet."

Icca's grip tightened on Caro.

Then she fell back, spine barreling toward the road and Caro barreling toward Icca, into the flickering press of their own shadows drawn faintly against the dirt.

FOUR

Year Zero Zero Ninety-Four, Winter Season

There Are 1006 Remaining Saints

CROUCHED IN THE WONDERLAND MUD, Carousel put a hand on the back of a crow's sleek neck and squinted out over the misted river. Her hood hid the light of the magic bubbling in her eyes; it dripped in blue beads off her chin, streaking out thinner and thinner in the water as it left her behind. Intently, she stared at the waterfall that slid over the stone quarry of the opposite shore, as if divining arcane truths from its froth.

Caro was not. Caro was hunting.

She pinched the back of the crow's neck, then dropped her chin further and spat on it; it didn't like it, the Birds never liked it, black feathers rising as it twisted to bite off her thumb, which was a mistake—Carousel met its eyes, and then they were her eyes, and she lifted her wings and flew off into the direction of the waterfall. To be exact, the cavern spiraling behind it.

Caro prayed as she drifted. She did not ask her gods to watch over her, to protect her. She asked for power.

She always asked for power.

The gods in her head were, of course, disparate from the gods in other people's heads. Now, in Religion, there were stories, not scripture choking out paths of morality like there had been in the Pallid Ages—the question that guided Religion was: Where, and in what, did one, as an individual knot of consciousness, feel the gods here?

All of them—people, Caro, history—had always been trying to guess at Divinity. In this moment in time, most of them—at least in Isanghan—acknowledged Divinity as the whole tableau of reality, but common practice was to select particular elements as personal gods, to play favorites—picking threads out of the fabric, so to speak. The gods were nature, the night sky and the winter season and wildfires, and rot. The gods were forces, love and cruelty and dreams—but Caro found that people were forces, too, and thought, perhaps like a heretic, that she had seen Divinity worn into the edges of those she had attached a fondness to, and that these gods were so much more startling than all the others because, simply, they were close.

There weren't exact names for the pieces of Divinity Caro had found in the twenty-one years she'd been alive, except maybe Cold, or Mist, or Birds, or Dawn—with its rose-frayed stare, there, always, after Caro was certain she wouldn't live through the night—these were what Carousel prayed to when she did pray, how she termed her deities in her head.

Maybe, at some point or other—but a long time ago, oh, too long ago for it to mean anything now, actually, certainly—smudged, maybe between Cold and Birds, there had been Icca.

And it wasn't until after Icca, perhaps even the very first moment after Icca, that Carousel remembered. She didn't know how she could have misplaced the truth of the world within which she'd been born.

Divinity was not only dangerous—it was hungry.

Why, just look at the state of the Saints (Caro always found this funny, that when old King Min Titus Kkul, the Red Queen's great-uncle, infused the Saints' magic with his own to stop the plague raids, he'd brushed whatever nasty spell that'd been with the intention of Isanghan's *protection.* The particularities of how exactly the King had created his spell remained a mystery, a secret of the bloodline, perhaps to stave off embarrassment or unsavory association—but clearly, Caro knew, he'd done a truly shitty job of it. The spell *had* worked, technically—the bolstered Saints had wholly vanquished the plague raiders' numbers—and some crueler, cleverer souls would argue that it was still working, even after the initial improvement the Saints' magic turned them into starved abominations after a handful of weeks. The King's intention still teemed within them, but the raiders were all dead and gone, and the Saints' own minds went with them, leaving them instead with the sole purpose of purging all the morose traits of humanity: grief and blood and anger and guilt and fear, all things they could smell as easily as a pie set to cool on a windowsill. But none they could sniff out so easily as a death trace, which was not an emotion, but an aura that attached to one's self upon committing a murder. And perhaps that also turned out for the best—after all, murderers would be sent out into Wonderland Forest to either butcher or sate the Saints, thus providing the Wards with some semblance of protection both from the beasts and from the killers, who deserved it, after all, even if they were small, terrified girls who hadn't truly meant it, and vowed one day to make everyone regret it, if they did indeed survive.)!

What had Caro been going on and on about in her head? If she still had fingers she'd strike them against her temples. Ah, yes. She'd been thinking about being devoured by the thing that made her feel the most herself.

Look how her magic—just a droplet of Divinity—still sought to corrode its vessel. Look at Icca—no, actually, don't look at Icca, Carousel snapped at herself. Look *here.* What was that, scuttling around in the dark throat of the expanse sheathed behind the sheet of the water? Was it possibly the Saint, on all fours in the teeth of the dripping stalactites, still biting the necks of the Merryweathers, scuttling around with the family's skeletal ankles clacking on the stone floor? Yes, Carousel mused. That was exactly what it was.

She coasted close to the drop, folded her wings, and dropped onto the slick stone alongside the waterfall's sheet edge. She tottered along its length and peered into the cavern, noted the Saint—who some had called Killian Tuttle, but who Caro currently called *very ugly*—skillfully disassembling the skeletons, lining up upon the floor a line of ribs here, a twisting path of finger bones there. From the Saint's cuticles, its black magic wept, smearing the white of the bones it had so precisely set.

It was calling upon something. Or maybe it was just decorating—Carousel didn't like to assume. She'd seen a Saint planting a garden once; Carousel would've thought it just a young girl, if it hadn't been in the middle of Wonderland Forest, if she hadn't looked closer and realized it was burying teeth instead of seeds, and, of course, if the Saint hadn't then caught her scent and dove down into the earth as if through a pond surface.

What she *could* assume about Saints without the fear of being a pompous ass when doing so was that, eventually, they would go along and try to eat someone. That and, of course—now having long claimed four heads and thus clearing her life sentence—her being paid for their heads by Hattie November Kkul, the young Red Queen of Isanghan, her dearest unnie.

Caro coughed back into her own body, grinning when she had teeth again, and tangled her fingers as she stood. Hell *yes;* Carousel loved this job, because Carousel loved *money.* She loved *things*, especially if they were shiny, or if they had some weight to them—metal rings, boots with good, thick soles and bronze buckles, sweaters stripped from entire lambs, cloaks and hoods that pressed her into the mud. And she loved her apartment in the Petra Ward, when she was there, and the iron balcony that looked out over the sleek spires of the Petra University campus. It was all so distant from the orphanage in Astara she'd been left at as an infant, owning nothing but the clothes on her body. Imagine how much prouder she could've been, growing up with tons of glittery stuff! Even the pathetic little knives that had been provided to her and Icca when they'd been sentenced to Wonderland had worn some glint of excitement into Caro's heart.

"Now," she whispered, the word wetted by the glow of the magic bubbling from her mouth, and threw back her head and thus her hood, her tangle of blond hair scraping the river bush curling around her. Caro had painted the lids of her eyes black, lined their fine edges, and shot the lashes through in red—she did like to decorate herself on hunting days—and under these black lids and through this sticky crimson thicket she peered down the riverside, and she felt the magic in her young, young veins sing. She was twenty-one years old, and her power still stung—but pain was like everything else. It was something she could best. "Now is such a good night."

FIVE

YEAR ZERO ZERO EIGHTY-NINE, WINTER SEASON

THERE ARE 1104 REMAINING SAINTS

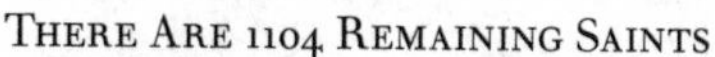

ALWAYS CAROUSEL AND ICCADORA. Icca liked it in her head, like that. Always Iccadora and Carousel . . .

Wiry limbs and sharp teeth, pinning themselves to the corners, they were bored of, and so ignoring, the orphan girls with whom they shared their space. The others were nice enough, but neither of the two ever really cared about niceness very much—it seemed such a flimsy trait. Both their parents gone from the same outbreak of saltfever, both six and small on the conservatory's doorstep the night after the pyres were set. They made themselves distant from all except for the other, and thus, made themselves strange.

It was only when they'd discovered Tecca Moore after they'd begun classes at Empathy that two became three, and three began to want more from their lives, from themselves. Soon they'd be in their beds after long days together, aching and shuddering after practicing their magic, bright with grins they could not press down even if they'd wished to. How silly it was, that all their classmates and all the people of all the Wards were so frightened of the pain that magic brought to its users—it seemed like pain for power was such an effortless bargain.

Under the shrouded winter sun, the light wasn't good, which meant the shadows weren't good, and thick, and then they were nowhere again, but this time the nowhere felt like the edge of suffocation, and Icca was dragging Caro through it.

They came out of the shade of the iron stove, shoved up against one another in the corner of the Moore kitchen alongside the angle of the morning glow.

Icca shoved Caro away. She was always shoving Caro away, as much as she was always pulling her closer, but it was in the shoving that Icca felt she had more of a grip on herself; her hands were moving of her accord and not on their own, drunk and distant with need.

The kitchen was empty and flushed with heat. Outside the windows, the normally lavender-colored limbs of the orchard were naked and thinning under gold-and-red flames. Smoke pinched at Icca's eyes, and she yanked her collar over her nose; it didn't help that the nausea shot through her gut from the darkporting. Caro was looking downright green under her black hood, the black roots radiating to pale yellow curls that pasted to the sweat on her temples.

The kitchen was empty save for them, save for the wooden mug tipped delicately over on the floorboards, coffee welling in the cracks.

And the blood.

And the blood pooling on the countertop. And the blood all over the forget-me-not wallpaper, blue flowers dripping in the flush of the smoke. And the blood already on the soles of their boots, the drag of their cloaks, and then, suddenly, on Carousel's sallow cheek.

Caro reached up a thin, long finger, and when she did, something warm plopped onto Icca's brow.

Icca had been mistaken. It wasn't blood on Caro's face, now on hers. Caro pulled away her touch and the droplet came along with her, the bead of softened flesh thinning, thinning, splitting, Caro's hands on Icca's shoulders, now, leaning, mouth twisted small and black eyes grotesquely splayed open, and the message was clear: *Ohmygodsdonotdonotdonotlookup.*

They looked up.

Icca heaved.

She had skipped the orphanage's breakfast rolls that morning, so what came splattering out of her mouth and onto Caro's front was clear and stinging.

Caro didn't even notice, white throat spilling up to her still-lifted chin—*How is she still looking?*—and Icca mirrored her. Icca looked again.

Skin wove across the high rafters of the Moore kitchen. Veins shone purple and blue from the press of the skylight hovering somewhere above; the weight of bones with their imprints easing toward the floorboards, still trapped in their sinews despite their new stretch. Above the central breakfast table, the fingers of a rib cage reached out of the thin, pale veil, the nubs of a spine spanning from it in a straight path, but dotted few and far between. Where the mess met rafter and wall it had been heated into a kind of glue as to hold itself in place, trickling downward—Icca couldn't believe that she hadn't been able to smell it past the smoke. Now she did. Now she couldn't stop.

"Icca," breathed Caro quietly. Carousel had never done anything quietly, and so it scared Icca, and she was already so scared that she nearly heaved again from the sound of her name alone. "It's a nest."

Saints weren't supposed to make it over the Walls.

Except when they were invited in.

Except when it was the holiday.

It could be no one else. Icca could barely breathe. "It's Kat Pillar."

Kat Pillar.

The Saint who was supposed to be on the other side of the Ward, entertaining the masses. Under the control of the White Queen.

Icca saw it then. She saw Caro saying they should run, and she saw herself saying yes, and then both of them living out the rest of their bleak lives hating themselves for it. She'd die at some blessed point and the moment before she did, Icca would think of now, of the flesh staining her cheek and the cowardice in her chest and Tecca, and leaving Tecca, because the unfolded form above their heads was not Tecca but Tecca's mother, because there was her weathered face grinning down somewhere past the rib cage.

And still Icca begged Caro, silently, in her thoughts, *Say we should run.*

Iccadora Alice Sickle was so, so scared. She would live a whole life of guilt, of self-hatred if it meant she could leave now, would do anything to crawl under the threadbare covers of her lumpy bed and pretend she wasn't a haunted thing.

Anything but say it aloud. She couldn't say it aloud.

She couldn't do that to Tecca.

And neither could Caro. Which meant when Caro spoke, it was only to say "Watch how you step."

Going quietly, quietly. The both of them moving across the blood, under the unwound Hanna Moore and into the dining room, which was empty, and into the hall, which was filled with Tecca's twin brothers, who before their unwinding had been small enough to tuck themselves under Icca's cloak at the same time. There was less smoke here, so it was here that Icca and Caro stopped to breathe. They filled their lungs, under the twins, tangled in their startling lengths around the hanging candleholders.

Eventually they moved for the staircase, which was spilling forth footfalls and a rhythmic, wet thudding.

Icca was a step above Caro, so they glimpsed the floor of the second story at relatively the same time, and at the moment they did, the Saint came out of one of the bedroom doorways at the far end of the hall.

They froze.

Saint Katarina Pillar was on five of its six pairs of hands and the pads of its feet, all seventy digits slick and crimson. It was naked, unnaturally tall, and lacking of fat, save for the indulgent bulb of its stomach. Every crook of bone tilled its gray flesh, and where the tips of its ribs met skin they tore through to the surface, and around these eruptions the Saint was weeping magic instead of blood. It was black and viscous—the Saint was over a century old, and even if Pillar wasn't dead its magic should have been by now, should have dried up like a wildflower fried in the sun.

In its frontmost pairs of hands hung Tecca.

Her head was hanging limp off her neck, her toes just barely gracing the carpet, carpet slowly staining with the blood dripping from an unseen wound beneath her chestnut curls.

Icca was hit with a sensation alike to her ribs being whittled, and opened her mouth to scream.

Caro lunged forward and muffled her with the palm of one hand, pressing her own silent sob flush against Icca's spine.

Beneath Caro's palm, Icca's lips moved. Her own magic filled the lines between her teeth, a drop of silver breaking at the corner of her mouth, and when the Saint looked straight at them, it didn't see them at all. Icca had taken Caro's hand and pulled the slant of the staircase's shadows around them both.

But that was it. Darkporting, this flimsy trick—that was everything she knew how to do. She couldn't even move without the enchantment sloughing off of her. They watched, frozen, as the Saint wandered into the bedroom closest to them, Tecca's bedroom, and the thud they heard next must have been Tecca dropping from its hands, because a moment later it wandered back out without her.

Pillar had a plain, slack face. It stayed unrememberable and unexpressive as it looked down to its ribs, multiple palms tracing against the dripping magic. Good gods—there were so many Saints left, too many to remember properly, except for the most horrific, like the one feet away, and the stories bubbled up in Icca's memories without consent. Katarina's magic had been elemental; a witch of the flames, she'd saved so many people in the plague raids. And now, it unspooled those people like thread, wove them into nests hot and bright. Pillar ambled in a twitching, insect way as it sidled up to the walls, drawing up runes that immediately began to smoke; it put its face to each, inhaling deeply, sunken brown eyes fluttering at each polluted breath, though it seemed a mere physical response, habit instead of pleasure.

It took ages before the Saint was out of sight, up the hall, and by then the wallpaper had ignited around the first handful of runes.

Then Icca was sick with her power. Her entire body went hot, then cold, and her vision blinked out. She came through choking on the magic clogging her throat, muffled by Caro's hand as she held her on the stairs. Her girlfriend was crying, shoulders shaking in horrific jolts, and Icca's first conscious thought was of her awe at Caro's complete silence. Dazed, she reached up, touched the high curve of Caro's cheekbone.

Caro tilted her face into Icca's touch, and Icca saw that, above, past the shell of Caro's ear, the Saint was on the staircase ceiling.

Spine rippling, its head was lolled back with eyes dropping wide, jaw unhinged past the point it should've been possible. Its twelve hands loosened on the rafters, and then it was falling, twisting for them in a mass of gray limbs, and again, again, and Icca screamed, and Icca shoved Caro into the shadows.

The darkport had them tumbling out from underneath Tecca's bed, drawn from memory upon giddy memory layered in Icca's mind.

Icca hit something soft, and Caro hit her right afterward. Her veins were burned with her magic; it was far from exhausted—no, it was excited and primed now, silver frothing from her mouth. Icca spat, breathed in smoke. The room was spinning, the four-post bed slipping up the periwinkle print of the wallpaper, the window of the reading-nook overlooking the orchard peppered with the books on the floor.

Caro shrieked.

She folded over Icca's stomach, hands grappling. The softness at Icca's left shoulder peeled away.

Icca turned her head, cheek to the room's hideous rug, and met Tecca's black, blank eyes.

"No," Icca moaned, as Caro's form broke over her ribs, *"nononono—"*

Tecca was gone. Her crown swollen and split, she was covered in her own blood, wet and warm under Icca's cheek. Now Caro was crawling over her, trying to reach Tecca, and Icca sat up to drag her away, to keep her still and quiet, but her own sobs were their own entities up her throat. Where was the shock? Where was the numbness, that sweet natural drug that was supposed to be in her head right now? She was feeling everything in full, and everything was too much, the grief and the guilt and the nausea and the *anger*, the anger was feeding her magic and she was drowning in it, silver bubbling out her lips and now slashed moonlike across Caro's hair.

"We have to go," Icca sobbed. Even though the next darkport might kill her—she wouldn't even care. "Please—*Caro*—we have to *go*."

But Caro had gone still, eyes huge and snapped to the doorway. It was then that Icca felt the Saint staring at the nape of her neck.

And it was because Icca was so completely petrified that she kept her gaze forward, and why she saw the first crow hit the window.

Its black body screamed out of the smoke, headfirst against the windowpane and crumpling for it with a cut squawk, deflecting lifelessly into flames below. It left a spiderweb crack across the glass that Icca thought, with a strange clarity, so entirely delicate . . . and then the next crow came and obliterated it.

The bird hit Icca's leg, embedded with, and soon dead from, the window shards it carried in. It didn't matter; it was one and suddenly it seemed there were hundreds, flooding in from the breach in a mass of black feathers and talons, and it was only then that Icca flinched, looked back to see Pillar reeling onto its legs to strike, to see the first crow hit its weeping chest.

Then Caro was doubled over Icca, body thrown over her own and the blue sap of her magic hot across Icca's skin, and everywhere, everywhere there were the crows and their cruel edges. It was the loudest moment of Icca's life, all three of them being shredded; desperately she dug for the memory of the gazebo, a mere half hour ago, the deadening hush of the courtyard mist, the drip of rainwater sliding off the gutters.

It didn't help. Icca was here, being torn at, about to be killed.

Icca reached out. Talons ricocheted past her outstretched arm as she searched for Tecca's small, cold hand beneath the feathers. Found it, slick with new cuts, held it tight. At least they were together. At least they were all going out together.

Almost.

The anger doubled in her, doubled again, and just kept going.

Icca felt dark. No—she was feeling darkness, odd, quiet spots she could sense but not see, but they were there, and they were everywhere. Where were they? In the middle of the morning, even? Almost slick, these pockets of dark...

Icca focused. Leaned for the source of these dark spots—in Caro, and in each of her crows, in Icca herself. Inside Pillar. And it was then she knew where such strange, warm shades existed. Cradled within internal organs.

Icca groaned to Caro, "Move the fucking birds."

She wrenched her head back as Caro drew her hands wide, splattering magic across the both of them, and Icca saw the gray stretch of the Saint's long torso flash into view amidst the thicket of crows. And Icca knew. Under that pale, sickly skin, Pillar's body cavity was clotted with dark. And here was an unnamed god, a new god, leaning forward with sick fascination, waiting to see if she knew what to do with it.

She did. Or maybe she didn't, but Iccadora was angry, and she just *moved*, latched enchantment to darkness to herself and *pulled.*

Something happened. What that something was, Icca wouldn't understand for a few years' time, but when she did—*oh*—but perhaps that was beside the point, because Icca at least saw what she had done, even if she didn't quite know how she did it. She saw the darkness blow out of the Saint, saw the shadows bloom from Pillar's very pores. The dark seemed to cauterize when it hit air, when it hit light, and the line of the burn was against the Saint's skin and the Saint was *writhing.* Black magic sputtered out of its chest and mouth, igniting whatever it landed upon, wall and floorboard and crow and Icca coughed, spasming within the power flooding from her form. She felt a sharp, startling ache in her mouth, gagged on something, and spat onto the rug.

The small lump of a tooth, no, two teeth—two of her left bottom molars—rose from the wad of silver spittle.

Icca, her weight on one elbow and Carousel's weight still pressed over her, lifted her head toward Pillar. The doorway was crowding with flames, with feathers, and she couldn't breathe past the smoke, could barely see past its sting in her eyes, but still she *stared*, met the glazed gaze of the crumped Saint with its internal darkness still corroding it down, down, down into the floorboards. Her magic bit into the raw flesh of her mouth; Icca flicked her tongue against the blood welling in her open tooth beds and she *grinned*.

"You are so sick in the head," breathed Carousel roughly, magic running down her cheeks, out of her nostrils. She leaned, her pale hair silver in the smoke, grabbed Tecca's wrist, and pulled her toward the both of them.

Icca smoothed Tecca's dark hair away from her temple. Caro's brow kissed the bottom of Tecca's ribs, and Icca's met Tecca's cheekbone. It seemed that, as one, the two living girls breathed in. Smoke filled them up; neither of them could feel it.

Icca took both of their hands, and took them away from that horrid, drenched place. They spilled out on the dry grasses clotted in the shadow of the neighboring farm's fence; there, the three of them had carved up obscenities and runes and their names across its creaky length. Icca was on her spine in the bone-dry thistles, staring up at the gray sky and the fence post, seeming to hold it up. It read as follows:

Carousel Rabbit + Retecca Rose Moore + Iccadora Alice Sickle say Fuck the Saints.

SIX

YEAR ZERO ZERO TWENTY-TWO, WHAT SOME WOULD CALL THE END SEASON, THOUGH WE KNOW, NOW HAVING WITNESSED OUR VICIOUS LITTLE CHAMPIONS CLOTTED WITH THEIR GRIEF IN A DISTANT WINTER, IT WAS NOT LUCKY ENOUGH TO BE SO

THERE ARE 1390 REMAINING SAINTS

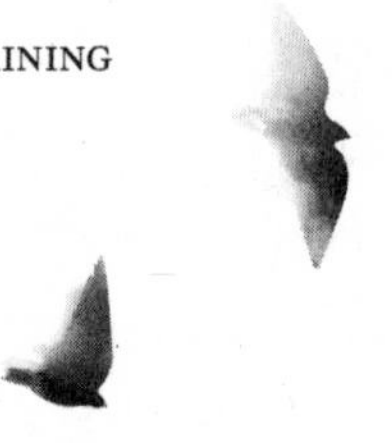

ONCE UPON A TIME—what is history but another tale, cherished readers?—at the end, there were four remaining entries, which a narrator posits with the hope that there might be found an ounce of comfort, that the world was not always like this; or, at least, was always like this, if one does find comfort in familiarity . . . yes, then, the world really was always so horrible, with its horrible human insistence, such monstrous efforts to hate and save and best each other:

On this the fourth day of Their Spring season, as deemed by Their humble servant the Church of Petra, the numbeur of living Saints, persons Divinely goode though wholly of human flesh, becomes Nine Hundred Sixty-Four, following the unction of Sainthood upon one Hilde Woodfast for Her actions of Holy caliber in plague raids of the Lojeumali Quarter.

Petra Saint Ledger, transcribed by Cardinal Oh
in Their Blissed Year Zero Zero Four

On this the twenty-first day of Their Autumnal season, as deemed by Their humble servant the Church of Petra, the plague raids are of an upfront, insistent travesty, at a gross assault of the benevolence and morality They desire for this mortal realm.

The end times are nigh.

Petra Saint Ledger, transcribed by Cardinal Oh
in Their Blissed Year Zero Zero Twenty-Two

On this, the first day of Their Winter season, as deemed by Their humble servant the Church of Petra, as to protect the earthly plane and following much deliberation of the Council of Petra and Their loyal warden, the King Min Titus Kkul, the rare ones deemed as Saints shall be bestowed with Their ancient powers, abilities of incomprehensible extent, to cherish and to wield as light and sword in these darkest of times.

By Their allowance of the distribution of Their most divine grace, we are saved by Their hand through this Army of Saints which will be our true salvation.

Petra Saint Ledger, transcribed by Cardinal Oh
in Their Blissed Year Zero Zero Twenty-Two

We fucked up! 우리는 좆됐다!

Petra Saint Ledger, transcribed by Cedar Kim, chimneysweep of Petra Cathedral,
in Their Blissed Year in Which They the Gods Certainly Mean to End Us All

SEVEN

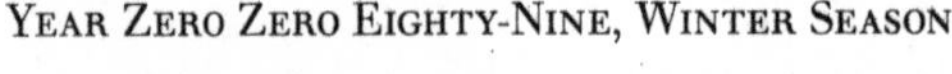

YEAR ZERO ZERO EIGHTY-NINE, WINTER SEASON

THERE ARE 1103 REMAINING SAINTS

BUT RETURNING, DEAR READERS. This was how the three young witches would be found, after the killing of Saint Pillar: down in the mud, slick with magic, and still—oh, so very still, once Icca curled into Caro's side, once Caro had reached her hand out to pull Tecca toward them both.

The ones who found them took Tecca away. But the day had sickened the two witches so much that they could only whimper as she was drawn away from them, and then could do nothing at all as they were collected into a wood cart, as the cart bumped beneath them up the dirt road toward the center of Astara.

"Icca," whispered Caro, when she could. "What's happening?"

Icca did not speak. Her grief was gray under the silver streaking her face, her tears bleeding magic onto the cart bed. Caro felt a hollowness set in her chest cavity, yet it was still heavy, so heavy.

Above, the sky had melted into the near-white fleece that marked the midday. Soon it was sheared down by the press of the cobblestone buildings huddled around Astara's market district. There were exactly five, four stout and square and huddled catercorner to a square plaza, with the church sitting on at their west, simple towers backdropped by a few colorless fields and then the rise of the Mugunghwa Ward Wall.

The Wall that was supposed to protect them from Wonderland. The Wall that was supposed to keep the Saints out. But of course its gates would always open lovingly for their White Queen, every year on her holiday. No matter what monsters she desired to trail along behind her.

How had Pillar escaped? Images rose in Caro's mind. A jeering, provoking crowd, wrists flashing the silk of white ribbons. Delcorta October Kkul's elegant neck, tipped back in her laughter. Attention frayed in her ecstasy, enough for the beast to skitter free of her influence. Perhaps the blank eyes of the Red Princess, calmly watching it go. Were they en route, to track Pillar down? Caro thought of the royal procession moving over the dusty roads of Astara and her body jerked. A bitter, silent twitching that was almost laughter.

Caro no longer felt hollow. She felt her anger as barbs, and they filled her up like her ribs were the edges of a bramble thicket and Caro *breathed,* breathed them in to feel them twist, to feel herself feeding them.

The cart stopped under the two huddled towers marking the front of Astara's church, *Mugunghwa* etched into the stone of their spires to mark the Ward: 무궁화.

Caro realized that she had regained enough physical function to sit up, and did, and looked back on Icca. She looked so tiny in the bed of the cart, and wholly unreal, all her crooks outlined in silver. *Alice*, Caro wanted to say, but—what on earth could she say next?

So she got off the cart and said nothing at all.

Icca was up, slowly, behind her when she reached the doors. The cart's driver, the Moores' neighbor and the one who'd found them, a lavender farmer named Ren Hunters, watched them go. Caro knew that he was watching to see if they would run, and that he'd pursue if they did; she knew that it didn't make any sense. They hadn't done anything wrong.

She saw that Icca noticed it too, a tic setting in her jaw, but she didn't stare at him like Caro was doing. Instead she knocked a rough hand against Caro's hip, urging her forward into the cool shadows of the church.

They stopped, when they saw, which was only a few steps in. They saw those dark pews and the path between them, like a cracked rib cage, and Tecca laid out on the wood dais at the end of that path, like a raw spot scrubbed onto Carousel's soul. She watched Tecca's beautiful hand, translucent and light on the runework, the same hand Caro had grasped in her own just the day before, walking her home with Icca ahead, always ahead, as if to scare their path clear.

Icca's face was blank, even as she reached a hand up, slid it from her mouth to her chin.

Caro wanted to shake her. She wanted to kiss her and then hate it as it happened. Why was she so angry?

Why was she ever not angry?

There was the Priest Huang, and the high sheriff Yon Miripta, standing up beside the body. It all felt very sparse, in the belly of the empty church, which was small but reached from its foundations, rose up, up, up to a patchwork of stone and dyed glass. Different shades winked over them as Caro and Icca began, inevitably, to drift forward. Carousel could feel the birds peppering the roof just out of sight.

It had started oddly, at first. Birds—crows, usually, since most of the birds in Astara were crows—would trail her from the orphanage to Empathy and back, peck at the window of the bedroom in the middle of the night in glassy notes. It was really Icca and Tecca who noticed them first. Caro had been too engrossed in the two of them, in their strange powers and their strange selves; she had barely noticed anything else. It was Tecca who coaxed the crows on the fence post to not spook, and Icca who pressed the stones into Caro's hand to knock them down in case they did. It was they who showed Caro how to weep her magic, the sadness and the desperation and the natural rabidness from which she could summon it.

She'd killed the bird, the first time; Caro still wasn't sure what she had been trying to do, and that's why it'd perished—her intention had been lacking, and so her enchantment peeled feather from skin from tendons until the crow was a dead and slick thing, balanced on the fence post. Tecca and Icca had tittered. They had shifted their bodies toward the next one.

"Girls," the Priest Huang rumbled once they reached the dais, stopping them a step outside of it.

Tecca was covered with a gray sheet, only the fingertips of one white hand visible, reaching out toward Caro and Icca. But not really, of course. It only looked it.

Miripta cleared his throat. "Perhaps we should wait for Madam Gim—"

"It doesn't concern her," snapped Huang, leveling Icca and then Caro with a black stare.

Caro had never had much affection for the old woman who ran the orphanage, with her twitchy, shrill manner—but now, she was sure the image of Gim lumbering down the pews toward them would be a comfort. She'd know what to do. Carousel didn't know what to do. She felt such a child.

"What drew the Saint?" Icca said suddenly, roughly, the look on her face hidden by the cut of her hood, stained silver. They were the first words she'd uttered since they'd darkported.

A beat of silence. No one, not even Caro, had expected that to be her first question.

"Her..." Miripta flicked an awkward, liver-spotted hand at the body at his feet. "Tecca's father, Quinn Moore. We found his body in the house—we believe he passed late last evening. A natural death."

Ajeossi, Caro and Icca always called Quinn, though he'd insisted before that Abeonim, *Father*, would suffice. How they had both laughed at it, a sentimental man and his quiet wife, not knowing how vicious their eldest daughter was, or the friends she brought into their groves. But there was love, in the Moore household. Had been love—Caro knew. She'd watched it. Caro, on her belly in the grove, in a bird, on a windowsill to peer into the small and comfortable home. She couldn't help herself. Kisses on the cheek, between Tecca's parents. The way their eyes followed the twins as they clattered around upstairs, and how their voices rang out over the grove to call Tecca in, to bring her home. Maybe some part of Caro would have wished herself to be in Tecca's place, if she'd wanted Tecca to be anywhere else. Caro liked the kind of love she saw, through the curtains. Love that was not fire, impulsive and burning, but habit, and easy for it.

Burning, burning.

How deeply the Moores would have grieved his death. They might as well have walked out into Wonderland.

One could open a vein in one's arm, and it didn't compare to the wound grief drew into the soul; mourning was of nearly equal ability to the death trace, in drawing the Saints.

"And the Queen?" Caro asked. The words breaking apart with the laugh in her throat. She was joking—of course she was joking. And now Icca joined in.

"Yes, where is Her Majesty?" she rasped. "Doesn't she want to come along and collect her Saint? Doesn't she want to come and meet the ones who felled it?"

"We felled it," Caro echoed.

"We won her Races."

"Yes, yes we did, where are our prizes? Our luxuries?"

"Oh, oh, no," said Icca. Caro had never heard her voice like that. A voice that darkened as it carried, a voice like bruising flesh. "That's all right. I'll just take her head."

Miripta and Huang exchanged a glance.

That same laugh was still moving up and down in her throat, or maybe it was a sob. Caro was breathing quite hard indeed. Huang's lips moved, and Caro didn't catch what they said, but now Icca's focus was away from her, and she was shouting something, something, and Caro on instinct snapped out a hand to hook Icca's arm as Icca lunged forward onto the dais. *What, what is it.* Caro tried to speak, but there was a ringing in her ears and the flush of her magic priming in her veins, a natural response to her panic, and oh, she was already so singed with it. She ached down to her marrow, and now Icca was screaming. Huang had taken the corner of the cloth covering Tecca and was drawing it away.

Where there was ringing in Caro's ears, now there was nothing at all.

Tecca's dark eyes were open, her lips parted. Her magic, a silken gold, just like her words, blotted at the corners of her mouth, peeked out of one nostril.

It was only a little bit. Caro had leaked more of it on her pillow the nights of especially vivid dreams. But it hadn't been there when they'd left the house together.

"No." This she could hear, the word out of her throat. Carousel's voice was small. She felt exactly her age. She was young, certainly, *oh,* so young, dear readers, to be feeling the world so deeply. "No."

Tecca had been alive. Lying in the dry grasses puffing around the fence posts, alive, alive, alive, while Carousel had closed her eyes to shut it all out.

Caro wished her hearing was still gone—the sound that was rolling out of Icca was unnatural, that serrated edge between a wail and a scream. Caro grabbed her; Icca snagged around her hold just as viciously. It tugged at Caro, these sharp affections, this childish, feral love of theirs.

"Icca. Icca." The words were breaking out of Carousel's throat. "We didn't know. We didn't *know.*"

It was the truth. They'd both believed Tecca gone, when they'd found her, those blank eyes, the open, glittering head . . . it just didn't matter.

There were cuts all over Tecca's body, clothes shredded from Caro's birds. Her fucking birds. Had Tecca tried to summon her own magic to get them away from her? Had Caro rendered her last moments a stinging agony? And Icca, pulling them all through the darkness, a perilous, tearing journey . . .

Someone shifted forward; Caro and Icca both snapped their heads up, aggressive, wounded animals—but it was the Priest Huang with his cruel mouth and crueler piety, and Caro felt cold, and small, and absolutely powerless.

"She might have survived," Huang said. "The Saint had a hand in it, alongside yours. But traces of your magic, both of yours, shone on her skin and on her clothes. It is—"

"Did she stop weeping in the cart?" Caro whispered, and Icca *growled* and when Caro asked again, *"Did she die alone in the fucking cart?"* Icca twisted in her arm and shoved her. It sent Caro into the ground; she caught herself but lay still after, dizzy against the coolness of the floor.

"Do *not* answer that!" Icca screamed, and Caro turned back to see her silver magic splattering the floor. Icca was breathing hard, the nodes of her spine heaving under her thin cloak. The shadows seem to lean, and deepen.

She doesn't want to know, I don't want to know, Caro thought in a haze, and then she thought something worse.

She twisted and was grappling at Icca, the panic drying her throat, and sobbed, "*Icca.* We've a trace in her death—"

"It's done," Miripta said, low and sharp. "The death trace is already on you. You're to be out before sunset."

"Out?" choked Icca, eyes so grotesquely large and white in her head, glossed in the fear stitching them together. And then Icca's voice was so small Caro felt it like a seed lodged in the bottom of her throat. "To Wonderland Forest?"

Caro felt so small, pressed to the wood of the dais, nothing more than a dropped coin.

They called them Jabberwockies, those with death like a tag in the palm of their hand.

"Please," Caro begged, bent over her stomach and the twine of her hands. There was no point of it. Nothing could be done, and still she was crying. "Please, please, please, we're mourning—they'll—they'll come to us in stampedes—"

"It's not our fault," Icca was shrieking. "The Queen. The *Queen.* I want to see the fucking Queen!"

There were some exiles who survived, some even who thrived, who paid off their sentences and earned their way back into the Wards with the heads of Saints—four for each life sentence. Three to dissolve the legalities, one for the White Queen Delcorta October Kkul to grind up and for the Jabberwocky to drink down, which obliterated the brand from their necks and the death trace, if they had one, from their souls.

Four seemed an impossible number—of course, some Jabberwockies were impossibly powerful witches. Of course, then it was often the White Queen they belonged to after that, up in her pale stone palace in the Petra Ward, which would always be safe because its protection was not a commonplace Wall, but a colossal, ringed Labyrinth that rose around the entire district.

It was hell in the Labyrinth too, of course, because the Labyrinth's knots were the home of the Queen's own captured Saints. The country of Isanghan would never crumble because the Petra Ward would never fall. Strategically, any invading army would find the Labyrinth a poor, crowded terrain, and their collective smell would bolster the maze's inhabitants better than anything else. Against any smaller groups of witches—well, the Saints knew the maze better than they would. That was the next step. If a Jabberwocky had already bested Wonderland, Wonderland then was a redundant punishment if they broke another law. The Labyrinth would not be. No one survived the Labyrinth.

"You can get yourselves along, to the south gate, before sunset, if you go quietly," the high sheriff said quietly, eyes low. "Have a chance to, ah, pack and . . . say goodbye."

It was a courtesy, a mercy; Icca and Caro would be able to return to the orphanage, maybe have a bath one last time. They could have lain on their beds in the gray light of the bedroom, feeling numb and real in the afternoon quiet, waiting for the sun to set, and pack their things.

They could have even, potentially, run away. Caro would think about that for years, how they could have ended up, if they'd been able to keep their heads for a time.

But they hadn't. They hadn't chosen to go quietly—nor, Caro thought, had they really chosen to completely lose it.

And maybe if they hadn't been so entirely drained, already so singed down to their marrow from their magics, their fighting would have amounted to something, something besides the other sheriffs piling into the church at the first hint of their powers weeping from them, something besides the sound of a single crow beating against the glass, and the cold weight of some enchantment slamming down, trailing unconsciousness.... The darkness came and Caro, for a moment, was sure Icca was in it beside her.

—

"Rabbit, *please*."

There was a hand on her shoulder—she had a shoulder, because now she was awake. It was being jostled harshly by Icca; the other was pressed to dirt. Good gods, was her head throbbing. Even the little light that remained in purple slashes across the cloudscape was jabbing.

And right in front of her, past Icca's form, rose the runeworked Wall of the Mugunghwa Ward.

They were on the very wrong side of it.

"Get *up*," Icca hissed, or to anyone else it would have sounded like a hiss. Icca's voice was cut from stone; when she spoke she hissed, or she shrieked, shrieked when she meant to only laugh. When she hissed now, her intention was to beg.

There was something on her neck.

Dazed, Carousel's fingers floated up to her own skin.

Two parallel dashes, angled and connected at their catercorner ends by a vertical line, drawn there in the flesh of her neck. The rune of death, an enchantment strung around her throat—the Ward Walls, marked somewhere with the paired rune, would repel her. Until she paid her sentence, of course.

So Carousel got up. She had on a thicker, darker cloak now, new gloves shoved onto her fingers. She had on better boots, and in one boot was a knife. She drew it out, looked blankly at its pitiful length, hardly longer than her palm, and then traced her eyes up, up, up to the top of the Wall, where High Sheriff Miripta was staring down at them with a crossbow in his arms.

"Get a move on," Miripta called, arrow steadily aimed. "You're drawing Saints with every breath you take. Don't be drawing them here."

Carousel hardly heard him. The last time she'd held a knife was when the three of them were carving the rings into their fingers.

Caro was distant with her shock—Icca, on the other hand, was flaming. Caro stared at the cruel curl of her mouth, the fix of her fists at her sides. She remembered Icca's grin after Kat Pillar had collapsed, its surprise and its arrogance and its hunger. Now Icca wasn't grinning. But there was still something in her that looked starved.

Miripta fired. The arrow cut the air next to Icca's neck and planted itself beside Caro's new boots. Icca stumbled back, and Caro caught her, spun her around and pressed her palms to Icca's cheeks, chest heaving against the buttons of her shirt. The look they gave each other was rabid, and knowing. But it had always been like that between the three of them—now, at two, Caro found it unchanged. She didn't know if she wanted to shriek with relief, or just—panic—

Icca, Caro, Tecca.

You're all so ridiculous.

I know, I know! Isn't it grand?

Grand and ridiculous. We should only ever hope to be grand and ridiculous. That's all the White Queen really is, anyway, and people fear her regardless.

Icca, Caro . . .

This was the knowing: Caro and Icca were Jabberwockies now, trailing death. And this was the rabidness: Carousel breathing, Carousel grinning at Icca with all of her teeth and none of her joy, and saying, "Oh, Alice, how late we are! Certainly late, for a very important date—we were supposed to go with Tecca, remember?"

Her eyes shone bright with tears—Caro did not let them fall free. It was all theatrics, her carrying words and their casual panic. It made the two of them vivid; it did not make them small things, so entirely small and exposed outside the loom of the Wall. They were not mourning. They were not scared. They were grand and ridiculous.

"Yes," Icca breathed viciously, immediately. "Yes, Rabbit, I remember."

"Come, then," Caro spat back.

She threaded her fingers through Icca's, and as one then they bent their necks back at Miripta.

"You better pray we die soon," Carousel called as they began to trail away, into the lengthening shadows peeling back from the rise of the Forest.

Wonderland Forest.

Thick with pine trees, with shadows, and with Saints. Once it had held roads, villages—Caro supposed there were still roads and villages, swallowed up here and there by the tangle of the thicket. Once, it would have held them—witches, enchantresses; they both would have been so much more powerful by their age if humanity hadn't been forced into the moorlands, the cleared Wardlands, if the Saints didn't prefer the dark of the woods, the thrum of whatever unquiet force was said to radiate from its strange roots. There were so many more gods in Wonderland, what with the growing things, what with the Fear and the Death, which were very powerful deities indeed.

Icca laughed, short and spiked. "Yes, Sheriff. You better pray the Saints get to you before we do."

He wasn't safe on top of that tall, tall Wall. Safer than they were, perhaps, but he could have his little comforts, his deathless air. Caro and Icca would bear theirs like they bore everything else. Together.

EIGHT

Year Zero Zero Ninety-Four, Winter Season

There Are 1006 Remaining Saints

BIOLOGICAL WARFARE, TECHNICALLY, was the thing of the plague raiders. Its founders were witches gifted with disease-influencing magic, but unlike others who used this ability to heal, they instead worshipped Sickness, believing the sallow god a cleansing fellow, that It left behind those who were truly meant to be on this earth.

Carousel was born decades after all the mess of it, and she truly believed it must be the most sheep-brained line of thought that would ever grace human brain folds for as long as human brain folds existed. No one was truly meant to be on earth, but sex with men was supposedly fun so people kept showing up anyway, and she knew intimately from her own seasonal colds that Sickness was not cleansing in the least, but actually involved a lot of mucus and tissues and feeling sticky and dull in bed.

Despite their skewed motivations, however, the plague raiders were why Caro was currently fighting a Saint. There wouldn't have been a need for Saints if there hadn't been a need for saving.

In his natural lifetime, Dorma Ouse had distinguished himself and his piety in the plague raids in the Larkspur Quarter. He'd used his magic to draw the spread of the rotting diseases favored by the sieging witches into himself. It was a clever trick, transforming the plague into a famine when it entered his body, saving his life. And it was a life of luxury, in those final days before the King would bolster his Divinity, hoisted up on a feather bed in some mansion of the Petra merchant district, being fed by the servants—even with the constant hunger pains, and the interrupted sleep; he had to be woken up to eat every few hours so he did not starve to death.

Death had come anyway, in a way.

And Ouse had stayed hungry.

Now, Ouse was thinking Caro might sate him. In that regard, he was no different from High Sheriff Miripta and the Priest Huang, all those years ago, and all the others who had built the criminal justice system of Isanghan decades before that—the Jabberwockies and the other rotted, Wonderland-sentenced souls either killed Saints or fed them, and either was slightly helpful in keeping them out of the Wards. But a Saint would never be full. It would eat until its stomach split. Sometimes Caro imagined what that would look like. Perhaps a popping sound, and then guts flying, like Caro was, currently, toward the nearest wall. . . .

Caro hit the stone arch of the cavern, slid down onto a floor littered with bones. Her breath left her—on the ceiling, gripping the stalactites with skeletal digits, the Saint wept magic from its slitted nostrils, its black flecked with her blue. Bringing her own power into itself. Ouse hissed; the magic weeping from Caro's mouth and eyes was being pulled off of her skin in glistening droplets.

"That's not yours," Caro croaked thinly, skin cracked along her knees. She was always fucking up her kneecaps. She'd be a cranky halmeoni complaining about stairwells one day. She was wholly excited for it. Thus she pulled her knives from their place lining her ribs a nick before the Saint shot itself at her.

In a dried-out rib cage a cowardly distance away, Caro had stationed a crow, steaming and slowly disintegrating as she periodically stole traits from it. The lightness of its bones, as she sent herself farther away from the Saint's lunge than she should be able, what with her marrow. The curl of its talons mimicked by the bone sprouted from her own knuckles. The higher, panicked beat of its heart in the veins feeding her body—Caro thought that one a neat trick especially; it spurred on not only her blood but her magic twining it.

The Saints never looked for the Birds. Not when there was a human in the vicinity. Their bloodlust stitched their entire world to the outline of her skin. Carousel did like the attention, in a way, up until one was about to kill her (she disliked these inconsistencies she found about herself, but she found comfort in the ancientness of her world, her gods. She had always better favored their attention above the Saints' anyway).

And really, she had become quite good at this.

The Saint slid from her daggers with that fogged, gray life already gone from its eyes. Caro gulped in her breaths and leaned down to shear its throat. Hattie November Kkul liked the heads, the Courts chittered, though the late White Queen Delcorta October Kkul had, too. It was just that Hattie was young, and there was the thing that perhaps she had murdered Delcorta for the throne, though no one, now, ventured to challenge her on it, after her harrowing display to prove it wasn't the case.

Probably.

But it's not like any of them cared about the morals of it anyway; the Courts liked to gossip, and they liked to titter about how horrifying the Queen was, with the same air as children daring each other to inch closer and closer to a very large and fanged spider hung on the wall, thrilled with their own rising heartbeats. The spider was safe either way—either such children wouldn't dare squashing it, or one would be brave enough to raise their chubby kiddy fist, and then the spider would lunge, and there would be blood everywhere, and as much as some of the courtfolk liked to preen, they also knew the thing about the everywhereness-quality of the blood.

And some of the Courts, like the majority of those in the Wards, did view Hattie as a religious figure—she had been the most pious royal on the throne that Isanghan could remember, a startling transition following the death of her mother. The god Hattie worshipped was Quiet, and she had never spoken in public. How Caro had hated Hattie as a younger girl, hearing about her apathy toward the Saints' Races, toward her mother's carnage—Caro hadn't known her as she did now. And she'd reformed the Saints' Races, too—it was only the monsters brawling with each other, now, no people. Not even criminals. Wasn't that just pleasant, then? Caro found it so—the last year she'd accompanied Hattie on her tour around the Wards, a kind of security detail. Not that Hattie unnie needed one, really, truly. There was nothing like seeing the Saints brawl in the pits—the *Races* portion of the name now only preserving the bloody memories of Delcorta's reign. Now it was Hattie's monster fighting monsters, the Saint count knocked down by the dozens by the time the tour ended, and the people revered Hattie for it—her wordless mercy, the deathly stillness she possessed as she observed from the edge of the ring, the red veil that covered her face, the serene, blank expression that surely lay behind it. She wasn't gaudy or cruel, as her mother had been.

Sure, they were terrified of her, too—yes, clearly, the Red Queen was insane.

It was her creation that skittered around in the ring, after all, a horror born of two Saints Hattie stitched together.

She created a new one every year, for the Races, during the Midwinter Tea Party that marked the commencement of the holiday, drawing the two bodies together in front of the Courts. The monstrosity would go along to clobber Saints in every one of the eleven Wards, then be retired to the Labyrinth upon the holiday's end, as a darling champion.

And Caro liked Hattie unnie a lot for the very fact that she horrified everyone so, even when the young Red Queen often carried herself with unassuming grace, knowing and contemplative and altogether calm, quite calm. She did *know* what the Courts said about her, of course; it was just she seemed to hardly notice other people, and so other people could not actually bother her—Caro believed only a very rare soul could truly irritate Hattie. It really did leave Caro in clutching awe most of the time, and Caro liked being in awe. It kept the boredom fastened back.

The crow skittered from the rib cage and came to land on her shoulder, feathers singed and sloughing, half fried from her magic. "Dumb bird," Caro murmured hoarsely, dropping the Saint's head into her bag, and limped back out toward the water. "You're such a little coward."

NINE

Year Zero Zero Ninety-Four, Winter Season

There Are 1004 Remaining Saints

ICCADORA CREPT OUT of the shade of a sage tree and balanced before the edge that marked the cut of the midday Light. She brushed her gloved hand against the Saint's head weighing at her hip, fingertips cold beneath the gloves—her magic always made her cold. She was always so cold.

She moved through the dirt streets of Yule, the central village in the Bajil Ward, on her way to the church, so that its Priest could identify her most recent Saint head and give her its bounty. Then the spoils would be put on the armored caravan that fed out into Wonderland, toward Petra, where it would be delivered and recorded. There'd been a time where she'd watch the steel trolley cars from the edge of the platform, turning over the thought in her head that she should buy passage into the capital Ward. Now, after she got paid, she immediately strode away for whatever tavern sat closest, in whatever ugly little town she'd glided into.

And it was especially ugly this week. Red ribbons everywhere, strung to door handles, threaded through grimy shutters. The Red Queen Hattie

November Kkul would be hosting the Midwinter Tea soon—then, of course, of course, it would be time for the Saints' Races.

Icca couldn't wait to get out of the street, away from the reminders of all of it.

She'd made the mistake, last year, of seeking out a village the tour was going through—she'd heard how the Red Queen had "adjusted" the holiday, and wanted to see for herself. Maybe, she'd mused, if she happened to be in the mood, she would knock off Hattie's head. There on cobblestones of some bustling town in the Malli Ward, pissed, with the winter cold crackling up her legs, she'd drifted through the teeming bodies, a shadow, no one at all. She'd followed the scent of blood, warm and tangy, spiking the frosted air. Stopping at the railing of the temporary arena, the crowd humming around her, Icca had ignored the monstrosities roiling below, the sound of tearing flesh. She'd caught sight of Hattie immediately. The Red Queen, done up in red—how imaginative—her small brown hands braced on the railing of the royal booth.

Icca told it to herself like that—she'd spotted Hattie first. Not the horrible blond head of hair that hung to the Queen's right, not the grin that cracked though the heart-shaped face, the teeth lined in blue from her excitement, her fervor, her *devotion*—

Icca stopped dead in the middle of the street. And then she did what she always did when the image of Carousel Rabbit beside Hattie November Kkul came up in her head—she imagined sawing off Caro's.

She imagined it hitting the ground with a *thunk*, and the *thunk* cleared her mind, made her calm, made her herself again, and she continued along, thinking instead of the comforts of whatever inn she'd find for tonight. She'd get a room and draw the curtains low to dull the Light and listen to the building ease around her, the usual routine. The shouts of the kitchen somewhere below, their ringing suffocated halfway through the walls, footsteps murmuring by. Watching the day flashing between the curtains lean and fade, thinking of how tired she was. Thinking of having tea in the morning. Thinking of how, from her place on her back, she could press on those Dark spots she felt wandering past the walls of her room until they burst. And she'd read, and it was because she read a lot that she could observe herself clearly musing and worrying and being habitually violent, and why she fancied herself an academic for sleeping a lot.

I sleep a normal amount.

Yes, a normal amount, if you're dead.

Don't tempt her, Caro. Alice is going to get ideas, and then we'll have to follow her, and the underclassmen will think they can take the bell tower as their own.

Icca pushed through the doors of Yule's church, her palm coming away imprinted with the 바질—*Bajil*—stamped repeatedly on the wood to mark it a part of the Ward.

"Your Priest," she said low to the nun crossing the entryway, whose eyes drifted to the curved shape weighing Icca's bag. "I've Saint Dorma Ouse."

"Oh," said the nun in an airy voice that Icca thought couldn't possibly be real—else her parents must have despised her—clasping her hands together under her long gray sleeves. "Oh."

She was still staring at the bulb of the bag, and Icca scowled, a sudden but predictable urge bubbling to chuck it at the nun's head.

"Well, how was . . . the Forest . . . ?"

Oh, of course, one of the *curious* ones. *Just go and see for yourself, already,* she wanted to snap, but gods, what would it amount to, and gods, how Icca hated *talking* to *people.*

She just wanted to be done with this and alone again—she wanted for the inn, in a way that she hadn't ever wanted a house or an apartment all to herself. It was not as if she couldn't come to possess the money for a permanent home—butchering Saints was a lucrative business—it was just Icca didn't see the point in it. Anywhere she went she'd leave again, eventually. She wasn't exactly sure if it was because she'd grown up in Wonderland, or, even if she hadn't, if the Forest would've called to her anyway. Perhaps, in her birth Ward, eventually, playing with her magic within the Walls wouldn't have been enough, and she would have crept past the borders. Taking the stretch of thistles between civilization and Wonderland inch by inch, until one day she'd look up, and see foliage blocking out the sky....

Icca chose a pew as the nun finally drifted away after a few more moments of glaring and stubborn, barbed silence, and sank down onto its dark wood, chin tilting toward the vaulted, glass-strewn ceiling. She breathed in, feeling the shadows like cuts of velvet against her skin, and breathed out a thanks to the Dark, and then to the Light—without one she would never have been able to discern the other. She liked that about her gods, how they leaned on one another. How completely they filled her world. She tugged her book from the smaller bag tucked beside the head-sack, balancing its spine on her knee. This one was about faeries; Icca liked that fictional trope, those nasty and violent and clever creatures. Her only tattoo was a string of tiny black mushrooms encircling her left wrist—a faerie circle ripped from one of her favorite stories.

In it, a Queen of a distant land thought herself to be the most powerful being in existence, and went to challenge the faeries for control of their woods. The fool stumbled upon their circle and danced until her bones shone through the bottoms of her feet, yet still, in her vanity, thought their laughter applause.

She was nearly at the end of a chapter when someone tapped on her shoulder. Above her was the Yule Priest Jang, an ancient woman with a small mouth that was already chattering, weary eyes already drifting toward the covered Saint's head. It had once been Dorma Ouse, recent devourer of a blacksmith's family in the Yuhwa Ward. Icca had hunted it down in some nearby ghost village in the Wonderland Forest, south of this Ward, and killed it just outside of its perimeter. It had tried and failed to flee her.

Well, if Saints had the fear to think to flee, it would have. The beasts didn't much care for their lives over their next meal. It irritated Icca to no end. Her favorite heroes and villains alike in all her storybooks always conjured some sort of dread in their opponents. Sometimes she supposed she could go and join the Red Queen's Culled Court of absolved Jabberwockies for a chance at it.

The thought always quickly grew tiresome.

She would find more amazement than horror for her peculiar powers, as it went with zoos.

The Culled Court was probably where Carousel Rabbit had ended up, since she'd become close enough to Hattie to be invited along to the Saints' Races. How Caro had always liked to preen, always liked to fantasize to Icca and Tecca about a glittering life in Petra. Icca, on the other hand, now liked to fantasize about Caro being dead. Anything but her living it up in the capital Ward, sucking up to the Red Queen. The secondhand embarrassment was too much for Icca to think about—thus certainly, readers, she never thought about it.

Besides, our dear Iccadora Alice Sickle preferred being with herself, with her books and their characters with all of their thoughts cracked open and bare against the page. Perhaps that's what makes her such a delightful creature, wanting nothing to do with the likes of us.

The Priest droned on, something ridiculous about how fateful it was, having a Saint brought in so close to the Races. Icca swept at her thigh, where the bandages were dampened—this most recent Forest visit had reopened the wound marring the flesh of her leg; she'd gotten it about a month back fighting a Saint in the Wonderland foothills. It was the picking more than anything else, really, that kept it from healing, more than the Saint brawls—Icca wasn't paying attention to the Priest's words; her focus was on her hand, observing her fingers curling absently to find a seam in the bindings. *I can see myself doing it*, she often thought, when she was poking at her opened skin, or pinching the multitude of spots on her face, and she thought now, *I am very aware of what I am doing to myself.* But she wouldn't stop. She'd bless her hands over burning rosemary every once in a while to scare the habit away; it would work for a few days, but the tic always came flitting back sooner or later. Icca didn't read too much into it. She supposed she simply didn't care as much about it as perhaps she should. Healing wasn't a god she found much Divinity in.

"I'll just take the payment," Icca cut in across Jang's chattering, thinking of being in a room all by herself—what bliss. She shut her book and offered the head-sack to the Priest for the identification, who smiled thinly and accepted it as easily as if it were a stocked picnic basket.

"Then the payment, yes, of course," the Priest Jang tittered quietly, barely looking, weighing the bag in one hand and the coin purse strung to her belt in the other. Icca felt herself straining as the Priest's wrinkled fingers failed once and then twice at the knot of the bag. The slow progression felt leisurely—matched with the fading gray Light bleeding from the windows, softening the stone of the church to seem like clay, like she could press at a wall and it would take the imprint of her hand—and Icca was too fresh from a Wonderland trip for the wholly unhurried moment to sit well in her gut. She wanted to say something to speed the Priest up but also preferred not to speak again, and compromised with a weak sound pilled at the back of her throat.

The Priest took no notice. She finally freed the knot, took a glance, and then untied the coin purse and held it out to Icca. The head bumped against her gray cloak.

The church doors flew open. Icca shot her gaze toward them; Jang turned more subtly, blinking blearily at the black-hooded newcomer. Icca searched for their eyes and found them painted, lined in crimson, flitting left and right.

Icca reached out to take the coin purse before she had to talk to another person. The Priest, however, moved to welcome them, the purse still pinched in her hand.

"Another Saint's head?" Jang called in her soft tones. "Blissed day."

The newcomer struck out a hand, a sack draped over the wrist, bulbed with the prize. "Saint Dorma Ouse, Madam Cleric," they spoke. "Fresh from Wonderland, fresh from his neck."

Icca froze.

She knew that voice, that unquiet, carrying thrum; that voice like rose petals, the smile always, always in it, the fringe of thorns. She knew it was Carousel Rabbit before Carousel Rabbit even drew back her hood, sent those black roots and the blond mess of curls rising from them into the gray Light, before Caro even met her eyes—she *knew*, so why didn't she run?

Carousel's hand dropped from her hood, and was limp at her side. Her jaw went slack off her skull.

Priest Jang—fucking Jang—said mildly, "How funny, it seems we have two Ouses. . . ."

It was petty. Icca knew it, and she immediately blamed it on Carousel. But suddenly she was sixteen years old again and she snatched the coin purse from the Priest's hand and dropped into the shadow of her pew.

Then she was running. Boots stomping down the dirt alleyway of some street over from the church—she had passed it on the way in, put its image in her head so she could use it as an escape if need be, as she always did—clutching the purse to her chest, heartbeat pressing against the coins.

Ha—what—what am I doing—indeed, dear readers, what the fuck was she doing?

Icca shot out into a cobblestone plaza sparse with carts and villagers, and slowed her steps. She tasted the metallic sting of her magic seeping out of her back gums—it'd been a while since it had been unintentionally summoned like this, but she drank it down, pulled close an enchantment around herself and smeared her physical body into a passerby's shadow. That carried her a little ways across the plaza and up the next street before she untangled herself, and immediately pushed through a nearby doorway and into an inn. "I need a room," Icca said to the innkeeper, and then she was behind shut doors and drawn curtains, just like she'd been fantasizing all day long. But the muffled movements of the building's inhabitants did not ease her.

She should have killed Caro last year, as soon as she'd set eyes on her beside Hattie. Why hadn't she? Why had she run now? It was just, seeing

Caro, so suddenly *real* again, it just all felt—gods damn it, how Icca hated *feeling*. Hastily, she brought back the saw in her head. She waited for the thud, but it didn't come. Caro's neck kept growing back; Caro's grin kept flashing in the Dark, and Icca's thoughts would not clear, and they would not slow. She'd left her book behind on the pew. She was pissed about it. Icca pulled coins from the purse and counted them out on her ribs. She was rich, again. She could buy more books; she'd buy herself a nice breakfast. She didn't think about the person in the church, and the strangeness of it, an outline cut from a very long time ago and stitched to a more current moment. Icca thought instead about the Darkness she could feel pooling on the streets outside. She considered the twin lightless spots on the opposite side of the room that marked her neighbor's lungs, pressed at them a little bit until she could hear him cough. She pinched at her face, and when that was exhausted and bumpy, she sat up to drop her cloak from her shoulders and went to unwind her bandage.

Such was an existence where one had grown unafraid of agony, and Icca was cognizant of the horrible and unflinching truth that self-inflicted pain was one's own right—her body and mind were hers to do as she liked with. Thus she'd battered away the fear of pain and the fear of anything else, and she was sure, Icca must be sure, she did it all on her own.

—

"You can't *actually* be *truly* afraid of the dark, Alice," Tecca had crowed past the door of the closet; Icca could barely hear her over her own shrieking. "It's only the possibility of what might be scuttling around within!"

"Let me out! LET ME OUT!" Her fists struck feverishly against the wood, but against the far side Tecca had leaned her weight, or perhaps jammed a chair against the door, and Icca was here, all alone in the dark, trapped, trapped, trapped . . . "For gods' *sakes—Carousel—*"

Caro had been somewhere out there, in the light with Tecca, speaking to her in quick, pleading tones—the hypocrite. Caro had been the one to tell her that Icca was afraid of the dark, prompting Tecca to throw her into the closet once last bell rang.

The girls had been around thirteen, and Tecca had already figured out how she could fuck around with the mice—and so what? She didn't have to drag Icca into it. Icca was perfectly fine ignoring the shadows that leaned for her; she did not want to be acquainted with them. Carousel—whose influence over the crows wouldn't rear its twitchy head until a few months later—preened and picked at Icca over all of it, too. About how she refused her powers out of her fear, and about how her fear was ridiculous, and, Caro had mused before, certainly masochistic. . . .

Within, Icca's screams bled out to rapid, choked gasps.

To be fair, readers, the dark that gathered around Icca was not a common dark. Night thickened and curled around her; it reached for her and swaddled her, and in the black depths of the classroom closet, Icca's thoughts were rapid-fire: *I feel I am nowhere, and there are no walls and it just keeps going on forever and ever, and I am so small in it that I am not sure not sure not sure if I am still here at all.*

Tecca was wrong, the bitch, Icca knew. She wasn't afraid of things in the dark; perhaps more accurate would be to say she was afraid of a lack of things, of vastness. She knew its nature in her bones; it was an entity of absence, always awaiting its moment to come crashing down. Why—*why* had such a vicious magic chosen her?

An age-old question, dear readers, that the people of Isanghan had been asking themselves for centuries, why witches were born with their affinities. There seemed no rhyme or reason to it, which was unfortunate, since such randomness often makes humans uncomfortable. But another question—could we picture Carousel Rabbit without her crows, or Iccadora Alice Sickle without the dark? In that sense it does not seem as random—it seems a thing of casts and molds.

But a contemplative narrator digresses—known to do so, admittedly—so back to it. Icca was locked in a closet, young and afraid, much too afraid to be furious at Tecca and Caro. Later, of course, she would pummel them, and drop their cigarettes into the mop bucket, and kill any mouse she found so that Tecca would have one less playmate.

But now, she was afraid; she was sure the dark made people cease to exist. When she died, wouldn't death look like this? Depthless, edgeless, and her, certainly nowhere and nothing at all. Even now—it swallowed up Icca's own hands in front of her face, and so she brought her palms closer until she could feel the heat of her own skin and then the tears on her cheeks, and she thought, *I'm still here I promise I promise I'm still here,* as Tecca chimed past the door, "Just *breathe*, Alice," and Alice breathed and she breathed.

Around her, the dark was oh-so-still; the rise and fall of her chest outlined her, distinguished her. She brought her hands away from her face, and then back, touching her lip.

And there—silver.

The magic stung at the cuts on her mouth, the furrows of her fingerprints. It did not glow and produce light—like some were known to do—but shimmered; Icca could see it when she moved.

She could feel it then, the dark that lay inside her, infecting her, but still she was breathing and breathing and alive, alive, alive, even as she was afraid of going away, of being lost in the blackness, or worse, unable to be found. She had never just *sat* with it like this, she realized—sat with what? The dark? No, no, that was always with her, always with everyone, in their lungs, the thin hollows under their skulls. She'd never sat with her fear like this. Observing it as something separate from herself. *Because,* Icca thought, even as it gripped at her, *because—that can't really be* me, *right? Cowering. Shuddering. It can't. It won't. I refuse.*

Every second her fear told her she was going to go away, and every second Icca continued. Breathing in the dark.

Until it unfolded around her truly, and she moved, and she was somewhere else. Dropped into the shadows of the closet, dropped somewhere else. And it was exactly like she'd pictured it being. Black in all endless directions, and she looked around, and saw nothing, and felt truly alone, truly afraid, and still, and still, here, here, here.

And Icca began to walk. She knew where to go, intrinsically—yes, yes, she knew where everything was. Dark was absence, and here Icca was in it, and so Icca must be absence, too, and needn't be afraid. She was already gone. . . .

I am the thing scuttling around in the Dark, Icca promised herself. *I am the only thing to be afraid of.*

She came out of the shadows off the wall, leaning away from the late-afternoon sun streaking through the classroom's dirty windows. Tecca turned away from the chair she'd indeed set against the closet at the back of the room; the front of her shirt was clasped in Caro's fist. Tecca dropped her head back and grinned, and Caro dropped her, jaw unhinging: "You—what—"

"Oh, *oh*," Tecca exclaimed gleefully, clapping her hands as Icca approached; even Caro's awe of her first darkport would not save them now. "We are so *dead*, aren't we, now, Carousel?"

—

It was there, perched at the edge of her bed, the fingertip of one hand under the first linen strip, that Icca saw the crow on her windowsill.

Just one eye, just the impossibly sleek cut of its beak, its razor tip clinked against the glass—peering in through the slit of the curtains.

Icca was gone. She spilled out of the Dark on the street below and pulled at the shadow of the inn roof, tilted both across her window and the crow tucked on the sill, ripped it out like a rug under its talons. The bird tumbled. If it had been a crow all the way through it might have caught itself. Instead it hit the dirt and Icca was upon it, upon Caro, snapping her foot quick and clean on its neck. It went still and did not move again.

Breathing hard, Icca scanned the skies, turning in a slow circle. The winter night pricked at her bare arms. She did not darkport back up for her boots or her cloak—she took off down the road in nothing but her trousers, tunic, and stockings. Carousel had to be close; she'd be weak, sick from the death. Then Icca could—she would—

Unless Caro was so used to dying in her birds that she had developed the stomach for it. Icca had certainly grown into her powers, over the four years since they'd separated. She could do awful, enormous things; Icca was powerful, and terrible, and had a magic in her that startled her, usually after she'd done something powerful and terrible.

It didn't matter if Caro had improved. It didn't matter if she was a fantastic witch—Icca always knew Carousel would grow to be powerful, if she lived. But Iccadora knew that she herself had grown to be something worse. Her gods crowded closer in her veins.

Icca turned into an alleyway, eyes hungrily snatching up the blue magic speckled and glowing against the dirt, and threw her gaze up the path, where a form was just turning the corner.

Icca took one step. Into a shadow and out of another the next block over. Soundless, she reached out and curled her hand over the back of Carousel's neck. The crow witch yelped as she was thrown back into the alleyway.

Caro lay still on her back, Icca's shadow draped across her thick cloak, the skirt and the tall, blood-splattered boots. Her silver rings glinted dully as they twitched against the dirt at her sides. A fan and a pair of gloves had rolled out of her pockets, pieces of decadence that had scattered so casually from her.... That made Icca absolutely boil.

Icca snatched up the fan and the gloves without knowing why, and then she could really feel it: those lightless gaps in Carousel's body, the Darkness one's form naturally cradled. The kind Icca could wind around her fingers and blow apart with nothing but her own pain as payment. With nothing but a thought.

Caro's lips parted. They were the same ribboned mess of chapped and torn skin as they'd always been. But she did not speak. And Icca did not think.

Carousel and Iccadora looked at each other. They *stared*, and Icca felt drunk—drunk down, swallowed up by Caro; Icca in turn was eating up Carousel. The way the cut of her cheeks had flattened from their childish curves. The brightly colored bird tattoos fluttering up the length of her left arm. The same auroral magic leaked from her fox-shaped eyes and into her temples, staining the strange shade of her hair, like the rich black of the roots had sloughed away to yellow once they realized the world they'd sprung into. Or maybe just the person they'd grown out of.

The both of them had grown up in Wonderland. They'd grown up as awful things; wholly horrible girls. They were still growing up. Icca knew she'd just get more and more terrible.

She didn't want to be anything else.

Good wouldn't keep her alive. It would barely keep her entertained.

And then Caro's mouth opened again, and incomprehensible, indescribable was the feeling in Icca's chest as she wondered what she might say, the first handful of words after all this time.... Icca used to want those words pricked on her skin. Icca used to want Carousel Rabbit's soul wound around hers like rot wound around a carcass, like Light chased the Dark.

Caro said, "I want my money."

"You *fucking*—"

TEN

Year Zero Zero Eighty-Nine, Winter Season

There Are 1103 Remaining Saints

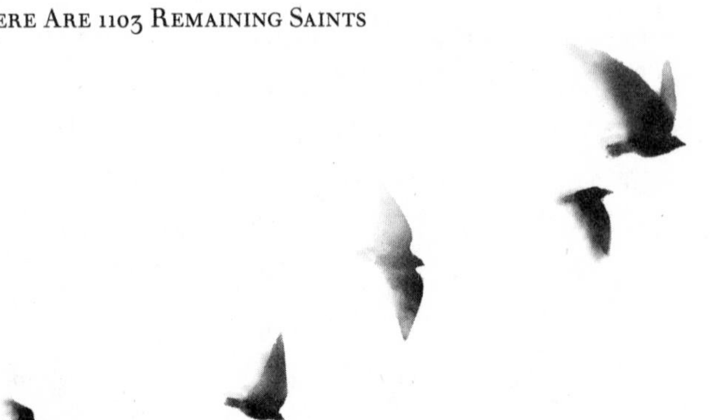

IT WAS ONLY A FEW HOURS AFTER THEY'D found Tecca, when the sun was setting and they were standing at the mouth of the darkening forest, that Icca realized that she was entering Wonderland as a heretic.

She wanted to shake the gods from their coward corners of the world—but they *were* the world, and even if Icca went to burn it all down, the Heat and Flame and Smoke were deities still.

But standing in the growing night, Icca slathered her hatred over as much of it as she could. It felt so much better than her fear, than her mourning— *Don't—*

"We can't think about it," Caro said, her hand in Icca's. *Can't think about Tecca.*

Icca started. She always started, when Caro spoke what she believed were her thoughts alone. Caro was turning, fumbling for Icca's waist as if she hadn't held it hundreds of times before. Her hands were cold, and trembling.

"We have to shove it down," she said, and Icca made a strangled, aching sound, and Caro kissed her, quick and hard; they snapped apart and stayed close, and Caro said again, eyes half-lidded, pleading, "Shove it *down*, Alice," and this time Icca was the one who wrenched her closer, who ran out of air and breathed in, in, in with their mouths still together, drinking down Caro's warmth, her terror, this frantic moment tangled between them.

I'm not thinking about it, and Icca knew the thought was mirrored in Caro's head, a perfect echo, *I don't ever want to think about it.*

It almost had nothing at all to do with the Saints. And not a one came skittering from the dark that night, drawn salivating by their mourning. They survived the first night, curled up sleeplessly on the Forest's edge, and were heretics for it. The gods were all natural things, and Icca and Carousel thinking nothing of Tecca, nothing at all—it was unnatural.

But they were good at that state. They didn't mourn—Icca knew Carousel did not mourn, that Caro had stuck Tecca in a black box at the back of her head because it was what Icca had done, because they would have been dead by now, a week later. They'd spent the days tracing the jagged perimeter of Wonderland, seeing the Walls of other Wards rise and then shrink behind them as they kept moving. The runes carved on their stone prickling the one burned into Icca's neck, keeping the Jabberwockies flinching back from civilization.

"It's itchy," complained Caro one day, scratching her rune.

"I'm aware," said Icca irritably. But they weren't looking at each other. Sitting between the thin stretch of moorlands between a Ward and the tree line, the wind playing in the thistles. Every time it came from the direction of Wonderland, the air smelled almost sweetened.

"*So* itchy," Caro strained, after a few minutes of silence. Now her gaze slipped a little, toward Icca. "Are you... hungry?"

"Yes," said Icca, even though it wasn't exactly true; they'd been eating wild onions and whatever bird stumbled within Caro's reach. Goose bumps tickled along her spine. "Aren't you... a little cold?"

More food, in the Forest. More firewood. Less uncomfortableness, without Walls leaning over them. All logical notes.

There was, of course, the thing about the flesh-eating Saints.

"Yes," Caro said, though her hands lay in the cooled earth instead of her pockets. "Absolutely freezing."

A few more beats of silence. Both their heads now turned toward Wonderland.

"Come on," Caro finally whispered, which was rare. She stood up. Icca let her take her hand.

"Why?" spoke Icca hoarsely, as her feet moved under her. *Why do we want to go?*

"I don't know." Now a note of giddiness colored Caro's voice. "Do you know?"

Relief. Food. Firewood. All viable reasons. But when Icca factored in the Saints, she knew—all lies. "No. I just..." She swallowed. "I want to know what it feels like."

Wonderland rose above them. Still, yet teeming. Silent, yes... yes. Something murmuring, Icca was sure...

—

So they didn't mourn. They did still have their fear, and their anger, which not all Saints had an appetite for, like they did for grief.

But there were some, of course, that did.

The two witches were sleeping in a tree, in the thick black branches shot out of a three-hundred-foot pine trunk. Never in her life had Icca slept so deeply as she did in Wonderland. Never had her dreams been so vivid—senseless and completely irretrievable, yet contained of colors so bright that, in the moment upon waking, she swore she could taste them melting on her tongue.

It was midwinter—Icca would realize later that this was important to note, that the Saint had found them because they'd both been slowly freezing to death, and their magic had roused to sting heat through their veins. And their magic was pretty—Icca was not a vain girl, but she'd cradle this truth. Hers cutting out of her with a silver sharpness. Caro's blue and luminous as the blush of the cosmos. Both shone from them. It outlined their features in the dark.

And Icca started awake, because she was choking on the magic that had pooled in the back of her throat. It splattered from her lips, and across the glassy, thin face of the Saint arched over her body.

Icca screamed.

Her hand was already around Caro's waist, and she felt the crow witch snap awake, and they were gone—Icca dropped them into the darkness veiled around them and they rolled out on the forest floor.

"Get up!" Icca shrieked at sleep-smeared Caro, head lifted toward the Saint scuttling down and down the branches above, lighted by her coughed magic. It dropped level by level, limbs fanning and tucking, methodic and horrifyingly quick for it. "Rabbit, oh my gods, *please*—"

Caro's eyes were outlined in blue. Icca realized that Caro wasn't there, next to her, at all, that the hand she was holding was that of a shell.

The Saint was thirty feet above their heads when a crow tore gracelessly out of the foliage and slammed into its jutting ribs. It tumbled off its perch, and even underneath its shriek Icca heard something in it crack.

Carousel's hand twitched in hers, and then she was back in her body, and collapsing to her knees. Icca was frozen.

"Icca"—Caro spat wetly through magic-slicked lips—"what are you doing—we need to *run*—"

But that sound. Those *sounds*—Icca was standing still, breath and heart heaving in her chest, listening to the dry rupture of splintering bone even as it faded from the air. Something—she was feeling something new. A tearing idea. A horrible, frantic thought.

Was it Wonderland, pushing such fantasies to the surface? Icca's suspicion twisted in her mind, yet she found only herself, only her fervor, only her mouth, which was watering...

And she was approaching the Saint, a twisting of limbs and shrieks in the underbrush. Caro begging behind her; that seemed very far off. And her knife was in her hand.

"Alice," Caro hissed. Her voice was strained—Icca glimpsed the sheen of crushed feathers under the Saint's hip, before it rolled over the crow and toward them, over broken knees. It reached its hand out and Caro flinched—Icca did not. "We need to—"

She stopped when Icca grabbed her wrist. When Icca's eyes were wide and wild in her head, when Icca breathed, "We need to get out of here, Rabbit. That is the only thing we need."

The Saint was downed, but painless and so ignorant of it. The crunch of dead pine needles, of bird bones, and Caro spoke quickly, as if triggered by the sound. "There's something here, Icca. I—*feel* different. Don't you feel different?'

Yes. Yes. Icca felt... raw, here, in the Forest, and she thought her terror would be a fog over her mind but instead she felt—clear. Every sensation and every thought seemed to have bold edges. The sting of her magic no longer simply burned, but felt like it was cauterizing. Cauterizing what? Icca didn't know. But some part of herself was sealing over, hardening. Strengthening.

The Saint dragged itself another foot forward, snapping its teeth at the ground, and Icca was... electric.

They'd been in a nothing Ward, looking at a nothing future. Now, the world suddenly seemed as vast and endless as a room in total darkness. Icca had been scared of that, once.

What would she become, if she conquered this, too?

Icca raised her knife. It caught the Light of the silver spilling down her cheeks. "Yes. I feel different."

She looked and saw that Caro had drawn her blade, too. Immediately.

She didn't know why she thought Caro would do anything else. Their souls didn't need to be wound, in the way Icca had daydreamed, viciously, that they would twine. They drifted into one another's heads so often that most of their thoughts formed with edges already fitted to hold the outline of the other witch. That was their love, their knotted and jagged and strange kind of affection. It pricked and stung and neither of them would like anything less—they were already such barbed girls. Such bramble-wrought souls.

ELEVEN

YEAR ZERO ZERO EIGHTY-NINE, WINTER SEASON

THERE ARE 1102 REMAINING SAINTS

PILLAR THEY'D KILLED. This Saint they destroyed.

They were animals. They knew what they were doing, the excess of it—the dozens of times their blades recoiled and found home again, even after the Saint had gone slack in the undergrowth. The sound of the act alien, slick against the cold and quiet press of the night. Blood and dead magic soaking up in their cloaks, weighing them down—but this wasn't heresy. This night was devotion; they were performing a rite with every blow they dug. The sun rose with their own heat curling off of them, and the day began with both of them worshipping a new god. It would be the only one that they shared.

Carnage.

TWELVE

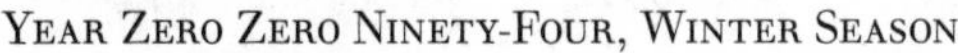

YEAR ZERO ZERO NINETY-FOUR, WINTER SEASON

THERE ARE 1003 REMAINING SAINTS

IT WASN'T BECAUSE OF CAROUSEL, why she never boarded the caravan to Petra; Icca knew it seemed like it was because of Carousel.

Yes, she had reasonably guessed that Caro, if she had indeed survived Wonderland, might have ended up in Petra, and yes, Icca still wanted Caro's place in the world to be an ash spot staining the gutters—but it's not why she had forgotten about ever going to the capital Ward. Icca was sure Petra would make her sick, with all of its glittering luxuries. With its steadfast safety. Icca liked safety, sure; she just didn't like the Red Queen. Or her maze knotting the Petra Ward borders. Or the Saints she stitched together every year, and set loose in its dark tangles, or how, upon the death of her mother, the White Queen, she fancied such an insane place to be her laboratory for the examination and experimentation of her beasts. That was one of the rumors, at least, as to why Hattie November Kkul slipped into the Labyrinth every month or so, the only one who wandered in who managed to wander out again, a few days later, unspeaking to everyone about her time within.

Some called her a scientist. Some, a mad scientist. Some, a Priestess.

Personally, Icca didn't care if she was playing scientist or if she went in to eat the dirt and dance naked for the entertainment of the Saints—whatever she was doing in there was all a part of her power trip, why none of her Court ever challenged her. The spectacle of it infuriated Icca; the Queen had never even been to Wonderland.

Icca had been to Petra once, when she'd gotten her four Saint's heads. She hadn't gotten into the city—the Red Queen met all the Jabberwockies in the Church Off the Labyrinth, set on the only Saint-free path of the maze where the trolley tracks fed through, connecting the Petra Ward to Wonderland.

Icca, of course, had been ignorant of the rest of the world during her time in the Forest, and so had been shocked when Hattie November Kkul had walked into the Church Off the Labyrinth instead of Delcorta October Kkul, who had died the year prior. Perhaps caught by that same spell Hattie held her Courts under, Icca had been transfixed, watching her approach. There was the young Red Queen's strange kind of beauty—strange, because Icca knew she must be beautiful, though her face was covered by a red veil. Icca could just see the valley of her brow and nose and lips, the dark brown hair enveloping her narrow shoulders, her delicate hands. Then there was Her Majesty's youth, only a couple of years older than Icca herself, who was eighteen at the time.

And the complete silence—Icca couldn't put her finger on it, unspeaking herself, it was just... some delicious charge, to that silence.

But what Icca most fixated upon was the enchantment. The Saint's head weighed in Hattie's thin hands, the rot she drew from its pores in threads binding her fingertips—she was called the Red Queen for the color of her magic, a startlingly deep crimson. It wept from her cuticles and nostrils, staining the veil, as she pulled the decay from the Saint, as she wound it around Icca's throat. The only time that Icca sensed something besides observance or disinterest in the Queen's energy was when she began to pull.

Icca blacked out. She woke up on the dais in the empty church, the brand gone from her neck, and she could feel it—the death trace gone from her veins. She lay there for a long time, free. Watching the Light move across the dark gray stone. Listening to the total silence of the Labyrinth rising around the church walls; Icca could still feel its loom. Feel those thick shadows it shed moving from the road and into itself.

She felt so . . .

Icca was so . . . different. Filling up the same limbs as the girl who had first stepped into Wonderland, and yet, such a far stretch from the one who had tumbled out.

This, in part, had been their dream—Icca, Caro, Tecca—that they should grow to be as powerful as Icca was now, limp and still on the cool stone. So powerful they could go anywhere, do anything they wished to.

Icca supposed they had meant to do all of it together.

Now, Icca, screaming at Caro—about being a thief, and a whore for capitalism—whose spine still lined the dirt, thought of that day. Of how she had wondered, limp on the church dais, if Carousel had already drifted through, felt the cold of the stone to her hip as Icca had then. If Caro hadn't, she would. And then she would think of Icca, too. Icca didn't need to wonder at that.

She thought how it was eventually Dark, and how still she was alone.

How she stood up and went back into Wonderland.

Icca was never lonely, in the Forest. She couldn't possibly be. It talked to her, in a way without words, and Icca liked to be wordless, too, sometimes. She knew, in some way, Wonderland observed her just as she observed it. That it delighted in her, when she indulged in her magic, in her pain, that it made her powers stronger in return, her mind clearer. She used to have people for that, to see her and be seen by her.

But now that she had Wonderland, what did she need anyone else for?

Icca's words ended. Her mouth turned dry, and she realized, with irritation, that she was about to cry.

"Alice," Carousel said, voice softened.

Icca flared.

And then she was stinging. Her magic wept from her, as she traced the Dark in Caro's veins and pinned it in place. Caro tried to move, and pain flashed on her face, teeth gritting in her jaw as her body snagged on its own lightless pieces. Icca caught a glint of something at Caro's neck; she leaned down and snatched the drape of the cloak away, revealing a pin attached to her collar. A white rose, no bigger than her thumbnail. The White Queen's symbol, and, after she'd passed four years ago, the emblem her daughter had taken as her own.

"You've joined the Red Queen's Culled Court?" Icca laughed over Caro, satisfied that her voice was deliciously cold. "I bet you make such a funny little feral pet, in high society."

"Oh yes," Caro breathed—thank the gods, all softness had evaporated. "You haven't heard of me? They call me the Red Queen's butcher. I'm Hattie unnie's favorite creature."

"Revulsion does make one pay attention." Icca flapped the gloves and the fan she'd taken. Unnie—the honorific for girls meaning *older sister*. It was abhorrent. Didn't Caro remember how they used to talk about scraping that whole bloodline out of existence? "She even dresses you up, your *unnie*. How cute."

"I am. I don't always look like this, you know." Caro's black eyes flicked down to her boots. Most of her was scrubbed over in mud, or blood. It was hard to tell in the Light. Her gaze stitched back onto Icca's, and she brandished a crooked, electric grin. "You've never beheld me in a dress. You could despise me as you do now, and your clothes would still drop to a puddle around your ankles."

Icca rolled her eyes. "And then where would yours be, I wonder?"

Caro pinked, but her tone was still the same sharp, biting curdle. "You needn't, Alice darling. I'd have you in an instant, and leave the deities wondering where the hell our hatred went."

"It's not going anywhere," spat Icca.

"I know," said Caro, just as viciously. She was not smiling now. "That'd be the joke of it."

Icca saw it then. The ember glint of Caro's loathing, burning low and constant. There was a joke, here, too. Even after all this time, all of this abhorrence—there were pieces of themselves mirrored in the other. And even more of a laugh: they both saw it instantly.

Tecca would have laughed.

It startled Icca. The thought of Tecca Moore.

Not just her voice, which chimed sometimes in Icca's head and drained away quickly, into the hole that Icca had drilled in her thoughts specifically for it. Caro and Icca had forced the girl away to survive Wonderland, survive their grief—but now it was as if Tecca could be standing right in front of Icca, between them, her curls and her vicious humor and the bite to her every word. Icca took a step back, the memory everywhere, and the first thought was of the hurt, and the second was that she wanted her book, any book, where the three of them never existed and neither did she, even, reading from far above. So distant from the worse parts. Still leaning in, when she got to a worse part . . . she had never leaned for the thought of Tecca, in the last five years, keeping her vague, keeping her nothing.

And neither had Caro, it seemed, having joined the Court of the family responsible for Tecca's death, responsible for the Saints to begin with. Hattie November Kkul sat on the throne and played with her monsters and toiled in the Labyrinth, and the people of Isanghan were obsessed with her for it. She made spectacles of the Saints—it made them feel safe. They weren't safe. They called the horror on the throne their protector, their *Priestess.*

"Crawl back to your Queen." Her magic slipped from Caro's outline. Icca spat her words in a way that would make Tecca proud. "Be so protected in Petra."

Icca turned and was gone. Stumbling out of a shadow near the inn, stumbling upstairs. She flung open the door and stared from its threshold at her wrecked room. There were black feathers and talon-torn bedsheets everywhere, strips floating in the breeze of the open window. Icca had shoved the coin purse under the mattress, and now it was gone. Caro had meant herself to be seen. She'd wanted Icca out of the room so her birds could have free rein.

Icca sat on the floor next to the bedpost for a while and considered burning the inn down, twisting around the stolen gloves and the fan in her hands, and thought of Saint Dorma Ouse. Caro would've gotten paid, once the Priest identified whatever Saint she'd actually brought in. The dumbass had probably been too impatient and left. Or maybe it had been Icca who'd misidentified the Saint. It wasn't such an idiotic mistake—Saints were varied, but they were also animals, and some had shared habits: the rolling around, the quadrupedal tendencies, the hobby of killing families and drying their bones.

There were no free Jabberwockies in Petra—not anywhere, really, but especially not in the capital Ward. Not with Hattie November Kkul inheriting her mother's sensory magic, alongside worse—a gift for flesh binding. The White Queen had filled the maze with monsters reaped from the world she ruled. Hattie made new ones.

Hattie, carrying around the magic that belonged to her bloodline alone, the only witch who could unstitch the death trace. Such rare ability was why, even after such unstitching, the absolved Jabberwockies, owing her nothing at all, still flocked to her.

Sure, Icca knew they couldn't possibly *all* be such sycophants, the Jabberwockies who'd joined Court life. Icca could respect witches who respected power—besides Carousel, because fuck Carousel. *Well, actually*, Icca decided, her hands wrapping the back of her head, as, distantly, she noticed she'd opened her mouth to scream, *yes, fuck* all of them.

They *were* sycophants—they were ignorant, and so they were *nothing*.

Hattie was cruel, and insane, and she made a joke of this world, with her experiments, her false piety. And Carousel. Could she not see how senseless it all was? Did she not remember that Hattie's mother had caused Tecca's death?

And Icca—Icca was senseless, too.

Senseless with the love that had scarred over, cauterized into something worse, and had done so *so damn fast.* She'd been a lovelorn girl one moment, and in the next, cradled a broken heart in her chest cavity. She hadn't even got a chance to catch her breath before the hatred had set in. It had always been like that, between her and Caro. No feeling of one for the other built up slow. Never a spark and always a pyre. Glowing health to full-body corrosion—Icca used to like that instantaneous decay. How her affection for Carousel Rabbit had wrapped her in full.

So now, by her own natural design—the one they shared—Icca hated Caro as much as she had once loved her. And so Icca really did need to kill her.

Laughing, a little to herself, now, to the empty and ruined room. Yes, yes. How could she have forgotten that? How could she have been so childish, flinching back, running away?

No more.

Icca's eyes cleared, and she began to laugh. Uncontrollably. Spasming back on the bed, hands curling the torn sheets. Her breath cutting her lungs like the bite of cold water. Glorious clarity shocked her system—she was awake. Of course, then. Of course Carousel needed to die.

Her, and her Queen.

The image of that white rose pinned to Caro's cloak burned in her mind; it wasn't a shield. Perhaps against the Red Queen, that loyalty barring her back. But Hattie couldn't protect them from everything.

She couldn't protect them from the Dark.

THIRTEEN

YEAR ZERO ZERO NINETY-FOUR, WINTER SEASON

THERE ARE 1003 REMAINING SAINTS

AFTER ROBBING ICCADORA, Caro caught the armored trolley out of the Bajil Ward, leaning on the railing of the passenger car, Cold limbs against the Cold steel—she was always Cold—as she watched the sun rise in the north, over the Wonderland trees.

She felt her tiredness as a second skin; but no, oh no, she wouldn't sleep until they reached the Labyrinth. She'd made that mistake once before, dozing on the trolley seats, awoken when a Saint barreled headfirst into the side of the car and sent the entire line off the tracks. Caro'd had a swollen brow and a broken arm when she'd reached Petra on foot, two days later than the Queen was expecting her. Late all the time, she was. Hattie had laughed at her—or at least smiled a little, which was equivalent—when she'd ambled into the palace, with two heads strung up on her back: one of them her bounty, which she'd had to pick through the tumbled trolley for, and the other from the Saint who'd done the tumbling, not knowing that it was The Carousel Rabbit aboard.

A joke. It wouldn't have left well enough alone if it'd known The Carousel Rabbit was around—Caro knew no Saint would ever fear her. Saints never feared anyone.

Besides the ones of Hattie's creation, that is. Hattie could make them flinch.

But Caro often liked to laugh at her. "They aren't Saints, Duchess dear, they're puppets," to which Hattie would glaze her over with those pale brown eyes and say quietly, "They're still Saints, Carousel. It's just I've put a little thread through them."

But Caro wasn't thinking of Hattie then, leaned over in the Cold, one hand under her cloak to thumb through the coin purse. She was thinking of Alice.

When she'd glimpsed that sickly face in the church, she really hadn't expected Icca to run.

Caro had thought about it a lot, how they would meet again, if they did ever meet again—though she hadn't let herself think about how she thought about it a lot.

But now the meeting had passed, and Caro thumbed through her fantasies as she did the stolen—and deserved—coins in her hand. Icca would be about to perish at the teeth of a Saint, and suddenly it would slacken and drop from above her, and there would be Carousel. Sometimes she was smug, sometimes she killed Icca right after; sometimes, when Caro really did think about it as if it could be true, she would stand over Icca and be so stunned by the image of all of it. Chest heaving with her efforts, the wildness in her eyes locked onto the wildness in Icca's own—coming back together as completely terrified and unquestionably real creatures.

But it had happened in some dingy and gray church. Caro hadn't gotten a chance to be anything but dumbfounded. And Icca had run.

And Caro had followed.

Oh, no, she hadn't particularly *needed* to rob Icca. She'd just wanted to.

And, readers, don't think it was solely because she'd wanted to see Icca again—Caro did want the money. She also wanted Icca to think of her, too, and robbing her did ensure that—Caro used to know in her bones that they thought of each other all of the time.

But over the last four years, she hadn't been so confident—well, actually, Caro had grown quite confident, most of the time flitting around Isanghan as an arrogant bitch, but in the case of Icca, she wasn't sure if the dark witch thought anything of her at all. She was sure it couldn't hold a candle to the extent Caro had thought of Icca, which now, as she was inventorying, she found had been quite often since they'd separated. And she wanted Iccadora to think of her, even—or perhaps, especially—if it was only to hate Caro. Because, after all, Caro did hate Icca, and fair was fair.

And if Icca *had* shown some sort of affection in the church, or in the alleyway, it would have disgusted her. Caro might have killed her instead of only sending the Birds to take the coins. She might have laughed, there, pressed into the dirt of the alleyway, until her ribs cracked apart with the effort.

"Ahg, shibal," Caro muttered low, slapping her palms to her cheeks. "Fuck, okay—snap out of it, Caro dear. It's going to turn out all right. She did fade from you, er, me a little bit there, didn't she? She'll fade again."

And she had other things to fret over, anyway.

Hattie was throwing the Midwinter Tea soon, after all.

And immediately after that—the Saints' Races! The glorious, blood-splattered holiday. Caro blushed just thinking about it—she felt she could appreciate it more than the general population, appreciate good, old-fashioned *fun.* The rest of them found the whole thing so significant, wringing out piety from brutality—Hattie killing Saints was a holy act. Hattie the protector, Hattie the High Priestess. Not that she had ever declared herself anything of the sort. Hattie hadn't needed to open her mouth to smear herself into a religious idol.

And now, the light flickered and dimmed.

Above Caro's head rose the Labyrinth. Its stone Walls sloughing Cold upon the trolley as the tracks snaked away from the Moorlands and into the capital.

The Labyrinth itself was a forest, yes, like Wonderland—it *was* Wonderland, caged and twined with maze.

But not quite; not with the White Queen's Saints, and then Hattie's, her amalgamations, her champions—but all branded with 꿀, *Kkul*, somewhere on their skin. The Labyrinth Saints belonged to the royal bloodline, not Wonderland.

Caro tipped her head back as the gray stone of the Labyrinth Walls blocked out the sky. And there was 페, and ten seconds later, 트, and then 라, and then 페 again, repeating, 페트라, 페트라, each syllable two hundred feet high and hewn into the stone to spell out *Petra*. Each carved letter was etched with tiny defense runes, thousands of them in a single block—Caro could feel their magic prickling at her skin as the trolley slid by.

She wondered if Hattie was within, now, doing whatever Hattie liked to do, silent, save for the soft sounds of her bare feet treading on the earth. Maybe the rumors were true, and she was experimenting. Caro honestly thought the better guess was that she walked in when she didn't want to talk to anyone and walked out again when she began to become bored, spending the whole time within making circles, or standing very still, just observing. . . .

With that thought, Caro felt the tightness slip from her shoulders.

Safety.

Whatever shit she had going with Icca—at least Caro wouldn't be devoured until she decided to leave Petra again.

Carousel would always decide to leave again, eventually.

Sometimes it was because she ran out of money. Sometimes Hattie fancied a specific Saint and sent Caro out to retrieve it, which had to do with getting attention from her unnie. And also with money. Sometimes, Caro just needed to go kill something. There were always *reasons*, yes, certainly. It couldn't possibly be that Caro missed Wonderland. Because if she *did* miss Wonderland—missed how it seemed to match her breath for breath, how her dreams were more colorful, how horrified it rendered her, because how *alive* Caro must be, to be so horrified—there would certainly be something wrong with her, and Caro thought certainly, certainly, nothing was ever wrong with her, because she was a perfect and ethereal being.

But she was tired today; she knew she'd be tired for a few days. She'd stay in Petra, and be alive for a short while longer. She'd sleep. She'd think about Icca, and cringe at herself for it, for how she, once, would have been content with living a nothing life in her nothing Ward as long as the dark witch was beside her.

How easy it would be, to attribute it to Caro thinking little of herself—but Caro had always thought a lot of herself. It was just that she had been sure, then. That it wouldn't have felt like a nothing life, with Iccadora Alice Sickle. That it would've been full and happy, far from grand, certainly, but certainly happy.... This is where Caro would smile to herself, assured, remembering with this thought how silly and young she'd been, to be undesiring of glory.

Wonderland had fixed that in her, with all of its dead things, all of her desolate thoughts. For—how dreary it all was! Carousel was more vivid than all of it. She felt so much more alive, trailing carnage while done up in glitter, personality and eyelids alike.

So then, after cringing and smiling, she'd put on a dress for the Tea and be a self-centered bitch all over again. Everything would turn out okay.

"Everything," Caro breathed, turning to the lad next to her—there'd been a lad next to her the entire time, while she was muttering to herself, and now he seemed surprised that she was addressing him directly, and even more startled when she gripped onto his shoulders—"is going to be *okay*."

"Please let go of me," he said.

—

Caro really did love the Petra Ward. The trolley slid through its gray, stoic Walls and straight into a cityscape scraped in indulgence—buildings of pale stone six stories high, wrought with twisting fire escapes and sprawling windows, roofs sloped and set like sharply styled hats, shutters painted over in pastels, bright-toned even under the perpetually stormy sky. Clean cobblestone met Caro's boots as she stepped from the trolley car and wandered in the direction of her apartment, passing by cafés smelling of milk bread and restaurants smoking pork belly on grills set on the sidewalk. Caro purchased a bag of jjingppang mandu from a street stall and paid with Icca's coins.

She winked at the vendor. "Keep the change."

Caro's apartment sat on the outskirts of the central-district Woods that the palace rose from. It was another reason why Caro liked Petra: that dark stretch of trees in the middle of all the urbanity. She was more powerful in the thicket of Wonderland, she knew, and the Petra Woods had its roots under most of these streets. It was a comfort, a violent one, being able to sleep in her penthouse and sense all the Birds' nests scattered through the tree limbs outside her balcony.

Then there was the Petra University campus, clustered in the Woods, lots of spiked gutters that crows in particular considered a favorite haunt. Hattie had encouraged Caro to take a class or two, and Caro had tried; she'd entertained going to college, once.

That's the point when Caro found she'd forgotten how to read more than three-syllable sentences. Which hadn't made any sense—she'd been literate when she'd left Astara, even as the shitty student she'd been. She'd tried to relearn multiple times, but found that it all trickled from her head when she went to sleep. Caro knew a curse when she saw one. Hattie speculated that she'd picked it up in Wonderland, off of some Saint.

Caro had wondered before if Icca had been hexed the same, but then she'd found Icca's book on the pew.

Caro had taken it, of course—now, as she climbed the stairs of her apartment, she retrieved the text from her bag, looking at the incomprehensible scratches on the purple fabric of the cover. Caro had killed twenty Saints—twenty-one, now. Around a fifth of all the Saints killed in the last half decade. Any one of them could have cursed her, but seeing as Icca could read, it had probably happened after they separated. They'd been powerful, bound together, two terrible witches making Wonderland their own. Maybe Caro would still know how to read if they hadn't. . . .

Caro was now through her front door and thus promptly dropped the book into the unlit fireplace, her cloak and bag and boots—blasphemy!—still on as she searched for a matchbook. A flame came alive in her hand and she let the matchstick fall, turning away as the cover went up in smoke.

"Hello, apartment," sang Caro as she began to take off her things. "I've missed you harshly."

This was true. Every time she left, even if it was just to get food up the street, she missed her home: the small foyer by the front door and the hooks lining it, suffocating under her jackets and scarves, the floor beneath lumped with her shoes. The cute kitchen it led up to, with its four-legged sink and the dark wood countertops, the breakfast bar with its rickety stools; the washroom with its little windows and claw-foot black tub just beyond that. Then there was the bigger room up the hall with the black walls, the one that let in a lot of light from the floor-to-ceiling windows and Caro's desk facing them, her spine warmed by the fireplace when she sat there to draw at night. Her four-poster bed would be at her right shoulder, dominating most of the room with its lushness, thick rug licking underneath it and the wardrobe by the entrance, filled with all of her pretty clothes. She liked the thought of the weight of her things further pressing the building down into the ground; it would withstand both wind and time better, that way. Thus Carousel ensured that her home would always be there for her when she got back.

It was winter, but Caro still pulled open her balcony doors, liking to air out the room whenever she returned from a long Wonderland trip.

Here was a crow balanced on the iron railing; Caro, in a good mood now, flashed her teeth at him.

"Birdie, birdie, babe, babe," she cooed, extending her ringed hand. In the crow's black eyes, she saw the singe of her magic gasp to life in her own. "I'll be borrowing you for a moment."

—

Carousel flew between the spires of the campus, over the Petra Woods to the palace, landing on one of the white, decadently detailed twists of metal that rose from its every edge. Purple tongues of wisteria shuddered in the Cold, enchanted to stay lively even through the frost.

Caro ripped off a length of them with her beak, and went a little ways further around the palace, toward a window in the highest tower. She dropped onto the sill and pecked at the glass. The young woman sitting at the desk finished off what she was writing, and lifted her head.

Her veil drawn back, the Red Queen peered at Caro with pale brown eyes.

Most of the time they radiated indifference—Caro had grown to know that this was half-intentional, and half-unintentional. Hattie didn't waste the energy to avoid seeming rude, because she *was* being rude, really; she had a lot of other things on her mind, and she wasn't going to look at you like you were the only thing she was considering. But Caro knew—as Hattie also knew—that, when she was growing up, before she'd begun to veil her features in public, people mistook this slack glint in her eyes for her being distant. Hattie November Kkul was not distant. The person she was looking at was never the sole object of her pondering, but she always, always paid them close attention. She knew when people were sincere, and when they weren't. She knew when people were afraid of her. She knew how much magic a person carried within them by the way they spoke.

"And how do I speak?" Caro had tittered once.

Hattie had thought for a moment, then said quietly, "Boldly, here and there. Frantically, here, and there."

Now, the Red Queen stood on the tips of her toes to be able to reach the window latch. She pushed it open and allowed Caro to step onto her small, gloved fingers. She hadn't spoken in public since the death of her mother; some of the Culled Court had never even heard her voice.

"Carousel," Hattie said, and Caro shivered.

Hattie pulled at the window to keep the Cold out. She took the wisteria from Caro's talon. "Is this for me?"

Caro squawked. She loved the feel of it, the full, extravagant jaggedness of the sound. It was another reason she preferred crows, and despised pigeons. She fucking despised pigeons.

"I've been notified that I have received your Saint's head," Hattie said, setting Caro down on her desk. Caro tucked her head in a mock bow, ruffling her wings.

This tower room was the Queen's study, a small space made smaller by overflowing bookshelves and tapestries plushing the walls. It used to belong to her mother, the White Queen. Caro hadn't known Hattie then, but had a feeling she hadn't changed the room much since her passing.

Hattie settled back into her chair. She wore a simple black dress that paired nicely with the richness of her shroud of deep-brown hair, half-tied back with a crimson ribbon. She seemed small—Hattie *was* small, enveloped by her mane and her fabrics, her heart-shaped face tucked within—and then she'd look up, meet your eyes, and she was the Red Queen. Even with that pseudo-distant look Hattie would pin to you, because most of the time she was bleeding her magic.

Hattie's mother's magic had been milk-white. It was said to have bleached cloth and skin and stone. Her daughter's was crimson, and it stained instead of bleaching, but the two were the same in the degree of their power—a power that they could not keep in.

Hattie took her red handkerchief and wiped absently at the magic dripping from her nose. Her skirt was wet with the drops she missed—this is why she always wore black, or red. Caro drank it in, this casual, habitual gesture that marked such absolute power.

"Hajima. You are going to make me blush," Hattie murmured at the staring Caro-bird, though Caro was sure that Hattie November Kkul had never once blushed in her twenty-three years.

The Red Queen tugged the letter she'd been working on out from under Caro's talons, plucking up her pen again and continuing from where she'd dropped off. Now she paid Caro no more mind; she'd look up if Caro insisted, maybe pecked at her thumb, but would go on with this action if Caro didn't, and Caro didn't. She wanted to stay and watch the movement of Hattie's hands, the gorgeous ribbons of her handwriting bleed across the page... but no, unnie had important work to do.

It was all right. Caro could admire her from afar; she often did, in Wonderland, when she needed something to scatter away the Forest chill. She'd think of Hattie's grace, her quiet manner, all of it an unassuming cover above the bottomless well of her thoughts. It was quite comforting, how Caro kept Hattie in a little room in her head, how in that room she could twist around Hattie's neck whenever she liked, to make her meet Caro's eyes. Once she told Hattie that she did this, which did make the Queen meet her gaze, and she called Caro strange in her soft, moth-wing tones, just a note, not a judgement, and this memory Caro put on a shelf in the little room and took proper care to keep off the dust.

Caro fell out of the crow. Slotting back into her body, she sucked in a breath of dewy air. She was on her side on the Cold stone of her balcony, slicked over in a winter rain, watering down the magic leaking from her eyes. A familiar nausea churned in her gut—she steadied herself with a breath of chilled air. Between the iron railings she glimpsed the Forest foliage, twinkling in cyan flashes as she blinked her power back. Her magic mostly came from her eyes, though sometimes it wept from her nostrils—like it mainly did for Hattie—or her back molars—like it did for Icca.

"Stop that right now," Caro groaned, gritting her teeth through the sting of her magic.

She forced herself up and wobbled for the doors, started drawing a bath, and balanced herself gingerly on the rim, shoveling down the rest of the mandu. She climbed down into the water and let it scald her, focused on her protesting nerves instead of— Damn it.

She really should've killed Icca in that alleyway.

Maybe. Caro didn't know if that would've been better; perhaps it would've only made the thought of Icca more sticking. There was also the consideration that Icca could've killed Caro instead, but that seemed a little thing, though Icca's power was not a little thing. Icca's magic had always scared Caro; and, readers, Caro was fine with admitting this to herself. Her own magic scared her, too.

"I'm exhausted," Caro stated suddenly to the empty, unlit bathroom. "I think I'll fall asleep right here and drown." It was a threat to herself, to her thoughts of Icca. When she didn't flinch, she smiled cheekily, water in her teeth. "Well. Perhaps to bed, then, instead of drowning. Oh, and then you'll be alive for tomorrow and you won't miss the Tea! You like the Tea, Caro dear, don't you?" Scrunching up the skin of her brow, now, she pouted slightly. "But the other Culled Jabberwockies can be so uninteresting, just coming to snack on cakes and gossip. It's o-kay. I'll keep you entertained, darling, you don't have to talk to any of them, or you can make fun of them to their faces! If you wish. That'll be fun. Don't you think it could be fun?" Carousel swirled a hand in the bath, thinking of her pretty hanbok dress. "Hm. Yes. I suppose. If you insist, darling."

Most people assumed she'd gone mad in Wonderland; there certainly were a lot who'd done so before her.

Carousel was sure she wasn't mad.

She was sure she was perfectly pleasant, and she loved herself a lot. Even though madness might not be mutually exclusive to these elements, it was these elements she liked to focus on. She hadn't beaten Wonderland by beating up its Saints; she'd beaten it because she'd wandered out of it still flirting with herself excessively.

"And, and," she added reassuringly, "you know, Carousel, Alice might as well be dead—you won't see her again."

FOURTEEN

YEAR ZERO ZERO NINETY-FOUR, WINTER SEASON

THERE ARE 1002 REMAINING SAINTS

AND AT ALMOST EXACTLY THE same time—as these things tend to go, readers—Icca was making her way through Darkness and thinking to herself, *That bitch thinks she's not going to see me again.*

Then the witch spilled out of a shadow and whacked her head on the wall lining the stairs tucked into the back of the Duchess Apothecary, leading up to Mordekai Cheshire's apartment on the second level. Icca groaned and rubbed her sore temple, hand flattening on the railing to steady herself, and, over her bitching, heard Kai singing over the bathroom sink.

"Ya, Cheshire," Icca called up the stairs as she pulled back her hair. It was longer than Carousel's was now, even though—if she had bothered thinking about it—Icca might've pictured that Caro would've still liked her own grown out, as she had when they were young, instead of the crow witch cutting those horrid yellow strands just beneath her collarbone. Icca's hair spilled to her waist when she allowed it to, liking how soft it felt against her arms. She hoped Caro had thought her a little vain for it. She wanted Caro to get the wrong impression of her.

The singing above abruptly stopped. Icca peeled back the curtain under the stairs to reveal a small kitchenette, and as she pawed through the cupboards for the barley tea, heard Kai shut off the tap and yell, "What do you want, Sickle?"

Icca began filling up the kettle, then muttered mostly to herself, "Tell me where else I ought to go."

"Depends on where you want to get to."

"I don't much care—"

"Then it doesn't matter which way you go."

"I was going to say I don't much care for your ridiculous knots of speech, today. Ever."

"Stay out of the tea," barked Kai in return.

Icca ignored him. She made up a cup and wandered beneath hanging baskets of jars and suspended herb bundles, toward the front of the unlit apothecary, peering out of its front window and onto the cobblestone street. She'd left Yule in the early morning to get here—the Polt village of the Beotkkot Ward, which sat a thin, jagged stretch of Wonderland away from Petra. She couldn't darkport all that distance from Yule, and had had to pick through a bit of the Forest in order to manage it. No Saints, and she found herself glad for it. She was too tired for terror this morning. Too pissed off to fight anything but sloppily, and her magic would weep in excess, and the resulting burning really couldn't be good for her organs and soft bits and the like.

Beotkkot was full of herbalists and potion makers, somewhere to make some extra coin gathering plants alongside Saints' heads in the Forest. It's how she'd met Kai Cheshire a couple of years ago. Now at least a couple of times a month she'd gather some horrible little plant in Wonderland for him to make a horrible little elixir out of, and then they might sleep together, or not, or just talk or eat or go chase down and beat shoplifters in the street, and then she'd leave again for a few weeks and come back to pick up work or sleep with him again, or not, again, and round it went. Icca often possessed, in a very neutral tone, the thought that Cheshire was her only friend.

Now he came down the stairs, all sparkling, lopsided grin and long limbs of deep olive skin, dark eyes lined in darker kohl at their perfectly angled corners. "Leave immediately."

Icca stayed stuck to the windowsill, ignoring him, while a blond, frazzled-looking boy came pattering down the stairs.

Kai shot him a wink, which the boy returned with a grin that was cute despite the string of hickeys absolutely staining his jawline. Icca rolled her eyes anyway.

"Annyeonghi gaseoyoh." Icca grinned sharply at him, meaning it in the most deeply literal meaning of the farewell, *Go peacefully*. Icca knew the thought of Kai was most often like a tack in the head.

Kai seemed to get her meaning, because the door closed behind the boy and he said again, drifting away to light the candles, "Leave immediately, Sickle."

But he didn't mean it. Icca was his only friend, too. Very poor friends they were, indeed, but language fell short of a more accurate description.

"He was just adorable. You seemed rather obsessed, judging by the sorry state of his face."

A jest. Kai Cheshire was only ever obsessed with himself.

He fancied himself above all the rest of the common Ward people, using his magic and musing how all the others in the village were safe, trite for it, but he would still die close to the rest of them, after a life hiding from the Forest.

What kind of life had Icca once hoped for? Graduating from Empathy, top of her class, and then—what? Perhaps she never gave herself a proper chance to think about it, knowing, in the deep black of her thoughts, that, without Wonderland, her end would be in a safe, distant future. Her grave in the same nothing Ward where her parents had been born and where they had died of saltfever, after a long life of that dreaded routine and wisteria farms, the same existence a generation down as a generation up.

Without Wonderland, Icca would've cultivated her magic over the years, for entertainment instead of survival like the vain boy before her, taking her burning slow. It would have hurt so much less. Caro and Tecca by her sides, the three of them bored out of their minds, growing more wicked by the day because of it.... So maybe it was always bound to happen. Maybe they would've done something horrible, eventually, just for the thrill, the variety. Maybe they were always fated to end up in Wonderland.

Maybe with Tecca alongside them.

Wonderland wouldn't have us.

Oh! And why's that, Icky?

You needn't ask, Caro, I know this one. Alice knows the three of us would send the Saints running scared, send them teeth over heels out into the Moorlands. It'd be a simple thing and leave the Forest blushing and embarrassed for it.

Icca took a long sip of her tea and said, brown eyes drawn to the gray Light teeming at the curtains, "I ran into Carousel Rabbit yesterday."

Kai looked up from the lit match in his fingertips, the flame glazing an expression that was first slack and then shocked and then grinning, again, and now, each tooth was thinly outlined in magic the color of lavender flowers. The matchstick died in his grip, but a moment later there was no grip, as Kai seemed to bleed out of the air in the same hazy, lazy fashion the smoke curled from the matchstick. It dropped to the table. Icca seemed to be the only person left in the shop.

She took another sip of tea. Here Kai was an outlier, just like her, one of the few of the population using his magic despite its sting. It was, she supposed, why she kept coming back. Habit, perhaps, to drift toward the bored ones. Everyone else... well, they were everyone else. They stayed in the same place; they probably would forever—wrapped up in their routines, chasing their small thrills, not thinking of the Saints, waiting for the Races to come around again. Maybe you'd move to Petra, if you had enough money, if you thought you could make it across Wonderland. And then you'd continue not to move ever again.

Icca thought the Kkul bloodline should count themselves lucky for it. If Petra people thought it a fine idea to leave the capital, they'd come back toting the horrors and traumas of Wonderland that they hadn't gathered from their insane Queen and the flashier Jabberwockies of her Culled Court—ultimately criminals who strutted around like celebrities—and they wouldn't be able to attend their classes or bake in their bakeries or build their adorable apartments any longer, with how much their hands shook, and the whole city would fall to pieces.

Kai reappeared a few moments later—soundlessly and not quite tangible, like the blank air was mist shrouding his form—now under the sage drying in the corner, one set of long fingers lifted to check its progress. "Carousel Rabbit, you say?" he murmured, as if disinterested, and then bled out of sight again. "And what fun did you have with Miss Rabbit?"

This latter question was spoken directly into Icca's ear; she tilted her head up and to the right, where Kai's teeth glinted in her peripheral but did not appear when she tried to find a set of eyes to meet.

"She claimed to have hunted and killed the Saint that was weighing my bag."

"How fateful."

"No."

"No?" Perhaps the corner of a grin, here; it was gone from the air when Icca's eyes tried to catch it.

"No, you don't believe it." Icca couldn't know for sure if it was Fate or not, crossing Carousel, but the concept wasn't one of her gods as it was. "You're saying it to get a rise out of me."

"Perhaps lucky, then."

Icca thought of her stolen coins and rolled her eyes. She said haughtily, "I almost made her organs implode from their own Dark."

"Almost," Kai tittered, now at her other ear. It had been a little unnerving at first, when she found Kai didn't have lightless spots in him when he did this, made himself unphysical, when he didn't have anything but that soft, cloying voice. Now she just found it dramatic. "Almost..."

"And she's invited me to Petra's Midwinter Tea." Icca set down her tea on the sill and dug through her bag, producing the fan that had dropped from Caro in the alleyway. She opened it, where across the first leaflet was scrawled 진심으로 초대합니다—*cordially invited*—and next to her boots she saw Kai's feet come into place, head bowed next to hers to read. "And it says I'm allowed to bring a date, to watch the Red Queen make her darling Saint for the Races. A high honor, truly."

She could feel Kai grin. "I thought you despised Petra."

"I do despise Petra."

"And Carousel Rabbit."

"I do despise Carousel Rabbit. So, do a little critical thinking, would you?"

"You're going to kill her." He knew right away, of course. He was just being an ass.

"Yes. I am."

Kai's grin split wider. "Oh, Sickle. Why? You were both horrible enough to one another, if what you told me was true." It was. Kai was the only soul she'd told the whole thing to. Not because he was particularly special to her, or deserved it. Just because he asked. She never meant her hatred to be a secret. And Kai, in turn, drank down the tale with the same amount of apathy she displayed for him. He liked the more wicked kinds of entertainment, just as she did. He liked boldness, and Icca was very bold with her cruelties.

Maybe if it were another, brighter world, without magic, without Saints, her viciousness would weigh on her.

But this existence was vicious. Her gods demanded to be felt, Dark at her fingertips, Carnage a thought to lean into.

Icca was a violent thing, and not often, but sometimes, she went senseless in her anger. She just didn't care. She didn't care that there really wasn't a fair reason for hurting Carousel, besides the fact that she wanted to hurt Carousel. She didn't care that she barely had a plan, that she was hunting down an impulse. She just wanted to fucking move.

"So, then," Kai said. "Why do we have to go to Petra?"

"Because," Icca breathed, feeling on the precipice of some greater version of herself, "I am going to kill the Red Queen, too."

Now she did look at him, eager and smug, for what would surely be Kai's appalled reaction. He'd think her a madwoman, a rare and genuine reckless soul.

Kai rolled his eyes. "Dear gods, Icca, this again?"

FIFTEEN

Year Zero Zero Ninety, Summer Season

There Are 1094 Remaining Saints

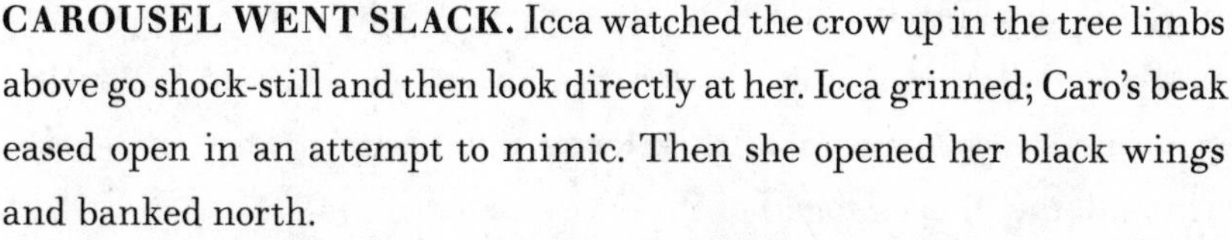

CAROUSEL WENT SLACK. Icca watched the crow up in the tree limbs above go shock-still and then look directly at her. Icca grinned; Caro's beak eased open in an attempt to mimic. Then she opened her black wings and banked north.

Icca watched her go with a swell of biting pride in her chest. Caro was so much better at flying, so much more precise with her power than she had been when they'd first entered Wonderland. And Icca had observed the same growth in herself—the two young witches feeding off that strange Forest influence. They were giddy with it, sometimes, certainly arrogant, and they figured they deserved it, after surviving a year here. After killing seven Saints.

And today, they would claim the last. Four heads apiece, then; it hadn't ever been a question, that they'd leave Wonderland together. They'd travel to the Petra Labyrinth hand in hand, heads in tow, and have the

White Queen draw the death trace from their souls. They'd get an apartment in Petra, perhaps. It'd have good light with glossy floors—even if Icca didn't like such decadence, Caro did, so Icca didn't care. They'd get dull jobs and come home at night and be high off their happiness for the rest of their days. They'd never go back to Wonderland. They had it all planned out, really. They were both so young. They had so much time to be together.

Caro spasmed back into her body, and then went completely still. Icca immediately doubled over to check on her, hand on her collar when Caro roused with a bubbling laugh, snatching to pull Icca down. Caro kissed her, and Icca snapped away, barking, "The *Saint,* Rabbit?" and Rabbit cooed, "Dozing in a tree a few hundred paces north, Alice dear, all's well in Wonderland."

And maybe it was even true—for them, anyway; Icca was sure some sorry Jabberwockies were getting eaten somewhere else in the Forest as they were making out in the underbrush—but as they *were* making out in the underbrush, dear readers, it must have been true. They'd almost frozen to death last winter and almost got gobbled up by every Saint they'd come across, and lay up at night, afraid, oh, so afraid, it felt they were just coats being worn by their terror. But it hadn't all been miserable. After all, they'd been together the entire time.

Night fell; they knew, by now, to wait for night to fall before facing a Saint. Because Caro was a chip of the Darkness in her crows and Icca—well. Icca was the Dark herself.

She could see the Saint perfectly well, in the tree.

Moonlight drew the shadows of its limbs down against the trunk. It didn't matter that Icca needed to get closer for the enchantment to reach; the moment the Saint snapped awake at their scent, snarling and already salivating, she was already weeping silver, already stinging, grinning.

Icca flicked her hands up, wound the Saint in its own shadow. And then, next to her, Caro flushed blue, and there were birds filling up the foliage. Tearing the Saint apart, and Icca was thinking of their apartment, of hot tea in the morning and hot baths in the night, of reading books in bed while Caro breathed next to her, their ankles intertwined.

But they hadn't known, about this Saint, or moreover, about this Saint's sister.

Do-San Tweedle slept in the trees. Dae-San Tweedle slept in the earth.

And now there were teeth around Icca's ankle.

Caro snapped her hand out, but Icca was already off her feet, on her stomach being dragged away from Caro as Dae-San unearthed itself and scuttled deeper into the Forest.

Icca reached out, shrieking and choking on dead leaves for it, scraping shadow with her fingernails as the Forest floor tore at her. She didn't know where she was. They were moving so quick that Caro wouldn't know where she was.

She could feel the Saint's black magic, bleeding from its molars and into the holes it wore into Icca's ankle, the air alive with the sound and smell of burning flesh. She could barely think of anything past the pain, didn't even realize she was praying until it worked. Until they hit a particularly lush patch of foliage shadow and Icca was over it, dropping herself like a stone into it, pulling the Saint down with her.

But because she was senseless with the pain and her own fear, she didn't have a destination in mind. And magic without intention was a burning, volatile thing, and Icca was wedged in it, in this absence she'd pulled herself into. The void of the Dark. Trapped in it, with the Saint.

It had let go of her. She was blind, stumbling through the blackness, trying to find a seam to slip into. It was usually dead silent in this place, no matter how hard she was stepping, or breathing, or screaming.

But now. Icca could hear the Saint's fingernails clicking as it searched for her, hear the drip of its black magic, the sounds drawn hollowly, like they were in the belly of an empty chapel. It was going to find her. She was too afraid for it not to know exactly where she was.

Icca wasn't sure how long had passed by the time it tracked her down, by the time it was holding her, and still she could not see it.

"You'll never get out of here without me," Icca croaked, even though it wouldn't understand, or even if it did, it wouldn't care. Not when it was about to feed.

She was so delirious with the pain of her own magic, excessive in this Dark place, that she barely felt the Saint pinch open her mouth. It wanted her tongue first, or maybe her tonsils. Saints did have some individuality to them. Some specific habits. Some insistent cravings. She and Caro had figured that out a while ago.

And just like that, with the thought of Caro, Icca felt an edge to all of this Darkness, and twitched for it, and she and the Saint were out of the void, rolling out on the Forest floor.

And then Carousel was on them instantly.

Her birds came down—they'd probably been combing the entire Forest. Icca didn't know where she was, and even as the Saint shrieked and clawed for a bite under the onslaught of talons, she was struck by her awe of Caro. How Caro could strike out her magic like a plague. She could send her birds to infect their brethren with her influence, and when she stole a crow to use as her own form—she and Icca had not found a limit to how far she could fly.

It was immense power. It hurt. Caro found Icca next to the dead, shredded Saint, and Icca found Caro shuddering above her with magic staining her cheeks. Her words came in a shaking line. "Alice? Are you alive?"

Icca lay very still indeed. For a time she did not speak, too clotted with fear. Caro lay down beside her, beside the Saint.

Eventually, Icca spoke. She felt like nothing but a child. "I don't want to be in Wonderland anymore, Rabbit." Her fingers reached out to clasp Caro's cloak, curled herself into Caro's ribs. She would hate the desperateness of it later, even though now Caro put her arm around Icca and pressed their cheeks together, so when a sob broke through Icca's next words, she could feel the warmth of Caro's magic against her lips. "I don't want to be here anymore."

And Caro said, "We're done, Alice. It's all right. We're getting out of here soon."

Icca thought it true. They'd four Saints' heads apiece. They were going to beat Wonderland. They were going to be happy.

But then they'd returned to their camp. It was clear it'd been ransacked.

They'd buried their seven heads. They found only two left, perhaps because they'd been hidden closer to the fire, where one would have to kneel in ashes. It made four total, including the Tweedles, one weighing at each of their right hips. Icca sank to her knees in front of the holes while the dawn sky thickened with birds, thickened with Carousel's scream. They would tear apart any other Jabberwocky who'd thought they'd thieved themselves an easy ticket out, but somehow Icca knew the crows wouldn't find anyone. It could've just as easily been wild dogs.

Icca tried to keep the thought away.

But it was a silent, dazed night. Both of them breathing, unable to speak past the shock, unable to touch each other without it being some kind of admission—*Oh gods, darling, darling, I don't think I can take it anymore.*

Still, they awoke as they did every morning: intertwined. Caro's heart beating steadily against Icca's spine—though, was it rising? Or was that Icca's own? The bad thought clutching, climbing through her. It rose up her throat and sat behind her teeth. Icca would not let it go.

Though, really, the thought was one she'd voiced to Caro before. One Caro had agreed with, not in words, but with the knife in her hands, with how she had slicked it over.

We need to get out of here, Rabbit.

That is the only thing we need.

SIXTEEN

Year Zero Zero Ninety-Four, Winter Season

There Are 1002 Remaining Saints

KAI CHESHIRE DIDN'T want to kill the Red Queen, because Kai didn't particularly want to die.

This is what he told Icca, and stood there while she laughed in his face. It was a truly ridiculous sound. It was like she was trying to break glass, with that laugh, but Kai stood there while she did so, because Icca laughing without scoffing was a rare thing. Then she realized that he was liking it and ceased.

"You are always saying you're off to end the Queen," said Kai, raising a weak wave to a potential customer peering into the apothecary. *Give me a moment here, please. This witch is trying to kill me.* It was of slight concern that now Icca was saying this while looking him in the eye instead of with her own drawn to the ceiling, her voice hard and sure instead of wistful and bitter like he'd come to know the thought to be. The murdering of Hattie November Kkul was often a topic after the sex. Kai didn't take it personally.

"I am not always saying that."

"It is an exhausted topic, Sickle."

Icca scoffed. "Fine. I'll shut up about it, then."

She only said this because she knew Kai did not, in fact, want her to shut up about it, then.

"'If I ever saw her one step out of the Ward,'" Kai quoted, tipping his head back to the ceiling to mock her properly, "'if I ever saw Hattie November Kkul one *step* outside of Petra, I'd knock off her head, I'd remind her of the world she is so sheltered from, and yet its evil she feeds off of like cherries off the stem—'"

"I," Icca said flatly, and he looked back down to see her dark, fine eyes pinning him down, "am never so pretty with my words."

A grin cleaved Kai's cheeks. Right she was.

"And it's not like she'd ever leave Petra anyway, the coward."

"All that proves is that she's saner than you, Sickle."

"No one is saner than me."

"Ha!"

But Icca's eyes flashed, and her voice came quieter, and when Icca was quiet she was calm, and that calm was lethal. "You know she killed Delcorta October Kkul, right?"

Goose bumps erupted up Kai's arms. He reveled in them. "Oh? I wasn't aware."

"Don't be flippant."

Kai flapped a lazy hand. Not because he was uninterested, oh, no, never, with Iccadora Alice Sickle. But because it would make her turn a shade redder, and he liked pushing her buttons. "Yes, yes, that was quite a scandal. Finding the Red Princess standing at the top of some stairs—"

"Overlooking where her mother's *body* had crumpled several stories below—"

"I'm regretting telling you that at all," Kai lied. Icca had been in Wonderland when the whole affair had gone down. The news had reached his own Ward only months after the fact, after Hattie November had been declared innocent of matricide and thus been crowned Red Queen. "And were you even listening when I did? She was proved to be without a death trace, sent herself into the Labyrinth to test it. The only one to go in and come out alive." He flicked Icca between the eyebrows. "Silly. See? Our Queen is just a darling girl." Nothing could be further from the truth—Icca's face sank another shade darker. "The Saints of the Labyrinth would've devoured her alive if she'd killed Delcorta, toting around that death trace, even before she could rip one of their heads off to remove it from herself."

Icca smacked his hand away when he went to flick her again. "And now that *Labyrinth* is her playground. I've heard she wanders in and out of the blasted place all the time."

Kai yawned. "So?"

"So!" Icca scoffed, indignant. "So people think she's a High Priestess of our times, and yet—"

"So why do you *care*, Icca, whether or not she's committed matricide? Aw—did you adore the White Queen?"

"Ha! I *care* because I don't understand how no one else sees it! I *care* because she got off scot-free, fooled everyone because she has some immunity to the death trace. She shouldn't have that. She shouldn't get to kill and then get crowned. She should be—"

"Sent out into Wonderland?"

"*Yes.*"

"Because she's someone who *actually* deserves to be?"

"She—" Icca stopped; Kai's smile was feline.

But it seemed, today, Kai had struck that chord a tad too zealously. The look that flickered across Icca's face told him as much, and so did the turn of her feet toward the shop door.

Kai leaned against the front counter and mused nonchalantly, purposely not looking in the direction of her departure, "Oh, Sickle. It's always been mutterings about killing Hattie November up until this point. What's changed?"

His musings had the intended effect. Icca stopped, one hand on the door. "You're implying something. Out with it."

Kai's grin softened—far from genuinely, just on the off chance it might coax more from her. "This is about Carousel Rabbit."

"It isn't."

"So why now? What's changed, besides that you've seen her?"

Icca's delicate features betrayed nothing, though to Kai it was as if she'd retreated for a moment, nearly imperceptibly, under the dark mass of her hair to think of some dark mass of a thing.

"It's not about her." She turned away from him, one hand floating up to her face, her poor, abused pores, before dropping. Curling at her side. "It's just. She's reminded me of something."

Kai let his grin split his face again now that she wasn't facing him. "And what's that?" He leaned, hand pressing to the wood of the wall beside Icca's head, to pick through her expression. Waiting to swallow down more of the horrible little tale that was Iccadora Alice Sickle. "Come, Sickle darling. You can tell me anything at all."

They had no future together. Really, it came down to this: Kai had no desire to go into Wonderland, and Icca couldn't leave it well enough alone. He'd heard of such madness being acquired in the Forest, witches drunk off the power they found while running for their lives above its roots. Seeing that madness up close was a thrill he'd find nowhere else, not in his little village, this dull Ward, not in the other girls and boys he brought into his bed. So maybe Kai did think of Icca when she wasn't here. Not enough to wonder where she was, or if she was thinking of him, or if she was safe, or finally slain and gobbled down by a Saint, but some.

And then Icca said, in her small, bramble thicket of a voice, "Seeing her. She's reminded me that the Red Queen's to blame."

"To blame for what?"

"For Tecca." She spat the words.

Kai liked this answer a lot. Still he pressed, "How so? Wasn't that the fault of the White Queen?"

"Delcorta is dead." Her expression was murder itself. "Hattie is alive."

"Ah, yes. Not untrue." Gods, did she hear herself when she talked? She clearly had no idea what she was doing. All Iccadora had was rage. Kai didn't mind it. In fact, if she was more self-aware, that might ruin the whole thing. He liked her like this. Senseless.

"Hattie deserves enough death traces on her that Saints should be stampeding the palace."

"I never took you for such a humanitarian."

"I don't give a fuck about the rest of them," Icca snapped, and turned and shoved him away, and then it wasn't enough for her, so she tried to shove him again, and Kai summoned up his magic and smeared his physical form out of the air. From the haze of consciousness he diffused himself into, he traced around on the ceiling, observing Icca standing all alone. She smoothed a white hand down her face—she'd been picking the skin again, he could tell, but it was never enough to cut out the prettiness there—and she said, quieter and more bitterly this time, "You could never understand what we all meant to one another."

He rematerialized behind the front counter, fingers—when he had fingers again—reaching to count out the change for the day.

"Hm, well, yes," he mused. He'd never been good at faking empathy. "So—what do you need me for? You can't kill her alone?"

The answer was yes, because no one could kill a witch as powerful as Hattie November Kkul alone, or at all, but still Icca scowled.

And then she drew her eyes up, and a chill traced its way down Kai's spine.

"I'll need a rose draught," said Icca, studying him and then bored with him, tucked up into her next thought.

"How now, darling, making a garden of the Queen?" Kai yawned, contemplating the request. It was obvious what Icca wanted to do—flower draughts made flowers bloom anywhere. Earth, or stone, or organs. Feeding it to Hattie would do the trick, but why not just use her own abilities? "What—thinking your own powers won't match up?"

"Please," she scoffed. Kai grinned. Of course not.

"And why a rose draught? I think my lilac draughts are much finer, or lilies would— Oh!" He almost shivered, he really did. "The White Queen's insignia. Oh, *Iccadora*, that is just—"

"I know the show she puts on with the Saints, every Midwinter Tea. I'm going to have one of her own beasts gobble her down in front of the Courts. The Saints' Races won't happen this year, not when she ruptures and her champion eats her alive."

"Come, now, you're going to ruin the holiday?"

Icca rolled her eyes.

"Well, answer me this. Is the plan, after the deed is done, to take the crown?"

"No."

"No?"

"I don't care for it."

"You don't care for it," Kai echoed. "Well, well..."

"Spit it out, you're *insufferable*—"

"I just thought you'd want the power of it."

"Ha! What power? I'd have to rule. I would have to *talk* to people. Even doing nothing would be a time-consuming effort, waiting for the country to collapse." She flicked a hand as if to clear the very idea from the air around them. "What power?" she repeated, murmured words all to herself, Kai knew. Her gaze had caught on her fingertips. "All the power is already here...."

Kai watched, fascinated with the act, all her strange acts. Was this truly not about Carousel Rabbit, but about the young dead witch, about revenge? Perhaps, perhaps... but here was a path, Icca's hand suspended in air.

Above all else, Kai dared to think, this was about no one else but Iccadora Alice Sickle.

She was a heartless girl, after all. He truly believed she didn't have the capacity to care for another.

And Kai thought—thought it with the utmost care, so as not to miss any detail of the future he saw sprawled in front of Sickle now—that if she actually managed the power to kill the Queen, it would only be the first taste. Icca would not be able to stop herself once she started; she'd crave her own magic, obsess over its growth. Another madness of Wonderland. Or perhaps a clarity. Pain meant nothing to her by now; death was power's only edge. How close to that line would Icca go, once she began to believe she could be the most Divine witch to ever grace existence?

Perhaps she would end up taking the crown.

Perhaps she'd be the one to end the Saints.

Or perhaps Hattie November Kkul would just kill her in a matter of seconds.

That would be interesting, too, though terribly anticlimactic. Still, still. Kai would like to see that.

He drawled, "Sure, Sickle. I'll provide you the rose draught, like I'd provide to any other paying customer. But why the hell would I go with you to Petra?"

"It'll be the farthest you've ever strayed from home. Are you afraid?"

He'd be a fool not to be. He hardly went too far outside the Wall of his Ward except to collect his herbs; even though he could dematerialize himself if he were ever in danger, he didn't fancy being hunted down. But this was simply Icca jabbing; she was stalling for something. Kai only grinned and waited.

Icca looked at the tips of her boots, then said disinterestedly, "Going with me, as my plus-one, would be the payment."

"Ha!"

Icca copied his laugh immediately. This time it wasn't genuine, but he didn't much mind that either.

"Please, Cheshire," the witch scoffed. "I know you'd hardly want to miss something like this."

Kai smiled and said, "Oh, it is always so good to be so known," at the same time he thought to himself, *The bitch wants a scapegoat.* "What happened to your money? Weren't you just out there, killing Saints, collecting coins?"

She ignored this. "One more thing."

"Yes, darling?"

"You're going to buy me a dress, too."

—

Hattie came to. Both her arms were asleep, sprawled across her desk; she lifted her nose from them and breathed in the scent of ink and old books. *I am awake*, she thought to herself, enjoying how the words came crisp and clear in her mind, despite the tiredness weighing in her eyes. *It is so strange, sometimes, to be awake.*

Dazed, she thumbed around her skirts until she found her pocket watch, checking the time, but it was gone from her head as soon as she snapped the silver cover shut. It was deep into the Night, anyway. She could feel that much, the press of the god at the windows of the study, even if It wasn't the one she worshipped.

She rose in a sluggish sort of way, kicking over a pile of books before she reached the door, her hand on the white stone wall, deep blue in the dark, to steady herself as she descended the spiral. Her bare feet soundless on the carpets licking up the halls, she followed up the east wing to find the dungeon stairwell. She knew the guards stood attentive at its entrance; Hattie paused and yawned before she made the last turn, sending the magic trailing from her nostrils over the curve of her upper lip, into her mouth. She flicked her tongue against the stream. She swallowed it down.

The enchantment, red and blushed with a rich glow, wove thin and threadlike between her fingertips as she spread them wide. The magic lit up the painting spanning floor-to-ceiling, a landscape of a moorland bright with midday sun. Hattie didn't like the painting, indifferent to it, really. Hattie preferred eccentrics, though she didn't consider herself an eccentric person, not like she considered Carousel Rabbit.

Hattie November Kkul didn't consider herself much of anything, besides powerful.

She closed her eyes.

She felt the breathing of the guards standing around the corner, used it to trace out the rest of their forms. Drawing out their outlines in her head, and then the eyes in their heads.

Hattie saw the empty hallway they were staring down with her own sight, the two of them splitting her vision in the strangest way. And her hands moved. And she stitched what she was seeing—what they were seeing—fast into place.

Hattie blinked back into her own eyes, and found them drowning in red. She took out her handkerchief as she rounded the corner. The guards did not see her blotting away the magic from her lashes and her nostrils—the latter with less effort, since she had long known it wasn't much use to do so; more would come—seeing nothing except the empty hall they'd been staring at all night long. Hattie found that stitching a sense temporarily into place was easier when one had grown used to what it was taking in, though she admittedly wasn't as proficient with forcing an emotion to hold fast. It was all those chemicals in one's skull, always moving—humans were always so finicky, so quick to change. The Kkuls had always worked better in flesh, anyway.

This was also why she liked Carousel. The crow witch was eccentric in her actions, but less so in her thoughts—there were parts of Caro's head that Hattie felt had snagged fast—no, fused in place. Carousel's fondness for herself, the way she looked after her own happiness—Hattie found that perfectly incredible. It was no easy feat, after Wonderland.

And Carousel's hatred for Iccadora Alice Sickle—Hattie found that some other game entirely.

Down, down went Hattie into the dungeons.

She just couldn't wait—she needed to see them. She was always so excited for the Midwinter Tea. Even though hardly anything showed on her face, she did think quite a lot, to herself. She was quite expressive in her own head.

The Midwinter Tea meant she could do her favorite thing in the world, even if it had to be a performance, even if it was important to brandish her magic in front of her Courts. She would much rather do it alone. She'd happily sit on the dungeon floor and stitch together the Saints right there if it meant she didn't have to look up and see a whole crowd of people watching her do it. And ruin her hanbok every single year with the blood, when she could have just as well worn a smock.

But people had always liked pretty Queens more than ugly ones.

Hattie went down the hall of the dungeon, bare feet moving over cold stone, stitching guard and prisoner sights alike, one by one. They would still hear her footsteps, maybe hear her breathing, or the tiny plops as her magic wept off her chin, but they wouldn't see her.

The White Queen always thought it was so darling, that so many thought the palace was haunted, when it was only her daughter not wanting to be bothered by people as she went about her things. Jageun yuryeong, her mother would call the little Hattie, *little ghost*, and Hattie would fix the Queen with a level, unimpressed look, and the Queen would flick an elegant hand and add, "Go on, now, you unimpressed child. Resume your spectral tendencies."

She remembered it all so vividly.

Hattie missed Delcorta a lot. She always thought of her especially around this time of year, around the Tea. It was when the White Queen would have a Saint captured and make it eat from the palm of her hand in front of the Courts before setting it loose into the Labyrinth, to cement the confidence of her people in their ruler before starting off the holiday.

As it was, Hattie knew that this confidence stood very close to fear, but as was the state of the world, with Saints in Wonderland. What a comfort, to have a scarier thing on the throne.

Hattie knelt down at the very end of the twisting dungeon halls, legs parallel before the last cell, its great iron door. Then she bent herself over her knees, set her cheek to the chilled stone floor and peered—magic dripping from her nostrils—through the slight gap at the bottom of the door. Already the Saints beyond were reeling closer at the smell of her.

A small slice of a black eye. Fingers, flushing at their tips as they tried to reach forward, under the slit of the opening. Lips and then teeth and then tongue, as one of the Saints opened its mouth wide. Its putrid breath blew the hairs around Hattie's face away from her temple.

"Hello," Hattie whispered.

Her nails curled on the cracks of the stone, stomach to the tops of her thighs. Something about bowing herself over felt holy, which was just. The Saints, inches away, wanting to swallow her down mouthful by dripping mouthful—they were the closest to Divinity that humans would ever come.

"It'll be all right," Hattie promised, quietly. "You'll like being one. More than you like being two."

SEVENTEEN

YEAR ZERO ZERO NINETY-FOUR, WINTER SEASON

THERE ARE 1001 REMAINING SAINTS

AS CAROUSEL MADE HER WAY through the Petra Woods, sky candied in sunset above her head, she thought to herself, over and over again like a mantra, *Gods damn, gods damn, Miss Rabbit. You're a very dashing witch this evening especially.*

She passed by other people of the Courts as she drifted through the palace gates and continued up the white stone path beyond it, still twisting through woodlands, but now with trunks that rose out of water instead of earth. Water lanterns floated silently on the surface, the yudeung painted over in good-fortune and protection runes. Bold, black strokes, like stitches over the blush of the paper.

Caro made it to the front hall of the palace and then turned away from the stream of people feeding into the massive glass tearoom that overlooked the water, instead stealing up another hall and around a few corners until she came up to the guards stationed at the Red Queen's wing.

"Why," Caro said to the guards, Chun-Ho and Aarnik, both of whom she already knew and who already knew her. "Me? A threat to Her Majesty? Please, oh, do let me pass! I cannot be expected to do any harm looking as adorable as I do now!"

Aarnik smiled weakly; Chun-Ho rolled his eyes under the brow of his helmet and said, "Miss Rabbit. You seem in high spirits."

"Maja, oppa." He was *so* correct. Carousel smoothed her hands down the silk of her hanbok and grinned all to herself.

As much as she liked to flourish all her bird tattoos, Caro couldn't help but admire the contrast of her blue wrapped top with the dress's chima—a skirt of deliciously pale pink—dropping from her ribs to the rug below her embroidered, stout-heeled shoes. A length of the ends of her sleeves were a spring green, as was the neat tie of thick silk ribbon at her front. She was so damn *colorful*, a pillar of pastels. Caro liked how it softened her look—no, Carousel liked how she'd seem soft until anyone bothered to look a little closer and see the dry yellow of her hair sprouted from her black roots, the harsh black eyes that immediately burrowed into their onlookers, the small bird tattoos peeking out from her silver rings. And below those, the half-healed scabs on her knuckles that her talons grew out of, when she wanted them.

"I hope you won't miss me too terribly, when I'm off to accompany Hattie for the Saints' Races," said Carousel, fluffing her skirts. "I know you cry whenever I'm in Wonderland, too, but I'll be back soon."

Chun-Ho coughed. Aarnik murmured politely, "Are you leaving with Her Majesty tomorrow morning, then?"

"Yes, tomorrow morning."

"Which Ward is the first stop? Which one did you grow up in, again?"

Caro was suddenly bored of the subject. "What do you want, an itinerary? Is Hattie unnie ready yet?" She set her gaze over Aarnik's armored shoulder.

"You can see for yourself," said Aarnik. Carousel Rabbit had free rein of the palace; she was the Red Queen's favorite Jabberwocky, after all.

"Oh, but you'll let me pass so easily? What if I harm her?" Caro exclaimed, and then erupted into a high peal of laughter that neither guard mimicked. They exchanged a look that Caro was used to—*What's so funny?*—and as Caro strolled passed them she thought to herself, *Why, that you're both absolutely useless here, of course.*

Caro couldn't harm Hattie if she tried very hard indeed.

She kicked off her shoes and made for the bedroom at the end of the wing.

In the silent room, the Red Queen sat before the vanity of her dressing table.

She was draped in a hanbok with deep-red sleeves and a black skirt, her small hands folded neatly in her lap. Obviously deep in thought, the quiet that surrounded her was not a usual quiet, not around Hattie. It was a kind of quiet that thickened the air, that reached down into a person, marrow-deep—the silence of an emptied church.

But her shroud of fluffy chestnut hair was in the traditional style, braided and brought back into a bun, and Carousel couldn't help but break the wordlessness with her exclamation, "Oh, your cheeks! I always forget how darling and round your cheeks are, unnie. Jinjja yeppeuda—you look like an absolute doll!"

Hattie ignored her. Caro didn't mind.

She'd lived in Petra two and a half years already, ever since Hattie had taken the death trace off of her soul. All absolved Jabberwockies in Petra were invited to join the Queen's Culled Court, but it was only Carousel Rabbit who got to waltz around the bedroom now, to look at all of the Queen's nice stuff—even out of the nobility of the Thia Court, who did whisper about the two of them in particularly passionate tastes.

"They say we're a scandal," Caro would whisper low to Hattie during a Court dinner. "We'll need to get married immediately."

"I am married, Carousel," Hattie would say distantly, sometimes patting the young King Il-Hyun Hyo's hand rested beside her, sometimes not.

"I'm all right with that," Caro would always remind her.

And Hattie would stare at Caro so contemplatively that she would snort her laugh and Il-Hyun would cover his nice mouth with a napkin to hide his chuckle.

"And where is the King?" Caro asked aloud now, as if Hattie was privy to the reminiscing in her head. Caro had knelt herself before a bookshelf of Hattie's old diaries, from back when she'd simply been the Red Princess. Caro traced her fingers upon the words she could not read—how could all those black marks look so pretty and so serious all at once? "Oh. You're still thinking. I don't mean to disturb you, really, I'm just— *Ag*. Hell, Il-Hyun. You scared me."

The King—who was really still a boy, barely a year older than his Queen—had been sitting in an armchair in the bedroom the entire time. Caro had glanced up from the diary page, and there he was, picking up his dark head of hair from the book balanced on his knee and looking at her over the rims of his glasses. "Good evening, Carousel Rabbit. You look wonderful."

Caro blushed. "Aw, oppa. And you're pretty," she said, and it was true. If he hadn't been betrothed to Hattie at sixteen, her at fifteen, he would've had all the noble girls fawning all over his delicate features. Maybe, Caro mused, if they didn't catch on that he was an academic, and incredibly kind, and already long best friends with Hattie by that time, growing up together, together all their lives.

Il-Hyun checked his pocket watch and shut his book, stood to lean his tall frame on the dressing-table before Hattie. Caro watched him do it, watched his mouth move and the focus draw back into Hattie's eyes the moment they did, and then Caro was thinking of Icca, thinking of herself saying, *I'm Hattie unnie's favorite creature.*

So what, if they weren't friends, her and the Queen. It had never bothered Caro before; there was a novelty in that, that she and Hattie liked each other without confiding in one another, without meaning the world to each other, especially since Caro knew Hattie didn't have anyone in her head except herself. Carousel had a lot of people in her head. She thought of Hattie a lot. She'd thought of Icca a lot, and then a lot less—tried to, because there hadn't been an Icca anymore, until a few days ago.

And now.

Now, Carousel had stood in front of her mirror earlier that evening, in her hanbok, thinking of how Icca's eyes would trace her head to toe. Thinking about how much she hated her. Who was the *she*? Who was the *her*—it was interchangeable, Caro knew, and so she shuffled them in her head like a stack of playing cards. *She hates her. She hates her.*

Caro watched Il-Hyun ease Hattie out of her trance, out of the depths of her head. The Red Queen stood—she barely came to her King's sternum, and he gave her a little kiss on the top of her head. Caro wanted to unravel all over the lushness of the bedroom. Before being lovers, and then, more than being lovers, she and Icca had been friends.

Stop that immediately, Caro thought to herself, and then softened. She did hate to scold herself, especially in her own head. It was *her* own head, after all! Ridiculous thoughts... yes, certainly, Carousel Rabbit had all she needed, right here. She doted on Hattie as viciously as a sister, and as deserved! Hattie could cleave someone down much more quickly than Icca could ever manage. Hattie could unravel the world. Hattie had nice clothes. Hattie had a pretty nose bridge. These were traits Caro deeply admired in a person.

It was no use.

"Caro?" Il-Hyun asked, studying her, an arm around Hattie's shoulders. Hattie was not looking at her; Caro knew that her mind was on her Saints. "Are you all right?"

Caro smiled at him, barely there. Her mouth moving on its own, small talk she abhorred. "Are you just thrilled for the Saints' Races, oppa?"

"I— Yes. Of course. And you?"

Caro did not hear him.

"Give Carousel and me a moment, would you kindly?" Hattie spoke softly, to Caro's equal surprise and thrill, as well as a stab of guilt. She'd never spoken to Hattie about Icca, but surely Hattie knew—even if she hadn't gleaned it off of the criminal records, which she noted when an absolved Jabberwocky wished to join the Culled Court, Hattie seemed to simply know things. Caro gathered her legs up beneath her as Il-Hyun left Hattie's side and passed her by with a small nod.

The Red Queen, having turned her head to follow the King's departure, now faced back to the mirror. Candlelight kissed the bead of red tucked at each nostril.

"This year is different, Carousel."

Caro wasn't sure if it was relief or disappointment that bubbled in her chest. Not about Icca, then—and why should anything *be* about Icca, anyway? "Because they'll serve eleven kinds of tea instead of ten?"

Hattie smiled, a little. "Because tonight, the number of Saints will drop from four digits to three."

"Nine hundred and ninety-nine! Or, I suppose, nine hundred numbers below that," shrilled Caro, though she did not care to ask Hattie how she could know this would happen tonight. The last count had come in at one thousand and one, if she'd read the newspaper correctly—and of course she had, Caro soothed herself, still being able to read numbers just fine. She bit at her thumb, quieting. "So what?"

"Three is a powerful number." Hattie's gaze did not waver. "Would you say otherwise?"

Caro bit at her other thumb. "If we're talking money, then three makes you dirt poor. But four's not far off from that either." She had run out of thumbs to bite—she put them in her lap and did not look at them again. Did not want to glimpse the pale scar circling her ring finger. "Unnie, what's this about?"

"You never did tell me about this last instance in Wonderland, Carousel," Hattie said, leaving Caro uncertain, albeit not particularly bothered, whether she'd been sidestepped, or if this was related to Hattie's musings.

"Oh, you know. Lots of dirt and trees and things in those trees and in those dirts," Caro said vaguely, toeing at the carpet. "Glad to be back in society, as per usual. The Saints aren't excellent conversationalists. Much less drama than I prefer."

"What about the Forest?"

"Hm?"

"Does it conversate to your satisfaction?" Hattie was still looking her in the eyes, or maybe just at Caro's cheek, but either way her own had been taken ahold of by their habitual glaze. "Part of the reason you keep going back, perhaps."

Gods, was the Red Queen wholly unnerving! Caro giggled in her uncomfortableness, then sobered and said with a wink, "I just like hunting. Keeps me sharp. Tip-top."

"Well, that's good, I suppose."

Caro beamed. "Is good conversation why *you* like going into the Labyrinth? Or is it just to be creepy and scare everyone?"

Caro did not actually expect an answer—that's not why she'd asked at all. No, certainly, she couldn't know too much about Hattie, or else...

"I go to pray."

"Really!"

"Really."

Could it really be true, that Hattie was some kind of High Priestess of modern times? Most of the noble Thia Court, along with the general population, thought it was true. The Jabberwockies of the Culled Court, on the other hand—albeit either hopefully or apathetically—all assumed she went to the Labyrinth to do only wicked, unspeakable things. Of course, there was the chance Hattie was lying. Caro thought she might lie a lot more if she were a Queen; though she lied as much as she liked as she was now, so maybe not. Caro glanced around the lavishly decorated room. "You could pray where there's a fireplace, or a smidge less murderous beasts stalking about."

Hattie's vacant eyes trailed around the space, and then she said with disinterest, "My gods are hardly ever here. They like the Labyrinth." She touched first her sternum and then the slick beneath her nose. "And Wonderland, I imagine."

"Oh, we can go whenever you'd like, unnie," Caro insisted, since Hattie did seem suddenly melancholy. "We don't even have to go into the Forest, if you think it'd be too much, just stand at the tree line. And tilt our heads back for a proper looking-at." Caro added this last bit because she thought that people didn't look at the tops of trees enough—she imagined *she* wouldn't enjoy it if people only looked at her from the neck down—and then doubled back. "I don't mean to say, of course, that you'd be scared to go in. I just know you—I mean, you *would* converse, wouldn't you?"

"Yes," Hattie said, smiling a little, which was gold to Caro. "Have I told you this before?"

"Nope. I'm just obnoxiously brilliant. And, well, you've mentioned how, if you ever *did* go on into Wonderland, you probably wouldn't entertain the idea of leaving." Caro blew her hair out of her face and sent two of her fingers onto their tips and walked them across the wood surface of the vanity. "You'd go in, but you wouldn't come out. I just didn't realize it'd be because the tree chatter would be too interesting. They're quiet, in the Labyrinth, then? Even if it was a part of Wonderland, before the maze was built up?"

"No, no conversing. It's the Walls, muddling things," murmuring Hattie. "The Labyrinth is easy to leave." *Behold,* thought Caro, thrilled, *the only witch in existence who could utter such a thing.* "It doesn't follow me out."

"And Wonderland would?" *Stop it this instant.* Caro kicked herself; she didn't quite like asking questions—well, no, the problem was she *loved* asking questions, but she didn't want to stumble across too many answers; too many answers would make her feel raw. Keeping Hattie as a terrifying caricature, shrouded in a quality that was slightly unreal, was for the best—Caro could be safely fascinated, unbothered when Hattie ignored her or pulled away, when the thought rose that Hattie, too, would probably leave her behind in Wonderland.

Hattie put one hand gently on Caro's, stopping her waltzing fingers. "Carousel, have you ever questioned why there is a Culled Court to begin with?"

Yesyesyes.

"No," said Caro with finality. *Good, grand, perfect girl.* She beamed once more, pleased with herself. "I just figure you're kooky, unnie."

Caro talked to her things and exploded Birds; Hattie created a Court out of Wonderland-hardened freaks and wandered into the Labyrinth for days at a time, always leaving her shoes at the gates—really, who didn't have odd habits? Caro didn't want to know reasonings; she was content to know such depths resided in Hattie without diving in. Diving in like she had with Icca and Tecca. She knew how that had ended, being down in treacherous waters for so long. With webbed feet and webbed fingers.

And Hattie smiled again, this time a little wider. Honestly it scared the shit out of Caro. Thus she was leaning closer when Hattie said, "Yes. I suppose I am." She smoothed her hands down her skirt, then observed the red magic smeared on her palms. "Well."

That was it; Caro could recognize when Hattie wanted to be alone. She blew a kiss and had slid away when Hattie said, "And, Carousel?"

"Mm-hm?"

"If your friend Iccadora Alice Sickle happens to make an appearance tonight, do be cordial." A pause. "Unless there's a context for it."

It was the first time Caro had heard Icca's name from Hattie's mouth. It shot chills down her spine. "What makes you think she'll show?"

Hattie shrugged without turning. The movement would've been lost in all her hair if it wasn't pinned up so nicely. "Some feeling."

"O-kay." Caro made to leave again but stopped, needing to say it. "But we're not friends."

It was impossible to see Hattie's expression. From the back, she was all grace and poise and fresh-pressed hanbok. She shifted, nearly imperceivably, then said, "Of course. My apologies."

Caro wanted Hattie to say something else—or was it that she wanted to say something herself? But what was there to say? She was out in the hall before she came up with the answer.

We were *friends,* Carousel thought, or maybe she said it aloud, out in the hall now, pressing the thought to the flowers carved into the wood of the alcoves. To Caro, often, it seemed a grander term than *lover. We were* friends.

But what would be the point of it?

And if it was the truth—why had Icca done it?

Why had Carousel done it?

EIGHTEEN

YEAR ZERO ZERO NINETY, SUMMER SEASON

THERE ARE 1090 REMAINING SAINTS

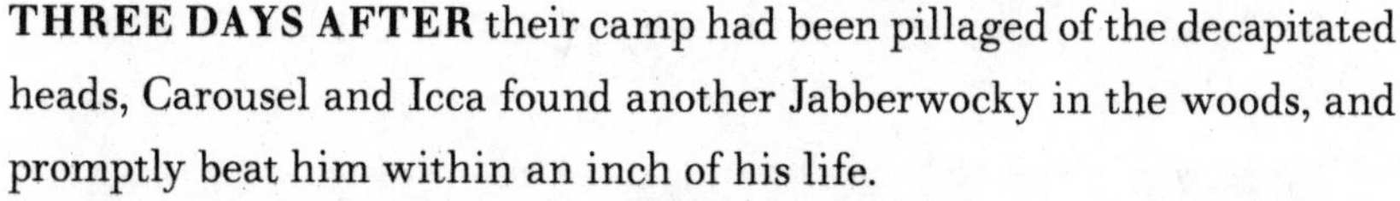

THREE DAYS AFTER their camp had been pillaged of the decapitated heads, Carousel and Icca found another Jabberwocky in the woods, and promptly beat him within an inch of his life.

It was a reasonable conclusion that they reached; Caro thought it quite reasonable. That he could've been the one who'd dug up their heads.

They'd stopped with their chests heaving in tandem. They knew they couldn't kill him, couldn't risk some other death trace slicking to them. Couldn't risk having to be in Wonderland a single day more than they had to.

He didn't give up the heads. Possibly because he hadn't been the one to take them; Caro knew this, really, and thought that Icca must know it too, when they returned to their camp in total silence, when they didn't eat anything and lay under their lean-to canopy of twigs and leaves and Icca didn't put her hands over her stomach to sleep like she always did. Caro knew it was because Icca felt sick, exactly like Caro did, and the weight of her palms and all the attached fingers and the blood outlining the cuticles would spur on the nausea.

Two weeks passed. They tried to kill two Saints and failed both times, nearly got themselves killed both times, like they almost did every time, but it felt different now. Caro no longer chirped about Petra or the lavish apartment that was waiting for them. Icca didn't indulge her in stories, or even snap at her, her expression fixed in an unsettling calm. They no longer cackled over the magic they could feel in their souls, feeding off the Forest.

Because maybe they had gotten it wrong. Maybe it was feeding off them.

They'd been fools for ever breaking the tree line. Wonderland had coaxed them inside, and now, and now . . .

It's never going to let us go.

Caro lay awake one night, thinking it. This time, unable to stop thinking it.

I am going to die *here.*

She was scared to die. Especially because she knew how she was going to die, because she knew she was powerful, that she was a fucking fantastic witch.

There was only one kind of thing that could kill her, and she knew how they liked to kill.

She hadn't thought about the Moore house in a while, to save her and Icca both from the Saints drawn to mourning, but now she couldn't help but peek at the memory. Caro had smushed it into a such a compact black pinprick at the back of her head that she barely could remember that Tecca had meant anything to her at all. Now, in her head, she moved through the house, room by smoke-filled room. The kitchen with its rafters woven with Hanna Moore, the hall light hazy with the twins. When Carousel got upstairs and saw Tecca, she hardly meant anything at all past the blood on her body, the slackness of her limbs.

It wasn't Tecca, bleeding out on the rug, with a horrible thing a few feet over in the hallway. It was Carousel. It was going to be Carousel.

Caro wasn't this. Lying under the lean-to beside Icca, starting awake from some nightmare that wasn't any better than the world she woke up to—she wasn't this terrified thing, this little girl. She wasn't herself, with this fear.

Because she never would have gotten up, if she'd been herself.

Carousel Rabbit wouldn't have peeled back her blanket in complete silence, and left behind Iccadora Alice Sickle, the love of her young life and her whole life, asleep, without a word, without a single fucking *word*, and left her all alone in Wonderland.

She wouldn't have knelt in the earth before where the first head was buried, wouldn't have dropped her brow onto it and begged the Night for forgiveness, for using it like this, begged the Birds for the same, because their devoted witch was such a wicked, sharp thing. Even though the gods didn't care if she was good.

And Caro remembered this, after a moment.

So instead, she prayed to Icca. Lips moving against the earth, and then she lifted her head. And she began to dig.

The head was gone.

Caro stared into the black hole for a moment, and then crawled over to the next spot. That one was gone, too.

"No." She laughed, fingers beneath the forest floor, searching for the third, and then the fourth, and then she laughed again, the sound pushed through grinning teeth. "Oh, no, no."

The night lit up blue.

Caro shot herself outward. That was a gamble, and she didn't care, pushing out the enchantment without knowing if she'd have a crow to land on. But then she was out of her body and in another, twisting through the rare, moon-shot sky, and she expanded her wings.

She coasted for a little bit; usually flying soothed her, but not now. She didn't even realize the bird was falling apart around her until she landed amid a flock of them up in a pine tree, but it was just as well. She'd just been using it as a contagion point.

She let out a caw. It thrummed up her teeny throat and burst through her beak. It tore her form apart, burst the bird like a spit bubble against its brethren. When she woke up—one arm limp and dangling over one of the head-holes—she felt the crows flinch and stiffen, heard the shift of their feathers in the back of her head. She had them now.

And they spread her influence. She felt herself in teeming multitudes as she infected the crows of Wonderland, the edges of her consciousness dissolving into tiny spots. Caro was boiling in her own magic as she rose, dripping blue, and it stung where it hit her chapped lips. She didn't care. They'd already found the person who'd taken the heads.

Caro could have called her crows down, all those sharp, fidgety pieces of herself, enough of herself now that she could've stripped the thief down without even moving. But Caro wanted to move. She wanted to be there when she tore them apart.

Icca might wake up and find her gone. She might go looking and see those dug-up holes and get the wrong idea—no, get the exactly right idea, really.

Caro would either come back and Icca would be up and be hating her, or she might come back and Icca might still be dead asleep. Caro would carry the secret like a seed in her pocket and never talk about it again, except to herself, except to hate herself.

So she set off into Wonderland alone, and she didn't think about what she would do when she got the heads back. If she would turn back to camp, to Icca. If she would just keep going.

It was nearly dawn when Carousel caught up to them. They had almost made it out of Wonderland; the tree line was only about a half mile or so up, and past that, the rise of the Petra Labyrinth. So close that Caro could feel the rune begin to hum on her neck.

And she saw the thief up ahead, in the lightening dark of the Forest, cloak bumpy with the heads hidden beneath.

The first crow hit them. A shot of black, and the person let out a gasp and was on the ground. Their cloak shifted, and there was the sallow curve of a rotten head against the undergrowth.

Caro hissed through her teeth at the sight, at the stab of pain that slashed up her throat as she summoned up the enchantment, as she sent the rest of the Birds down.

She felt herself—felt them hit nothing. The Birds twisted upon themselves and the undergrowth, shrieking as they tangled, but Caro detached her influence with a snap that felt like hitting ice water, turning, already seeing the flash of the cloak up ahead—how had they moved so quickly?—and was running, and she was faster; she realized she was *faster* with a rabid stab of clarity. *I'm going to get you.*

Carousel was on them. Sending them both into the earth. Weight on their stomach, Caro snatched one bony wrist in her hand and wrenched the thief to face her.

And suddenly, she wasn't scared anymore. Not of Wonderland. Not of the Saints.

She sat back on her heels, chest heaving. Seizing. Her hands curled into her knees, dirt worked beneath every nail; she'd dug like an animal.

Caro knew exactly how she looked. How her lips were parted, how her breath scraped at them. How wide her eyes were, and how very pale she'd become. She knew right away, because it was how the witch below her looked. They'd always been mirrors of one another.

"Oh, Alice," Carousel spoke, her voice hollow and infinitesimally small in the gap of the Forest. "I thought you asleep."

NINETEEN

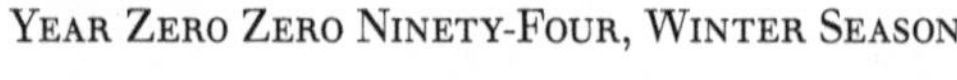

YEAR ZERO ZERO NINETY-FOUR, WINTER SEASON

THERE ARE 1001 REMAINING SAINTS

REALLY, ICCA DID HATE Petra. She paused on the earth walkway snaking through the waterlogged palace face, hands curling in her black hanbok skirt. *Don't you know just what's protecting you?* She wanted to grab the fine clothes of the courtfolk passing by in high spirits and shake them until they saw sense. *Don't you know how they could tear you apart?*

They did know, of course. They knew everything—the Kkuls had never kept it a secret, what teemed in the Dark of their Labyrinth, what could kill even the Jabberwockies who had survived their Wonderland sentence. The Queens—first White, now Red—had made the horror story of Petra's protection into a revered tale. Witches with their Labyrinth Saints shield. Witches making flesh and mind and Divinity alike teem at their fingertips, and so it didn't matter that an old King of their bloodline had corrupted the Saints in the first place.

Kai had stopped without complaint beside her, a pillar of deep blue silk in his hanbok, save for the strip of white at his brown throat. He looked perfectly regal as he studied the rune-painted water lanterns bobbing beside the path.

"You look ridiculous," Icca snapped at him, because she didn't really want to move forward. The glass vial of rose draught was cold on her skin, strapped to her forearm beneath the pale green of sleeve. She'd been fidgety the whole trolley ride over that afternoon from the Beotkkot Ward. Would the guards be patting people down? She was suddenly so hyper-fixated on the feel of the rose-draught vial she could feel how Kai had merrily scraped the words DRINK ME! in spindly letters into the glass. She'd already set up an escape, memorized a shadowed bit of the Petra Woods that they'd passed on the way in.

"And you look stunning," Kai returned immediately, and he might have meant it—the hanbok he'd purchased for her shimmered as it dripped off her limbs—but it was also an automatic response he would've said to any human in his proximity, and so was the lowering of his black lashes and the utter focus in the eyes beneath them, and so was the arm that rose ever-so-subtly for her to take.

Icca did, her hand wrapping in the crook of his elbow. And her fingernails curled. "Whenever you decide to run away like the coward you are, Cheshire, don't bother telling me. I'll be too busy to give you a proper goodbye."

"You never make time for me," he said mildly as they began to walk toward the guards stationed at the palace entrance. "I know the real reason why you brought me, Icca." Well, she'd expected that. Some part of him had to have gleaned the truth of why she'd brought him: as a potential scapegoat. Also to throttle him immediately if the draught was a dud. "Did Carousel Rabbit call you a loner? Did you feel the need to prove companionship, bringing me along?"

"What the *fuck*?" The only reason she didn't immediately shove him off the path and into the water was because it'd make a scene. "*Excuse* me?"

"No, no, excuse *me*. Who am I to judge? I love making people jealous," Kai said, and grinned that wide, thin grin of his.

Now, dear readers, our Iccadora did turn this over in her head for some morsel of fact, because she was indeed an academic and championed the general truth of things. However, this introspection lasted the length of a lightning flash before she recalled that Kai was a bitch and she absolutely abhorred the idea of him having a hand in a fruitful self-reflection, especially in the case of fruit as foul and prickly as this: that Icca had come with him because she had not wanted to come alone. And Icca loved being alone, and she would not be deterred from this grounding aspect of herself. So instead she pinched his arm to the point where he yelped.

Other guests in full finery milled around the white mouth of the entryway, and Icca's eyes roamed over them all, picking at the smiles and the bright cheeks, all under a night sky suffocated with clouds. Most of the people before her had probably spent their entire lives in Petra, set to live full and long existences behind the massive Walls of the Labyrinth. The thought struck a bitter taste against Icca's tongue, and then it congealed to the gritty memory of smoke breathed in deep, of cooled skin yielding beneath the press of her fingers.

She'd been so *sure*, sixteen years old and small against the rug, that Tecca was already gone.

Or maybe it was just her panic, her fear, that had chased that thought into her. The assumption. That a Saint made death a given.

For all their arrogance, all their talk of storming the palace Icca now stood before, and all their musings about how Wonderland would cower before the three of them, and Icca had stood in those smoke-filled rooms of Tecca's home and thought not one of them would make it out alive.

Because that's all they did, those in the lesser Wards, the distant Wards, with their small Walls and false securities. They feared—it was in the air, even if quelled by the notion they might be safe—and then they died.

And here, in Petra, they just died.

So it wasn't fair.

It wasn't fair, this party, all these people who wouldn't spend a single day looking over their shoulders. The absolved Jabberwockies that flocked to this Ward, to its Queen, were pathetic, wasted creatures; they'd all stood above Wonderland's roots, had seen the true nature of this world, and chosen to hide from it. To play pretend, play spectacle.

And Kai had been correct. Icca was far from a humanitarian; she did not kid herself over thinking so. She wanted to kill the Queen because she blamed Hattie November Kkul for Tecca's death, blamed the blood in her veins. She wanted to kill Hattie because people thought her unkillable.

And because killing Hattie would make Carousel depressed.

And because, fuck it, it sounded like fun; Icca wanted to kill Hattie because Icca wanted to.

"Now you look like murder," Kai murmured to her, which Icca found she liked better than *stunning*.

Still, because now it was time to talk to people, she fumbled for the fan invitation in the parcel bag on her hip. She held it out awkwardly to one of the guards flanking the entrance, and said, quick and bumbling, "A-annyeong hashimnikka."

The guard smiled as she glanced at the invitation and handed it back to Icca. Kai snorted as they passed into the front hall. "You're so incredibly formal and polite, Sickle. Might you be a little nervous?"

"Never," spat Icca, though... Was she nervous? She hadn't been in a while, in this palpable, jittery sense; usually she just went for spots on her face or her wounds. But she couldn't pick at herself here to calm down. She had to be perfectly pleasant. Perfectly focused.

The glass tearoom was a feat of airy decadence, and Kai hummed as they glanced around, clearly pleased with the setting. On either side past the glass sprawled a view of the waters where the paper lanterns floated, and directly ahead, doors had been flung open to reveal the grove of the palace courtyard. Icca could glimpse the tips of its trees through the domed ceiling, past crystal chandeliers hoisting fat, sloughing candles of pale green and white. Two long tables spanned the space, clothed in gray lace and silver pastry platters, misted in the vague fog wafting from the pots of tea set every few feet. The air smelled sweetly of jasmine flowers and peppermint, the earthier scent of brown rice mixed in with the green tea; place cards with frilly borders were upright before each pot, and Icca read BARLEY and CORN on the nearest ones before such an intense bout of indignation struck her that she could look no further.

"It's like being in a fishbowl," she scoffed.

"You're delusional," Kai returned cheerfully.

Hovering near the entrance of the tearoom, Icca could tell who was part of the Culled Court and who belonged to the noble-born Thia Court just by the way the two cast their glances upon the other. The former meeting eyes and baring grins, brandishing gestures, and sending the latter skittering away into nervous conversations with their own people. The nobles stood with ramrod posture, their movements softer, Icca noticed, while the Jabberwockies seemed unable to keep their bodies completely still. Fingertips twitched, words were thrown sharper, food was gobbled down with less ceremony—perhaps that was just because it was harder to care about pomp and poise when one had seen Wonderland, which did wonders for stripping away any significance to societal civilities.

And there in the midst of it was Carousel Rabbit, in a pink-and-blue hanbok, already reclined at one of the great tables while the Courts drifted and mingled.

The crow witch had been watching the door—of course she had been watching the door. She'd always liked to people-watch—Icca's mind recalled, without her consent—it was one of the reasons, besides the finery, that she'd wanted to move to Petra.

And so Caro saw her right away.

Small chin set in her palm, her silver-ringed fingers stuttered on her jawline before the look in her eyes flattened, and they slid away to sample the looks of another partygoer like a finger sandwich. It really was an impressive display. Caro looked like she was believing her own ambivalence.

Now Icca was grinning.

Kai twitched next to her when he saw it. "Good gods. What now?"

"I'm perfectly pleasant," Icca said, and when she quieted her voice like this, the sprawl of her voice was more hoarse than barbed. *Smoke instead of brambles,* Caro had drawled to her once, Icca's head on her stomach, Caro's fingers in her hair. Icca had adored how Caro spoke, a poet's tongue in her mouth, when she wasn't being ridiculous—which was most of the time, admittedly—but Icca had liked that, too. More than once, Icca had told Caro she should write.

"Nah." Carousel would flap a hand. "No one deserves to be graced with my golden prose."

"I do," Icca would say.

"Hm. This is true. Well. Maybe someday, then."

"Uh-huh," Kai said now, unbelieving.

"I'm perfectly pleasant," Icca repeated, and then moved away from him, muttering to herself, "and that bitch has my book."

Icca dropped herself into the chair beside Caro. Caro didn't look at her, just picked up her tea casually and leaned back into her seat, her hanbok shimmering under the candlelit chandeliers. She sipped and spoke. "Do you think you can sit so close to the Red Queen, Alice?'

Icca imagined wrapping her hands around that delicate throat and squeezing. She watched Caro's skirt shift as the crow witch crossed her legs, uncrossed them.

"I've heard the Queen is very progressive. No seating chart, no requirement for noble blood at these things, or perfectly clean souls." Icca traced a fingertip down the cold, flat metal of the chopsticks beside her plate. "She knows power is the only thing that matters, and it isn't determined by how close people sit to her."

"Oh," purred Caro, and now, suddenly, she was looking at Icca. Her hair was loose—instead of the traditional bun style Kai had twisted Icca's jagged ends into—combed and clean but still wild and full, that truly awful yellow stark against the pale blue of her hanbok top. "So you just wanted to be close to me, was that it? Is that why you're here, Icky?"

And Icca was angry, with Caro's black gaze upon her—studying her like she had a right to study—and completely cold with her anger, a cold like glass in her veins, and Icca moved very precisely so as not to shatter it, so as not to make the lightlessness that stained the air in Carousel's lungs burst and corrode.

Icca took one of the nearby clay teapots and poured herself a cup. She blew on it carefully, carefully, took a slow sip—and Caro was still watching her, amused, and then the crow witch was cackling a horribly delighted laugh when Icca pulled her cup away.

The tea glinted silver at its surface. The sting of her own power tasted of jasmine and blood.

But Caro stopped when Icca turned her head, when she said, low and quiet, just how she knew Caro liked, "Oh, Rabbit. Did you take my book?"

Caro hesitated, then tried to say easily, "That can't be the only reason why you've graced the Courts with your sickly prickly presence, dear."

"Oh, dear, it's not," Icca assured her, leaning closer, and Caro was very still, with Icca's hand on her thigh suddenly, with Icca's silver lips parting next to her ear. "I've come to win you back, see? I realized you'd never beheld me in a dress, either. Is it working? Are you mad for me yet?"

Icca pulled back, grinning. Her own heartbeat had spilled up to her ears. Caro was smiling, too. They were inches apart—anyone looking on would have thought them nothing more than giddy girls laughing over cruel, petty pieces of Court gossip they'd exchanged between them like pieces of yeot-gangjeong. But Icca knew better—of course Caro had gotten the joke.

Of course they were mad for one another.

Just not in the way they had been. Not in the way they'd gone into Wonderland being.

"It's working," Caro said, fingertips tracing a light, slow circle on the side of Icca's knee. "I am completely enchanted by you, Alice."

I want to see your brains glistening across the tea table, Alice.

"Well," cooed a voice above. Both witches glanced up to see Mordekai, standing behind Icca's chair. "Isn't this a sight."

For a panicked moment, Icca was sure that Kai was going to misread the situation, and try to kiss her to help her spur some childish bout of jealousy in Caro—upon which Icca would've throttled him. Instead he pulled out the seat beside her and struck his long legs under the table, the toes of his formal slippers peeking behind the dark blue hem of his hanbok. Then he leaned across Icca and took Carousel's hand, and now Icca *was* really going to throttle him—

"Kai Cheshire ibnida," he introduced himself, and Icca just rolled her eyes instead.

"Carousel Rabbit, or Caro, or darling," Caro immediately returned, electric grin already in place. She shook Kai's hand heartedly. "A pleasure."

"You're gorgeous, Carousel Rabbit," Kai purred. "Icca's told me a lot about you, but she failed to mention the entire extent of that detail."

"And I also told you that she's a massive lesbian, Cheshire, remember," spat Icca.

"Oh, yes," Caro said, but her tone had shifted. Icca took her glare away from Kai and pressed it to her again. "You've told him about me?"

"Well, yes," Icca said flatly, confused by her tone.

"Oh."

"What?"

"Nothing. It's just—I haven't ever told anyone about you." Icca continued to stare, and Caro smiled again and spat, "Not because I wanted you all to myself. Not even that I don't want to stain another head with the thought of you, either, Alice, dear—please don't think that. I just don't think about you enough to speak about you."

Carousel sneered. Icca sneered. Kai, apparently completely bored now that the attention was off of him, took a bite of a brown-sugar hotteok from one of the hand-painted plates on the table and said mildly, "So, who the fuck are the Queen and King?"

—

The crow witch flashed another darling grin, and pointed to a clump of Tea-goers gathered at the head of the table.

Growing up, Kai had always loved the holiday of the Saints' Races. The clamor of excitement that took over his village in the weeks leading up to it, the maggot-wrath of white ribbons tied to the storefronts, snapping in the cold wind. The Races often took place in the larger town a few miles over from his own, and he'd trail his neighbors across the cobblestone road that joined them—first with his parents, and then alone once they had passed, one death starting the autumn season and the other concluding it—the air abuzz with anticipation. He could recall, as a small child, the metallic tinge of bloodshed spiking the hazy air as soon as they reached the border of the hosting town. He remembered the White Queen's delicate hand extending, dull light glittering off her rings, plucking unfortunate souls out of the crowd to have hauled into the arena. The words she spoke had bled out of his memory, but their cooing tenor was never too far out of reach. The White Queen always stood down there in the ring, with her lottery winners, her chosen ones—they were not alone. Royal and commoner—they'd face the beasts together. While the others pissed themselves and went sheet-white from the fear of the charging Saint, there then flashed the red cut of her smile, spilling the honey-coated sweet nothings that'd make the monster go slack. She'd hand the commoner a blade. Laugh, pleased, when they'd brought their own. Delcorta would step aside to let them slay the Saint—that was the defining moment. They needed to be intentional in their carnage. If they did not kill the Saint immediately, if they balked at the sensation of flesh giving under steel and hesitated, then Delcorta would lose interest. The Saint would awaken, and the Queen would step to one side.

In the best years, the chosen ones would bleed magic, do something really extraordinary. As a teenager, Kai had always wanted to be chosen. He wanted to impress Delcorta, with the pain he'd bring into himself with his magic, how much he could manage without flinching. But she'd never been cruel enough to select a child. And when Delcorta died, he heard that the merciful Red Queen had abandoned the lottery, and the Saints' Races would now consist of Saints only. What was the point of going, then?

He'd missed the senseless drama that had accompanied the White Queen. What was this country coming to, he thought, pivoting toward the supposed piety of her heir? But Religion had always bored Kai. Ever since the Red Queen's coronation, he'd stayed home from the Saints' Races, every year lamenting about how he'd never again feel the shiver of the White Queen's power.

But now he was seeing Hattie November Kkul's face.

He'd been correct—he'd never again have the feeling of the White Queen's magic as it felt for his flesh, his senses, his own magic that churned through his soul, that little drop of Divinity nestled in such a profound, unfindable place within his existence.

Because he knew, right away, that the White Queen's power paled in comparison to the Red Queen's.

Kai was looking right at that small, featureless face—save for the two wet beads on her veil that marked the magic bleeding from her nose—a face that was turned away from his own, and still, Kai could feel her magic outlining his every piece.

Drawing out his marrow, his bones, his veins in nice, thick lines.

Tracing around his magic, his little mortal Divinity, and where it had become physical in his back molars, following its trail down his throat as he swallowed hard. Kai was a piece of fruit ready to be harvested—*no*, his *pieces* were fruit ready to be harvested, plucked up by the magic dripping from the Queen's nostrils.

He could feel her feeling out that drop of Divinity like a seed in her palm, and she wasn't even paying attention.

Kai glanced over at the other two witches, his fingers unmoving from the handle of his cup the entire time. Carousel Rabbit must be used to it by now; Icca was definitely feeling it, too, judging by the way she'd stiffened in her chair, but not to the extent he was—not to its true, burrowing extent. Kai became his magic more often than others; he was quite good at smudging away his form and building it back up again. He'd grown to know his corporeality and his incorporeality very well, and now he knew this was more than just a bad feeling, more than just a powerful witch before him.

Good gods. Icca was about to get herself slaughtered.

Now things were settling down. People were taking their seats, and the King and Queen took theirs with spines to the windows that overlooked the water, a few spots down from where Kai and the girls sat. Carousel leaned forward a bit to wave at the Queen as the King filled her teacup.

"Icca," he said quietly. "We should leave."

Scapegoat or not, he'd come for the spectacle of it. A dead Queen, and Petra a mess, and he'd float back to the Apothecary and wait for Icca to figure a way out of her new death trace, or just live in Wonderland and be perfectly content with it. He'd come because he hadn't known about Hattie November—how could he have known?

Icca merely grated her teeth with a scoff. She was definitely focused on the Queen. "You know she killed her mother, right."

Kai settled back. This again.

Caro flapped her hand with a dismissive air that had matched Kai's own; thus one he had to admire. She dropped yet another sugar cube into her tea. "Eh. Probably not."

"*Probably,*" squawked Icca, indignant.

"Ah yep." Caro leaned forward excitedly. "Didn't you hear how she wandered into the Labyrinth to prove she didn't have a death trace?"

"That's—"

"That's *hardly* proof!" Kai chimed. He selected a jelly pastry from one of the lace-lined plates. "That's what you'd sound like, Icca."

"Will you shut your trap—"

Caro flapped a hand. "Proof or not, people haven't really cared since she wandered back *out* of said Labyrinth."

"Cared!" Icca scoffed. "Of course they wouldn't show that they cared, when she terrified them all just by doing so!"

Carousel promptly began stuffing her face with a red-bean bun. "Yeah, I guess. It's kind of old news, Icky. Why do you care?"

"Why the fuck do people keep asking me that?"

"Because you're loud," Kai muttered.

"You didn't used to be," said Caro.

"Is that really true?" he asked. "Because that's—"

"Your Queen harbors some obsession with the death trace," Icca interjected. "Why else would she make her Culled Court a Court of Jabberwockies? The very concept is—"

"Why do people keep asking me that today?" Caro objected, then shook her head. "Or—I'm just sick of this question! You there—um—with the rainbow magic—how the hell did you survive Wonderland—and have such a horrid sense of style?" These latter two bits were under her breath. "You, Scena Lin!"

The absolved Jabberwocky apparently called Scena Lin looked over at Caro and Icca and Kai. Icca was clearly shocked and dismayed—why the hell had Caro called out to Scena, who was separated from them by two others sitting between her and Kai? Scena leaned over her tea, obviously annoyed. "*What*, Carousel?"

"Why is it that Hattie likes Jabberwockies?"

"The fuck are you on about?"

Well. That laid clear how the rest of the Culled Court regarded Carousel Rabbit—were they affronted by her bubbly brightness post-Wonderland, perhaps, or was it jealousy for her moniker of the Red Queen's butcher? Well-earned, certainly—Kai had read the nickname multiple times in the papers—the Saint count was scraped off here and there by absolved Jabberwockies and criminals shucking around in the Forest, but none who had the talent to be so distinguished (and he doubted there were other witches here like his darling Sickle, slaughtering Saints without seeking fame for it). Of course they'd abhor Carousel for her flaunting. Kai thought Icca would look smug if the dark witch wasn't so downright socially awkward, hurriedly sipping her tea so as not to have to speak. Kai poked at her.

Caro shrugged, unbothered. "I dunno. Somethin' about Hattie liking the death trace—"

Icca hissed, "Being *obsessed* with it, more like—"

"—is what Icca here is squawking about—this is Iccadora Alice Sickle, by the way, we used to be lovers, and now—"

"Gods, I do not care," Scena snapped.

"Thank the gods," Icca murmured, and finally slapped away Kai's hand. "*What?*"

"I'm telling you, we should—"

Caro flagged down another Jabberwocky, this one even farther down the table. "*Hey*, so—"

"Oh, I take it back! I don't care!" pleaded Icca.

"Really? Because you seemed—"

"*Stop,* Caro—and *you* stop." This was said irritably to Kai; again she batted away his poking. "Just run along. I told you not to say goodbye."

"You don't know—"

Icca flapped a dismissive hand, shot him that dark glare. "Go observe from that coward plane of existence you fancy. Then you can even pick out a scared noble from the crowd to soothe once I'm finished."

Well.

Of course this was what he had meant: that *Icca* should leave. All the time, Icca would have a body that could die. Kai didn't. Kai wanted to stay close, pressed to the chandeliers, and watch and feel how the Queen's magic would follow him still; he knew it would.

"Goodbye," he said, magic stinging his throat, and then he was unraveling, fading away, as Carousel stared at him excitedly until there was nothing more to stare at, and Icca ignored him until there was nothing more to ignore, besides his voice next to her ear. "You're going to die."

Caro leaned closer to Icca. "You heard that too, right?"

Icca just rolled her eyes, part of their arc following Kai up as he tucked himself against the heat of the candles burning in the chandelier. He could see so much better like this.

He watched as the Queen stood and greeted everyone with a small bow, her hands clasped. He saw her and her King tuck their heads as the Courts began to pour their tea and take their treats, giving silent thanks to their chosen gods.

He could see into the Queen's teacup, the rounded shadow its rim cast into its porcelain depths.

He could see Icca shake out her sleeve, a little, nothing motion. The first drop of the rose draught rolling silently from its hidden place, tracing its way down the pale line of her pinkie finger.

And the droplet, the same white color as the roses he'd strained it from—of course Icca had insisted on white, wanting to mock the White Queen, the Culled Court, all of it—getting fat along her cuticle, more and more, and then it broke, and it fell toward the floor.

Fell toward the thin shadow of Icca's chair leg, and disappeared.

And the surface of the Queen's teacup rippled slightly.

Holy hell. This was going to be quite the bloodbath, one way or another, wasn't it?

Cheshire smiled. He was sure his teeth were glinting in the light.

TWENTY

YEAR ZERO ZERO NINETY-FOUR, WINTER SEASON

THERE ARE 1001 REMAINING SAINTS

"WHO IS THAT, NEAR Carousel, November?"

"That's Iccadora Alice Sickle, darling." Hattie didn't glance up. "The two of them are in love, but they think they don't deserve each other."

As usual, in public, Il-Hyun was leaned in very close to her, so he could hear her words when the others would only find unbroken silence. He smelled of cinnamon. And under that, of course—the scent of his blood.

Hattie tore the hwajeon Il-Hyun had given her in half with her fingers, splitting the purple flower at the rice cake's middle, and paused. Maybe she shouldn't eat this, either.

Just as well. Her veil still hung softly against her nose, the bow of her lips. Hattie felt very private, very dear and secret to herself, behind that veil.

"Really?" Il-Hyun asked. Sweet boy.

"Yes."

"Do you remember her?" Il-Hyun queried, always the curious one out of the two of them. He meant, did she remember taking the death trace off of Icca's soul? It was obvious the witch was an absolved Jabberwocky. They did have a more jagged air than the nobles of the Thia Court.

"Well," murmured Hattie, glancing sadly over the table. She really was hungry. "I doubt I would have if I hadn't known Carousel first."

People were so inconsistent, but more than to themselves, they were so extraordinarily disparate from one another. It had fascinated Hattie's mother, too. The startling detail of human individualism was a feat of Divinity all on its own.

Which is why Hattie had been stunned. Hattie had never been stunned before.

She'd found Carousel strange—Hattie was sure everyone did, actually—but it had been before the crow witch had even opened her mouth. Because Hattie had been feeling out Carousel's soul in her hands, reaching for the death mark cracked like rot through its profound depths, and there it was. It felt, to Hattie, like a cord. A steadfast piece in that haze . . . Really, Hattie hadn't been able to help herself. She felt for what it was, and thought to herself, *Oh, my, it's hatred.*

Hatred for what? Carousel wouldn't say. Carousel said a lot, but she'd never even hinted at it, and Hattie wanted to *know.* Wanted to know about the loathing that held up Carousel like a blouse to a clothesline.

And then the answer walked into her Labyrinth's chapel, reeling from the sting of the rune on her neck she'd had to brave to get there, to get the death trace removed by Hattie's hand.

Hattie searched for it, like she'd done with Carousel, and all the others before.

And her magic tripped across that same cord. The same exact hate.

It wasn't the same after that. Hattie had read Carousel's records prior, ravenous with her need for the story, but seeing Iccadora Alice Sickle's name, a list of her features in ink, and her history a scant line—parents taken by saltfever, a wholly common end, placed in an orphanage so early she could barely remember being anywhere else—it wasn't the same as feeling that cold, steadfast line drawn through her soul.

It wasn't the same, with Hattie knowing that if she had wandered down that length of hatred in Icca's heart, her magic would end up clotting in Carousel's chest.

It was incredible. It was very strange indeed.

It was incredible that now, Iccadora and Carousel had ended up at Hattie's Tea, sitting side by side and not throttling one another, and it was strange that, after all this time Hattie spent thinking about Icca, considering what type of person she might be around all that hatred, now Icca was trying to kill her.

And Hattie really was hungry. She needed to keep her hands occupied or she might nibble on something absentmindedly, or drink the tea. She held her cup in her hand to admire how the color hadn't changed from whatever Icca had dropped in it, and whispered to Il-Hyun, "Can you collect my Saints, darling?"

"Of course, love," he replied, and went away to do so. Through the red of her veil, Hattie watched the back of his head with affection. She could love him, certainly. Even if they'd only married because she, eventually, needed an heir. He was immensely kind, and brilliant, and didn't mind that she wasn't thrilled that they had to touch one another past the cheek kisses and the embraces and Hattie's head on his lap as she read at night, or vice versa. "To be fair," she'd told him more than once, "having sex with anyone doesn't exactly liven me, I find I have no opinion on it." And to this he'd laugh, not at her, but at the situation at its primitive whole.

Hattie stood.

The room immediately quieted, which meant even the softness of her voice could carry. But of course she did not speak.

She did not need to. Hattie moved toward the open doors at the back of the tearoom, her feet shifting onto cool grass past its threshold, and there was the scrape of chairs, the shuffling of feet.

A round courtyard spread out amid the water, hosting a small patch of woods and jars of fireflies suspended in the branches—no path, no furniture, no dais. Hattie stopped at the clearing at the edge of the water. Her Courts, knowing the tradition, hovered near the tree line. The glass of the tearoom rose behind them and above that, one of the palace's pale spires, rising toward a shrouded black sky.

Hattie went to take off her slippers and realized that, in her excitement, she'd forgotten to set down her teacup. But she liked the weight of it, even if she looked ridiculous, holding the cup with her slippers and socks off now, toes against the earth. She liked the thought that Icca was somewhere in the crowd, looking on anxiously to see if she'd take a sip.

And now, that crowd was parting.

Il-Hyun was leading a cart, piled up in flesh.

He motioned for the guards to stop at the tree line, and they worked to haul the cargo off the platform and lay them out—gently, as ordered—before Hattie's bare toes.

Her captured Saints, slack in their sleep.

She looked up, and Il-Hyun wiped his magic from his eyes, dark like jasmine tea leaves. The littler Hattie and him had played fun about it before—though really, Hattie knew now, it wasn't a very fun thought—how they would have beaten Wonderland, him with his sleep magic, her with her stitches.

He gave her a bow, came up with a softened smile that she thought revealed his true beauty. She smiled too, one he couldn't see, and tasted the sting of her own magic on her gums.

Turning her body to face the water, Hattie reached back and drew the veil away from her features. The night air kissed her cheeks. It was in these little sensory instances that she felt blessed by the world. Felt lucky to be alive.

She reached up to touch the streams of magic from her nostrils just as they reached her chin, dripped off into her teacup. It was blooming in the water when she glanced down, and she saw her hanbok already speckled with it.

Just as well. It was all about to be drenched, anyway.

Hattie knelt down before the Saints.

Bowed her head, sent a prayer up to her favorite god, Quiet, who always hovered close. Who was the quality of her veins, the space between the beats of her heart. Who was the state in her head where she found herself as a dreaming being, a holy soul.

Who—Hattie knew—awaited her in Wonderland.

Like her mother before her, Hattie could influence the senses. And it was the senses that one took in the world, that bled its magic, that translated its aspects, which were its deities.

And, so, cherished readers.

There were so many gods in Hattie's veins.

Magic stung her throat. It stung her eyes and the cuts on her lips. She could barely see anything. She didn't have to. She felt her magic threading between her fingers, and she felt the existence of the Saints before her, and a Saint's existence always felt so distant from human existence.

How bored Hattie was, of human senses.

But those of a Saint—gods, gods.

She was electric, as she blurred her focus on her own senses and instead pinned her attention to the sleeping Saints. The transition like drinking down a cup of static, fresh and sharp and teeming. And it was like this that the Red Queen hewed herself in two every single year.

There was, to Hattie, nothing like such cleaving.

She knew she was the most powerful witch on the planet. But sometimes, sometimes... *Yes*, Hattie thought. *How strange. Sometimes I'm something else entirely.*

Something like a Saint? Perhaps. The beasts were not witches, not anymore. Their amplified Divinity had made them feral, inhuman, but that Divinity was still very much within them. It was still very much *them*, now. And were Divine things not gods?

And if one stole the senses of Divine things, what did that make one? What did that make Hattie?

What did it make her—what did she make herself—when blindly, she found the left wrists of the two creatures unconscious before her, and began to stitch them together?

The little gods awoke, of course, when their flesh began to fuse.

And so Hattie made them blind. She made them forget their feet.

They could smell her, and past the thick red gleam of the magic pooling in her eyes, she saw them get to their knees. Hattie felt the saliva pooling at the backs of their throats, the animal kick of their famine. But already she was wearing them—wearing their senses, their Divinity—and confusion curdled in the hunger of the beasts, as they found only themselves upon her skin.

Because they fit her perfectly.

They always fit her perfectly.

And so, even with the smell of her skin, even when Saint Natasha Jun twitched its blank expression to Hattie's collarbone to inhale along its length, even when Peter von Rutterlin's head twisted back and its teeth closed on the air over her hip, they did collapse, did not gobble her down, screeching and flailing before her Courts. How embarrassing it would be, certainly, for all of her revered Quiet, if she left the world like that, splitting the air with noise. Well, well. Behind her veil, Hattie smiled.

What a fraud they'd all think her, then. . . .

And wouldn't that be just, the Queen torn apart by her own freakish display?

Disappearing into the Labyrinth for days at a time, no one quite knowing how she toiled within its Walls. Playing at her mother's Saints' Races. Playing at piety. And the Courts—always scrambling between believing her and ridiculing her, between loving her and hating her. And Hattie knew at some critical point between two such human instincts, love and hatred, there was a chance she'd at last be understood. It's how she'd come to understand Wonderland. But she knew it was a long shot, with human beings. People were people were ridiculous people, and they lived in their own heads, obsessing over the stories of their lives, making villains and heroes and religious figures of one another. Wonderland, lacking language, didn't make up stories, didn't judge her. It didn't judge anyone. Wonderland was Quiet.

She smoothed her palm across their waists, finger trailing red threads from her cuticles, trailing a closing seam between the two bodies. Fitting their ribs together like intertwined roots. She drew the corners of their mouths together, shuffled their teeth.

She kept one eye from Jun and one from von Rutterlin, and stitched the others closer together—brown on the left, and green on the right—so they sat low and comparatively small above the lengthened mouth. Perhaps if there were a beating heart, or some kind of soul between the two, if they were anything but empty husks of magic, the flesh and bone and muscle wouldn't slough into her desired form.

Perhaps they wouldn't be like clay between her fingers.

One thousand and one Saints, and Hattie was going to pinch together two bodies of that number to make it one thousand and zero. But, yes. One more would fall off the count, tonight. It was hard to say how she knew. She'd had some dream, perhaps. . . .

Her senses were becoming less split, stitching on top of one another like clouds shifting over the moon. Then she was seeing out of two eyes instead of four, and feeling from twenty fingers and twenty toes of one form instead of two. Hattie sat back on her bare heels, knees in the grass, went to wipe the sweat from her temples. Her entire face below her eyebrows was a mess of her magic, and she blinked it back, swallowed it down, so when she had to speak again, her words wouldn't sound so clogged.

Her newest Saint lay on the ground before her. Although it wasn't quite a new thing, together, but certainly not their old selves. Its limbs dragged against the earth, testing its weight. She'd snipped off its senses from her own but even now, it still wouldn't hurt her. Her magic was a part of it, now, and they knew it, knew that Hattie was the one keeping them together.

She ghosted a hand, fingertips quivering with her effort, over her Saint.

Soon it would rouse itself and try to eat up her Courts, so this was always one of her favorite moments. Watching it take in the world as a new thing.

Because when it did try to eat the Courts, she wouldn't like it as much. Or maybe, more accurately, it would be that Hattie would no longer care about it at all. It was the art of it she liked. The way her magic fit to their bodies like their edges were meant for one another.

Because, really, Hattie was making monsters.

She never forgot that. She would never forget that.

Yet Hattie couldn't help but understand them.

She, too, was attuned to the emotions of other people. Their strange reactions to being alive.

No, her mouth did not water at their mourning; at the depths of their despair, she did not desire to unhook her jaw and swallow them whole—though, sometimes, smeared in the morning Quiet, freshly from the warm haze of some dream, Hattie would think, *In pieces, perhaps...*

Delcorta had created the Saints' Races to soothe and startle the general population with the power of their bloodline. Hattie would admit that the Midwinter Tea was for the Thia and Culled Courts—nobles and absolved Jabberwockies, respectively, and the bolstered part of the Petra population—meant to remind them that they should be afraid, even in the higher rungs of society. But for the holiday of the Saints' Races that followed—Hattie's intention wasn't simply terror, for her subjects, like Delcorta's had been.

It was fervor.

Here was the terrible secret Hattie and the Saints shared—the people of Isanghan were numb.

They had numbed themselves, to survive the creatures that would seek them out in the depths of their despair. Hattie sought to be the thing that would remind them of such depths, by exposing her own.

She wasn't simply creating horrors, drawing two into one. She was making her pain incarnate. She was whispering, *Here is my agony, skittering around on hands and knees. Here it is, killing creatures.*

Here I am, alive, alive, alive.

Be alive, with me.

Before her, the fingers of her new Saint began to work in the soil. The pads of its feet knocking up clots of earth.

Her Saint swiveled its head toward the onlookers. Hattie frowned at it, then down into her poisoned teacup. And there, as if she were divining from tea leaves, was the curl of Iccadora Alice Sickle's anger, and her hatred, and her mourning.

Such vividness struck Hattie.

Struck her like a dream of Wonderland, and Wonderland Hattie did see, then, foliage whispering in the back of her mind. Telling her . . . She strained to listen.

Yes. Yes.

Hattie snatched a hand out, fingernails digging underside her Saint's long, long jaw, peeling open the slit of its mouth.

Then the Red Queen took her poisoned teacup and emptied the contents into its throat.

TWENTY-ONE

YEAR ZERO ZERO NINETY-FOUR, WINTER SEASON

THERE ARE 1000 REMAINING SAINTS

CAROUSEL GLANCED AT ICCA. It startled her, for a beat, that she *could* glance at Icca, that Icca really was standing right beside her, the top of her head just to Caro's temple, the height difference unchanged though they were both a little taller now—why wasn't Caro killing her again?

She looked around at the courtyard, at the paling faces juxtaposed against hungry eyes, as the Courts watched the Red Queen lean back from her new Saint. Right. This wasn't really the place to be snapping necks. Caro certainly didn't want to take the attention away from Hattie.

"Look at that, Icca," whispered Caro feverishly. "We've hit one thousand! We'll be Saints-free by the time the sun pops from the sky, at this rate!"

But Icca wasn't paying her any mind. Caro looked back toward Hattie, toward where the Saint had begun to twist on its many knees and its gnarled knot of a torso, toward where, now, the Red Queen was wrenching open its creepy thin mouth and feeding it her tea.

Unnie's very fucking weird, thought Caro affectionately.

"What is she *doing*?" hissed Icca.

Caro shrugged. She watched Hattie raise a hand to stave off Il-Hyun, who was waiting like a good boy at the front of the crowd for the Saint to come a-charging.

But it didn't.

Maybe there was something wrong with it—anatomically; there was definitely something wrong with all Saints in general, Caro knew, ugly motherfuckers as they were. But the Saint's hesitation was not why the hairs on the back of Caro's neck were standing at attention. It was Hattie's posture. Still kneeling on the ground, but now completely still, her chin raised with the magic-soaked veil clinging to her neck. Moving as she swallowed. She was waiting for something to happen.

Caro was so thrilled at the prospect that she hardly cared that Icca's dark little presence had vanished from her side. She didn't care at all.

The Saint took another step—did things on all fours step, or did they crawl? Caro would definitely describe the motion on the Saint more as crawling than stepping, though she didn't think deer crawled, or cats—and then it paused.

And it...

The sound of stretching skin—Caro hadn't known there was such a sound—and the Saint's two-toned shriek, and it—erupted.

Carnage splattered Hattie, the crowd, spraying the surface of the water, and the Saint collapsed with a force that sent the foliage above Caro's head shivering.

Quiet, she wanted to hiss to the reeling crowd, if she could speak in that moment. *Don't you want to see what's happening clearly?*

The Saint was slumped on the ground over all of its limbs, shifting but certainly, certainly not of its own accord, but because of the plants that were sprouting out of its back. Bright green leaves curled off of thorned stems, and when the bulbs were a few feet high they burst into roses of deep, perfect red—even under the Saint's black blood, Caro could tell.

The petals were the exact color, Caro knew—she *knew*—of Hattie's magic.

Now the Court was really screaming—the noble Thia Court, that is; the Jabberwockies of the Culled Court were straining for a better look—and past the fleeing bodies, Caro picked out Icca, who, in the excitement, had pushed to the front of the crowd.

And Caro knew the look on her face—absolute murder.

Absolutely fucking not.

Caro pushed past the sea of scattering hanboks and then she was on Icca, grabbing the back of her dress and using it to throw her against the trunk of a tree. Icca's breath left her, her knees crumpling, but Caro held her fast in place, the bird tattoos on her fingers sinking into green silk. She leaned close.

"Now," Caro breathed. "Why did you say you were here, again?"

Though it was obvious, now. Something had been in the Queen's tea. Something that would've made Hattie a rose garden. The suicidal, *vile*—

"She killed Tecca," spat Icca. "Your Queen is perfectly safe here and she let Tecca die and it didn't even *matter*."

Tecca. The name clattering down Carousel's ribs.

She hadn't been prepared. Her fist shook around Icca's dress but held fast; Icca shifted her feet and dropped into the shadow of the foliage, slid right out of Caro's fingers like the ground was a pool of water. Caro whipped her head around, and caught Icca sliding out of the dark opposite the clearing.

And Caro had known Icca must have gotten stronger.

But now Icca's fingertips were spreading at her sides, and now the shadows of the courtyard were angling toward her, stretching beneath Carousel's feet. They clotted beside Icca and then, when they were good and black and thick, slipped up the trunk of the tree behind her.

Caro had known. She hadn't known enough.

Icca was weeping magic and grinning through it. Icca was making a door.

From the shadows clotted against the tree trunk extended a clawed hand, reaching out from the dark, and into the light.

TWENTY-TWO

YEAR ZERO ZERO NINETY-FOUR, WINTER SEASON

THERE ARE 1000 REMAINING SAINTS

OH, YES, **ICCADORA** thought to herself, as the Saint crawled out of the shadows, out of the door she'd made leading from her black, in-between realm, *Oh* yes.

Icca hadn't been sure if the Queen's created Saint would go after its maker, even with roses sprouting from its chest cavity—she'd planned for the carnage of the rose draught to send the Saint reeling for Hattie—but Icca had planned for this, right, right, and she'd brought her own monster, she was the master of the universe, because Icca was the fucking Dark witch, bitch, she was—

Being lifted clean off her feet by a clawed hand around the back of her hanbok, and Icca was twisting to see her summoned Saint opening a jaw that split halfway down the sides of its throat to quite literally swallow her whole.

Her magic gave a rabid kick in her veins alongside her frustration. *You—imbecilic, disgusting animal—you're killing the wrong—*

And then Icca was surrounded by imbecilic, disgusting animals.

The crows tore in a rupturing line up the Saint's arm, some lodging down the spiral of teeth winding down its throat, and Icca was dropped to the ground. Outraged, she recognized she'd been saved. She immediately lifted her head and screamed, "I didn't need your help!"

Carousel, halfway across the clearing, hands spread at her sides and pupils and whites drowning under her weeping magic, looked directly at Icca and grinned. "Ha—I'm not helping you, Alice!" She wiped her eyes and flicked blue against the ground, the grin turning into a rictus. "The Saint doesn't get to be the one to tear you apart!"

At her words, the birds peeled off the Saint's shrieking form and were upon Icca. A talon scraped a long, bright line down the length of her neck as she dove for the shadow of a nearby tree, and then she was in it, down in that Dark, quiet place.

Her magic stung her more and more with every second she sat there in the black, but she did sit there and breathe and breathe, and then scream.

Had the Queen seen the draught drip into her tea? Why in Divinity would she have fed it to her monster?

And past the incredulousness, Icca felt a bitterness so dry it was rupturing within her—that Saint was *hers*, gods damn it, not the Queen's, it had been down here in this shadowed place for an entire year, and still it had come out ready to swallow her whole. It should have feared her by now. It should have crawled out mewling at her feet.

Icca had thought she'd always have to hold on to Caro when they darkported, but then Dae-San Tweedle had followed her into the shadows all those years ago, had been able to wander in all on its own. It hadn't really been intentional, with the Saint now loose in the palace courtyard—Icca had been fighting it a year ago, and something similar to what happened with Dae-San had occurred, where the Saint was tangled to her and she dropped down here, into her other realm, to break away. But she was focused, and a step later she found herself on the Wonderland earth with no Saint in sight. She hadn't known where it had gone until the next time she darkported, and it was there, in that place she thought all her own, and it was chasing her.

For a year it had been chasing her, whenever she stepped into the shadows. She'd kept her darkporting distances short—more time than that and it would've been on her. Really, Icca should have known the first thing it'd try to do upon release would be to swallow her up. Perhaps—she thought it deliriously—she got caught up in the story of it: surely, her character was one of the greats, who did not know the cold bone-touch of fear because it radiated from her. She who was both the slayer of monsters and the worst of them.

But storybook creatures did not Saints make, apparently.

She hadn't had the place to herself for a while now. It was a little nice, sitting there, down in the stomach of her Dark deity, screaming her throat raw, while gods knew what was going on in the Light.

She could run. She could feel the shadows of the Petra Woods loom in her mind's eye, the escape she'd set for herself just past the palace gates. But now Icca was mad, and maybe, she thought, maybe she was always a little pissed off, but not always in a way that fixed her focus like this—like she'd never be able to enjoy anything again if she didn't put everything she had, right now, into crushing Hattie November Kkul out of physical existence.

Icca swallowed down her last scream. And then she went back up—or, dear readers, perhaps down, or sideways, or through . . . a narrator restricted by language apologizes for the uncertainty of terming particularities of magic, which detests being termed to begin with.

But continuing—Icca blinked into the soft candlelight of the courtyard to see her Saint's mouth crowded with a final glimpse of the King's legs, which were jerking. There was no scream to be heard—Il-Hyun Hyo's head had already met the teeth that lined the plush flesh of the Saint's throat—only a wet *crunch, crunch, crunch.*

Icca thought as she began to move, *Gods damn it, you dumb beast—that's the wrong godsdamn royal.*

Crows were scattered everywhere, both them and Caro herself attempting to fight it off, and the Queen stood small and quite still at the edge of the water—in shock, or in apathy?

The courtyard was cleared, and Icca's approach to the Queen was over grasses flattened by panicked feet. Good gods, was the Culled Court laughable. She'd seen how they'd reeled with interest, at first, before her Saint—one without a leash—had come into play. And where was the Queen's guard? No hard feat to imagine they had turned tail and run; especially with Hattie standing so perfectly unshaken, bare toes on the earth. Icca knew she didn't need protection. Knew Hattie thought she didn't need protection from Icca. Between them, red, red roses rose from the stitched monster's chest like the furrows of its ribs were tilled earth, slicked over in its black blood. A breeze came licking out from over the water, brushing by them.

And Hattie's hands were moving. Icca braced for an attack, but the Queen was only drawing back her veil.

She had the daydreamy expression of a lost child. Beneath all the red, of course.

"Roses . . ." murmured Hattie, and it was a surreal thing, her voice. Faraway, and curious. She wasn't even talking to Icca.

Oh, Icca thought. *What the fuck?*

Her husband was being stuffed into the stomach of a Saint a few dozen paces away, its shrieks parrying against those of Caro's crows, and the Queen was considering, considering. "How random . . ." A joke, perhaps, if Hattie was even able to make jokes. She must have known Icca had chosen the flower as a stab at her entire bloodline, to disgrace the White Queen's image, and Icca wanted a reaction to match that. She wanted hurt. So why did Hattie look so—*calm*?

Kai had explained it to Icca, once, that roses were for romantic magic, in their purest form. But, perhaps as a result of this trait, they could also take to hatred quite beautifully. "Feed off of it quite ravenously, yes," Kai explained—not that Icca had asked. "Not exactly the same they are, love and hatred, certainly, but oh, dear, certainly not too distant." Kai grinning, grinning, Icca bored as she gathered up her clothes, but listening a little, maybe—readers, and only just maybe—thinking of Carousel. "Both requiring attention, passion to sustain. Both just past that fine, fine line of being alone in one's own head, and moving over to allow another room."

Icca was close enough now. Her magic welled in empty spots where her back molars had once been, and she bit down on the sting as her power pawed for all of the Red Queen's lightless spots.

Icca had intended hatred, so that's what the rose draught had come to be by the time it had dripped from her fingertips—a rupturing, ravenous thing, reflecting her loathing, reflecting the thought of Tecca in Icca's head.

It was too bad that Hattie had noticed it. It was too bad Icca's Saint was so fucking sheep-brained.

The Red Queen smoothed a wistful hand down the front of her blood-soaked dress.

"Oh," said Hattie November Kkul quietly. "I see what you're doing."

And Icca was on the ground.

She'd completely lost feeling in her legs, and when she sucked in a gasp, she stopped breathing—her lungs stayed unmoving and uncomfortably full, like they'd forgotten how to compress. But that wasn't it. The Queen had stitched them into place.

And Hattie's Saint, inches before her, was blinking awake. Of course it was still alive. It didn't get to die without her say-so.

"You're going to regret that." Hattie's voice was as calm as her expression, so entirely, awfully calm. "You're going to regret all of it."

Icca's chest ached. This was really happening. She was either about to get eaten without moving or she was going to suffocate with her lungs full. She'd lost her focus; all the Queen's lightless spots slipped out of the reach of her magic, like silk pulled through a keyhole. She could see her own hand pressed uselessly into the dirt, the scar encircling one finger. . . .

No.

And then, somewhere behind her, the thud of a body and the low, keeling moan of a girl. Even with the Queen's stitched Saint rising on its forearms before her, roses rippling, barely alive and still excited to eat, Icca thought, *It's Carousel.*

The stitched Saint opened its mouth, teeth scraping her cheekbone. Its throat radiating the stench of rotting meat.

And then, incomprehensibly, Icca was underneath not one but two reeking bodies, and her form was her own again.

She let out her breath in a pinched, painful exhale and as she did, attached herself to one of the body's shadows, momentarily filling its outline before she crawled out of its far edge, a few feet away. Choking on her own magic, Icca glanced back to see her Saint fighting the Queen's in a flurry of limbs. The stupid beast. It would never win against the amalgamation—though it *was* weakened. But why did it want to fight the twined creation when there were humans to devour?

Some horrible, clean *crack* rippled through the Queen's monster. It went limp beneath Icca's Saint, and then Icca's Saint—it was...

Eating the roses?

And then there was the arch of a foot in Icca's ribs, and she was on her back. And Carousel was leaning over her, breathing raggedly. Her lip had been split, but there was magic in her eyes and a dagger in her hand, the blade already to the crook of Icca's neck.

"I feel a twitch of that nasty little power, Alice"—Caro laughed, the sound black and jagged—"and it's off with your head."

It was quite a natural thing, the fear that bloomed in the base of Icca's throat. Icca truly did believe her. Caro's cheeks were bright under the streaming blue, her voice wild and clutched to the idea like it fascinated her.

—

It did fascinate Carousel. How years ago they would've burned down the world for one another. And now. Caro really could cut off Icca's head and savor every wet, sawing moment of it.

But somewhere beside her, Hattie let out a little gasp.

Caro looked over, giving a little pressure to the knife to tell Icca she was still paying attention. This is when she noticed, *Oh. There's Icca's Saint, I was wondering where it went, it really is almost right directly above me*, and also when she noticed that the Saint was not currently eating her alive.

And it was Hattie, because of course it was Hattie, keeping it at bay, but Hattie's hands were empty of any enchantment, and she looked just as stunned as Caro felt. Caro saw a thought cross Hattie's face, blatant and incredibly rare for it, and then the Saint—moved away from Carousel.

It lay facedown on the earth, its full stomach crushing the grass. And it stayed there, perfectly unmoving.

Caro's eyes drifted. She knew Icca's were doing the same, and then Hattie's, and then all three witches' attention was pinned to the roses rising out of the stitched Saint's chest. A few stems were bare, the apple-sized blossoms swallowed down; a few more had the obvious imprint of teeth.

The Saint's black blood shimmered under the fireflies, covering petals the exact shade of Hattie's magic.

Hattie was controlling the Saint.

"Oh, oh, Hattie unnie," Caro breathed, and their eyes met. The expression across Hattie's face was completely bare in the realization—in the instinctive kick of hubris at the act. Hattie had never been ignorant to the extent of her power, but this—Caro had never, ever seen Hattie relish her ability, even with the steely calm that contained it. Like a marksman pulling back an arrow and knowing it a perfect shot, that it'd hit air and then skin and then muscle and then organ. "How are you *doing* that, you miraculous creature?"

Hattie didn't answer, wrapped up in her own head, but Caro was excited, so she chattered about it to herself, how Hattie had fed her stitched Saint that rose draught, and it had sprouted roses the same color as her magic. Now those roses sat in the stomach of the other Saint, and Hattie had made it quiet with a thought. Certainly *that* was magic, newly discovered! Her unnie would have such fun peeling it apart—she was such a scientist. Like Icca, in that way, with the academicness of it all. Perhaps Caro liked that trait in other people, though she was sure Hattie wore it much better.

Hattie's fingers dropped to her sides. She fell back to her knees, all of the grim satisfaction evaporated from her look. She was looking at Icca, still pinned by Caro's knife and Caro's knee against her shoulder.

"She killed Il-Hyun," Hattie said. Her voice was devoid of emotion. She was just making a note. But it must be bothering her, a little, Caro figured, since the Red Queen's fingers were twitching at her sides.

"Oh, it won't hurt if you don't think about it," Caro said.

This was the best she could offer. She didn't actually care very much about Il-Hyun. Hattie might focus more on Carousel now, and didn't that sound nice? It sounded so nice that Caro began to laugh, splattering Icca with blue.

"Oh, off with her head indeed, my Queen?" spoke Caro through her giggles.

"Carousel."

"Arasso, arasso, unnie, I know. I was just kidding. Nighty-night." This last bit was meant for Icca, who realized this and tensed a moment before Carousel stood and kicked her in the side of the head.

The dark witch went limp immediately, chin snapped to the side.

Carousel took a very measured step back, and then another, to ensure she wouldn't keep going.

TWENTY-THREE

Year Zero Zero Ninety, Autumn Season

There Are 1089 Remaining Saints

AND THERE THEY WERE, dear readers, in one of the worse parts, what must be, they thought, surely the worst part.

Aching with her magic, Carousel had let Icca up. Silently, they had walked back to camp together, and more than once Caro thought of reaching for Icca's hand, but she didn't. The Saints' heads were in the way. The thoughts in her head and in Icca's head were in the way.

Icca had known too, of course, that Caro had planned to leave the same as her, even before they reached the dug-up head-holes Icca had been so careful to cover up again.

Two weeks passed. Summer slipped quietly into fall. They didn't go hunting for Saints. They set up the heads in a line by the fire pit even though the birds would get to the ones with meat still on them—Caro would awake from a restless sleep because she felt them outside the lean-to, picking, eating, and would let her magic leak so she could snap their necks without getting up. Birds for breakfast, birds for dinner. They still hadn't said a single word to one another, and Caro felt that lacking like a pit opened up beneath them both, eating its way down, down, down into the black earth.

Carousel really did hate herself.

Because she was sleeping so poorly, she had plenty of time to examine this new feeling that had taken root in her. She examined how she wanted to never move again. She examined how her magic disgusted her, how much she wanted to cry when she felt it bubbling up. She examined how she'd like a Saint to come crashing through the place and how much she wanted to fear for her life, to have the world whittled down to that pin-width of terror because it might scrub her clean—before she died, of course—it might be her repentance, swallowing that pin down, waiting to feel it catch.

And there it was, another inconsistency, in this little fantasy of getting ripped apart—she knew that she'd fight the Saint off. It wouldn't be her fear moving her body, pinching her puppet strings—she'd be herself the entire time, wanting to live, live, live. She might even win. She turned over in their blanket and hated herself even more.

—

And Icca, awake beside her, had her head filled with similar thoughts with similar sharp edges, the self-loathing like ink in her veins. Staining her blood, staining her magic—which was probably for the best, because multiple times she tried to feel for the lightless spots in her own lungs to pop them out, send them corroding, eating her away, just a little, and came up blank. Came up with that same feeling of dread that had woken her up that night, that had her hands in the soil in the dark, but it wasn't the Saints that terrified her any longer—had she really been worried about the Saints? Now she was constantly fantasizing about them crashing through the place, so the fear could clutch at her . . . Oh, but, cherished reader, you've heard this part already. . . .

—

They were so busy hating themselves, really, that for a while they didn't have much time to hate one another. Or maybe, they thought to themselves, in the dead quiet of the night, that it was so much easier to think of hating themselves than hating one another. Because how could one hate the other?

They loved one another more than any other soul in the world.

And still, they'd tried to run.

The other had still tried to run.

They could blame Wonderland—a sorrowful narrator believes, truly, our darling champions should have. They could blame its Saints, or whatever had stolen the heads in the first place, or they could have even blamed Tecca. But none of those fit quite right. None of those were breathing beside them when they tried to sleep, when they couldn't.

One night Carousel rolled over. There'd been a twig or some shit under the small of her back, and she hadn't rolled over to face Icca since that night. And Icca was awake, her skin moonlike in the dark, little dark eyes glinting as they snapped to Caro's, and as one they took in a breath. Some breeze flitted through above their heads, knocking pine needles into pine needles. *Tsk-tsk-tsk.*

Carousel put her hand to the slight curve of Icca's waist.

"Don't," Icca said, but she'd been talking to herself, and Caro started to pull away, and the next *Don't* was a frantic kick in her head because this one was meant for the other witch, and Icca moved closer and kissed her.

It was grappling, sloppy, like they hadn't made out a million times before, in a million other angers, and they broke apart, chests heaving, feeling the thought begin to press in, take form—*this didn't feel right*— and suffocating it before it could latch, back together, stomachs together, Caro's fingers on Icca's spine and Icca's fingers in Caro's hair, and then traveling lower, moving like she knew how to move them to send Caro's breath thin and high and—then her trembling was over, and they pushed away from one another at the same moment.

Icca was up and Caro was following her to their dead campfire, autumn cold already drowning the heat of their skin, the lingering heat of the other's skin.

—

"You—" gasped Carousel. It was the first word she'd spoken in weeks, and it came out rasping. Her magic stung in her eyes, sent blue washing over Icca's face. Caro loathed the giveaway of it—she could damn well stop herself from crying, but not her magic from feeding off her aches. "Did you— Was it all in my head, Alice? How you feel about me?"

It might not have been what she meant to say, but it was in the air now, and now Caro knew it to be her darkest thought of all. She couldn't stand it if Icca hated her as she hated herself.

"You know that's not true," spat Icca in a cracked voice, silver beading at her mouth. Caro watched her swallow it down. "You did the same. You were going to do the same. It has nothing to do with how we feel about one another!"

"It has everything to do with it!"

"Deities, I *love you*, you bitch, and you love *me*, don't you?"

"You're a fucking academic, Alice." Caro tilted her chin back with a laugh, letting the magic trickle down her temples. She was seeing the night in a blue, glittering sheen. It was entirely surreal. Now she was just chattering. Chattering like one of her birds, thinking the rumors were true. People did lose their minds in Wonderland. "Oh, my, my, aren't we hopeless! It doesn't matter. It doesn't matter!" Her hands flitted around her head, as if to scare away the hurt. "Come on. Come on. Just touch me again, Alice, won't you? Tell me to give you the rest of the Saints' heads. Tell me to get on my knees. Tell me you're leaving me."

"Stop it," Icca rasped.

Caro did get on her knees then. Laughing, laughing, pulling Icca in by the waist. Her lips brushing her navel. "Tell me you would do terrible things for me."

"I would. Gods, you know I would."

"Forgive me, then."

"I do. I do." But Icca was crying now.

"I forgive you, too," Caro said, feeling cruel.

"Get off of me."

Icca squirmed away and Caro let her. There she knelt on the forest floor, absent her altar. Caro said, "I don't believe you, either."

—

"I was scared. Weren't you just terrified, Rabbit?" Icca whispered, and Wonderland took the tremble in her voice and swallowed it whole.

—

But it all made Caro so bitter.

How good it had been, how close they'd been to beating Wonderland, to being so ridiculously happy together for the rest of their lives. She'd messed it up.

But Icca would've left her first.

It was a logistical thing, Caro knew, a chance tic of her sleep cycle, that she'd caught Icca in the woods and not the other way around. Yet still, the thought wouldn't unstick—Icca couldn't really love her. She couldn't. She couldn't. She couldn't.

But perhaps more pertinent was the fact that Caro couldn't really love Icca.

They couldn't be in love with one another, because this wasn't love. This couldn't be *love.*

And the realization embarrassed her, throttled her. How deep had Wonderland sunk into their veins, that they'd been so delusional?

"I was scared," Caro heard herself finally say. She met Icca's eyes, knew her own to be smeared away under the mess of her magic. "I was scared, and I should have killed you. I should have fucking fed you to the birds."

—

Icca took a step back, hurt flashing across her features first, just for a moment, before the anger hit her throat, the tips of her fingers.

"You betrayed me, too," Icca spoke, the words lifted with her quiet disbelief. "Don't forget that for a single moment, Rabbit. You were going to leave me here, too."

Her own voice rang in her ears. Every word she spoke was true. Icca had spent all this time hating herself, like she was the only one to blame, the only thing around that deserved to be blown apart. So what? Icca hadn't wanted to hurt Caro, and Caro hadn't wanted to hurt Icca, but that's what they would have done by leaving, by saving themselves. How the hell was it any different now?

How the hell could they be in love, now?

"Apologize," croaked Icca.

Carousel barked a laugh. "For all of it? Like *you*—"

"No, you twit." Squeezing her words out of a tear-tight throat. "For that nasty thing you just said."

"Oh, about the birds. I'm *so* sorry about the birds. I would have used them to check in on you, every now and then, Iccadora darling *dear.* See how you were faring."

"Why are you *doing this?*"

"Because we're delusional, Alice, we've succumbed to that genuine Wonderland sucker punch of madness! A minute ago we thought we loved one another, and now—I can see it on your face. Where are we now? What are we to one another, now?" Carousel laughed again, again, again.

"Stop it," Icca rasped. "Just shut up—"

"We wanted to leave so badly, so let's, Icca." Caro leaned over the cold weight in her chest and snatched up one of the Saint heads. She threw the rotting weight at Icca. "We were going to leave anyway, right? Now we have an even playing ground. Let's see who can get to Petra first. Don't look me up when you get there. And don't haunt me if you die; you'd make such a frigid little ghost."

"You're being mean," said Icca, holding the head, and felt like a child for saying it, for feeling so small.

—

And Carousel tried to stop herself, hearing the truth in Icca's voice—she was being mean, she was being awful. She just didn't care. She could now very clearly feel her heart broken and with it had settled a kind of clarity. "I can be mean to you. I was going to let you die anyway. What does it matter how awful we are, now? We've already done the worst."

—

What does it matter? Icca was boiling. She was seeing red, and past that, silver, silver, silver, its sweet sting down her throat. *What does it matter—but—it has to* matter.

Did it matter?

Did it matter, when Icca knew that if she had caught Caro leaving instead of the other way around, she would've killed her, in that initial hitch of the anger and the hurt, made the darkness in Caro's lungs burn her down?

How were they supposed to live, now?

"Do a problem with me, Icky Alice the Academic," Carousel was singing now, and kicked another skull toward her. It rolled to a stop at Icca's boot. "What do you get when you have two witches with violent tendencies in love, and you take away the love? The maths are easy, easy. You get two witches with violent tendencies. . . ."

Caro continued to ramble. Icca looked down into the Saint's empty, rotting sockets. The decapitated head, that reminder of death—her as its harbinger—struck her with a clarifying calm. She'd been hazy, so unsure of herself lately, but, yes. Now Icca recalled—she wasn't like this. She didn't let things hurt her. Nearly every creature that had tried had perished.

"I haven't," she said, and Caro paused.

"Haven't what?"

Icca met her eyes. "I haven't done the worst yet."

—

And the night thickened.

Carousel took a step back. She tripped over one of the heads she'd been messing with and was back on her hands and heels, feeling cold under her fingertips as it seemed every spare shadow in Wonderland stretched toward Icca's feet. The witch's features would be the picture of calm if not for the magic flooding them. *She's going to lose all of her teeth,* Caro thought distantly, as shadows tangled in Icca's fingertips, as, before Caro's eyes, she was becoming something else entirely. *The idiot is going to be a seventeen-year-old halmeoni with a grin full of gums. . . .*

But then Icca did grin, and each tooth was there, carved in silver.

"Are we doing this?" laughed Caro, and the sound was frayed. Her fingernails curled into the earth. "Do you really want to do this?"

"Oh, now, it's so funny, Rabbit. I think I really am seeing clearer, and so quickly too," said Icca, and now she was laughing too—no, no, she was shrieking, shrieking her next words as dark spilled like liquid from her rising fingertips. "I thought you curiouser and curiouser with every moment more I knew you, and now you're on the dirt, and you're boring me!"

Then all at once it was dark, so, so dark; Caro raised her hands instinctively but couldn't see past her wrists. Icca's laugh seemed to resonate from all directions, and then something like a rock cracked against Caro's ribs and she was on her side, gasping, and Icca was saying, "Feed me to your birds, Rabbit darling, just like you wanted to, come on, give me something more challenging. . . ."

—

Icca was just behind Caro, the rock she'd plucked up weighing her hand. She raised it. Her gathered Dark snapped around her, pulling at her edges, but the pain didn't matter—the stone was real and solid and so was the side of Caro's head. Icca was a whole different person. She felt so much better. She was going to crack Caro's skull apart and she would feel so much *better*—

And bodies came flying out of the Dark.

Icca hit the ground with a screech, her focus shattered, her shadows fleeing from her. Past the initial, blinding flare of agony she saw the crow sprouted from her side, talons hooked under her skin, felt one set of claws curl around a rib. Black wings flailing, it pulled. Icca screamed as she had never screamed before. It hurt so much that briefly she was no one, she was nothing but her own pain, and then her magic flared and the bird let out a horrible sound as its lightless spots fried it alive.

Icca simply grabbed the next crow, which was going for her eyes, and flattened it against the ground with a *crack*. She was vaguely aware of Caro's body twitching a few feet away—so the bird in her fist *was* Caro, and Icca took out her knife and cut the bird belly to throat. . . .

—

Caro spasmed back into her body, the ghost feeling of the knife still itching across her sternum, but she didn't give herself time to scream at it—she twisted, and Icca was still over the dead bird, and Caro threw herself at her, knife already in hand. The two witches went rolling, smashing through their lean-to and sending the tarp down on them both. Icca let herself be swallowed up by its crashing shadow, and then Caro was clutching nothing but their blankets, trying to untangle herself and knew when Icca was above her, even before the dagger sank into her shoulder.

Caro bit down on her cry and kicked outward, hitting Icca in the shin and sending her stumbling back, and Caro was untangled and lunging yet again, onto nothing but another damn shadow. But she'd figured it out by now, that Icca liked the cheap shots, liked Caro blind when she took her hits, and so Caro spun around and slashed her blade through the air, and she hit skin, and so did Icca, both daggers moving at the same time.

Both girls stumbled back, hands on their faces.

Icca traced a line starting just under her right eye, angling into her cheekbone and then under it, ending at the crook of her jaw. Caro, meanwhile, drew her palm over her eye, peeled it back to find blood mixed strangely with her magic. The cut, white-hot, dropped from the top of her left brow to the bottom of her crow's-feet. Icca hadn't carved out her sight, but she'd gotten close. She'd meant to get closer.

Carousel had, too.

"Go," rasped Caro, blood dripping off her jaw. "Just take the heads and *go*, Alice!"

—

"We're not finished," Icca breathed. She couldn't leave it like this. She hadn't won yet. She smeared a hand across the blood marring her cheek, her other tightening around the grip of her knife, outlined in red. She needed to *win.* "This isn't over—"

—

"I'm not going to kill you right now. I can't—*kill you* right now," said Caro, horrified by the sob in her voice, horrified that suddenly, she was on the ground on all fours. Hair slipping over her eyes as she dropped her head, and she squeezed her eyes shut and screamed, "And you're not going to kill me either, so just *go*!"

And when she opened her eyes, Icca was gone. So were two of the heads. Caro rolled to her side, shrieking laughter she hadn't intended to bubble up, but the lack of control with it—the Saints she might draw with it—seemed the most distant thing.

—

She's going to draw them, thought Icca as she stepped out of a shadow two hundred paces away. The birds in the trees above seemed thoroughly unnerved, casting skittish glances in the direction of the laughter, high and tearing. Which was probably for the best. Icca would've run down anything that looked at her as she cried, feet carrying her deeper into Wonderland, would have killed crows or Saints without giving them a chance to run, which was probably a good thing.

She was in mourning. She was going to draw them, too.

TWENTY-FOUR

YEAR ZERO ZERO NINETY-FOUR, WINTER SEASON

THERE ARE 999 REMAINING SAINTS

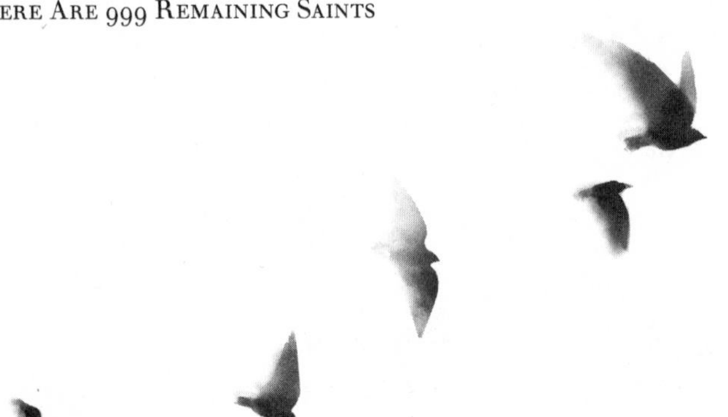

NOW, OF COURSE, readers, our Carousel Rabbit was completely fine. Caro was having a pretty good night—even though the King was dead and he'd been nice and all, and Hattie might have discovered some supercharged power with the roses that would leave Caro fighting for her attention, plus the funeral (and the need to wear dreadful black clothes instead of her preferred brightly colored everything), of course, Caro wasn't insensitive—actually.

Caro had just finished hauling Icky Sickle down, down, down into the belly of the palace dungeons. She threw her like a rag doll into one of the dirty, Cold cells. Icca immediately dove for one of the shadows in the corner and crumpled with a groan when she hit solid stone, and Caro shrieked her laugh and ran her knife gleefully against the bars, *tingtingtingting.*

"They're runeworked, dummy. No magic in here."

Then Icca, of course, attempted to dive for Carousel. But Caro had always been better at the hand-to-hand stuffs, which is why she was taking her sweet time getting out of the cell and locking the door behind her—she'd hoped Icca would try something like this.

And now Icca was on her back, and Caro could tell she was startled by the quickness of it, which really did wonders in fattening up Caro's ego. As did the anger burning to life in Icca's dark brown eyes as Caro leaned over her.

"I used to think I wouldn't be able to live, if you hated me, Alice," she breathed, gathering up the front of Icca's hanbok in her fists, and she smashed her brow across the bridge of the dark witch's nose. Icca shrieked, and Caro ignored her completely, head tilting back with Icca's blood and Icca's magic smeared across her grin, euphoric in the sting of it. "Now I kind of *love it.*"

"You're different from how I left you," spat Icca wetly as she sucked in a breath. Her nails curled into Caro's wrists. "You're all twitchy. A flighty, nervous thing."

"Nervous?" Caro said. "Just because I'm twitchy doesn't mean I'm nervous. Maybe it means I'm *bored.* Maybe you're *boring me*, Alice—which means you're different, too. You were always a quiet little witch, wanting to be that mysterious sidelines observer pressing herself into the dark. You must like it, that you've achieved it, it fits you so well. Being so utterly insignificant."

A witch of Icca's caliber could've been so much more. She could have been one of the legends. The part of Caro that was a romantic had fantasized that Icca was dead. But the part of her that was an absolute genius knew that the dark witch had survived Wonderland. And all this time, Icca had just been hunting down the bounties the Crown dished out for Saints—whether the hunter was noble or commoner or absolved Jabberwocky alike—not even setting foot in Petra. It was such a quiet life, and it irked Caro, how Icca had seemed to keep to herself. Like she never needed anyone else. Like she hadn't needed Carousel to begin with.

"Aw," Icca cooed beneath her, bleeding onto the stone. "Why, I'm never quite sure what I'm going to be, from one moment to another, between me being insignificant and me being so entrenched in your head—aren't I, Rabbit? Would you make up that scattered mind of yours and then *let it rot between your temples*—"

"You know, I've pull with Her Majesty," cooed Caro, even though it wasn't true, even though Hattie would always do whatever the hell Hattie wanted to do. "Don't roll your eyes at me, dear, it's quite rude—it's quite *damning* when you consider the situation, that you killed her husband—"

"Do you feel a death trace on me?" Icca shot with a wound of a smirk. Carousel didn't, of course. Icca hadn't grazed a hair on Il-Hyun's pretty head. Not like she'd pulled Tecca through her dark, scraped the barely-there girl with her magic; not like Caro's crows had clipped Tecca's skin. Her throat went dry at the thought.

"Fine, you only summoned a Saint to eat him alive in front of her. That's so much better, of course, but of course, there's only one punishment for absolved Jabberwockies." Icca's gloating hesitated across her features and Carousel drank it in, lips curling as she said, "Oh, yes, so, Alice dear, it's damning, that you're not *begging me*, when I could save you from it."

Carousel felt Icca's heels scrape against the floor, a jolt of her body that did not show in her calmed expression. But it showed in her voice, just a hair. "From the Labyrinth?"

This was reminding Caro of something, which was irritating. She didn't want to be reminded of something. But there was Icca's paled face, and the two men before them with their pity drawing nausea and anger in Caro's throat, and Tecca's body, so still . . . and Icca, and Icca, and Icca saying in the smallest voice Caro had ever heard, *To Wonderland Forest?*

"How bad could it be?" Icca rasped, attempting to gather the sharp bits back into her voice. "Hattie November Kkul's playground. In and out she goes, right? I've heard the rumors. And she's in one piece."

"One piece, certainly!" laughed Caro, cloaking her own hesitation behind her the cheery tone. "Well, well, of course that's the case! Her own creations can't harm her, of course, and she probably doesn't even draw any other Saints that might've ended up in the Labyrinth, calm and fine all the time, as she is."

"That's not natural."

"Well, but isn't it interesting—"

Icca's eyes suddenly shot wide. "*You* don't even know what she's up to, in there!"

"Hattie goes to the Labyrinth to pray."

"Bullshit."

"You little—" Caro made to grapple the front of Icca's hanbok again, and shook her harshly before remembering and pausing abruptly. "Oh, well, you're right, actually. I guess I don't know for *sure*. Good thing I don't care. I'll leave the pointless obsessing to you, Alice."

"She killed her mother."

"You've already exhausted this topic."

She flicked Icca's nose. Gods, was she irritating, and she didn't actually care, just wanted to make excuses. Couldn't Icca just be happy with being a horrible person? She should really just try and love herself as Caro loved herself.

Now Icca was ranting, and Caro was still ignoring her and thinking, *However, I am not so disagreeable, and certainly easier to love.... Her not being in love with me right now, in fact, just speaks to poor taste. And she's still* talking—*though*... Icca's insistences tugged at something in Caro's brain. What was it? A memory, perhaps... one forgotten, or misplaced, half-hidden under a floorboard that Icca had just ruptured with her words, and now Caro could see, half-exposed to the light, an instance where Hattie had mentioned—something about her mother, right?—Caro could just *almost— Gods*, who did Icca think she was, ruining the glorious and gleaming floors in Caro's head! "And why do you even *care* so much?" she spat, cutting Icca off.

"Because I hate her, and her blood—she shouldn't be on the throne. The Kkuls should've been scraped from the earth for creating the Saints."

"What, she should be scoured for the sins of her uncle? *Great*-uncle?"

Caro laughed once more. "He was just some man; they're always the ones to start the wars. Why should Hattie not work with the world that's presented to her? Aren't *you* doing the same?" She poked at Icca's collarbone with a sharp fingernail. "How your life must be so dull, having to reap this ridiculous purpose! Oh, oh, your hatred, Iccadora Alice Sickle," Caro cooed, tilting her head this way and that for each part of the barbed name. "You and your hatred and you and nothing else and no one else—does it keep your belly full and your limbs warm at night? Who knows, maybe the Labyrinth will be good for you. There's nothing like being gobbled down alive to click things into perspective. Perhaps in your last moments you'll abandon your hatred and find love everywhere, the entire way down the Saint's throat, and be at peace for it!"

Icca's eyes flashed.

And then she smiled.

"Oh, Rabbit," she said, words taking their time to unfurl, her hand tugging at the scar encircling her finger. "And where the fuck has love ever gotten me?"

—

Caro's footfalls were heavy up the hall, her skirts whispering up the dungeon steps as she left Icca on the cold stone. Alone at last.

If this were one of Icca's storybooks, now would be when the hero recognized just how scared they were for the next part, and breathed in the terrible inevitability of all of it, knowing that they must do what must be done, regardless of their mortal fears. This would mark them as brave, which was an admirable trait in storybooks—did the brave ones tend to live longer? Icca hadn't kept count. It certainly wasn't the case in this world.

Was Icca brave, as she lay on her back in the Dark, and grinned?

She was going to the Labyrinth. It would have terrified her, more than it was terrifying her now, just that morning. But the day had been long, and she'd found out a new magic, cradled in those roses painted over in the Saint's black blood. She loved finding out new magic, how it blossomed around her in the most horrifying of times, just like how it did for heroes and villains alike in her faerie books.

Perhaps all the Jabberwockies Hattie sent into the Labyrinth discovered what she was toiling with within; this seemed to be exposure the Queen was content with. After all, it was Hattie and Hattie alone who went in knowing she'd wander out again.

Icca didn't know, for herself. But she could guess.

They would be coming to search her, soon.

Icca plucked the rose-draught vial from the band on her arm, and held it to her eyes. Any other witch wouldn't have been able to see the few remaining drops settled at its bottom, the scrawling on its glass in the Dark.

DRINK ME!

She opened her smile and dropped the vial whole down her throat.

She nearly choked. She rolled onto her side and curled into a fetal position and gagged silently, swallowed again and again even though it hurt each time, until it was down, and into her stomach.

Icca swallowed again, drinking down the magic she'd summoned up in her empty molar beds.

She'd been such a good student, before Wonderland had put a prompt end to her education. She knew no suppression runework could sink into her more than skin-deep, not without a matching rune on her body. And so—fingers on her stomach, now. Eyes closed, sipping down her Divinity. Feeling the shape of the vial settled into the lightless spot of her gut.

She focused, and then it was gone. So was a portion of her stomach contents, likely, swallowed up by her own Darkness, dropped into the strange, not-quite-place of a place she'd kept the Saint in.

Drink me!

All of Hattie's monsters in her Labyrinth. All of the knowing in the world that the Kkuls would never fall, because the Kkuls had their holy beasts on leashes.

No, thought Icca, with vicious excitement. *Eat* me.

TWENTY-FIVE

YEAR ZERO ZERO NINETY-FOUR, WINTER SEASON

THERE ARE 998 REMAINING SAINTS

HATTIE WAS WRISTS-DEEP in the guts of the dark witch's summoned Saint when Carousel returned to the courtyard. She didn't have to look up to see Carousel picking around the dead birds, jostling them to see if any good charms could be made from their bones. The absolved Jabberwocky was being Quiet to seem as if she were keeping to herself, though Hattie knew she was testing the air, seeing if she should say something. She should not say anything. Hattie was busy.

Busy seeing if Il-Hyun was still alive.

He'd been swallowed up almost as a whole thing, but Hattie found that the Saint had teeth all the way down to its stomach, found him very much gone when she opened it to the courtyard's soft light.

But there were also rose petals, slick and intact. Things less savored, gobbled down in euphoric haste.

Hattie sat back and took a soundless, shaking breath. The Saint was dead now, of course, but when she'd first gone to look it'd been awake, watching her, unmoving, because she'd thought, *Do not move, you pathetic, wicked shell.*

And it had given not one twitch, as she cleaved it apart.

Hattie rolled her neck around. She was quite tired, and quite sad, so immensely sad it seemed she was nothing else besides her sadness, just her alone on its blank, gray plane. She'd always taken her moods Quietly. People thought her cold for it. She'd lie awake in her bed at night for a while and feel the silence in her marrow. She might cry in the tub a few times, or eat more than usual, or a lot less—maybe she did feel less than all the others, who had more physical reactions without having to think about it, letting their flesh carry at least a smidge of that promised, profound human grief. Hattie hoped it was the case. What she held was quite a lot as it was.

Carousel was holding a up a crow by its spindly black ankle when Hattie murmured, "This is a private moment."

Carousel immediately dropped the bird, apologizing, "Mianhabnida, unnie, I just—"

"Oh, no," Hattie said with a slight smile, rising to her feet. The earth was warm under her bare toes, like it had been drinking in the heat of the fight. "Geogjeong hajima. Stay, you're not bothering me. I wasn't talking to you."

"Oh. Then who—"

Hattie pulled at a string of her awareness, attached to a consciousness that was floating above their heads. And the form of a young man unraveled out of the air.

"Ack," Carousel said, jumping as he fell a few feet, and scrambled upright, dark blue hanbok stained with the ground overturned from the night's events.

Carousel recovered quickly and was upon him, knife in hand and against his throat as Hattie neared, brushing her stained palms halfheartedly against her skirt. Such a waste of a dress, every year.

"Now," breathed Carousel, "what is it? Harmless, pathetic voyeur, or the second dimwit tonight thinking their magic holds a candle to hers?"

Such flattery. Hattie peered at the boy's face, which was a very nice face, startled now, but it seemed a smirk might usually fix his features, neatly done kohl lines deepening his eyes. And, as he had already heard her speak, and the courtyard was cleared, Hattie asked, "What is your name?"

She felt the witch try to dematerialize again, right out of Carousel's grip, but Hattie wiped at the magic dripping from her nostrils and stitched his form to its physical state. Her late father had had a magic similar to this, which is why she knew how to control it—Delcorta October Kkul had taught a littler Hattie.

"Answer her," ordered Carousel, grinning as she realized what Hattie had done to him, as he realized it too, now rapidly paling in the crow witch's fingers.

He hesitated, and Hattie silently riffled through all his physical and metaphysical seams in her head, really more out of curiosity, but she knew he could feel her doing so. Her father had always felt when Delcorta went peering.

"Cheshire," he said finally, his own name a gasp. "Mordekai Cheshire ibnida, Your Majesty."

"You've a hand in this, Mordekai Cheshire." Hattie gestured with a stained hand, back toward to the mess she'd left in her wake. It was not a question. "You should know that, at dawn, before the royal caravan departs for the first leg of the Saints' Races, I plan to send Iccadora into the Labyrinth."

Hattie felt every aspect of him seize against her, and she followed its pulse up, her magic light—but still very much there—against its electric thrum, like one of the water lanterns on a storm-wrecked ocean.

Still, the young man said immediately, "A fine choice, Your Majesty."

"Fine indeed!" echoed Carousel.

"Well, you know, I'm not a Jabberwocky myself, so the Labyrinth would be unfitting in my case. And Wonderland"—Cheshire scrambled, fighting to keep his voice level—"well, it'd be a waste, really. I'm a fantastic alchemist. Certainly the palace is—in need?"

"You were the one who created the rose draught?" asked Hattie.

"Well, yes. Sickle said she'd commissioned it as a gift for Your Majesty. I came to make sure that was the case. She's always talked about killing you."

"Ah." Hattie picked at the blood crusted in her cuticle. "You came to protect me."

Carousel's grin flashed as Cheshire's wavered.

"I excused myself as soon as I knew you didn't need me," he attempted. But Hattie didn't care about his lies. She already knew she was going to let him rot under the palace—he had spoken some truth. Wonderland would be wasted on him. Besides, now Hattie desired to study the controlling magic of the rose draught, and Cheshire would provide her all the product she required for a proper experiment. When the Saints' Races were over, of course. People were expecting a holiday.

"I do," said Hattie, "need you."

How she knew it terrified him.

Lulled by the jump in his heartbeat, moved by it, Hattie knelt down in the grass. "You have talent," she spoke, and Carousel made a low noise in the back of her throat, nervous when Hattie doted on other people. "Not only as an alchemist, but as a companion. A confidant to the likes of Iccadora Alice Sickle. What a feat, truly."

"She's a heretic, to go against you."

"Hm." He was still trying to flatter her. "Do I really look like a High Priestess?" She tilted her head. Her voice came Quieter. "A conduit of Wonderland?"

And what came out of his mouth next still did sound like flattery, but it was the way he could suddenly not look at Hattie that told her that he, at least, believed he was telling the truth. "You feel like one."

Hattie shifted his eyes.

Through them, she peered at herself, at the blood-like magic that caked her small form. Cheshire was letting out little, choked gasps. She felt them bob in the back of his throat, echoing in the base of her own, like sweet, desperate creatures she could cup in the palm of her hand.

"Well, I suppose I can believe you," Hattie mused. "I *am* practically wearing your skin."

Carousel bit her lip to keep back her laugh.

Cheshire shuddered, eyes closing. "She's such a fool," he murmured. "And I was a fool to follow her here. Of course you'd sense magic in your teacup. And Sickle still thought to let the Saint out. She was never going to win."

Hattie made his eyes open again. Made him look at her. Wasn't it such an honor, anyway? "Let the Saint out of what?"

"I don't know. I don't understand it. The dark, I suppose."

Hattie bit at the tip of her knuckle. "The dark..."

"Oh." Carousel flapped a hand, waving around her knife. Knowing Hattie had him pinned, she stepped away from Cheshire and flopped down on the grass, blowing out a bored breath. "It's nothing. I mean, I'm pretty sure it's *actually* nothing. Some between, in-between space. It's how she darkports."

"A void?"

Caro shrugged, her bloody hanbok whispering against the grass. "I guess. What does it matter, unnie?"

Well, it was just...

How Quiet such a place sounded. Residing within Iccadora.

And Hattie knew she herself was no High Priestess, really. The masses only called her that because she indulged in her favorite god, because her veil and her silence rendered her a blank slate to cast their hopes and fears upon. They desired a religious figure, a protector, a martyr, a tyrant, a creator, a destroyer, and Hattie could be all of them, for them.

Meanwhile, she would go along doing whatever she liked.

Wandering into her Labyrinth, seeking the Quiet in its Wonderland roots, in the blank shells of the Saints that teemed in the dark around her.

She'd told Caro that what she did in the Labyrinth was prayer; others, who did not worship her god, would call it meditation. When Hattie breathed and breathed and for a moment it seeped into her head, the Quiet, and she was briefly nothing, no one, only recognizing she had been nothing and no one when some thought came pulsing back. It was there, in her deity, where Hattie lost and found herself, over and over again, and how she adored the game, the internal hide-and-seek. She imagined it was a little like being dead, and then being reborn. Lost, and then found.

What would she find, she wondered, in Icca's dark place?

And they were talking about wastes. Sending Iccadora into the Labyrinth to die, carrying what might be some aspect of Hattie's god...

Hattie looked behind her, at the Saint she'd torn apart. Il-Hyun's bones jutting out of its erupted gut. She gave a little melancholy sigh.

She was so intrigued by Iccadora Alice Sickle—but how desperately Hattie wanted to see her ripped apart! It was certainly a conundrum.

If it were any other time of the year, Hattie would follow Iccadora into the maze and watch it happen. But the caravan was to depart for the nearest Ward by dawn, to start off the Saints' Races.

Oh, how they bored her, since she'd taken the human element away.

She thought it would be good, removing her mother's habit of roulette, to start off her reign. And it had been. Most of her people believed, now, that she hadn't killed Delcorta for the crown—the High Priestess was too good for that. She'd spared them from a chance participation in the holiday events, after all. But perhaps she'd sheltered them too much. Her mother had meant to drive the pursuit of magic back into the general population when she'd started the Saints' Races. Hattie meant that, too, with their continuation. But though she displayed her strange, wonderful abilities, she was detached from them. Hattie wasn't down in the ring with her creations. And even if she were—it wouldn't have the needed effect upon the masses. They'd never watch her bleed. Never see her flinch.

Because Hattie wouldn't flinch, if she had to fight.

She wouldn't cower or scream or cry. She didn't shy away from death.

The physical world was barely real to Hattie as it was, not like it was to other people. Not when she could tear it like paper.

She knew she wasn't like anyone else, in this way. She didn't know how it felt to be afraid of the Saints. She barely remembered what it was like to fear anything at all.

She supposed that's what the masses needed. Fear. Emotion. They needed to see witches who felt it all, who survived the Saints anyway. Hattie was so bored of the numbness around her. So sick of being surrounded by empty shells.

But Iccadora was not an empty shell. And neither was Carousel. And now they were back in one another's lives. It would be a waste, to break a connection like that, so rare was their bond, cauterized by Wonderland. There was something to be done, with a connection like that.... Yes, Hattie could do something wonderful, with that.... She kept the smile from her face. Yes. She supposed the Labyrinth could wait. First, first. Iccadora and Carousel must remember that they were in love.

"Iccadora wishes to kill me because my mother let a Saint loose during one of the Races, yes?" said Hattie. She had read the reports, of course. It hadn't been a particularly uncommon event, during her mother's reign, for a Saint to escape its cage. "Saint Katarina Pillar. It killed one of your friends. Tecca Moore. But her death trace still slicked to you both. Tricky thing."

Carousel stiffened on the grass.

Cheshire's grin unfolded once more, less strained, this time. "One of the reasons, yes, Your Majesty. Sickle's also just a murderous person."

"And why don't you want to kill me for that, Carousel?" queried Hattie, gently.

"Because I'm a perfectly lovely person," shot Carousel irritably, picking at the ground and avoiding Hattie's eyes. "And I'm not a moron, either. You're not your mother."

"Hm."

"Cheshire's right, anyway, she's generally and genuinely unpleasant, really, really. She hated your mother, sure, yet she squawks over the rumors that you..."

"Killed her?"

Carousel shut her mouth. "Mm-hm."

Hattie waited for her to grasp the obvious, that Iccadora had come to knock off Hattie's head because she wanted Carousel's attention—her hatred, if not her love. Instead Carousel fumed and scoffed on the grass and understood nothing. Forced herself to understand nothing. But Hattie could cure her of that. It was going to be so lovely.

Hattie leaned over the crow witch.

The attention shifted her mood instantly. "I don't want to kill you. I love you," said Carousel. She reached up and slid her fingers into Hattie's hair.

"I know," said Hattie.

"I would do terrible, terrible things for you."

The crow witch's fingers caught on a dried blood clump in Hattie's hair. She retracted her hand, but Hattie caught her around the wrist, held her there. The heartbeat beneath the delicate patch of skin fluttering.

"Carousel?"

"Yes, unnie?"

"What about gorgeous, incredible things?"

TWENTY-SIX

Year Zero Zero Ninety-Four, Winter Season

There Are 997 Remaining Saints

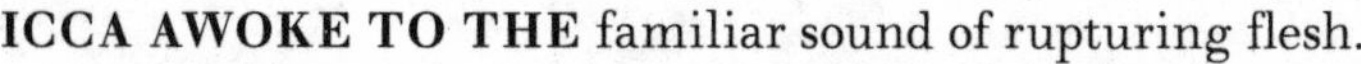

ICCA AWOKE TO THE familiar sound of rupturing flesh.

Blearily, she blinked at the grinning figure crouched past the bars. It was Caro, of course. Icca knew even before her eyes focused.

"Come to take me to the Labyrinth?" Icca murmured, veiling her excitement. Somewhere up the corridor, there was the unmistakable shriek of a Saint. Wait—Icca listened—two Saints. No doubt it was the darling Red Queen, creating. Icca had ruined her champion for the holiday, after all. Her lips twitched at the memory. "You'll miss me, won't you, Rabbit?"

"No, no," Caro cooed. "Hattie wants to play a game first."

The words snapped Icca out of her haze and back into reality. The warmth of her violent fantasies scattered; she lay on the stone floor, her limbs cold. "What?"

"You're her champion now, Alice."

Icca blinked. Another twin arch of Saint screams lashed up the corridor, and then both abruptly cut out. Then she could only hear the blood in her ears as she pulled herself upright. "The fuck I am." She had plans for the Labyrinth. She couldn't be ripped away from them now, to perform for some guise of a holiday. "I thought the High Priestess didn't use humans in the Races anymore. Isn't that what makes her *so* adored, being kinder than her mother?"

"Perhaps she knows a monster when she sees one," Caro mused, but Icca watched the subtle twist to her mouth. There was the usual amusement, of course, but tinged with displeasure. "What can I say? You have such a flashy power. It intrigued her."

Icca let out a disbelieving laugh. "Holy fuck, you're jealous."

Caro rolled her eyes. "You're delusional. What's there to be jealous of? Humiliation? Certain death?"

"Oh, I do *adore* how Hattie unnie *adores* me."

Pink now tinted Caro's cheeks. "Such sick-sickly-sick ideas of affection, Icky! Where *do* you collect them from?"

"That is *rich*, coming from—"

Icca shut her mouth at the new scream that shook the air. It was akin to a newborn's wail, but two-toned, and so vibrant it clattered at the back of Icca's skull. Despite herself, cold, curdling fear unfolded itself in her chest cavity.

Caro immediately pressed herself closer to the bars to observe, and Icca immediately tried to take her eye out. Caro danced away.

"So what?" Icca spat, keeping her expression annoyed, bored. "It'll be me fighting that thing? Holiday's going to be finished after the first Ward." She flashed her teeth. "Or does she just expect me to lie down and die?"

"Oh, no, no, Icky," Caro said, twirling in the middle of the hall. "Hattie wants you to live."

This unsettled Icca deeply.

"You gave her an idea—what was it she said? Encouraging magic back to the masses, they've been scared of it for too long, with the pains and the Saints being super-gross and whatnot. Delcorta, I suppose, didn't help—she tried to frighten them into pursuing their witchcrafts, but, oh, Icky! You can dazzle them instead!" Her tone rolling out sickly-sweet. "You won't just be a champion. You'll be her hero. You'll be everybody's hero."

At this, of course, readers, our dear Iccadora thought, thoroughly appalled, *I'm her fucking* villain.

Didn't Hattie know that?

Of course. Of course she did.

The story that Hattie had fed Carousel was full of shit. It must be. What did the Red Queen want from Icca, really? To humiliate her? To have her die in public, instead of in the privacy of the Labyrinth? It couldn't be anything so superficial. Not with Hattie. Icca had tipped her hand too much, and the Queen, with that blank-yet-digging stare, had seen something in her, something to reap.

"Bored of her Saints, is she?" said Icca, retreating back to her arrogance, her armor. She didn't trust a godsdamn word about Hattie's intentions.

"No, no, it's just, you're just *so* interesting, Sickle." The flirting was overgrown with thorns. "Cheshire certainly had a lot to say about you."

"You caught him." Icca had predicted that.

"Of course. He's going to sit nice and pretty in the dungeons forever, Hattie says that a power like his would be good to have around—"

"He's really to blame for all of this, you know."

Caro's laughter arched clear and bright.

Icca rubbed her temples. She'd fried her head with her own magic yesterday, and the details of the party were blurry. She remembered teeth snapping the air. The smell of blood. Hattie November's serene expression, once she'd pulled back her veil.

Serenity, when Icca deserved horror, or at least anger, or at least *something*.

"And I suppose you've been employed to keep me in check?" Icca was watching for the pulse in Caro's neck. "Make sure I don't go off-script?"

Caro smacked her lips. "Perhaps, you don't behave, Cheshire will die. Perhaps I'll cut off his head. Make sure there's a body attached to it first, of course. Else, how would I—"

"I don't care if he dies." This was probably true. "I'm not participating. Just send me to the Labyrinth."

"If you survive the Races, Hattie says you don't have to go at all."

"Lies."

"Well, perhaps. You did kill her husband." Caro slid up to the bars again. "Come on, lovely, tell me what you want, in exchange for your participation. I'll give you anything." There was a pout to her lip before it suffocated under her smirk, her eyes roaming Icca up and down. "You know, I used to give you whatever you wanted, don't you remember? Because *I* remember *you* enjoying it. I remember the noises you used to make just before you—"

"So she has you whoring yourself out for her, too?"

"Nah. For you, darling, I'd do that for free." Caro winked. And the pouting returned. "Just tell me what Hattie can give you to get you in the ring, don't be difficult, and I know you'll love the rush of it, anyway—"

"I want a rematch," Icca shot without thinking. Because who would be there to send her to the Labyrinth, after that? And this had to end with Icca in the Labyrinth. She had its Saints to feed her remaining rose draught to, after all. She had a capital to overrun with monsters, a home to burn from Carousel's head. . . .

"With Hattie! You're asking for your death. You're suicidal—"

Caro continued to fling insults upon the bars while Icca's mind reeled—she was *such* a *fanatic*. The thought built bile at the back of Icca's throat. Her vision dotted red, and then black. *I'm Hattie unnie's favorite creature.*

And if Icca slaughtered such a creature, before its keeper?

The Red Queen barely batted an eye over her husband being gobbled down. And Icca didn't want Carousel dying ignorant. She wanted to ruin the image of her Queen first, obliterate her faith before sending her off to oblivion.

But perhaps Hattie would do that for her.

Icca pictured the faces of the crowd the one and only time she'd deigned to attend a holiday event. The way they cheered and recoiled and drifted back, always drifted back, to the edge of the arena. Looking away was impossible.

They hung on to every shriek, every staccato splattering of blood.

Icca remembered the thrill biting into Carousel's features, and beside her—Hattie's absolute stillness.

This fucking holiday.

The Queen expected her to participate, play the games that led to Tecca's death? That led to all the rest of this—Icca behind bars, Caro gloating on her high horse, the two of them blown apart? Did Caro remember *none of it*?

"—a masochist, really, Icky, I mean genuinely—"

"You," Icca said. "I want you."

Down in the ring with her.

And the moment Caro tripped up—the moment Icca tripped her up, perhaps—and Hattie's creation got ahold of her, the moment she realized her Queen, her Priestess, her *unnie* wouldn't lift a finger to save her, it would be over between them.

Oh, yes, Hattie November, Icca decided, *I'll play your Races. I'm going to blow your holiday apart at the fucking kneecaps.*

"Don't you want to be her champion, too?" whispered Icca. Caro's expression had frozen in a rictus mask, assessing.

"Need me to protect you from the horrors, darling?" came the expected taunt.

"Haven't we always shared our punishments, dear?" She watched Caro's throat move. "Come on, Rabbit. It'll be just like old times. Just like Wonderland."

—

The new Saint crouched below her. It extended its twined torso, shrieked, as if pretending to feel pain. Then it soothed under Hattie's touch. Her finger stroking the warm, bald ravine that ran between its two skulls, fused at the browbone. Like reverent, whispering lovers.

Perpetually fixed in profile, staring at one another. At itself.

Hattie November didn't mean to be cruel, dear readers. No, no...

After all, every time the Saint reached out, it found itself again.

Sometimes, when Hattie was creating, all that went through her head was, *Don't be lonely. Don't be lonely....*

Now, of course, that the Saint was one instead of two, it couldn't remember being anything else. It didn't mind being what it was now. There were no past selves to mourn.

"It'll be just like old times. Just like Wonderland." Iccadora's jagged voice splitting up the hall, now, and Hattie thought, closing her eyes in the bliss of it, *Yes, yes, please.*

TWENTY-SEVEN

YEAR ZERO ZERO NINETY-FOUR, WINTER SEASON

THERE ARE 997 REMAINING SAINTS

HATTIE BEGAN TO TWITCH as soon as the train passed out of the Petra Ward Wall.

Immediately, Carousel knelt at her feet and stared up, her hands a query on the empty seat next to Hattie. But Hattie paid her no mind, which usually meant she wouldn't, so Caro left her and went to play cards with Icca. She was sitting nicely in one of the booths on the opposite side of the car—glaring, yes, but Caro knew that was just her face. Really, of course, Icca was ecstatic. Carousel was ecstatic. Carousel was a champion!

Carousel won every card game because Icca's hands were shackled with runeworked manacles that were threaded into her seat—murderous intents and the like—so Caro played for her. "You're really terrible at this game," she chattered. "I can read you like an open book."

The game—Caro throwing cards onto the table between them and giggling when she got a high number. Sometimes she threw them at Icca's face. The two of hearts was caught in the black depths of her hair.

"You were always shit at reading," Icca muttered.

Caro blinked. But then, why wasn't she breaking Icca's nose? So then she was lunging to break Icca's nose. Which would also be rebreaking Icca's nose—there was a nasty bruise across it, from yesterday. . . .

Icca recoiled with a shriek, her teeth scraping Caro's wrist, and then Caro was shrieking too, or laughing, and then they both went silent. It was like Carousel's voice had closed up in her throat. But being under this harmless string of Hattie's magic—Hattie's attention—relaxed her, so she sat on the edge of the table, stroking her throat contemplatively, boots planted on fabric booth-back on either side of Icca's shoulders. Icca had gone completely still, eyes flicking past Carousel's shoulder.

Don't mind Hattie, Caro would say, if she could talk. *Unnie just gets creepier and creepier the closer we are to the Forest!*

But Icca was boring, really, when she was not screaming, so Carousel slid off the table and returned to Hattie's feet.

It was early morning, and rare sunlight flashed golden through the window behind Hattie, making the lace of her veil look delicate, weightless. Except where it was beginning to stick to the slickness of her nose and her eyes and the corners of her mouth. The cuticles of her unpainted nails beginning to bead with red where they lay still against her lap. Save for the occasional twitch. *How it must* hurt, thought Caro dreamily, knowing if she lifted Hattie's veil—she'd *never*—she'd find not an ounce of agony across her features.

In the other armored trolly cars linked to this one—some people of the Courts? Some guards? Hattie's newest Saint somewhere, presumably? Caro didn't see why such inventory mattered. It was just the three of them, in this moving room, and such a setting felt deliciously intimate. The pale-yellow wallpaper and the tweedy furniture mimicking a domestic setting, Caro pondered. Yes, like a lovely living room. Caro would not let Icky Sickle's unfortunate presence ruin that. Even though she felt bitter that last year, it had just been her and Hattie. Oh, and Il-Hyun, Carousel supposed. *Rest in absolute pieces, you dear, sweet boy*. . . .

Below them—the hum and jolt of the train's wheels, rumbling across tracks running across the strip of the moors that lay between Wonderland and Petra. They were skimming northward, slinging around the grand curve of the Labyrinth, toward the Malli Ward, the nearest providence to the capital. Hattie was faced toward the Forest.

Caro felt the stitch on her voice unhook in her throat, which was not an unpleasant sensation—it was soft, almost, like someone was pulling back the edge of a bedsheet from the mattress. Caro glanced back, knowing that it was a great possibility that Icca was about to be rude.

"What's wrong with her?" Icca murmured, dark eyes fixed on Hattie.

Caro rolled her eyes. *So* predictable.

She was stunned when Hattie actually answered. "Do you not feel it? The tug of Wonderland."

"Wonderland doesn't tug on me like *that*."

"But it speaks to you."

"It doesn't."

But of course she was lying.

Caro, too, could indeed feel the Forest rising at her spine, the rustle of the foliage streaking past the windows. In the back of her head, images flashed without prompting. She felt Wonderland's cool, clean dark sliding under her clothes. She could smell the fresh, sleeping earth. The murmuring of its crows . . .

Hattie said quietly, "It doesn't speak in words, so you have trouble understanding. Let me tell you what it's saying." Carousel startled when Hattie's hand brushed her cheek. "Come back. Come back."

The touch was there, and then gone, leaving magic that stung like a burn across her face.

"And what does it say to you?" breathed Icca. "Does it call you a coward, Hattie?"

But Hattie had fallen silent again.

"I told you," Carousel said affectionately. "Fucking creepy."

—

"She's not just mad. She's unnatural," Icca murmured.

Caro paused detaching Icca's shackles from her seat to flick the side of her head.

Icca barely blinked. Her eyes had a hazy look in them that Caro remembered meant she was in the middle of thinking and thinking and thinking. Dangerous acts. Both the thinking and the remembering.

"Is she always like that, outside the Walls?"

They'd reached the Malli Ward, the train sliding into Ecceret, the single village in the Ward that possessed tracks. Hattie had not spoken another word the entire three-hour trip, just stood up from her seat and departed when the guards came a-knocking at the door. Caro was to drag Icca over to the arena that had been constructed in the town square.

"Come on, come on, let's go!" Caro chattered, ignoring Icca. "Doesn't it feel like—"

"Answer me first," Icca said.

"You're obsessed," Caro shot, then braced for Icca to shoot back with *Jealous! Jealous!*

"She's *unnatural.*"

"She's eccentric."

"Wonderland shouldn't affect her like that."

Caro shrugged. "Y'know, it's a High Priestess thing, duh. A Wonderland-conduit thing. *Duh.*"

"Bullshit. Bull*shit.*"

Caro hooked her hand in Icca's shackles and yanked them above Icca's head. She felt Icca's leg ramp up on a seat to land a gut-kick, but Caro only leaned forward and loomed her grin over Icca's face. The kick hesitated. "Did it look like bullshit to you?"

"You have to be bothered by it," Icca breathed, "that she reacts like that. Scared, even? Come on, Rabbit. You can tell me."

"Mm. Nah." Caro shrugged easily. "Hattie says we all react to Wonderland. *'Its shadows are a looking-glass, Carousel…'* Is that right? It's somethin' like that."

"Is that what she preaches?" Icca's brow twisted. "What the fuck does that even mean?"

"That the Forest brings out what lies in the darkest depths of our little Divinities. Our darkest magic. Our darkest selves."

Caro only realized the weight of what she was saying when her words were bleeding out in the air.

Icca's eyes flicked across her own, right, left, right. The sun coming in golden from the window was igniting the brown in her pupils—a lightness Caro's own did not possess.

It was difficult, not to believe Hattie's wisdom about Wonderland, though Hattie herself, of course, had never been. It was difficult because Icca and Caro had witnessed those dark selves, spilling out of them, out of each other.

Caro internally flinched. Externally, she only tugged at Icca's handcuffs absentmindedly, said dreamily, "But! Hattie's also cuckoo." She let out a heavy sigh. "Isn't she just wonderful?"

Icca's voice came low. "What happens, if she does go into the Forest?"

"Oh, Icky. What happens to all little girls who get lost in Wonderland?" She cupped Icca's horrible, beautiful face in her hands and imagined squeezing until her brains were painting the train car. "Come on, come on, you know this. We've lived this. They become powerful." Carousel smiled and smiled at her. "And then they become something worse."

Icca looked her dead in the eyes. "I was always meant to be like this."

The sudden quiet of her words startled Caro. What had she once thought Icca was meant to be? Prickly and antisocial and unpleasant and educated and comfortable and cherished. Just as she was, with everything she wanted.

"What, Alice?" she said, pantomiming such gentleness. "A basket case? Suspicious of everyone? Lonely?"

"I'm not lonely." And she said nothing else. Her eyes had hardened.

Once, Caro would have screeched and demanded elaboration. And, once, Icca would've handed it over.

Caro drew back. "Alone, then."

Outside, the holiday was rousing. Caro towed Icca out of the train car into the shade slanting on the station's simple wooden platform and paused, squinting in the light, trying to remember where the hell she was supposed to go.

The line of gray-and-black-painted storefronts that faced the track was serrated with red, moving cuts—ribbons marking support and welcome to Hattie and the holiday. The general public was drifting for the arena—*That's where!*—heads bobbing past on the sidewalk below the platform, twisting toward them.

Already, word had reached the Wards that the High Priestess of Isanghan had something different in mind for this year's Saints' Races—two absolved Jabberwockies would be her champions, and they would remind the masses of the extraordinary magic they all possessed, if only they could withstand the hurt. What glory could be found on the other side of agony.

Are those really the Red Queen's champions? the passersby wondered, as a doting narrator desires to remind dear readers that our darling champions had always been the strange, out-of-place ones, even while set at the center of this particular tale. *They certainly have that manic Wonderland look in their eyes. That twitchiness—brains fried in magic. Such tragedy…*

"What the hell are you looking at?" Icca snapped to the rubberneckers. Gazes immediately darted away. Caro cackled.

Icca seethed and shook her hands uselessly in her runeworked manacles. The air pricked with the scent of her zapped arm hairs—the result of whatever bit of magic she'd just tried to pull. Her mouth opened—to squawk and bitch, Caro assumed—but then she stilled. Slowly, her dark eyes turned over her shoulder. Caro followed that silent gaze.

"Something to say, Alice?"

It'd been dark, when they'd boarded the train.

"A transport fit for a High Priestess, isn't it?" sighed Caro. "Doesn't it just look *holy*?"

Icca hadn't seen all the runes hacked into the metal of the car.

"It looks mad." Icca's eyes searched. "Grounding runes. Cleansing runes. Fortune runes."

Such a show-off. Caro yawned. "Keep-Hattie-sane-around-Wonderland runes . . . oh, Alice! What a grave little expression you're wearing! Are you finally realizing you're out of your depth?"

—

It hadn't been entirely true, that Icca had left last year's Saints' Races rather quickly, in an angry haze after seeing Carousel celebrating the holiday at Hattie November Kkul's side. Well, the angry haze was true. But of course she'd hung around the events all day, as Hattie's creation tore the Saints captured from Wonderland limb from limb. Of course she'd been waiting for Carousel to slip away, to kill her right there and then and be done with it. Slipping from shadow to shadow, flickering in and out of sight.

Flickering in and out of Hattie's reach.

So Icca had faded into someone's shadow and had emerged from another someone's on the other side of the ring. The crowd's cheering split up into staccato blotches of noise and void, noise and void. She'd barely paid attention to what unfurled in the arena below, her eyes always attaching themselves to the royal viewing box. Upon completing her last darkport, Icca realized that Hattie had disappeared from the place she'd stood unmoving all day long.

That Hattie had slipped over the railing, that her veil was drawn back, and she was climbing down into the ring.

No one else seemed to notice as her feet hit the dirt floor, as the young woman moved for the writhing mass of raw flesh that was her creation tangled with another Saint. Her slippers and the dark skirt of her hanbok dragging through the black blood that had pooled against the saturated earth. She approached her creation as it tore, with a mouth that smiled from the base of its throat, the competing Saint's head from its shoulders.

The crowd roared.

Icca flicked her gaze to Carousel, up in the box. Saw Caro throw an ecstatic smile to the empty spot where Hattie had been fixed throughout the event.

When Icca looked back down, cold shot through her blood.

The Red Queen was looking straight at her.

Eyes the color of earth-muddled water. Features so serene and still that they looked lifted out of a parchment painting. The shouts of the onlookers dulled and died in Icca's ears.

Hattie looked away. She extended a hand—her creation dropped the Saint's decapitated head and curled its way toward her on its many limbs. It revved up to its full, terrifying height before her, all its mouths clicking open, but Hattie looked down at its feet, as though uninterested.

"How did I miss you?" There came the High Priestess's enigmatic voice. It seemed, to Icca, as if thrown to her from the other end of a tunnel. It was hushed, sounded vaguely dazed. "Where did you come from?" Hattie's head tilting. The veil attached to her hair, drawn back in the traditional style, rippling slightly, delicate as tinted air. Except where the Queen's magic had dried, clotted in the lace.

"What are you doing?" Icca murmured, unsure if she meant *To me?* Or *Down there?* There was nothing but Hattie's voice and the thud of Icca's heartbeat, as if the two of them existed in a void, or the Dark place.

"I don't know. I suppose . . . I've grown bored. Perhaps next year . . . next year . . ."

For all the hatred for the Kkuls that had curdled in Icca over her young life, she found herself at a loss for words, brushed with this small increment of Hattie's attention.

It was warm.

At first.

And then Icca's vision smeared.

For a moment, she misplaced where she was, in a Ward, on the holiday, watching the fights. Icca swore . . . Where was she?

Yes. Right. She was in Wonderland.

She could tell because it was talking to her.

Its foliage was whispering over her head. What was it *saying*?

No, no. Icca's vision knit back together. Her magic stung in the back of her throat.

It was Hattie who was whispering, Icca realized, down in the ring.

"What?" Icca shook her head. Her gaze flicked to Caro, who was still smiling brightly at Hattie's spot, as if the Queen had not moved. It must have been what everyone believed. Whatever spell Hattie had conjured over the crowd, it'd missed Icca during her darkport. And now she was essentially alone with the Red Queen. An intimacy that Icca found herself ill prepared for. "What did you say?"

"Does it look like me?"

"What?" Working out her breath from around the sting of silver in her gums. "Does—Wonderland—?"

"No. Not Wonderland." One of her hands wiped at the stream of red magic bleeding out from her nose. And her other, now, upon her created Saint's face, crowing over her. Its many features threaded together, pallid skin seamless, as if they'd never been apart. Never been two.

"I don't know what you mean." Icca didn't understand what was happening. Why wasn't she killing Hattie, like she'd always said she would, if she ever had the chance?

Carousel had said she would, too.

But look at her, now.

Icca was looking at her, now. . . .

The sickly blond head, the sicker rictus grin. How much Icca wanted to tear it away. How much Icca wanted to scream at her, first, demand an explanation, demand her guilt, her penance. *How could you? Do you not remember Tecca? Do you not remember* me*?*

"Would you rather die, than experience losing her?" came Hattie's voice.

How Hattie could know what they had meant to each other was beyond Icca. But the answer still rose clearly to her mind—once, yes. Icca would have chosen death. She would've gone into oblivion willingly, clutching the thought of Carousel Rabbit the entire descent, until at one point, she was no longer Icca, no, she would find nothing of herself and only the other girl—

"Ever since I cleansed your death traces . . . I thought, if anyone could understand, it would be you two."

"Understand what?"

The question crept from Icca's throat, breathless. She could not recall at what point she'd moved forward, stomach flush against the wooden railing.

What was that look, Hattie's face? It couldn't possibly be—*sadness*, could it?

Icca's lip curled, vindicated at such sorrow. Didn't the Queen's precious piety protect her, from such emotions? Didn't her madness expel the rest?

Hattie's eyes drifted back to her Saint. Her monstrosity. A monstrosity formed from monstrosities, and why? Before, Icca had believed such magic to be frivolous. The Red Queen was simply showing off, just as her mother had. So why did she have that godsdamn look on her face? Her touch, aimless and gentle upon the Saint. Like it was a thing to be treated with such care. Like she could understand its murmurs, divine its thoughts in the shape of the blood splattered against its flesh.

"How impossible it is," Hattie said, tears and magic in her eyes, "to conceive of being apart."

Icca's laugh beat out of her.

"Comparing us to a *Saint.* That *freak* of nature, *especially*—"

"Freak of nature?"

"Obviously," Icca spat.

Hattie tilted her head.

"Oh, Iccadora." And then, the worst thing—a smile was cutting across the Red Queen's face. It grew and grew and grew and it was Wonderland earth unfurling under Icca's boots, the snapping of its foliage flooding her ears, it was talking to her, it was saying, laughing, "I didn't mean the Saint!"

And when Icca blinked, that smile seemed to smear, and when she blinked again, the Queen had vanished from the ring. Now she was back in the royal box, still as stone, hands folded before her as they had been all day. As if she hadn't moved, all day. The red veil draped back over her features.

Carousel flitting around at her side, chattering. Icca had been waiting around to kill her, remember? Remember?

Everyone thought, behind her veil, the Queen's face was always passive. Pious. Contemplative. But now Icca knew. Knew that Hattie was smiling. And that smile was tracing its way across Icca's skin like the cold tip of a blade.

Icca's feet had dragged beneath her. Backward. And then she was running.

TWENTY-EIGHT

YEAR ZERO ZERO NINETY-FOUR, WINTER SEASON

THERE ARE 997 REMAINING SAINTS

NOW, A YEAR LATER, in this shitty little town again, with its shitty little arena. Shitty, shitty spectators—

"Stop muttering *shitty*," Caro clucked at Icca. "Get more creative. Hideous. Dinky. Foul..."

They were down in the dirt ring of a temporary arena that had been constructed for the holiday. Icca glared at the onlookers up in the wooden stands—their heights carved with runes to prevent the Saint from scaling—at Hattie, draped in red, up in her box. The sun had disappeared again behind the gray haze. The threat of a downpour scented the air like perfume and static.

No riveting speeches would be made this year, of course, not without Il-Hyun. What was there to say, anyway? The carnage would speak for itself, would it not? *Behold, witches in prime. Revel in the power we possess within us....*

"Fuck this holiday! You're all fucking blind! Fuck you, Hattie November Kkul!" Icca screamed. She stomped her feet. She knew she was essentially throwing a temper tantrum. She knew the crowd barely cared—Jabberwockies acted in such vicious ways, wasn't it just *so* entertaining? "You insane bitch!"

"Your fault for giving her a public platform, unnie," Carousel called. Then she casually smacked Icca in the back of the head.

Icca immediately spun and dove at her, but her hands were still shackled and the lunge was awkward. Caro simply sidestepped, and Icca sprawled out on the dirt. There she fumed. Part of her wanted to just stay down and get eaten up by the Saint that chattered within the massive cage supporting the royal box, hidden behind black silk.

That would put a damper on the holiday, certainly, our darling Dark witch pondered—a dead champion in the first town of the tour. Nothing to feed to the Labyrinth, after that.

Luckily for us, dear readers, our Icca knew that dying just to embarrass Hattie was a sorry trade.

Because the High Priestess, of course, couldn't be embarrassed. Hattie, of course, didn't give a fuck about her public image, no matter what rumors churned in the population about her intentions. This was all a part of some grander experiment that she was playing out on an excessive scale, because she could. To what end, Icca did not know.

Hattie had damned Icca, that day now a year ago, when Icca had missed her spell, had been trapped in that strange, disorienting moment. Damned her to see her as other people did not. And Icca still did not know exactly why Hattie had allowed such an instance.

Oh, if only Carousel knew they had shared that private moment, how she would boil with jealousy.

If she would even believe her.

Icca got up from the dirt.

"She's not right," Icca murmured, looking up at Hattie. Who was looking at her, perhaps. Who was ignoring her, perhaps. . . . "There's something not right with her, Carousel."

"So you've said, over and over. Why do you give a shit, truly, Alice?" Caro slung an arm around her shoulders, jostling them. They were facing the cage, the black silk of which was rippling from the breath of the beast it contained. "We might be about to die—oh, no! Now is the chance for a last confession. None of that she-killed-her-mother or her-mother-killed-people stuff. Or admit you don't have a fucking clue, that you're just a terrible person. Just tell me the truth."

Icca turned her head. Met Carousel's pitch-black eyes.

She scares me.

She should scare you, too.

And maybe Icca was admitting too much, with that, to herself.

Some seedling of a thought bubbling up—that Caro should run far, far away from Hattie.

It couldn't be true. Icca didn't care about Caro like that, not anymore. Maybe it was just that she couldn't leave well enough alone. Poor Alice, always in her own head, touching the things that terrified her. The Saints. Carousel. Hattie. Wonderland. Seeking them out in the Dark of her thoughts. Never comfortable with comfort. She didn't trust it. Didn't trust the world not to burn it away.

"I'm just a terrible person," said Icca.

And because Carousel was Carousel was a ridiculous creature, the crow witch blushed. "My, my, Alice . . ."

And then the dull roar of the crowd was arching above their heads. The girls looked away from each other, up at Hattie, who had shifted closer to the railing. Icca watched, disgusted, as Carousel took a bow. The knives strapped to her legs glinting in the dull Light. Caro flicked her wrist, and a key appeared in her hand. She ghosted it over Icca's shackles.

"Are you going to try and run as soon as I unlock you?"

"No." Icca was exactly where she wanted to be.

"Kill me?"

"No." Right? Icca wanted Caro to die by the hand of Hattie's Saint? Knock the worship of the High Priestess right out of her head. Right? That was the plan?

But then Caro was unlocking her. But then the shackles were falling away into a metal heap upon the dirt, sending freshly freed magic pumping through her veins once more. But then Icca was thinking, *Oh, never mind, then. I can't fucking resist*, her head flashing with pain as she prepared to—

Caro grabbed her by the shoulders and swung her around, so that they were facing the cage once more. The tip of a blade teasing between Icca's ribs. "Please," came the scoff in Icca's ears. "You'd really kill me, here, in front of everyone? Where's the intimacy in that? Come on, we have a Saint to kill. Look *alive*, Alice, we—"

The end of the sentence never came. There was the soft thud of the silks over the cage being dropped away, but this whole thing was ridiculous and beneath her; Icca's head was still turned as if to glare into Carousel's hair.

But then she felt Caro's body go tense.

Not battle-ready tense. That would be paired with a rictus grin striking her features. But all her amusement had evaporated. Icca blinked back yellow strands and—why did Caro look so—shaken?

"No," Caro breathed. "We already—didn't we—"

Icca felt a long, thin shadow uncurl from the bars of the cage and slip silently across the length of the arena.

Her eyes slipped from Caro's expression, traveling down into the dirt. The shadow was fraying.

No, uncoiling.

Uncoiling limbs upon limbs.

Icca finally looked up at the cage. She didn't fucking want to.

"It's not," Caro was murmuring rapidly, attempting to soothe herself. "We killed it." She was saying it over and over again.

They had. Icca's thoughts came to her as if out of a haze; the roaring of the crowd had dulled to a distant buzz. They had. They had. They had. Yes. The heads. Look at the heads. Two of them, twisted toward one another. Glazed eyes bulging, a mess of teeth and tongues chattering beneath them. Necks double-barreled upon fused shoulders, constructing a ring of collarbones. That was original. That reeked of Hattie November's amalgamation style. But the grotesquely long body that dripped below all of that, churning with limbs . . .

The Saint coiled down into itself like a snake, and then it lunged.

Blocking out the sky with flesh . . .

Icca didn't think. Just moved down into the moving Darkness of its shadow. She didn't remember the point she'd taken Caro's hand. Then they were in the black place together, that familiar full-body-bruise sensation filling Icca up, but it seemed a distant thing. She did not move to bring them back into the arena. Her hands pulled at her hair. Was she screaming or whispering? Hard to tell, down here. Either way . . .

"No fucking way. Not a chance. She did not make it look like *fucking Pillar.*"

It's what Icca wanted, that shell-shocked look on Caro's face.

But Icca was too—sixteen, again. Holding her breath, in the kitchen, on the stairs. With Carousel clutched to her.

Snap out of it.

Snap

out

of

it.

It was Carousel who did it for her.

Caro, throwing her head back in the Dark, and laughing. Laughing like she never wanted to breathe again. Laughing like—she wasn't laughing. She was sobbing. Panicking. Was Icca panicking, too? Caro was tugging at Icca's sleeves. "We need to go back. We're late. We're late."

"Gods, just let them all die of boredom, Rabbit, what does it *matter*?"

"We need to get Tecca." Caro's were eyes black stones in her head, flitting around. "We—"

Icca's blood pumped cold. "Stop it."

"Icca, we have to." Now she was really crying. "She's all alone, why don't you understand that?"

"*Stop* it, you ballistic creature! She's dead! Tecca's dead, we killed her—"

"*Nonono* it wasn't us it wasn't us it was the *Saint* and it's still out there—"

How Icca hated and hated and hated her. How suddenly her treasured arrogance had dissolved, how clearly and precisely Icca could see the extent that Wonderland had messed up Carousel's head. The Forest should have killed this frantic child now babbling before her. Icca thought the helpless teenager in herself had died, too, but seeing Carousel like this—it was some kind of horrible resurrection, and Icca despised her for it, at the same time she clutched Caro's face, at the same time she sounded like she was pleading when she said "It's not Pillar!"

"We have to—"

"Rabbit, Rabbit, look at me. It's not Pillar. Hattie's just fucking with us. She's just always fucking with everyone. Don't you see that she doesn't care about you?"

"Don't say that. Tecca cares about us. You know she does. How could you say that?"

Icca slapped her across the face.

Seeing Caro sprawled with her cheek tinted pink, Icca reached for her. Opened her mouth to say sorry, she didn't mean it. Then she shut it. Snapped her hand away. No. It wasn't just Carousel being delusional, reverting. They weren't like this, now. They weren't terrified teenagers, doing their little magics. Look. See—Caro's eyes had cleared. And now they were flashing blue. Flashing with anger. Yes, they were remembering to exist just as they should. Icca, throbbing with the pain that came with being in this place. Caro, now in a similar state.

When Caro spoke again, her voice had found even ground. She touched her struck cheek.

"Oh," Caro said. Shrugged. "My bad, Icky. Silly me."

Icca stared at her, chest heaving.

Caro stood up. "Come on." Extending a hand. "Don't you want to go kill something? Doesn't it sound like fun?"

TWENTY-NINE

Year Zero Zero Ninety-Four, Winter Season

There Are 997 Remaining Saints

CARO WAS RIGHT (of course)! *Darling Caro, Carousel, Caro dear, you're always right!*

This *was* fun.

Over and over again her blade found flesh and then bone and then flesh again. Arms and crows peppered the ground of the arena. She kept fucking tripping over them. Sections of the crowd had been splattered with black blood; she could barely see anything past the blue of her magic filling her eyes. Hattie must be thinking she was glorious, her darling champion, weaving around the spring-lunge attacks of the Saint, breaking its own teeth against the earth she'd been in the instant prior. It had bit off one of its tongues, and it lay like a slab of wet obsidian under the royal viewing box. Its remaining one sliding mournfully down its other throat, searching for the lost companion. Down between those two necks was where Caro had been attempting to plant bird-bombs, its collarbones and face splattered with small bones and black feathers.

And still the Saint wasn't dead. Wasn't dead. Wasn't dead.

What was Alice doing? Messing around with the dark. Every time she tried to wriggle an enchantment through the beast, it spun for her. "You need to distract it!" Icca kept shouting at her, frustrated and sweating.

"I don't want to be the distraction. *You* be the distraction."

Of course Caro loved showing off. But then she was getting tired. The Saint was not, would not.

This is so *fun!* They were both off their game. *Why would we be off our game?* Caro kept glancing up at Hattie—this is what Caro did now, while Icca slid around in her shadows and the Saint coiled and uncoiled after her, leaned against the slick, runeworked wall of the arena with her chest heaving, and gazed up at the royal box. Hattie, unknowable behind her veil. Unknowable without it. Had Caro embarrassed herself, when she'd frozen upon first glance of the Saint? When her vision smeared, first to Wonderland, then to— No. Carousel didn't do embarrassing things. *You're wonderful, darling. I know, darling. Everyone knows. How couldn't they? Hattie knows, too. She just. With the designing the Saint like this. She just…*

Icca was suddenly beside her, risen out of her shadow, spitting, "What the fuck are you doing?"

Caro tipped her head back, disoriented. The faces of people she wouldn't remember staring down at her. If she killed the Saint now, it wouldn't escape. It wouldn't escape and find a mourning family on a wisteria farm. Why wouldn't it just die? Was it all shot? Was all of it meant to happen? She looked back to Hattie, like a reflex. Clutching her remaining blade to her chest, the other one jutting uselessly from one of the Saint's collarbones. It must have bit her; she had teeth marks on her forearm. It hurt. Gods, it all hurt so much. Her fingers probing the pushed-backed skin like the golden nodes of an instrument. Icca now in front of her, hands on her shoulders, screaming at her to do something, to *move*. "*We have to go.*" Caro gazed into her dark eyes and the silver storm of her mouth.

It all was kind of smearing away. Wasn't that nice? The Saint across the ring doing that coiled-up-spring thing again. Across the ring? What ring? Caro meant, surely—the other end of the hallway...

Yes, dear readers, she was losing it a little. More than her usual amount.

Icca had brought them back into the light through the shadow coming off of its excessively long spine, and braced forward on its first four knees. It hadn't turned around—just tipped backward like a wave of flesh and limbs. Its two heads hanging upside down. That's what Caro focused on, the heads, which now, she supposed distantly, were moving rapidly closer to her... heads that had been lovingly pushed together by Hattie, for Carousel, her champion. Hattie would never hurt her, see—specifically and intentionally, she had used multiple heads to remind Carousel that it was *not* Pillar.

(Because remember, Carousel, it'd only possessed one ugly mug.... Yes, that *was* right, certainly, Carousel, promise, promise, don't you *remember*? Well. It was hard to remember. Because every time Carousel thought of that house. Stop. Because every time Carousel thought of the kitchen ceiling or the hall beside the stairs or the bedroom—dear gods, the reek of it all—no, no, no. Carousel. What do you remember, Carousel? Stop remembering it, Carousel. Remember it like this, Carousel, this is how it happened. The air smelling like wisteria only. No cauterized flesh, in her memories. No bodies unraveled, filling the rafters of her beautiful head. No nearly dead girl on the rug upstairs. No Saint. No pain—never, ever, in that house. She always had her shoes off, in that house. Her feet stamping on plush carpet. Hands brushing clean tiles, the little flowers pressed into the picture frames. Carousel, so filled with warmth and comfort and not knowing what to do with any of it, not wanting to look too closely, never ever, because don't do that. She might scare it away. She tended to scare most people, but not these people. Who was in the bedroom, upstairs, cradling their little magics? There was just Caro and Icca and Hattie—no, that wasn't right, it was Hattie and Caro—got something wrong, what had she gotten wrong—stop. Yes. Nothing wrong, Carousel, dear, nothing wrong . . .)

"Rabbit!" Icca screamed. "What are you—"

Caro's feet had left the earth. She was being held. Crushed. Tears and magic stinging her eyes in tandem. Oh gods, oh gods, where was she? What was this place? She was so confused. Caro blinked past the mess in her eyes and saw the double-headed Saint, its jaws opening for her, smiling at itself, and between those two smiles Caro glimpsed silver, clouded sky.

They'd failed. Pillar was going to kill her, and maybe Carousel deserved that. Then it was going to kill Icca, and maybe Icca deserved that too. For never mourning. For saving themselves in that way. For carving that habit of unfeeling, for opening that door into abandoning each other. But gods damn it, what were they supposed to do? Caro was so fucking sick of it. Sick to her stomach over hurting all the time. She was a beautiful soul and she had done it all to herself.

"I'm sorry," she was murmuring. "I'm sorry. I didn't mean to. I'm sorry. . . ."

She glimpsed Icca, under that gray sky. Standing stock-still in the inkwell of the Saint's shadow. Just watching. She looked so small, down there, even with the vicious smile on her face.

And it was such hatred that brought Caro roaring back to herself.

The bitch was going to let her die.

No. Hattie.

No, no, no. It couldn't be true.

Carousel kicked and screamed, and somewhere within her shrieks was embedded a prayer. All thoughts of her gods fleeing from her. She was only thinking of the Red Queen. The High Priestess.

And then—she was being dropped.

Dropped onto lush, Wonderland earth. Breathing in the Forest.

She blinked and it was gone. She wasn't looking down into lush grasses. There was dirt and black blood on her hands and knees. No trees rising before her—only the Saint, two of its limbs still outstretched as if it were still holding her. Faces blinking at each other. And then. Then there were delicate red lines striating its gray skin. It was from these lines that the Saint came undone. Unraveling right down its middle into two parts, then more parts. Then it was small. Then it was dead, and it was nothing.

THIRTY

Year Zero Zero Ninety-Four, Winter Season

There Are 996 Remaining Saints

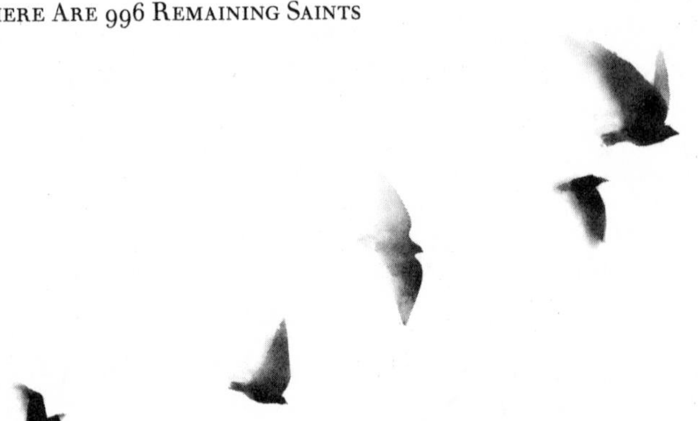

CAROUSEL GLANCED UP just as Hattie's hand was dropping back to her side. Crimson was winking from her cuticles.

The crowd was going berserk, of course, readers, they adored Hattie so. They adored being told, with this gesture, this small magic of hers, *Feel everything. Come completely apart, I'll protect you, then, too*... or so they thought Hattie must mean, with such a display.

But behind her veil, Hattie was frowning.

She hadn't truly expected Iccadora to let Carousel die.

Just as Iccadora hadn't expected her to allow Carousel to live.

The dark witch thought her so wasteful. So cruel. As if Hattie hadn't spared her from the Labyrinth. As if Hattie hadn't just saved the other end of her soul. Gods. Both witches stared at her from down in the ring, chests heaving in tandem. So in synch, even now. How could they not see it?

It was all so predictable; Hattie knew what was going to happen next.

She sighed. Nearly rolled her eyes, as Carousel turned and lunged at Iccadora.

Hattie missed her maze, as the two witches went screaming and rolling among all the blood and detached Saint parts. Oh, how she missed its Quiet.... The shrieks of the crowd tired her. This holiday. What had any of them learned? She could only hope that the strange magic of the two girls spurred some in the crowd a node of interest in pursuing their own arts. That's what she'd told Carousel she intended, with Iccadora's participation. But in truth, she'd known already that Iccadora would want Carousel suffering along with her. That they couldn't leave each other alone.

Behind her veil, her frown twitched.

And below, oh, her blood-splattered champions. Brawling. She was so disappointed in them. So unimpressed by them. *Stop*, she thought, and they stopped. Pinned by her.

This time it was intentional, missing Iccadora with her spell. Stitching the crowd's sight as she held still, so everyone else would only witness her standing impassively, and not moving closer to the railing. Lifting her veil so she could see Iccadora in her true coloring. How the shadows thrummed against her like shivering ink.

"You were going to let her die," said Hattie. Slightly startled, by the shock in her words.

Icca smiled, vindicated by it. "Godsdamn right I was."

"Just like Wonderland," Hattie murmured, remembering the conversation down in the dungeons. But no. She hadn't pictured it like this. It wasn't supposed to be like this. No. No. They were supposed to come back together. Hattie had tried to bring one of their nightmares to the surface, she wanted them to remember what it was like, remembering that love, to be clutched by the indescribable feeling of fearing for another's soul. How Hattie wanted to watch them protect each other. Realize they couldn't be apart. And then Hattie would have made it so.

"Just like Wonderland," Iccadora said. Perhaps without meeting Hattie's eyes, this time. Perhaps Quieter. But there was a ringing in Hattie's ears, now. Her own voice sounded distant to her.

"You don't understand. You could be so—happy."

"I knew it. This wasn't about the masses. This is all some freak experiment. What are you trying to do? Tell me." How bold she was, demanding, still pinned to the dirt. Caro had hit her in the face, and there was blood and magic caking her features. And still she clutched her cruelties like bouquets of pride. So blind to what was right in front of her. To all she could be, if she loved Carousel Rabbit. "Tell me!"

Iccadora had been right. This wasn't about the masses.

This was about Hattie.

Down she climbed into the ring. Just as she had the year prior. She had so appreciated their conversation, then. But then Iccadora still had potential. Iccadora had made Hattie think, *Maybe, maybe*...

"I wanted you to love each other," Hattie whispered. Leaning over the two pinned witches.

Caro lay on her side, looking at the earth. Icca looking up at the sky. And now at Hattie. That grin flickering into a grimace. "*Why?*"

"Because it hasn't worked, creating Saints. They're empty shells. They're nothing, always nothing. Even when I put them together." Hattie closed her eyes. "No matter how many I put together."

"You're mad—"

"I'm not mad. I'm just—here." Breathing in and out, Hattie touched her arms, her throat. Wiped at the magic trickling from her nose. "I swear I am."

It was no use. The red flowed out and out from her nostrils. Streaming over Hattie's fingers. Splattering against the ground. *Drip. Drip. Drip. Drip.*

"Just admit you love her," Hattie heard herself say. "Just admit you love her, and then I can sew you both together like I want to and you'd never be apart."

Hattie had been having strange dreams, dear readers, ever since she'd met our Iccadora Alice Sickle and our Carousel Rabbit.

Wonderful dreams, where she threaded their throats and smeared their bodies and ran her fingers through the warm, sloughing mess of it, until a new girl lay shivering in the carnage of what had been her two past selves, who had loved each other, so, so much. It would've been like painting. Gods, she would have been art. She would've been gorgeous. And Iccadora had ruined all of it. The girl she could've been, with Carousel. Iccadora had ruined her, and so now she had no use.

Hattie's magic dripped onto Iccadora's face.

And Iccadora would flinch, if Hattie had allowed her to move. She was allowing her to speak, but Iccadora was saying nothing. Hattie could see the whites of her eyes.

"You would've never been lonely again. And then I wouldn't have been lonely, either. Not with the person you were supposed to become."

Ah, well.

Now, Hattie supposed, she desired Iccadora to die.

How deeply, deeply disappointed she was in how all of it had turned out. All she had wanted to do was to create something lovely. Oh, dear readers, how they would have understood one another. Because Hattie was something lovely, too.

THIRTY-ONE

YEAR ZERO ZERO NINETY-FOUR, WINTER SEASON

THERE ARE 996 REMAINING SAINTS

THEY RETURNED TO the Petra Ward a little before Dawn. Caro had gone to throw Icca into a cell while they prepared her Labyrinth rune-brands, kicked around the palace for a time. Mostly wandering back and forth before Hattie's chambers. The Queen's guards told Caro she was sleeping and was not to be disturbed. Caro blushed deeper and deeper each time. Hattie was cross with her. Hattie hated her. She hated her enough to end the holiday early, to not speak a word to Caro the entire train ride back. Caro had disappointed her. Caro hadn't been able to kill Pillar. "I tried." She'd been so weak. "Don't say that." She was so useless. "You're being so mean!" She clutched her arms around herself tighter and tighter, holding back tears. "Don't cry, it's all right, darling." Eventually she crept back down to the dungeons. There was only one thing to do to feel like herself again—kill Icca. Yes. That'd get the nausea out of her gut. Icca had meant for Carousel to die in the ring. Icca had failed to kill Pillar and had disappointed Hattie, too.

But Icca was busy, she was being held down, and she was screaming as the guards pressed a red-hot iron brand to her neck. Then heaving and gasping as her palms ghosted over the rune steaming on her skin—the one that would mute her magic anywhere else besides the Labyrinth, and muddle her head within its maze. The smell of it made Caro feel better. She went back upstairs and washed her hair and had a bit of coffee. She was feeling better, really. Hardly thinking about anything other than how pretty she was.

Then finally—it was time for Icca to depart for the maze! It was time for Icca to die!

She found the dark witch just as she'd left her, still on her back, gaze unfocused at the ceiling. She unlocked the cell door and leaned against the chilled metal of the threshold, staring, seeing if the dark witch might try to charge her. She didn't.

"You're thinking a lot, again, Alice, and that makes you forget to talk," Carousel cooed. "I remind you of this item of yourself because this is the last time you'll get to beg me to try to spare you from the Labyrinth."

Still Icca said not a word. She had been like this ever since they'd left the ring. Being boring. Being somewhere else.

Quiet the whole carriage ride over, past empty cobblestone streets and the smell of bread as the Petra bakeries began to start their days. Quiet as Caro hauled her out, and they stood before the great rise of the great Wall with its great, massive letters. Even with her head tilting back, back, back, the Labyrinth blocking out the sky, and the tips of its trees reaching even farther, Icca chewed on a thought, and a line of goose bumps sprouted down Caro's spine. This wasn't right.

So Caro slung an arm around Icca's narrow shoulders, leaning her weight casually on the stiffened frame, and cooed brightly, despite the unease rippling through her. "What is it, Alice? Come, come, you can tell me. You're going to be all alone in there, except the Saints, and a skeleton or two—if they haven't been made into spells or soup yet—they don't listen a quarter as well as I do."

She leaned in excitedly as Icca opened her mouth. "Hattie . . ."

"Oh, here we go again," Caro scoffed.

To her surprise, then, Icca shook her head. "I'll talk to my gods."

Caro blinked, and then deflated. "*Pft.* Heresy more becomes you. And to think, all those years ago, you wanted to leave Wonderland so terribly."

"You did too. You don't spend all your time here, in this glittering blight of a Ward." Caro realized she'd miscalculated, because now Icca was turning her head to meet Caro's eyes, and they were suddenly quite close indeed. "You need the Forest as much as I do."

There were at least a hundred Saints in the Labyrinth that the Kkuls had stockpiled over the decades, and they'd been powerful witches, too. Petra was the only Ward in Isanghan that was physically a part of Wonderland, instead of being forced to construct out in the moorlands that ribboned the Forest—it had been a fortress city, long ago, bracing for and surviving the initial onslaught of the Saints, perhaps because it was still fed by Wonderland's magic, its roots deep even under the cobblestone façade, and richer still in the Petra Woods, a preserved part of the Forest itself. When no one had known what was happening, when the Saints started to turn, when they started to die and then get up again as something worse, the strongest of them had been in Petra, fighting for the Kkuls' army against the plague raiders. And then when it *was* known, the Labyrinth, which then had been merely the outer barracks ringing the city—originally a cherished landmark, constructed simply to be a pretty, grandiose thing to distinguish Petra—had been used to quarantine the Saints until everyone figured out what was going on. They had never been let back out.

Now, the iron gate hewn into the Wall—enchanted so the Saints and the sentenced Jabberwockies, both with Labyrinth runes on their bodies, saw it as solid stone always—was yawning open, sending a cool breeze licking out of the undergrowth of the maze, thick with the feel of magic and gods and worse things still.

"You're going to die in there," Caro reminded her, because clearly Icca needed the reminder. It was making Caro restless, the contemplative quality to Icca's voice.

"No I'm not."

"Deities, *yes*, you *are*, you lun—"

Still half-tangled in Carousel's arms, Icca let her head drop back, and she smiled. Caro's words faltered. The rune-brand shone against her neck in the weak morning sun.

"I am going to be Queen," whispered Icca, each word barbed, heavy with dark elation. "I'm going to be Queen of the Saints."

Caro stared.

And then she rolled her eyes, and took her weight off of Icca. *Ah, never mind, actually*, she thought. *She's completely mad.*

Some conversation, floating up out of the black. Caro with her finger in Tecca's hair, Icca acting the irritable philosopher as always: *I don't think anyone goes mad in Wonderland. And anyone who did was a little mad to start out with.*

Like Tecca? Caro had asked, and Tecca had grinned.

Don't answer unless you want me to send the orphanage rats chewing on your toes tonight, Alice. And Alice means you, Carousel.

Dead. Dead. Thoughts that were meant to stay dead.

This holiday had shaken Caro—shaken things loose. But she was fine. Really. Caro cut the throat of every memory that came up. Not everyone could cut the throats of things that did not have throats, but of course Carousel was quite an accomplished person.

The guards supplied Icca with a pack of clothes to replace her shredded hanbok, new boots, two new knives, a skin of water, a box of matches, and enough food to sustain her half a week, or give the Saints an appetizer. Caro had also been killing time preparing her own parting gift, and placed a parcel in Icca's hand.

"Well, open it," Caro said. "Don't worry about having not gotten me something in return—gratitude is the only thank-you I need."

From the paper wrapping Icca drew out a book—in fact, the same book she'd left on the Yule church pew. It was a nicer copy, with a better, thicker binding and a prettier cover. Silver-painted edges. It'd taken some time to find—Caro was still cursed and such and had only vaguely remembered what the letters on the cover had looked like, but the palace had a gorgeous library with an ugly little librarian who'd proved very helpful.

"I threw your old one into the fireplace," Caro said. "It was rude of me, spectacularly childish. I do hope this can make up for it in some capacity."

Icca stared at the cover, her expression passive, but Caro watched hungrily as Icca's fingertip, as if on its own, traced its silver edges. Her dark hair fell over her temples and eyes as her head tilted over the book. Good deities, the girl really was pretty, in that cruel, delicate kind of way that Caro had never seen fit so completely on another person.

"Is the ink poisoned, then?" Icca spat finally.

"I'd argue that reading does poison one's head," responded Caro. "All those thoughts can't be good for you—and with no pictures, even! Renders a book useless, to be without pictures."

Icca scoffed.

"You love it," Carousel said, gaze scraping the thin scar marring the angle of Icca's cheek. "Do you want to make out with me now?"

"Neither of us would enjoy that very much," Icca said promptly, and pressed the book to her chest. And then she walked into the Labyrinth. The dark head of hair did not turn back to look once, and the gate closed behind her.

"Well," Caro said aloud to herself, a bit stunned with the abrupt close, "that was extraordinarily underwhelming."

She poked the scar dripping from her own eye in a bothered, hurried fashion for a moment, before forcing her hand away from her face and turning back for the carriage. "Enjoy the book, Alice. I did have to tear out the last chapter, for old times' sake, of course, but up until then . . ."

THIRTY-TWO

Year Zero Zero Ninety-Four, Winter Season

There Are 996 Remaining Saints

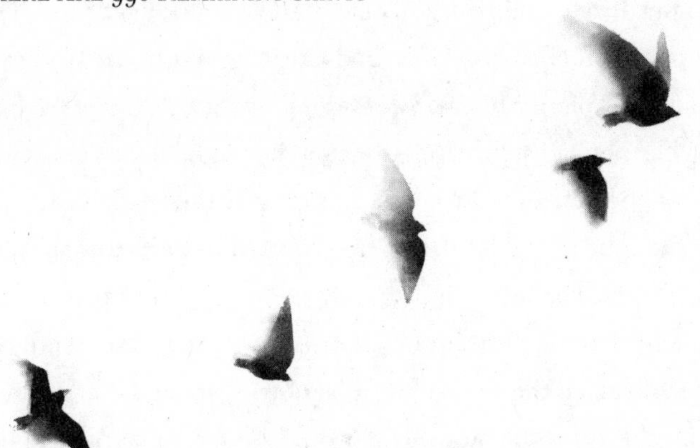

ICCA WALKED QUITE confidently away from Carousel, clutching her perhaps-poisoned book, straight into the Labyrinth. She was wholly satisfied with the display, how Caro would pick at the unadornment of it in her head, thinking, really, it was the last time she was ever going to see Icca.

She was wrong, of course.

Though it felt, a little bit, like it could maybe be right, when the gate closed behind her, and then Icca did turn back, and saw only a thicket, like she'd walked straight out of the undergrowth. The top of the Wall flickered what seemed like a mile or two in the distance, dark stone flecking between far-off trees. She scratched irritably at the rune on her neck.

All forests were mazes, really, so the massive walls tangling this particular hewn section of Wonderland into a Labyrinth seemed excessive. But it wasn't just the physical elements that made this place inescapable. There was a strange magic at work here, slowly twisting and twining human thoughts—the runes on the walls sloughing confusion, the rune on her neck their door.

Icca, at least, had paid attention in Madam Killington's geometric runework class. How most runes had to come in pairs to work properly, like finicky puzzle pieces.

At least, for now, Icca could recognize how unclear her head was. The instinct hadn't been knocked from her body, or the magic cut from her soul—she trusted both plenty to carry her along.

Icca touched her neck absentmindedly, took her hand away, and then brought it back as she continued to walk, picking at the tender edges of the brand. She thought irritably of Kai, the coward. He'd never survive Wonderland—Icca barely believed he'd survive jail. He wouldn't even have a death trace on him to declare he had a little grit, if Hattie changed her mind and sent him to the Forest—he'd be one of the lesser criminals gobbled down by the time the sun set. It would be rather hard keeping him out of the Wards, of course—even though he might go *pop* when he materialized again with the criminal rune still on his neck, but Kai could shed his physical body for as long as he liked, the lucky bastard. His affinity even allowed him to cheat the pain of it. It was no wonder he was such a rotten person.

Did you feel the need to prove companionship, bringing me along?

Icca scowled at the memory. He truly was a dimwit. She had certainly *not* balked at the idea of facing Caro alone. No, in fact, Icca had seen her and had wished the rest of the room were empty. Because—then she could kill her in private. . . .

Her stomach let out a growl. Only then did Icca realize she was starving, and her feet were hurting, and that she'd been a little bit of an idiot this entire time. She didn't need to go looking for Saints. They'd find her, eventually.

She was at a three-way split in the path, before two massive slabs of runeworked stone and the Wall barring them on their opposite sides, thick moss and a handful of massive trunks hugged up against them. It was all very strange and further disorienting—this felt like Wonderland, in Icca's bones, but the turns of the Labyrinth structure reminded her of the human touches at work here.

Here, the Kkuls' morals, or the lack of them, made up the Walls clustered around Icca. It wouldn't be harder reaching for her gods—maybe for a lesser witch, or one whose deities weren't everywhere—but it would certainly be irritating, with the magic the Labyrinth secreted clouding her head. There was still a sense of *Wonderland* that existed here, some hum in her marrow, the cognizant feeling of her lungs stretching and deflating and the weight of her body; maybe if she hadn't had the rune . . .

Hattie goes to the Labyrinth to pray.

Icca turned quickly, scanning from the trees behind her to the path she'd come up from. For a moment she was twitchy, wringing her hands and darting her gaze about. Just as in the Forest, Icca felt as if she were being watched. Watched by an arcane force without eyes, without limbs to run after her with, an entity old enough that it didn't need such form. A bird or else another creature shrieked in the distance; a high wind sent the foliage chattering. Icca scratched at the back of her head and forced herself to face forward once more.

That couldn't *really* be true, could it, Hattie coming *here* to pray? Of course, now that she'd really met the Red Queen . . . if anyone would choose such an insane place to be pious, it'd be her, with her vacant gaze and teeming magic. But Icca decided then and there to simply refuse to believe this. Hattie had proved herself insane and nothing else.

How long had Icca been standing here, before the fork, just being pissed about all of it? It was dusk now.

Icca drew her hand away from her neck, the rune newly raw and her fingernails bloody, and sat down where she stood. On the bump of a root, she took off her shoes and wore her toes into the soft earth, drinking down the growing cold of the air and the deepening of the shadows around her. She ate dried rice cakes and some horrible jwipo taken from her gifted provisions—the fish jerky having been prepared without sugar, which

Icca thought obscenely wrong, and it left an aftertaste like the underside of a pier on her tongue.

Am I scared? Icca asked herself as the Darkness pooled. *What's changed, really? I'm doing the same thing I usually do, generally. Waiting for something to come along and kill me. Waiting to pull it apart.* Hattie hadn't shaken her so much. Icca was scarier than she was, she reminded herself, and was comforted. Then she was feeling very wicked indeed and finding, as usual, she very much liked it.

Legs folded beneath her, Icca waited for the night to fully settle around her. Then she was in shadow, and she breathed it in, let it go.

And now she felt it. Lightless spots moving about in the split of the path before her.

It had caught a glimpse; she knew the Saint had caught her scent, because it was panting.

And then it was charging.

"Oh," Icca said quietly, unmoving, that familiar tic in her throat. The little fear, thrumming within her like it possessed its own independent heart . . . she didn't mind it. She wanted to feel so viciously alive, up until the moment where she would lie so very dead. "Oh, no, no . . ."

THIRTY-THREE

YEAR ZERO ZERO NINETY-FOUR, WINTER SEASON

THERE ARE 996 REMAINING SAINTS

A FEW DAYS PASSED. Caro kicked around Petra and pinned back any bounties to check at a later date. For whatever reason she didn't call on Hattie at the palace—it just didn't seem any fun, it wasn't even about Hattie being maybe cross with her. And Caro was feeling lethargic, anyway. She was quiet and satisfied in the mornings, what with her always waking to soft gray light and the patter of rain on the cobblestone streets. And then she did nothing all day and was casually disgusted with herself by nightfall. It was a routine she was used to; she very clearly knew the importance of rest. But it felt different this time. She wasn't savoring her food, or messing around flying in whatever landed on her balcony; she wasn't talking aloud to herself as often, and it made the apartment feel cavernous.

Of course she wasn't sad that Icca was currently settled in a Saint stomach right now, but still, Icca being dead was... quite dull.

Maybe it was because their parting had been exhaustingly unspectacular. Caro had been expecting to be physically hurting when she finally scraped the blight of Iccadora Alice Sickle from the face of the earth. She had expected to come back to the apartment and lean her weight on her sink and admire all the new bruises and cuts in the mirror, and think to herself, *You got close, Alice, and it was fun and all for it, but really, what did you expect…?*

Caro had gotten a few bruises from the Midwinter Tea and their post-Pillar brawling, but she found she didn't get much triumph out of them. Mostly, when she peered into the mirror, she found her eyes drifting to the scar on her face. She'd always liked it, thought it was just edgy enough to give her look a little bite; it fit her quite nicely—like all her features did—even if Icca had given it to her. Caro didn't always think of Icca when she was looking at it. It was on *her* face, after all.

But now Icca was dead, and when Caro looked down the scar's thin, raised path, she had an image in her head of the dark witch walking into the Labyrinth without turning around.

"That was fun," Caro said, not for the first time, to the empty apartment—to remind it and herself. She was standing in the middle of the bedroom, looking around at all her pretty things and daring them to say anything different. "It would be a very queer thing if you did," she told them. "It would be such a very queer thing if you said 'It *was* fun, Caro dear, but it doesn't feel like it, does it? In fact, it kind of feels like when the tea leaves won't steep properly because the water's gone Cold' that I would be very obliged to give you some of my raging sapphic-ness and clasp it to you like a darling button."

Caro's fists dropped from their place at the top of her hips. She turned a hundred and eighty degrees and repositioned them again. The apartment curled over her like a stomach, eating up what little noise her feet scuffed against the floorboards.

"Well, fine, I guess I could use a bit of a walk," she declared to herself haughtily, and partially to jab at all the things that had rudely refused to answer her. "Maybe I *will* go and see what Hattie's up to."

Caro put on her thick cloak and her thick boots and stole out into the street, making for the Petra Woods. It was the middle of the week, and the University's classes had just gotten out, witches strewn about the trees talking or hurrying into the gorgeous library that sat the closest to the palace, where through the swinging doors Caro glimpsed heads bent over tomes and great clusters of candles washing over alcoves and tired students in yellow and orange light. The University was the only thing that Icca had been really excited about when Caro talked about living in Petra, once they beat Wonderland. Caro had been a bit excited for it too; uni would be nothing like the nothing girls' school they'd attended. She'd study transduction morphology, the type of magic that she and Hattie could do where they could borrow another living thing's senses; Icca would study something with just as fancy of a name, or maybe just literature because she loved it, and would finally have the chance to be the entire academic she'd always wanted to be.

But truly, dear readers, if by this point in the story you are still seeking comfort, enough so that you are picturing our darling, gruesome champions engaged in habits so domestic and casual as the pursuit of higher education, even toting around a god such as Carnage, then a concerned narrator must ask after you—are you very much all right?

"And now she's *dead*," sang Carousel, startling a few college students passing her by. Caro twisted her neck around as she passed through the palace garden wall so that they got the context. "It's a holiday season now! Reject your schooling and live as feral, happy things!" She was fully walking backward now, one tattooed arm shooting out of her cloak to flap insistently at their retreating backs. "Iccadora Alice Sickle is dead!"

THIRTY-FOUR

YEAR ZERO ZERO NINETY-FOUR, WINTER SEASON

THERE ARE 996 REMAINING SAINTS

ICCADORA ALICE SICKLE was alive, and laughing. She was laughing and rolling to the side, and the Saint barreled past her—the sad, horrifying thing one of Hattie's creatures, judging by the number of heads. It turned and stood, a full eight feet tall, as her magic stung down her throat, as Icca flicked out her silver-stained tongue and painted it over her smile. And then she brought the night crashing down.

Hovering over the Saint, pinning it under its own Dark spots, Icca reached into that black place and drew out the rose vial. *Drink me.* How long ago it seemed, tucking it away! Like she'd seen Hattie's magic drip from the mesh of her veil into her teacup, Icca brought her thumb to her mouth, silver on her nail, and dashed it against the lip of the potion. Gave it a good shake.

Then she wrenched open the Saint's mouth and shoved it down.

Icca didn't fuss around with a trinket magic like alchemy—she hadn't known that, had Hattie drunk the poisoned tea, it would've killed her long before her demonstration. This magic was breathlessly quick. A twitch, the blank eyes rolling back, and the beast erupted into a rose garden.

Black blood splattered across Icca's features, a thread of it connecting her lips as she parted them in her low, sharp laugh. She dropped to her knees and ghosted her palms over silver petals. Gorgeous, gorgeous harvest—there were so *many.* Enough to raise an army. Was it really so simple as a marriage of Saints and roses and liquid magic? Perhaps the Carnage was a critical factor, yes, the catalyst being flowers cracking apart rib cages; perhaps the spell liked the noise of it; perhaps it was the willingness to have some part of herself consumed, her little Divinity; perhaps it was complete nonsense, all nonsense, painting roses...

Once she had control of a few Saints—barring the possibility that this new rose magic wasn't vicious enough to fry her in her own body—she'd see if she could get them over the Wall, if her insistence could overpower the influence of the runes keeping the Saints pressed down into the Labyrinth. And then the path of the plan was a string with a frayed end—Icca didn't want a neat conclusion. She wanted total chaos.

She'd spill her Saints through the Petra streets. She'd let not another fool think there was anywhere truly safe in Isanghan.

Queen of the Saints, that's what she'd told Carousel. But Icca didn't want a crown, or a country.

She'd learned her true purpose, pinned in her body, that body on the warmed courtyard ground. Hattie November Kkul had barely even bled for it.

It was an embarrassment, but a taste nonetheless.

Icca didn't just want power like that. She craved something more.

More, and nothing else.

There was no *why* of it, really, the want to be the most powerful witch in existence. Certainly it was not what she had originally set out to accomplish—a dead Queen, for an avenged Tecca. But with each and every mad thing that had passed out of Hattie's lips, Icca's want had mutated more and more.

Now, when she palmed for it in her head, it felt like a need.

And so—her life would be a devouring thing. She'd be an existence as insistent as decay. How pious she was, to want nothing more than to let her magic, her Divinity, swallow her down. The High Priestess had nothing on her. Hattie would have nothing. . . .

THIRTY-FIVE

YEAR ZERO ZERO NINETY-FOUR, WINTER SEASON

THERE ARE 995 REMAINING SAINTS

"ICCADORA ALICE SICKLE," Hattie said thoughtfully to Carousel when Caro blew in, from the rug of her bedchamber where she lay quite still, "is not dead."

"Gods damn it." Caro flopped down onto one of Hattie's love seats. Then she changed her mind, instead rolling off the love seat and onto the floor, and came to a stop next to Hattie.

Side by side, their two spines lined the rug. Caro looked up into the ceiling, which was striated with colored glass. She could see it had started to rain, and she interlaced her fingers on her stomach and listened to it and Hattie breathing beside her—how lovely, Hattie *wasn't* cross with her (Hattie was never cross with anyone of course, being a person of an even temperament and all)—but it was kind of hard to relax, because Cheshire was bound to a chair a few feet away and it had uneven legs that clicked against the hardwood floor as he shook.

Hattie was not staring at the ceiling like Caro was. Caro guessed that, in fact, even if she'd peeled open Hattie's eyes, Hattie would still not be staring at the ceiling, or then, at Caro leaning over.

Comparatively, if Caro did the same with Cheshire, she'd probably find that behind each set of dark eyelashes and each closed lid there was a hollow in his skull.

It'd been careful work, certainly, and Caro imagined silent, deliciously grave and serious Hattie with her mouth drawn in a line, as she slid and stitched her sight under Cheshire's. And then she could see what he was seeing, so she could simply send his eyes curling out of the physical plane, out of their sockets and flitting out into the Labyrinth. This was the cleanest way to do it. It would really be much more of an effort if she used his whole body, much less of a mess to leave all of his organs and consciousness and such here. She could have very easily asked Caro to go check in on Icca in the Labyrinth, but what kind of punishment would that be for the pretty, traitorous boy? It was better like this. Caro and Hattie on the rug, like gossiping schoolgirls. There was something particularly warm about being on the floor with a loved one. Carousel adored a good floor-lay.

Though, again, her unnie wasn't really there next to her, one hundred percent. So Caro got up and stepped over the Queen, and eased herself onto Kai's lap. He stiffened and let out a startled cry, and Caro ignored him, tracing her fingers on the lines of his wonderful face—the parts that weren't blindfolded, and gagged, that is.

"Oh dear, darling," she purred. "Gwaenchanha—why would you think it's not okay? You'll come back perfectly intact; unnie's quite surgical with it. It just must feel a little funny is all." Caro traced a fingertip down the nice, straight line of his nose. "Hm. Are you really just a boy? Because you really are gorgeous, and usually I'm not so keen—"

Hattie jerked upright, and Caro jumped and almost slid her finger into Cheshire's mouth. She felt slimy at the close call. *Good, right, then, definitely a giant les—*

"Unnie?" Caro said, now with her arms looped around Cheshire's neck. "Gwaenchanhayoh?"

The Red Queen was sitting up on the rug, spine a tick less relaxed than her usual sure posture. Her hair was particularly frizzy around her shoulders from the scratch of the rug. She was in her own thoughts, and then Caro saw her draw back from them, now rising, eyes lifting, and Caro slid off of the now-limp Cheshire and followed Hattie out of the room.

But Hattie stopped short at the end of the wing, now between her guards, and she was speaking quietly. "The Petra Ward is locking down."

Aarnik and Chun-Ho bowed and ran off. Carousel, meanwhile, let out a little shriek of glee. "A *lockdown*? Oh, what did you see? What did you peer? What's sickly Icky Alice up to—"

Hattie brushed past her, back into her rooms, and Caro trotted behind. The Queen went to Cheshire and drew away his blindfold and his gag, and then dug her small hand into the underside of his jaw. Caro could absolutely faint with the thrill of it. She really was going to beg Hattie to marry her—how could she not, with that little doll-face entirely calm, as the red bled down in two straight lines from the pleasantly soft nose, as Cheshire twitched in Hattie's hold, as Cheshire *screamed*. . . .

"The suspense of it!" exclaimed Caro brightly, peering curiously down Cheshire's throat. "The boys back at the apartment are going to be sorry they missed this, but I'm so glad to have left them now. . . ."

"—swear she didn't tell me anything!" shrieked Cheshire—Caro must've missed Hattie asking him a question. "Gods, gods, I swear it, Your Majesty, I didn't know what Sickle meant to do in the Labyrinth—"

"Carousel," murmured Hattie. "Cut—"

"Hooray!" shouted Carousel, knife flicking into her grip, and she slashed Cheshire sternum to shoulder-tip. He screamed again, and Hattie was rolling her eyes.

"—his binds, Carousel."

"Oh," said Caro, blushing, and twisted the knife in her hands bashfully for a moment before slicing the ties away. "I'm apologetic, Cheshire."

Hattie brushed absently at the magic flecking her skirt and said, "I will have to borrow your eyes again at some point." Cheshire opened his mouth, and Hattie added quietly, "You can say no, but only once. I'll be sending for a carriage to Wonderland when you do."

You sucker, thought Carousel, as Cheshire's mouth closed. *That's an easy out.*

—

"*Unnie,*" Carousel whined under the chime of the lockdown bells. "What did you see? Now you're killing me. The *anticipation*!"

They moved through the filling palace halls. Hattie was focusing on her breath, out, in, out again—there couldn't be disquiet in her head when disquiet was the outside state. She needed to stay quite focused, and calm, so as to figure out what to do next. That's what Hattie's mother would have done, her rationality a majestic thing. Hattie wanted to be a majestic thing, too, to uphold the royal Kkul name, the rich tone of their magic, lethal and elegant Divinity.

Nothing like the power of Iccadora Alice Sickle.

Down there, in Hattie's Labyrinth, the dark witch's magic spilled from her, jagged and devouring and absolutely feral. Hattie had been slow—it'd taken her some time to practice using Cheshire's power, Cheshire's eyes—and she'd found Iccadora had already killed a Saint, had already used the rose draught she must've smuggled in to make it a garden.

Hattie had seen Iccadora surrounded by Saints, kneeling on the Labyrinth floor, saw them chewing, chewing, chewing not the dark witch but the silver flowers she'd grown. Hattie had seen her hand rise, watched her beckon one of the beasts closer, her dark brown eyes bright and glittering. Watched her cut it neck to ankle, just to see if it would stay still the entire time, and it did, of course.

Watched Iccadora tilt her head back, white throat hitching, swallowing like she was about to cry.

And then Iccadora had laughed.

She'd laughed, and the horrible sound had chased Hattie all the way back to her own body.

This is what Hattie told Carousel on the spiral of stairs up to the study, speaking still as she sat down at her desk and began to write off letters to her Jabberwockies of the Culled Court. Hattie needed living Saints; she needed to make more monsters, because she did not know if she'd be able to control the ones Icca would attempt to send over the Labyrinth Wall, into Petra.

Hattie November Kkul was rarely angry. It wasn't in her nature, because it hadn't been in her mother's nature. Rational, majestic. Lethal, and elegant.

But it all did feel quite personal. It was art, what Hattie did, what Hattie created; her magic was art and she—she was an absolute prodigy. But Iccadora's magic was chaotic and ragged, and she was smearing it all over Hattie's Saints, Hattie's work. Hattie didn't like that, how messy Iccadora was being with all of it, the violence decadent and imprecise. It felt like an insult.

She could've been so much *more.*

So maybe it was childish, Hattie setting down her quill and turning to Carousel now. She could call upon any other Jabberwocky of the Culled Court instead, and any number of them; though, truly, Carousel was the best of them.

But Hattie really was, just a little, angry.

She didn't like it. The emotion clouded her more than thick, sickly-sweet drink. But it was already on her tongue, and no, no, she didn't want Iccadora to simply die.

She wanted Iccadora's heart to twist around in her chest cavity a bit before it was ripped free, and Hattie knew it would, because it would be Carousel doing the ripping.

"Carousel," Hattie spoke, meeting the crow witch's black eyes. "I'll be contracting you to kill Iccadora Alice Sickle now."

Caro squealed her excitement, boots tipping on the study's rug as she dropped the quickest kiss to Hattie's temple. Hattie smiled, surprised first at the gesture and then at the warmth that rose in her chest from it, brushing the spot with her fingertips as Carousel clapped her hands and spun around.

Eventually she collected herself quite nicely, Hattie thought, and gave a curt curtsy, her head rising, her smile a sharp little thing on her lips.

"Of course," Carousel said through the split of her grin, words sweet and dripping, eyes already lined in blue. "Anything for you, unnie."

II

THIRTY-SIX

YEAR ZERO ZERO NINETY, AUTUMN SEASON

THERE ARE 1087 REMAINING SAINTS

AS HATTIE DROPPED Delcorta over the edge and into seven stories of open air, she had the peculiar thought that the circular rise of the tower study was alike to a throat. And the stairs going round and round—licking up to the platform beneath Hattie's feet where she stood at the door of the study—that was a kind of strange tongue.

Perhaps, dear readers, it was because of such a peculiar thought—the likes of which tend to be of the more hypnotizing sort—that Hattie lingered so long at the door, peering down at the blood blooming from Delcorta's broken body, and was thus witnessed by the servant who eventually came by to collect the tea tray the White Queen had requested for her and her daughter around an hour prior. And still when the servant was shrieking and drawing the guards and any wandering nobles, Hattie stood transfixed at the top of the stairs staring down into the throat, the base of which must surely be swallowing up Delcorta, because before

Hattie's eyes it seemed her mother was getting smaller and smaller, farther and farther away, certainly . . .

"She fell," Hattie November Kkul lied, when it was time for her to speak—the last words she would ever speak to the general public—thinking all the while, *I am running around in my head, chasing my personality.*

THIRTY-SEVEN

YEAR ZERO ZERO NINETY-FOUR, WINTER SEASON

THERE ARE 995 REMAINING SAINTS

ICCA WAS CRAWLING. . . . Which of her was crawling?

No, that wasn't right. She was sitting. Yes, she was sitting very still and trying to keep the head—the one that was just her own—above all her—the others. Her others. She was getting to be so many others, now.

And Icca had always liked this, dissolving herself.

It was in other heads rather than in her storybooks, now, but, oh, how deliciously familiar it felt. Being somewhere else.

"Stop it," she hissed from beneath the cast of her hood, to whichever one was crawling. The Saint stopped immediately; she felt it lie down, good, yes, all of it felt very peculiar indeed . . . *Keep going now* she kept going, now, now.

She'd been mistaken again; she hadn't been the one sitting still. She was on her knees, hands moving, leaning over the Saint she'd killed her first night, the one that had barreled for her and whose throat she'd tipped the rose vial contents—spiked with her magic—into. The one she'd made her garden.

Now, Icca was harvesting.

The Saints had come skittering out of the Labyrinth at the sound of her laugh, and it'd been the most curious thing, that they had then skittered right on past her to feast on the flowers instead. Icca found she'd been able to tug them back with nothing but a thought once they'd stolen a taste.

She still had so many blossoms left. So she ripped off the roses by their necks, pressing them slick into her faerie book—sending a jagged thanks to Carousel. She'd have little focus to read for a while.

The roses still dripped with the Saint's black blood, but beneath, the velvet of the petals shone the moonstruck silver of her own magic. Icca's fingers paused over a blossom, suddenly dazed with its color and weight, like cheeks, and thought about how nice they would feel on her tongue, how soft they would sit in her stomach. . . .

Icca snarled back the thought, which wasn't her thought, really—her Saints wanted to feed—and then abruptly sat back on her heels. Well. Was it perhaps slightly concerning that their whims were bleeding over into her head . . . ?

"No," she laughed quietly to herself, brushing away the notion and continuing her work. "No. . . ."

It wasn't concerning. Icca was much more tangled up in them than they were in her.

Icca did wish that it hadn't been one of the Red Queen's stitched Saints that had come first, a few days ago, that she'd turned into the rose bed. She would have preferred having it under her control instead. Currently, Icca only had one Saint beside her other twelve that was Hattie's creation, and she felt the distinction—how it was heavier and would still move the fastest, when she did get along to making it move. She wanted another. Then she'd be ready for Petra.

For now, all of her—them—all of them were gathered close by, slinking around in the Dark. They were hungry; Icca was quite hungry lately, no matter how many birds she had brought to her and laid at her feet, just because she could make the Saints do so. She could make them bow their heads.

Maybe now she could admit it: she'd always been a little jealous of Carousel's power, of the Kkuls'. They didn't have to live in their own bodies all the time, in their own heads. Icca was so much more than her own head, than her fragility, the circles under her eyes, the sores on her face. She'd never felt more physically close to her crueler qualities. Never felt more seen by her gods.

—

Never quite sure when she was sleeping, now. Never quite sure when she was awake. The mental toll of her conscious's edges being blurred, shot across different bodies—she felt she was dreaming all the time. So perhaps Icca awoke, when pine needles began to shake above her head. Or perhaps she only snapped back to attention.

She pressed herself upright, flinched, flinched, until her own eyes clicked into place in her own head, just as the new Saint shot out of the shadows.

"Oh," murmured Icca, fingernails curling into cool earth. "Oh, *yes*."

It was one of Hattie's amalgamations, barreling toward her.

Icca made herself very still—after all, what was all of this, if she was not confident with the magic she wielded? She'd left one full rose in the garden plot of a Saint, now tender with its decay, and the new monster stopped dead in its tracks just before the soft bowing of the blossom.

It began to eat, and Icca let out a low sigh, lying back down on the earth again, as she began to seep into it.

This stitched creation had all of the features of both of the Saints from which it'd been born, four eyes cluttered together and four nostrils strung beneath them, two mouths a little ways apart, so that they slipped up around the cheekbones. Icca felt her way through each treat, each violent, unimaginative tendency—there was no rage or sorrow that drove the need to rip human beings apart, just an animal hunger. Hattie was right—it was just empty shells upon empty shells. This was really where Icca could distinguish herself. She was an unmistakably vivid thing amid the rest of them.

But this newest monster... there was something different about it. Icca knew, because Icca felt a little different. Her fingers traced upon the ground.

"Hana," she called, though she didn't really need to—she could have just as well thought of the first of Hattie's creations she'd influenced nearing her and it would have—but she was trying out the name, *One*. Not particularly creative, but she didn't think much of these creatures as it was. She wouldn't name the rest, the Saints without stitches.

Hana dropped down from its skittering about the pine limbs above her head. Icca sat up and peered as it came closer, as it sat down beside her new Saint, who she would now call Dul, *Two*, following her uncreative streak.

"There's something..." Icca murmured aloud, or in her head, as she now crawled around the sitting Saints, inspecting. A few times her focus stuttered, and then she was looking at herself through their eyes, and had to pause to collect the order of perspectives, tugging hers back to the top, much like how one would pull a coin from the bottom of an unorganized pouch. "There's... The two of you aren't..."

Hana had felt distinct from the other Saints, echoed with Hattie's magic, the same cloying press that Icca had felt wound around her in the palace courtyard. Icca had expected Dul to feel the same.

"You *are* hers, aren't you?" asked Icca irritably, smacking Dul so it twisted a little and she could glimpse the "꿀" brand stamped on its ribs. "You don't feel like hers, really... yet... almost... and who else could've..."

She pressed a hand against Dul's clammy skin. Its teeth chattered above her crown, twenty fingers ghosting at her shoulders and her neck, but Icca could barely feel them as she thought, and searched—had she really been so scared of Saints, before? So scared of Wonderland? That version of herself seemed such a distant, limp thing.

Hattie November Kkul was the only one who created new monsters. That's what made the Red Queen so revered, so feared. It was a fact of this world, that Hattie was unlike anything that had ever graced existence before.

But now, now. The monster keening before Icca was not the Red Queen's work, Icca was sure, sure, sure. . . .

She smiled. She made Dul roll over, made Hana bow to her, laughing at the ease of it, dizzy and giddy with the new knowledge. Someone else could stitch Saints together, too. The Red Queen was hiding something. Hattie November Kkul was not the witch everyone thought her to be.

—

Shrouded in the nearby foliage, a solitary crow observed the scene. It was shaking rather curiously, because Carousel was shrieking her laughter in its head, and the bird-throat couldn't spill her chuckle.

What the hell—she was attempting to gasp—*What the hell is wrong with her?*

THIRTY-EIGHT

YEAR ZERO ZERO NINETY-FOUR, WINTER SEASON

THERE ARE 995 REMAINING SAINTS

ABOUT FIFTEEN MINUTES PRIOR, Caro had strolled up to the stout wooden building that crouched outside the gates of the Labyrinth, battering her hands along its side before sliding up to the open window and leaning her weight on the lip of the counter there. "Hello," she said to the startled guard. "I'd like to go into the Labyrinth."

"You— What?" The man had been tipped back in his chair and now straightened, sloshing the coffee cup in his hand; Caro blew yellow hair out of her eyes with a puff of breath. Gods, how boring this post must be—sentencing to the Labyrinth was rare, and Hattie had her own key to the gates, probably, or maybe she could walk through walls; Caro had never asked.

Caro flung her pointed finger back to the rise of the Labyrinth behind her, a monstrosity of dark stone and lettering. "That one," she clarified for him. "The Queen's asked me to."

"Did you . . . do something wrong?"

Caro threw her head back and laughed. "You are potentially very interesting and funny, aren't you! Well, I'll tell you. I'm going in to retrieve someone."

The guard looked away from her steady eye contact—Caro's was of the more unnerving sort, dear readers—dropping his gaze down into his cup. "Their body?"

Well—potentially very interesting and funny, if not a little slow. "Well, if I'm retrieving Icca . . . yes, I suppose her body, too."

Now he stared at her again. And because Caro didn't care about him, it was difficult for her to remember what he looked like even as she was currently looking at him, hence, for a narrator to avoid being deemed a lazy one: perhaps he was tall, or had a little mustache, or had the thought to himself, yes, he supposed he could let this young strange-haired girl into the Labyrinth, as the Queen had apparently wished, but it wouldn't be fair, since she'd never come out again. Perhaps this is why he said to Caro then, "It wouldn't be fair," not knowing Caro's attentions had been stolen by a crow that was perched on the gutters of a nearby apartment complex; instead of responding to him Caro said firmly to the crow, "You stay right here in case I need you later," and the guard said, "In case you . . . ?" and Caro said, "You're a pretty one, aren't you?" and the guard stammered, blushing, "Well, that's . . ." "Pretty, pretty, pretty, shiny . . . Well, will you let me in or not?" This last part was actually to the guard, and the guard got up, perhaps on tall legs or perhaps not, gathering the keys off the wall hook—which Caro noted—and perhaps thought to himself as he went to unlock the gates, *Nothing is fair; nothing is fair at all*, because the girl who had called him pretty was definitely going to die.

—

So Carousel had waltzed into the Labyrinth rather confidently, without a rune on her neck to muddle her senses, with her Birds everywhere—save for when a Saint smelled her influence on a crow, and that little dot of her awareness would get swallowed down with a squawk.

Prior to the aforementioned confident waltzing, Carousel had scoped that Icca had a healthy stock of Saints, and was now—in a less healthy method, for them—sending them to smash themselves against the Wall of the Labyrinth, over which Petra sprawled under a midmorning rain.

Caro surrounded her body with crows to keep watch, and then tucked herself into a gnarl of tree roots, wept her magic, and found wings, which she lifted and flew in the direction of the *thud, thud, thud* of Saint bodies against stone.

Caro dropped into a tree to find Icca squinting and cursing in her usual prickly fashion to the Saints as they rolled from the Wall—squinting, of course, because Icca couldn't be seeing the Wall with the eyes in her own head, the rune on her neck rendering the scene before her as continued forestry.

On the grayed skin of Icca's beasts, burns festered from the scorch of runework. The smell of it burned in the air like sulfur, and Caro imagined it would have tickled at the flesh of her nose if she'd been truly using her own. Ah, she loved her nose, the subtleness to its tip. She missed her nose, whenever she was a crow.

As if answering the thought, the limb that Caro was balanced on shook slightly. Caro picked up her bird—chin?—face and saw a Saint balanced on its hands and feet at the end of the branch, spine arched like a kitten's. Then its slack face was rapidly nearing her. She tried to fly away, as was the initial instinct. At least she was eaten alive rather quickly.

"Damn," she breathed past the stinging stream of magic on her lips, when she had vocal cords again. Icca definitely knew she was here now. Caro pushed back her nausea and wrenched herself upright, drawing her knives, and began to move for deeper Labyrinth. "Okay, okay, it's okay—knew there was going to be a show of it, anyway . . ."

Caro stood, stroked a fingertip in an affectionate line down her nose, and then there was something skittering for her, said the Birds, said their eyes in the trees. Caro reached a place with nice, tactical grounding. Plenty of area to hop around in, onto logs and thick roots and such for the higher ground, yes, it'd suit nicely....

She pulled back the hood of her cloak, rolling her cheek over her shoulder to glance back into the shadowed thicket. Her makeup was probably a mess already—of course she'd decorated—and she liked how it looked, even if she didn't exactly know how it looked. But she could picture it. Her yellow curls casually wild in the tuck of her cloak, the angle of her cheekbones glazed in blue. Her magic filling the lines of her eyes and the lines of her smile—as the Saint who'd gobbled down one of her more disposable selves came tearing out of the dark at her spine.

"Well!" Caro exclaimed, flicking the knives at her sides. "You are totally missing the art of the moment, aren't you, Alice?"

And the air was thick with feathers, and talons.

Her Birds seemed to dissolve the Saint, even as they were snapped aside, torn to bits. The sheer quantity of them was indulgent, but Caro thought they were more appreciated here, rather than picking at crumbs about the Petra University campus from where she'd plucked them—what with all the witches with their noses buried in books as they were, and truly, dear readers, not appreciating just how effortlessly a crow's talons can slit skin.

Caro shot back her hand, and a line of the Birds cleared, and through the silky black there was flesh, and then Caro sliced and there was blood. An arm came snapping out, the attached hand startlingly massive, but Caro didn't realize this until it folded to encase the entire left side of her torso, clammy and Cold, and—

The image of Icca laughing, such a rare thing, slight form balanced on the orphanage's window-frame, dewy breeze licking in and—

Staring up into the cobweb patchwork of the hospital's saltfever wing, and her hands very small and cold at her sides and her umma—

Tecca at her side as they chased Icca through the darkened wisteria grove; they could never, of course, catch her in the night unless Icca let them, and she always did, the earth cool and plush under Caro's bare feet and—

Her parents on the pyre, hissing under the drizzle but still burning, slow, slow, and sure—

Caro pushed her knife through skin, tendon, and then bone, and the hand detached from her, from its own wrist, thudding to the earth. She reeled back, struggling, keeping her focus on the Birds as she sucked in her breath, forced herself into the present from beneath the influx of memories. She hated the head magic, the in-your-head magic.

"Now," Caro rasped, limbs twitching from the excess magic boiling up at her startlement, the ache following it, "that was the last time you'll get to do that, to anyone, I do hope I was worth it. . . ."

Carousel lunged, a knife in each hand—she and the Saint went down in a cloud of crows; Caro wouldn't even have been able to see the forest around her, if she'd looked up—but she didn't look up, readers, such the professional she was. She slayed the Saint under that fluttering black, peeled herself from its slack form and immediately felt better, even though she was stinging as she rose, victorious, having to keep somewhat of a hold on the Birds; her day was not yet over.

The crows cawed, still swirling around her as she stood, as she tilted her head back to search for the sky.

"Alice!" Carousel called. "Oh, you saw what I just saw, didn't you? Don't get so caught up in all those memories—I'm not."

Icca, the hospital, and Tecca, and Icca, and her parents' funeral. Carousel had been so many people. A sick child, a grieving orphan, a lovestruck girl. What was she now, with her head dropped back, so used to the steady corrosion of her magic, of her youth?

Her favorite self, certainly.

A butcher. An arrogant bitch. A witch, flocked with her crows, knowing exactly how strange and delightful her power was.

"But you know not to put too much stake in memories," Caro said to whichever of Icca's ears was listening. "Else we already would have dropped everything by now, yes? You wouldn't be here, in this prison, refracted and sieging a city. I wouldn't be about to cut your head off. Don't send another Saint—what if it does end up killing me? You'd feel a little left out of my death, wouldn't you? Aren't you glad, I didn't die on the holiday, that you get another chance at it? Come on, darling, come out and right your wrongs!"

Caro looked through the veil of the crows, peering for an influenced Saint skittering from the dark of the foliage, and saw not a one. Icca had gotten the message, then.

Really—Caro knew Icca wouldn't be able to resist. This ended with them.

Carousel knelt down on the green earth, dispelled her Birds, for now, besides her watchers. Now she had at least a minute, before the sickly little dark witch came gliding out from the shadows. This felt right, the stillness before their final fight. Caro dropped her brow to the moss to drink in her gods.

They wouldn't mind that she grinned as she did so; Carnage especially liked her excitement, of course.

THIRTY-NINE

Year Zero Zero Ninety, Autumn Season

There Are 1087 Remaining Saints

HATTIE KNEW SHE COULD leave if she wished, but for a time attempted to sate herself by gazing out the window of the tower study.

First lay the lush teeming of the Petra Woods, the sweeping stoic roofs of the University buildings half swallowed by the foliage, and past that, the sprawl of the city proper—the residents of which would have already heard the news of the White Queen Delcorta October Kkul's death, but not necessarily of Hattie's imprisonment in the tower following. She had not yet been crowned the Red Queen in a proper coronation, and thus still held, formally, the title of the Red Princess, but Hattie—on her knees in the velvet of the desk-chair in order to do such peering—had already brushed the banner away in her head. The moment upon Delcorta's demise, the Red Princess was no more; oh, dear readers, how Hattie was so certain, and furthermore, *must* be certain, that little Hattie was no more.

Hattie November Kkul was the Red Queen.

She'd had Delcorta's blessing in it, even if there were certain members of the Thia Court who believed otherwise. Thus Il-Hyun's insistence that she resign herself to the tower, as an act of good faith for her Court, until things could be "sorted out," so he said.

Which means, really, they did not know what to make of Hattie. Could this mild-mannered young woman have really committed matricide in order to ascend to the throne? And the Red Princess and the White Queen had seemed so viciously close, too.

Hattie had not opened her mouth to say to any of them that, if she'd particularly wanted to, she could have easily made those who discovered Delcorta's body be ignorant of her watching from the top of the tower-study stairs. She did not say that she could, of course, take the throne by force. This had to be played out in a more delicate way.

Well, it did not *have* to be, of course, dearest readers. Hattie November Kkul's ascension to the throne as the Red Queen of Isanghan could have been the most shocking, carnage-ingrained event since the creation of the Saints, but Hattie preferred order; more so, she preferred people to be unsure of her. Uncertainty could be wielded as a tool in and of itself; the smear between fear and reverence birthed less-volatile loyalties.

"Suggest to them the Labyrinth," Hattie had thus mentioned offhandedly to Il-Hyun, too busy in her own head to give him, or this matter, her full attention. Ever since Delcorta's death, Hattie had been trying to decide if she actually existed. It was such a difficult thing to prove.

"What?"

"If they want to see if I have a death trace, if I killed my mother, it would be a way to do it. Even my sense-magic wouldn't be able to make me invisible to them if I'm truly a Jabberwocky. It's more efficient than sending me out to Wonderland—closer quarters."

Il-Hyun had smoothed a hand down his weary face, sending his glasses halfway down his nose, which was a very regal nose indeed. "Closer . . . quarters. For the Saints to find you."

"Drawn by the death trace. Should I have one."

"They'd just find you anyway."

"Perhaps."

"No one has ever survived. You know this."

"But, if I do live, it would solidify the Thia Court's confidence in me. Even if it's not enough to convince all of them I'm innocent, then it'll at least prove that I'm witch enough to rule." Which might be the more important of the two. She paused, mired in two conversations: the one going on in her head and the one outside of it. "And if I survive, then I'll marry you. Your family has great pull in the Court. That will be an act of good faith, too."

"Gods, November."

Was she being cruel to him? Cruel to his heart? Half of her wanted to check his expression and the other half knew it didn't matter, and this latter part of her claimed victory immediately. She'd sat still and waited for his answer.

Hattie was Queen, and only the gods reigned over her; Logic, she supposed, was one she found Divinity in.

"All right," he said, and Hattie knew he, like the rest of them, was unsure if Hattie had done the deed. If she'd truly pushed Delcorta over the edge, to her death. But still Il-Hyun had come to see her. Still he held gentleness in his voice when he said, "I will bring the idea to them. But you must stay here, in the tower, November, please."

Hattie had shown no complaints.

She was still . . . getting used to all of it. The thought of being alone.

The thought of being some other self, now—but wasn't that going to happen regardless? Delcorta had been ill for a while now. She was going to die, sooner rather than later, and leave little Hattie all alone either way. Little Hattie had been destined to change, either way.

And it had been her idea, after all, to make the transformation so—total. So complete that the Red Princess was obliterated, and now the person who sat in Hattie's skin on Hattie's mother's chair was no one but the Red Queen, coronation or not, possessing the love of her people or not.

Past the stone patchwork of the city streets rose the Labyrinth. Rose the tips of the trees within it, and, of course, beyond that, those of Wonderland Forest.

Even from here, Hattie could feel its pull, its unquiet sprawl.

She'd never been able to hear it before Delcorta had died. It didn't used to whisper to her so. There was the proof, then. She had become someone else.

Somewhere in that Forest, of course, readers, it had been a handful of days since our darling Carousel Rabbit and Iccadora Alice Sickle had gone their separate ways, unknowing that the White Queen had been found crumpled at the base of the tower, that the Red Queen—who, around a year later, would wander to the Church Off the Labyrinth to remove their death traces—had been found at the top of the spiral stairs, believed to be responsible for Delcorta's graphic death.

But there would be no evidence to be found.

Evidence didn't matter. The Saints would serve as the final judges, jury, and executioners. Of course, the Saints found everyone guilty, but if she truly had the death trace, within the close quarters of the Labyrinth, they'd find her with such frenzy even she would not be able to stop them.

And days later, after hours of mediation and thinking and inventorying, Hattie would decide to be done with her time in the tower. There was too much to do. She'd write a note to Il-Hyun telling him to notify the Thia Court of where she'd gone, that she'd leave one shoe outside the Labyrinth gates and the other within to prove she'd entered. She'd bleed her magic and coax the guards who came to deliver her dinner that night to unlock her door. She'd go down the spiral steps, past the spot where Delcorta's blood still marred the stonework, and she'd remove her shoes at the threshold of the palace gates.

And she'd move for the Labyrinth.

Three days, she'd written Il-Hyun. *Three days and if I don't come knocking on the gates, I'm dead and guilty. If I do, I'm innocent and the rightful Queen.*

Some of the Thia Court might not believe it was enough. Hattie herself certainly wouldn't have bought it, knowing the witch that she was. But this was about image. If she survived the Labyrinth, she would be the first, and she'd emerge, perhaps covered in carnage, perhaps holding one shoe. She would not smile, and she would not run from the horrors that she knew she'd be leaving behind.

Hattie would put one foot in front of the other, and look over everyone who stood there awaiting her return.

And watch them bow.

FORTY

YEAR ZERO ZERO NINETY-FOUR, WINTER SEASON

THERE ARE 993 REMAINING SAINTS

ICCA WAS NOT particularly impressed—Icca was not really only Icca, now, yes, but she was sure she was not particularly impressed with Carousel's display.

Icca, of course, could kill the crow witch while she prayed, waiting for Icca herself to come along—although, dear readers, an attentive narrator does observe there has been a quantity of *coulds*, by now—kneeling like she wasn't a capitalistic heretic on the Labyrinth floor. But Icca didn't want it like that. She wanted Carousel Rabbit on her feet before Icca knocked her down. She wanted Caro looking at her when Icca plucked the Light from her eyes, so she could see it bleed away, like rainwater sucked down through gravel. Then—she wanted to eat her alive?

"Not really," Icca reminded herself, thumping the heel of her hand against her temple as she made her way through the woods—it was amusing to her that she hadn't gotten too turned around in this so-called Labyrinth; of course, it had been something of a tourist trap before King

Min Titus's time, and its scale kept it from being too convoluted, so, really, what had been the appeal of it without the Saints...?

With that thought, Icca felt a pang of longing for Wonderland.

And then she squashed it down the second after, because what a ridiculous thing, to wish for something for the horror of it. Yet still, for a moment, her feet paused and her hands wrung and wrung, and once again she looked behind her and around her, feeling horribly claustrophobic and very wrong indeed. To have trapped part of the Forest like *this*—and to have thought to *privatize* Wonderland as a tourist attraction, all those decades ago! At least now, she hadn't had to pay to get in.

Though the thought was hardly comforting.

Icca thumped her hand against her head again and forced her feet to move.

She needed to remember very clearly and constantly that she was leaned into Hana's head, and it was the Saint that was seeing Caro pray, and the Saint that wanted to gobble up Caro.

Icca was seeing... Icca focused to see what she was actually seeing.

Forest, and the rise of the Labyrinth Walls, her gods, the Dark and the Light, eased up against everything, as usual. Watching herself watching Carousel—kind of. She really was getting cloudy-headed.

"What do we know?" she murmured. "What do I know? That I don't usually talk to myself, aloud. That's good, to recognize it, so what else... once upon a time—what?"

Icca breathed in.

"No, that's right. That fits; I like to read. I like the stories that start like that. Which of me—which of you don't? Didn't? You're fucking dull. Where was I...? Once upon a time there was a young girl named Alice. She followed Rabbit into Wonderland, because I was in love. Very much so. Now I'm not. Now I've got to kill the Rabbit, and send the Saints up and over—don't you see your dearest Red Queen is mad, having your shield so swollen with monsters? Coming to *pray* in such a place... not that I believe it to be true. *I* certainly don't find *my*—well. But *my* gods are everywhere. Just—please don't forget what this world is at its heart. Please remember how hungry I am—I mean, *it* is—damn it." She scrubbed at her face. "Once upon a time, Alice hunted Rabbit through a forest, which was a Labyrinth, which was a prison, which was a protection, which was her harvesting ground. . . ."

Shadows stretched toward Icca's feet as she stalked along, greedy things, or perhaps curious things—whenever she was riled up they tended to come crawling along more hastily. Now, Icca came upon the small clearing where Carousel knelt, under the blue bruise of the fading daylight. It was raining steadily now, drops light and thin like clipped threads. Caro lifted her chin, water trickling down her temples. Icca pulled back her hood and took another step forward.

"You're quite late, Alice," Caro cooed.

Icca thought it might be true. She was having an awful time—keeping track of it, that was. "You're right. I should've finished this ages ago."

Caro rose, shaking out her cloak, one tattooed arm fluttering from the black folds to extend at her side, the other palm pressing to her chest as she bowed low—the start to a true gentlemen's battle. Icca did not return it.

"Your Queen's taught you all the formalities, has she?"

"I might like Wonderland for the change of pace and the wholeness of my gods, but yes, Icky, I've learned lots, in the highest rafters of society." Caro peered at her intently. "What have you learned, preferring yourself a feral Forest creature? It *is* rather pious of you, but I wonder the long-term damages it might do to your head." Then Caro gestured seemingly vaguely around the Labyrinth arched around them, though most likely to the pair of Saints Icca had waiting in the deeper shadows. "Well. I guess I don't have to wonder, actually. What is your purpose here, again?" Caro gave another condescending wave of her hand, tattooed fingers catching rainwater. "Right, right. You're bored and you're a narcissist, and you have power you can wield and so you are."

And, readers, Caro was right, mostly. Icca didn't care about being good, or being bad, much alike to her deities, and all Their other Selves. She was the magic she possessed, and she really did like how it felt. To let everything spill up and over, to burn down within her own power—all the witches who couldn't relish the sting were dead by now, or worse, mediocre.

But there was one point besides that. And the fact that Caro seemed to have missed it, seemed to keep missing it, made Icca boil.

"And Tecca," Icca murmured. "This is for Tecca, too."

"It was a *lifetime* ago, Icca!" Oh, and Icca had been mistaken; the crow witch's voice and the anger in her expression was so quick to rise. Rabbit had been waiting for this. "A whole reign ago; Hattie's building up the Walls in the Wards, but it's a bit difficult and slow-going, you know, because there's a couple or so Saints in Wonderland; you know the Forest is *massive*—"

"I don't care!" Icca laughed, spreading her arms wide. "Her bloodline's to blame; your precious unnie is still creating monsters." Icca paused. "She's not what everyone thinks she is. There's someone else who holds her power."

Caro cackled, clearly disbelieving. "Okay? So you're going after them, next, is it?"

"I damn well intend to find out who they are. I'll act accordingly when I do."

"By all means! Be the jury, be the executioner. Be the Queen, and judge their black hearts and knock them down, one by wicked one, Alice, so you can live all alone with your own in your chest." Caro's tone had changed; it was light, and she was singing her words, but she was also bleeding her magic; she was laughing, and the foliage was teeming with crows. "Take mine, first, then! It's one of the darkest you'll find out there. It's night, it's ink, and best of all, it matches yours perfectly!"

Icca's vision flashed silver.

And then she was covered with birds.

Icca slashed an enchantment across them, felt them go off as a chain reaction, crows corroding in their own lightless spots even as their talons were under her skin. They sloughed away and she opened her eyes, and past the glow of her magic Caro was descending from the distant crack of sky above, from the swirl of her dying animals. But her knives met only earth; Icca was spilling out of the end of Caro's shadow, trailing shortly behind her heels in the fleeing daylight, so close when Icca rose that she could have tilted her chin up and been kissing the nape of Caro's neck.

Icca knocked the crow witch forward, and down.

Caro twisted on the earth as Icca went to drive her own knife between Caro's ribs, and from the ends of the crow witch's knuckles glinted bone-talons. One pair caught Icca's blade and wrenched it right, knocking it soundlessly into the forest; Icca put her full weight on her knee and sent it into Caro's stomach. Caro made a choked sound before she planted her palms in the earth and threw her legs up and back, sending Icca tumbling over her head. She landed hard as Carousel nimbly continued the roll backward, her knees to the ground before she was up and off of it.

Caro hadn't even lifted her chin fully before she was snapping her knee around, catching Icca directly in the cheekbone. Icca's vision snapped from silver-stained to a dead-quiet night, bursting with white stars.

She reached forward, blindly, sending a nearby shadow stretching for her fingertips—Caro's boot crushed her wrist. Her vision was returning, but she was unfocused and still had her consciousness scattered over a dozen other bodies, and she saw woods and the Labyrinth Wall and—Petra streets!—before it fixed correctly, in her own head, and she saw Caro's knife flash against the dusk, tip angled beside the split of her grin. Her hand was around Icca's throat.

"I've made the Wall," Icca scraped out. Caro rolled her eyes.

"And this was so ridiculously easy because of it, dummy. You're here, but you're also there, and there. . . ."

Icca tasted blood and her magic, welling at the back of her throat with nowhere to go. She tried to speak again, her hands clawing at the talon-lined fingers crushing her windpipe.

Caro leaned in enthusiastically, knife still hovering by her ear, twisting in practiced, excited fingers. "What was that? A last word, for me, Alice? Let's hear it."

Once upon a time, Alice followed Rabbit into Wonderland. *What do you get when you have two witches with violent tendencies in love, and you take away the love?* Alice still liked Rabbit's face, the press of her skin, the strangeness of her magic, because she was powerful and thus often bored, and whether it was love or hatred between them, it was always electric, and entertaining for it. *You get two witches with violent tendencies.* What horror, what horror... Alice still wanted Rabbit in her head, even if Rabbit lost hers. Even if it was Alice taking it away.

"And there," Icca rasped.

And the dusk was blocked out by flesh, and by teeth.

The Saint ripped Carousel off of Icca.

Icca clawed away from Caro's kicking feet and lay there spasming on the earth, choking on the influx of air. Her skin was flushed, face a mess with tears and magic and blood, but still she twisted and squinted through it to behold the glorious sight of Dul with its four hands clamped on Caro's arms. Icca's mouths—Dul's mouths were salivating from their angled places on its cheeks, snapping as Carousel shrieked and kicked to get away. The air thickened again with feathers, but Icca didn't care; Dul would let itself be picked down to the bone and it still wouldn't let go of Caro, simply because Icca didn't want it to let go.

"You said—" Caro gasped, her panic full and bright now, magic flecking at her cuticles. "You said no Saints—"

"I didn't," said Icca, the words throbbing up her half-crushed throat. Why wouldn't she use a Saint? It was fair game enough; it was, after all, somewhat Icca herself....

"This is it? You're just going to let it eat me?" Caro was incredulous. Then it seemed her curiosity got the better of her. "Will you feel it doing so? Is its hunger your very own, then, maybe, I'd have to be less *totally fucking pissed*—"

"Obviously it's not eating you, Rabbit," Icca breathed. "Who said anything about it eating you?"

And, oh, Icca savored this part, when Caro heard the grin in her voice, when the crow witch snapped her head back to look, black eyes wide over the cut of her shoulder. Caro couldn't mean to look so entirely terrified; it was just something she could not help. Icca liked that. She liked seeing it click for Caro; that, at least for now, Icca hadn't been intending to kill her at all. Not yet.

Icca reached into her cloak. She pulled out the harvested petals, their coating black, their velvet beneath a silver all her own. She was so entirely thrilled about this next bit that, as Caro's crows came screaming for her, Icca barely had to think about corroding them in their own Darkness, dropping them straight out of the air. Her path, these next few steps, was fixed.

Icca thought it, and Dul flattened Carousel to the ground. Icca knelt below the arch of Dul's massive torso, keeping out the rain, and pinched Caro's nose until she opened her mouth, and pushed the petals down her throat.

Caro choked, limbs and cheeks white with her terror. And then she tried to bite Icca's fingers off, but was startled away by Icca's other palm against her temple, freeing the blond curls glazed beneath her sweat, the movement gentle. Icca meant to be gentle. Carousel on her stomach, Icca lying down on her side so that they could only look at each other, under the canopy of Saint. Her hand had stilled on Caro's cheek, thumb to the end of the scar she'd carved over the crow witch's eye.

"Geokjeongma." *Don't worry.* No, she wouldn't want Rabbit to worry. . . .

"I'll still try to hate you," promised Icca quietly, as she felt yet another edge of herself began to blur. She wouldn't have trouble keeping her word; she was already so many other bodies, and still she lacked sympathies for them. What was one more monster on top of it? "I know you'd think it an insult, if I thought of you bittersweetly, just because I won."

FORTY-ONE

YEAR ZERO ZERO NINETY-FOUR, WINTER SEASON

THERE ARE 989 REMAINING SAINTS

START OVER. Hattie needed to start over.

She pinched her forefinger and thumb together and used this point to draw a line across the air. The Saint before her unraveled—first into its original two bodies and then into a heap of slick parts, rolling across the already-slick cobblestones of the dungeon cell. She kept the heads attached to their spinal cords, of course, so they still were alive, blinking at her, while she contemplated.

Hattie shuffled their parts. Hattie tried again.

The Saint rose anew. But no, Hattie didn't like this version, either. Took it apart. Put it back together. What was wrong? What did it matter? All she needed was a handful of beasts to clobber the ones Iccadora planned to send over the Wall. They didn't need to be beautiful—they were never beautiful, of course—but they were lacking their usual synergy. She was missing the meditation of it. Her head felt so loud. Again she dismantled the Saint with a sigh.

Hattie had been restless, creatively blocked, ever since she'd ended the holiday early. Ever since Iccadora had disappointed her so. She hadn't felt quite like herself, misplacing her curiosity, her joy in her arts. Every Saint she pinched together was the same nothingness incarnate, over and over again. Void feeding into void. Hunger feeding into hunger.

They never appreciated what they were, how miraculous it was to exist so strangely.

And so Hattie was haunted by who Iccadora and Carousel could've become, if she'd sewn them together. She was haunted by the art that she knew existed within her own soul that would never become tangible; she would never grace it with her fingertips and feel so seen. But love needed to be present between them for such a process. If it wasn't, Hattie knew the girl they'd become would come out so—ordinary. Self-loathing, flinching away from her own thoughts. She wouldn't be able to hear Wonderland over her own self-chatter, she'd fear its shadowed depths, which Hattie knew, would really only be her own shadowed depths. . . .

Hattie reordered limbs. She rolled and tilted and smushed heads, threaded ribs. Then there was a new thing hissing at her and she leaned back against the wall, sweat-soaked, breathing hard. Gods, how she hated it, the beast. And it hurt Hattie so, to hate her creation.

Il-Hyun would have been telling her to slow down, now, Hattie recalled, the memory tinged with fondness.

And then it was gone, replaced by the memory of the fullness of her own gut, after Iccadora's summoned Saint had swallowed Hattie's magic-painted roses in the courtyard. After it had swallowed Il-Hyun.

Hattie knew what it was like, now, to eat someone alive.

She flinched as a particularly full bout of her power swelled up, so harshly her magic splattered both wall and disassembled body parts. For a moment she stood there, watching what had been inside of her glimmer against what was around her.

She remembered it had soothed her, to take Cheshire's eyes out of his head. To be somewhere else, like this. So she drifted away from her work, up the corridor toward his cell.

He shrank from her immediately when she opened the door. But Hattie found she could only look at him tiredly.

Hattie could always feel, if she focused, the roots of Wonderland shot underside Petra. Feel the Saints in her Labyrinth skittering over them, over, over, over... The first of them had just gone over the Labyrinth Wall....

She sighed. How perfectly ridiculous it all was.

"It's such a particularly cruel magic, the roses," spoke Hattie. "She's just getting further and further away from herself...."

"Just nasty work, Your Majesty," crowed Cheshire. He didn't understand. But perhaps you could, dear readers, you who know how our Hattie November Kkul thoroughly enjoyed her magic. She knew in full the existential art that was transduction morphology, the ability to borrow or wear or influence another form's senses or physicality. But Hattie was always herself when she did so—she very much liked being herself all the time. Other forms were cloaks, handkerchiefs she kept in her pockets, pieces of fabric lined up before her: items distinct from herself.

But Hattie hadn't worn the Saint in the courtyard, after it had eaten her roses. She'd blurred into it.

"Will Iccadora stop," murmured Hattie, "when she feels herself fraying?"

Despite herself, the thought filled Hattie with the strangest feeling of longing. What would *that* be like, to fray so completely? She didn't want to lose any part of herself, but to come undone, to dissolve without moving, just breathe and breathe until she forgot she had lungs and a body, until she was simply *being* instead of being *something*?

How she breathed and breathed when she was in the Labyrinth, waiting for it to happen. Waiting to be so whole. To be everything else.

But she knew it would never happen there.

And for a moment she let herself imagine it. Rising from the dungeon floor, out of the palace and out of the Woods, past the city in havoc, past the rise of the Labyrinth, until she was standing before the mouth of Wonderland. How it would greet her as an old friend, and she'd smile and remind the trees and the earth and the roots, *We haven't all met before*, and they'd chatter back, *Are you sure, darling girl, are you sure*, and she'd say . . .

"No," said Cheshire.

Hattie appreciated this truth. Then she said, "Now. Hold still."

—

Kai felt his eyes being fed back into his sockets, and he gasped down the damp dungeon air. He was slack on the ground. Looking up at Hattie November Kkul leaning her small frame thoughtfully on the ajar cell door—ajar so as to break the magic-suppressing runes on the bars, and etched across the floor to match. So that she could break him.

He felt absolutely sick at the sight of her, the quietness of her expression, like she had not just peeled his sight away down to its slick, diving roots.

"Iccadora left her alive," murmured Hattie finally, and wiped at the magic dribbling from her nostrils. "Alive . . ."

"I don't care. Fuck Sickle. Good gods. I never should have come."

Kai heard himself croak a laugh. He was too violated to retain his groveling. Groveling would do nothing. He was barely there to Hattie. Just like he'd been barely there to Icca. These fucking witches, existing on entirely other planes, and everyone else rendered toys. Hattie had clearly not even heard him. Kai, on the other hand, had heard her. For hours upon hours now—the wet tearing of skin.

"I think they might really be in love." So casual and quiet as she said this, dreamily, with her hands folded over her stomach, as if her palms and dress were not slick with black blood, glinting in the dull light.

And then the Queen smiled, actually smiled, and it even looked a little shy, and Kai thought, *She's crazy, she's off her fucking rocker...*

"Well," Hattie November murmured in her small way, when she had effectively turned over whatever was in her head. She wiped her brow with the back of her hand as she closed the cell door once more, and made to return to her projects up the hall. "Back to it, then."

FORTY-TWO

YEAR ZERO ZERO NINETY-FOUR, WINTER SEASON

THERE ARE 988 REMAINING SAINTS

CAROUSEL BLINKED AWAKE on the Labyrinth floor to find Icca on the ground before her, convulsing, with her eyes spinning in her head.

Good. Caro rolled onto her back and ignored her.

Night had settled fully. Caro tried to breathe in the stillness of it before the nausea ruptured in her gut and she was back with her cheek to the earth, trying to keep it level.

"Oh, don't feel good, not good," she slurred. Icca was still twitching a few feet away; they were generally where they had been when Icca had made Caro swallow the petals, when Caro's vision had gone Dark.

Despite her nausea, Caro took quick inventory. She could move her hands all on her own, could still feel her skin when she pinched it, watching the flesh darken at her insistence. She had such gorgeous flesh. It was no wonder that Icca had wanted to control it. It was also no wonder that she'd ultimately failed—gorgeous flesh can only be commanded by a gorgeous mind, and Caro imagined that Icca's had the damp-and-dreary quality of a moldy cave, especially after all the monsters she'd been allowing to trudge through it.

Caro recalled the stitched Saint that had arched over them prior to her loss of consciousness—where had it wandered off to?

"That one was an ugly one, unnie," she murmured as she dragged herself to Icca's side. "They're usually ugly—you usually leave them with only two eyes, and you like to knot the torsos. This one must've been from when you were a messy child. I can't picture you a messy child.

"Alice." Caro shook her arm, found a heartbeat in the wrist that was light and fluttering. "Look at my head—I still have it! You were trying to control me, and look where it's gotten you. What did you expect? Don't you remember? I've kissed you so tenderly—I've drunk down your magic before, dear, and you mine. . . ." Caro knelt, her brow on the line of Icca's shoulder, as another wave of nausea hit her before continuing. "And roses are roses—it's just that Saint blood that's making me ill. I'll get over it. Are you twitching because you're collapsing under all of your other consciousnesses?"

Caro freed her smallest knife from her boot, and went to cut Icca's throat when it was clear she wouldn't be able to reciprocate a proper conversation. It was dull because Caro was so entirely ill she could barely focus on how much she was about to enjoy it.

But the Labyrinth was wholly quiet. Caro sat back on her heels, and after pushing down the desire to hurl, lifted her head to glance around. She had no more crows attached to her, but she could still sense them there, in the trees, feel out their mood. The Birds always knew first, when Saints were about.

They felt docile—about as docile as the skittish things could be—and moreover, Caro couldn't hear the *thunk, thud, thunk* of Icca's Saints throwing themselves against the Wall. They'd made it over, then, into Petra. Perhaps they had scalded themselves all the way up the runework only to fall three hundred feet over the opposite side, and all the Culled Court Jabberwockies were on cleanup duty instead of fighting them off.

But Saints tended to be durable. And there was no telling how much brutalizing Hattie's created ones could take. There was a reason no one made it out of the Labyrinth.

"Oh! Besides me," Carousel chirped, and began to gather up Icca. The other witch wavered on her feet, and when her eyelids fluttered, Caro saw only white. She traced a thoughtful fingertip against the rune ribboning Icca's neck. "You won't be able to use magic outside of the Labyrinth, Alice dear; that's the only reason I'm bringing you out. Well, the second reason—I think I have to bring you out instead of killing you; I'm not sure if Hattie will be able to put down your Saints, but you sure as deities can."

Icca was not making her kidnapping easy. She was on her feet, but it was almost useless; her entire weight listed against Caro. Caro, with one of Icca's arms slung around her shoulder, patted Icca's cheek as they limped along toward the entrance, dipping into crows every once in a while to see that they were heading in the right direction.

Caro's head was cloudy from the disorienting runes on the Labyrinth Walls—but only a bit more than usual, which she figured was probably clearer than most of the population, boring lot as they were. It would be different if she sported the same rune Icca now wore, these enchantments working only as a matched set, if Caro recalled Madam Killington's dull geometric runework class—Wall runes as the charge, and skin runes to render the person a lightning rod. Luckily for Icca, the Labyrinth runes didn't repel their wearer from the Walls—some of the passages here were narrower, and it wouldn't be any fun, Caro figured, if the sentenced Jabberwockies died by being singed down in a slimmer bit of maze, rather than being eaten alive.

Caro recalled when she'd first passed through the Petra Ward Walls, making for the Church Off the Labyrinth to get her Wonderland rune removed, along a thin, bone-lined footpath marked for incoming Jabberwockies. Every step had stung her, and if she'd laid one toe over a femur, the shock from the rune would've shaken her to dust. She'd waited for Hattie on the church dais, bowed when the Red Queen came in at the message sent by its Priest, that another witch had beaten Wonderland.

Caro hadn't wanted to bow; she'd kicked herself for bowing as an instinctive thing, until she'd been around Petra for a bit, and learned that Hattie didn't care at all what she did or did not do.

Caro was sure Icca hadn't bowed. Was even more sure that Icca hadn't followed Hattie home.

And so what? Caro was sure Icca didn't bow to a lot of things that Caro did: to her closet, or to the walls of her apartment when the Light hit the pictures right, or to the trinkets that *did* (every now and then) feel like conversing, to be polite and to encourage them further; to particularly rosy Dawns, of course. And as for following Hattie . . . well. It had become clear that Icca didn't need anyone, had never needed anyone, content with her books and with her great plans and her greater view of herself. Caro supposed she . . . well, she didn't certainly *need* anyone, either, what with all her occasionally talking trinkets, but she wasn't so dull that she pretended she didn't *like* company, didn't dote on Hattie or chatter with another Jabberwocky or nobleperson of the Thia Court when she saw them in the street (until they told her to go away, or fell into an unnerved silence when crows inevitably started to gather).

It was funny how, until Icky Sickle's presence had showed back up again, much like a poorly handled termite problem, Carousel hadn't realized she'd still be toting around some fragment of the idea that she and Icca were one and the same. Even the reason they'd split in Wonderland had supported that. But now Icca was doing things Caro wouldn't dare mess around with, that she couldn't have begun to think up. At a younger age, it would've fascinated her further. She probably would've regarded what Icca was doing so dreamily that eventually she would've found some part of herself that also yearned to move in the same deliciously despicable direction. But perhaps there shone some other truth in that, too. That to find oneself in another wasn't some rare, serendipitous feat of fate—just the evidence that someone changed, maybe without even realizing it, that they were shifting over parts of themselves to allow this other presence more room. Undoing the nails of floorboards, knocking down walls. When it was all set and over with, what did the original house even look like? More wretched, surely, one must think, one surely *had* to think, since it was impossible to put things back to where they'd been.

Partially the reason Caro felt such fascination around Hattie was that she was sure Hattie hadn't ever moved around any part of herself for anyone else. Caro imagined where others might sit in her head—as portraits on some wall, neat and orderly in their frames, which Hattie did visit every now and then, but otherwise she was busy building halls and libraries and dungeons, her own private Labyrinth.

"Alice," Carousel sang, nudging Icca, whose head was lopped on her shoulder. "This is really helping me, actually. I was still thinking you were pretty, you know, but feared it was more than a logistical observation. Now you're leaning on me, and we could be dancing, and—I would still think you're pretty, of course, I do have eyes—and I would hate you all the same. What relief! Let's try it, dancing, actually." Caro looped Icca's twitching wrist in her grip and sent her other arm around Icca's waist, and tried to spin. It did not work. Icca folded over limply, and Caro almost emptied her stomach at the movement and had to take a moment to set them both upright again before continuing along. "Well. That was embarrassing. But you're barely there as it is, so worth the try, at least… Oh! We've arrived."

The gate had come up on them rather quickly—or Carousel's head was an ounce foggier than she'd thought. She almost sent them crashing into it. Momentarily, she slouched her back against the metal, eyes weeping her magic, and blinked into the gutter crow she'd had wait for her on the other side. Thus then she was standing in a gutter, looking out over her bird-feet and under the roof of the guardhouse. Empty. All the guards must be preoccupied, what with the chaos and all. Hattie had needed to take these dramatic precautions, it seemed, with the lockdown; though as Carousel peered about, it'd been perhaps a bit useless in practice. She just saw the heels of a Saint, flesh burned with Wall runes, kicking in the pastel-blue shutters of some penthouse up the street before it disappeared inside.

Caro fluttered through the window of the guardhouse and found the key on its hook. With some fiddling she fit it into the gate lock, rolled out of the crow, and blinked back to Icca's deep brown irises looking up at her, glazed as they both slouched against the gate.

Caro was glad this was the moment she was conscious—viciously, she gathered up the front of the dark witch's cloak and breathed, "Alice, your Saints better not touch my stuff. If they fuck up my hardwood floors there'll be hell to pay."

Icca's lips parted, half-blue, like a forget-me-not sprouting new in the springtime—of course, readers, Caro surely was only peering at them out of her raw battle instinct, she reassured herself, and was bolstered in this line of thought when she glimpsed a moonlike flash of her magic somewhere down Icca's mouth. Caro promptly shoved open the gate and dumped Icca over its threshold, kicking it shut before hauling her back to her feet.

"Whew, that was close!" Caro exclaimed, shaking Icca a bit, for fun. Silver foamed at the corners of the dark witch's mouth, but she did not melt out of Caro's grip, into the shadows pooled at their boots. Caro glanced around. "But you still have control over the Saints, it seems?"

That made sense. The Labyrinth rune sealed a witch's metaphysical abilities within its Walls, but this influencing magic was acting on a higher plane: playing at consciousness, profound (non?)individual existence, or whatnot, or whatever.

"I don't see why you'd dilute yourself, Alice," mused Caro, as their boots began to move over cobblestones. It seemed that the chaos was northward—the streets were curved and obstructed her view, but Carousel could hear the clamor and the shrieks and the like as they moved deeper into the city. "Well, I guess I would, if I were you. I'd be bored with myself enough, too, then, to split myself as you've done."

"Of course you don't understand," Icca murmured.

"Oh, *No one understands me, no one could ever understand me*—the edginess of it! Does it ever get old?"

"Plenty of people could understand me." Icca's voice was dry and quiet. "Just not you, Rabbit. Not now. So there's no use in you contemplating it."

Caro stopped walking. Now they were standing in the middle of the street. She found herself missing the Forest; here, the buildings crept up to the gray of the sky. The lockdown kept the Petra population out of the streets, but the stillness of the city was different from the stillness in Wonderland. There weren't many witches in the Forest—a strange collection of bounty hunters, Jabberwockies, Saints, gods—but Caro could feel them here, in Petra, unmoving behind their walls to wait out the breach. It wasn't so much sensing a thrum to the air as noticing the absence of one.

"But I used to," Carousel said, unsure why she'd paused them, or why this seemed to be an important thing to note—no, she did know why. It had been important. Just because they hated each other now, it didn't mean they couldn't have once meant everything to one another—more monstrous transformations had happened in Isanghan. Caro's words tumbled from her. "I understood you in full, Alice." If Icca was pretending that hadn't been the case—how could Icca pretend that?

But Caro turned her cheek to find that Icca had fixed her with a startled look. It was a peculiar moment, Icca's surprise knocking Carousel into her own, and for a beat of silence they stood there staring at each other, before Icca said, "Yes? I know?"

Caro couldn't help but chuckle at her bewildered tone, in a lost sort of way. "What?"

Now Icca just looked irritated, her brow scrunched up, like Caro could press the edge of a coin into one of the lines and have it stay upright. "What? Why did you say it like I didn't know? I know. I knew. Obviously."

Caro cracked a grin. *Obviously.* "Oh. Well, why couldn't I understand you now? I'm quite varied in my empathies."

"Because I don't want you to understand me now." It could have been cruel; it *was* cruel in practice, but Caro knew that was a side effect and not Icca's purpose—she had answered the question with full honesty.

"You're missing out. Unnie says I'm good company."

"The Red Queen enjoys questionable things to begin with."

"Ah, she's an odd duck, but don't hold it against—"

Caro snapped her head up.

She could hear it. Something was moving up around the curl of the street. The cobblestones carried its hiss.

"Just as well," Caro chirped at a whisper now, beginning to move them once more. She put her lips to the shell of Icca's ear, so the girl could feel her grin. "I've got an Icky-pricky shield as it is."

But Icca was looking behind them as they moved up the block, the striped awnings of cafés drawing dull colors against the cut of her cheekbones. It was clear one of her Saints was trailing behind, out of sight. Caro wasn't going to over-concern herself with it; now, she could just snap Icca's neck if she were about to get eaten down. It might not kill the Saint, but there had to be a moment of confusion at its conscious edge snapping away from that of Icca's—Caro often only needed a moment, a lucky shot.

"Rabbit."

"Almost there, Alice. I think I've been slow, but unnie's used to my being late, or she should be, by now. She'll want to watch me knock your head off good and proper."

"*Rabbit,*" Icca hissed, clawing at Caro's arm. "It's not mine."

"Your head? Oh, I know. *Obviously*, as you apparently say. What did you expect—"

"The *Saint*, Carousel!"

"The—" Caro looked over her shoulder. The street was blank and quiet behind them. "Huh . . ."

Icca lurched her weight into Caro.

They went tumbling into the door of one of the bakeries, and, with the knob jabbing between the back of Caro's ribs, she saw the Saint hit the awning they'd been walking toward in a flurry of limbs, and tear through.

It landed with such force—because it had thrown itself from the rooftop with such force, Caro supposed—that now it lay still on the pavement. Caro gave it a once-over: head pushed down into its shoulders like a half-sunk seed, and those shoulders sprouted with another hand apiece, so that it would seem to cup its own cheeks tenderly—if not for the molar that rose at each finger-end instead of a nail, clicking into one another, now, rippling over its mouth and nose as a second jaw.

Good gods. She was far too pretty to be about to be eaten by the ugliest creature she'd ever seen.

On its ribs was stamped the 끌 brand, Caro saw, as it lifted its chin—and thus its body—and stared with vacant eyes at the two witches pressed into the arch of the entryway.

Silver glinted in Carousel's peripheral, but Icca's magic was locked up in the Labyrinth. And this was not her Saint. How could it not be her Saint? Had other Saints within the Labyrinth gotten wise, watching their brethren throwing themselves over the Wall? Sheep, all of them...

Carousel spoke very quietly. "Okay, so—"

The Saint lunged. Caro's hand was already on Icca's shoulder, and she sent them both dropping down; its hip or something knocked against her temple, but its weight smashed in full against the door, and obliterated it.

Caro could feel the weakness in her bones from whatever shit Icca had fed her—she couldn't outsprint the Saint; she had to take it down *now*. Her grasp left Icca and found her knives, and she started the line at the Saint's gut, drew it up, would draw it out... it revved up, a shin clattering against her stomach, and Caro was thrown into the bakery's small dining area. Chairs and a table scattered at her impact, shattering a display case, and she twisted to see the Saint already halfway up the opposite wall. It was bleeding black up the lavender-print wallpaper, joints already tensed to spring. Static pooled in her limbs; magic stung in bursts at her eyelids. It wouldn't be enough.

Caro had always thought she'd die in Wonderland, not in Petra, not in this perfectly adorable bakery that smelled, past the blood, of sweet red-bean paste, with mujigae-tteok smushing the broken glass of the display case in sticky-rice rainbows. She would've much preferred roots under her back than this pastel patchwork of tile, much rather have been closer to her gods.... The thought of it was a quick ache; Carousel was much too afraid to linger on it. Now her lips had parted; she'd said, "Well, fuck me," without intending it, but now realizing it had left her, liked how it was quiet, and to herself, and closed her eyes. She heard the wall crack as the Saint pushed from it.

And she was still alive.

And Icca was screaming from the street.

Carousel was on her feet. Now she could feel crows nearby, drawn to her panic. Like fingers dragging through Mist, Caro pulled them into her, their lightness, their heartbeat, the growth of their talons. Cradling her nausea, weighing it against the sting of her magic, she clattered from the bakery's front step and pointed, with a bone-lined finger, at the Saint lifting Icca clean off her heels.

Well. There was no accounting for poor taste.

"*Ya.* What, seriously—you really prefer her?" she snapped, and the crows chittered along with her. "If anyone's going to kill the bitch, it's going to be *me.*"

FORTY-THREE

Year Zero Zero Ninety-Four, Winter Season

There Are 988 Remaining Saints

THIS MADE TWICE in the past week that Icca had been picked up by a Saint like a cat carrying her kitten. She was wholly disgusted by it.

Feet braced against its broad chest to keep it from pushing her into its chattering finger-jaws, Icca again reached for her magic. It bubbled and stung uselessly in her empty molar beds; she could still feel the lean of the Dark all around her, but it resisted the hook of her enchantments. So instead Icca reached into the Saint's head and ripped out its eyes—not because it would help; the beast would still be able to smell her out just fine—but because she was really getting pissed, now.

And then there were more fucking Birds.

The Saint's grip loosened under their sharp, black cloud and Icca twisted away. She tried to catch herself, but her vision stuttered, and then rippled, like she was fanning out pages of a book . . . she was on another street, tearing apart a guard. No—she was in some apartment, throwing her weight against a door, shadows moving under its slit, silent in their terror and it didn't matter, she could still . . . She was underneath the pinking sky, in a mess of her own black blood, a Jabberwocky she'd glimpsed at the Tea grinning as he dug a knife into her throat.

With a gasp of effort, Icca pulled her own head back to the forefront. *Damn it.* She hadn't accounted for this. She'd clustered her Saints in the Labyrinth, but they'd dispersed in the city. They'd spread her thin.

Carousel was yanking Icca to her feet. Then her hands were on Icca's waist, wandering. Icca froze. They were only a few feet away from the Saint, shrieking under the thicket of Birds.

"What are you—"

Then Caro's hand retracted, and a weight left Icca's hip. "Robbing you. Again."

She saw in Caro's palm the book of her harvested petals and immediately lunged for it, even though she now knew they were why the Saint had peeled off Caro and shot for her, instead. She didn't care. She needed those roses, she needed *more—*

Caro tossed the bottle high and far.

The Saint, still tangled in crows, dropped to all fours and ran blindly in the direction its shattering rang from. Icca was momentarily stunned, and then her next coherent thought was of the single petal she'd stored away in her pocket. A kind of keepsake. She should have stashed them all. She should have sewn them to her form.

"You—" Icca began, a shriek to start, she was sure, but then her focus split again. It danced all over the city, into eleven different Saints before she remembered her body again, and by then, Caro had dragged them through the Petra palace gates. On instinct, Icca twisted and fell out of her arms.

Above her, Carousel scoffed.

Then she kicked Icca in the ribs and sent her off the side of the road, into the water of the flooded Petra Woods.

Icca gasped first at the cold, and then at the depth. Her toes didn't find ground—but that wasn't right, she'd seen the shallow bed of the water beneath the lanterns, when she and Kai had come through. She—what?

Oh.

Apologies, readers. It is hard keeping track of our Iccadora; she can hardly keep track of herself at this point—yes. Icca was Hana in a penthouse apartment, hanging from the rafters with its four hands, now, here was the dangling of her feet as she skittered toward the family huddled in the corner—and—yes. Here again. Icca was drowning.

Caro pulled her to the surface, barely submerged up to her knees, hand around the back of Icca's cloak as she shook her, laughed at her. Icca coughed, drank down air.

"Good gods," Caro hollered. "You really *are* completely out of it!"

Icca almost snapped at her then. *You nit. You don't even realize I've been pulling your strings this entire time, with those petals in your stomach,* but she held her tongue. They were only dozens of paces away from the palace entrance. And Icca was sorely wanting a word with the Red Queen.

Caro plucked Icca up and both went dripping up the path.

Icca could feel the strange, fine line that marked the edge of Caro's soul, easing along the border of Icca's own. It definitely felt different from being a Saint—Icca was far from being Carousel, she supposed, because Caro was much more alive than anything else Icca had attached herself to. That's what Icca had learned, over these past few days. She was influencing Saints, but she knew she was opening herself up to them in turn. This realization thus begged a more delicate practice with Caro—the Saints were nothing, shells; they could look at every piece of Icca and Icca wouldn't care, because they couldn't care.

But Icca was careful now, peering along that fine line of Carousel Rabbit, leaning on her thoughts just so. *Take Icca to the palace. I think Icca has to be alive to stop her Saints.* Those nudges had been easy, and Icca would've been hungering to force Caro into greater actions if it weren't so clear that Caro was, really, such a burden. Icca didn't doubt she could've had a dozen more Saints under her control without being reduced to the fraying mess she was currently, if she hadn't taken on Caro.

What would have it been like, years ago, when they'd both been convinced they were practically the same cruel, bored soul? Icca wouldn't be stumbling over thoughts of Caro's apartment, a place with big windows and a Dark, gleaming bathroom—Carousel missed it, so Icca missed it, soaking wet and shivering in the chilled air, missing the crackle of the fireplace—*where I burned her book*—the bitch. The bitch had burned her book. *And to think! She was supposed to be there with me*—what?

Icca glanced at Caro, whose expression betrayed nothing as she hauled Icca closer to the palace entrance. But Icca was in Caro's head, and so Icca saw. Saw a flash of an image—Rabbit had always had such an imagination—saw her own black head of hair, messy against white sheets. The harsh corner of her mouth, tucking downward. It was so odd that Icca stumbled over her own feet, catching herself on the road, hands and knees.

She was looking at the path between the branch of her fingers, still seeing herself in Caro's head, even as Caro tittered and jeered and then yanked her back to her feet. She spat in Caro's face just to make the image break, and it did, bled away instantly into another—now Carousel was picturing throttling Icca. There. That was better. That was right.

"You're blushing," Caro said, silver spit streaking her cheek. "You're disgusting. Is that what Cheshire likes?"

Icca said nothing, Caro's delight a distant thing—much too close, really, but more distant than Icca's own startlement. Of how easily that image of her had come up in Caro's head. How quickly Caro had suffocated it. Icca didn't suffocate the thought of Rabbit like that. She let it all spill out and over. It was a habit that Icca had never truly ventured to cease, just like how she picked at her skin. She replaced and she picked because what the hell else would she be doing? Stop? Just stop?

Caro stopped them, looking momentarily dazed. Icca shut off her thoughts, and they began to move once more.

Those petals would work their way out of Rabbit's system eventually, in a way they wouldn't with the Saints. Then Icca could have more.

This was her edge. She felt so ill with the rose magic that she was vaguely disgusted with herself, a shaking physical body to match a sloughing mind. This was her edge—she could bear it. She'd keep returning to it.

Because, really, Icca did like the rush.

Even with most of her weight against Caro's side, she could feel her power stretched around her like she was a girl lying in a flower field, like that sadistic little witch in the old creation tale. Icca imagined herself stretching, hands brushing thistles, worlds crumbling as she breathed in.

This lovely thought dropped into Icca's head as they took the first step over the threshold of the front hall, having passed a pair of guards who'd parted in their recognition of Carousel, and then Caro stopped.

"Alice," Caro breathed, her hands now transferring to clutch the front of Icca's cloak, and leaned over her. Icca immediately started sweating at the effort of keeping on her own feet. "Why is it I'm thinking of creation tales?"

"The scramble of your brain has nothing to do with me," Icca snapped, and leaned against their shared edge. *I must be reminiscing because she's close.*

She saw the thought settle into Caro's eyes—and then Caro snapped her head to the right. And then the left. Then she came back center with a grinning snarl, and then was dragging Icca up the hall, so that Icca's heels and the backs of her calves burned against the stone.

"Hattie unnie!" Caro was screeching as they passed Jabberwockies wearing their white-rose Court pins, brandishing weapons and clothes stained with the glitter of their magic, some with more pep in their step and fervor in their expressions than others—perhaps *so sad* about the collapse of their darling safe haven—alongside guards toting armor. Caro tore through a tall set of doors into what looked like a bedroom wing, while Icca half choked on her own cloak, which was being pulled up taut around

her neck. Promptly, Icca was deposited on a lavish rug, Caro's boot crushing one forearm immediately following. "Unnie—"

Icca twisted her chin around, and saw the frame of a four-poster bed. A moment later, there was the Red Queen, crawling on her hands and knees to the end of the bed, peering down at Icca, and then up to Carousel.

"*Jinjja?*" Icca shrieked a short peal of laughter, absolutely incredulous with the sight. *Really*—had Hattie been *dozing* while Icca sieged her city? "Did I disturb your royal rest, Your Most Honored Highness?"

The curtains were drawn, the room still thick with the stillness of the night.

But then the Queen lifted her chin a bit higher, and all of Icca's amusement, all of its attached fury, died in her chest. Replaced by cold shock.

Hattie November Kkul's face gleamed from the eyes down, her throat slick. A drop of her crimson magic broke from her jaw and fell soundlessly over the edge of the frame.

"Actually," Hattie spoke, hands dusting her soaked gown front absentmindedly, "I've been awake quite a while, now."

FORTY-FOUR

Year Zero Zero Ninety-Four, Winter Season

There Are 987 Remaining Saints

HATTIE HAD BEEN fighting Saints all night, and found it a tricky practice. Not to say that she wasn't quite proficient at it, readers. Our Hattie November, of course, was quite proficient in all of her magics.

She couldn't be the Saints she controlled—she didn't *want* to be them, like how Iccadora seemed so intent on being. But Hattie had attached her threads—she was keeping watch. She had four of her amalgamated Saints out right now. She'd let them out of the dungeons and then stumbled back to her chambers, disoriented by the sensation of their movement, the outside air on their chilled skin, hands on the bedroom wall to guide herself. Crawled into her bed, in the blissful dark.

She could not see through their eyes, not at this distance, but what little emotions remained carried—could one call hunger an emotion? Perhaps *desire* would be more fitting.

Staring up into her blackened canopy, Hattie felt Quiet, hands on her stomach, tangled up in her Saints. The pangs of their hunger carrying her like the thrum of bells in her bones. Bleeding magic in the empty dark, she lay there, drowning in her bed, in her own power, as she twisted their threads. As she devoured monsters in the streets.

She pinned the cravings aside, as they rose as within her Saints; they could smell the hiding witches, her people, behind the walls of their homes. Hattie tucked the Saints' hunger beneath everything else, a stockpile of famine. When her Saints neared one of their own, one of Iccadora's—or otherwise, now; she could sense that not only Iccadora's monsters had made it over the Wall—there was a familiarity that sunk like an ache.

Then Hattie would move her hands; she bled her magic, and stitched ache to the stored hunger, and pulled the suture taut. Hattie wasn't the one eating, but she couldn't help but swallow. She listened to the action in the dark, her tongue over her lips.

But now Hattie was out of threads, snipped from her fingertips and her magic as her Saints were killed in turn. She figured it the work of the stitched Saints under Iccadora's control, so much stronger, simply larger.

Hattie herself had only created one of Iccadora's two, of course.

But she knew how these things went—the stitched ones were hungrier than the naturals; two starving tendencies sewn together.

Hattie's last thread had been snipped, the Saint killed—brutally, at the hands of her own creation, deemed Hana by the dark witch, from the last year's Midwinter Tea and the prior holiday's champion—a few minutes before Carousel had arrived, kicking in said dark witch.

So maybe Hattie had been resting, just a little. Just a few moments on her bed, feeling her outline, remembering she was always feeling the weight of her own body.

Now Hattie peered at Iccadora, thumbed through the dark witch's metaphysical edges, which were a mess, like a sleeve unhemmed in beats. She stumbled across something familiar, and tilted her chin toward the crow witch to say quietly, "You are not quite yourself, Carousel."

"I figured it," she muttered, and Hattie could see Icca's fingertips flushing dark under the weight of the crow witch's boot.

"It's repairing itself," murmured Hattie, eyes drawn low, her magic observing the edge Iccadora and Carousel were sharing. "Should be out of your system, soon; perhaps a quarantine would be suitable. . . ."

"Can I have a cell?" asked Carousel excitedly.

Hattie tilted her chin quizzically. Carousel usually liked herself in luxury. "There are plenty of empty bedrooms."

"I've business, down in the dungeons."

"Business." A smile touched the corners of Hattie's mouth. Strange, strange Carousel Rabbit. "All right."

Carousel took her weight from Icca, who now twisted on the rug in the direction of her departing heels.

"Don't," the dark witch rasped.

And Carousel did pause. But only to turn back and bear down on Iccadora with a black-eyed stare and chuckle, one elegant fingertip rising to tap her temple. "It's very done, Alice, I know you're in here. And I'm very good at compartmentalizing, so now that I do know, you can go sit in the indifferent box alongside all the other versions of you I have in my head. It's a very dull place."

But Iccadora only grinned, even as she rubbed the boot-bruise on her arm. "I know you're lying."

"You're right. It's not dull, not for you—it's actually a very horrible and dangerous pit that I've thrown you and all the others of you in. Do watch for the spikes, and for the bears."

Carousel strode up the hall and out of sight. Then Hattie and Iccadora were staring at one another, beside curtains slowly fraying with the morning.

"You're not hating it as much as you thought. Sharing a head," Hattie said as she slid off the bed, just to note the fact, and not particularly to start a conversation. Though she was interested to see if Iccadora would assume that as her intent; Hattie could gather up a lot about a person from how much they chose to talk, sometimes even more so than from what they had to say.

Iccadora didn't say anything. Hattie could admit to herself she was a little pleased at it.

She drifted over to the curtains and had the thought to look past them, but decided against it, instead running her hand across the velvet, considering.

"Did you intend to have Labyrinth Saints follow yours up over the Wall? Ones outside of your control?" Hattie asked, wanting an answer, but not necessarily needing one. The beasts were empty shells, but seeing ones, too. They'd probably observed Iccadora's Saints being able to fling themselves over the Wall at her insistences. They were quite predatory, after all, and predators tended to learn. The White Queen had called that ability *deliciously terrifying*; Hattie wouldn't go so far with the prose, but she would certainly deem the horror of the implications *interesting*.

Iccadora again did not answer. Hattie took it as a *no*. The witch was certainly brazen in her recklessness, snatching up power in fits and starts, as much as she could bear. And she couldn't bear much more, Hattie knew; she could sense that Iccadora's individuality was warbling like heated glass. But at least Icca was present enough to know not to lunge for Hattie, even though the dark witch was not bound yet—remembering how useless it would prove, Hattie supposed.

"I'm sorry," Hattie said, but it wasn't exactly true. She wasn't apologetic, but she did think herself sympathetic. She was very much aware of the world they were in—knew her own throne was secure simply because of the vast sprawl of her magic. Iccadora knew, too, that power was the only thing worth being so horrible over, the only thing worth anything at all. "I'm sorry, but it's not going to work, Miss Sickle. I am not going to die. The Petra Ward is not going to fall. There will be casualties; my Courts will whisper about my handling of things, which is why we'll need a trial for you, and an execution. You'll end. All of this will end, the Saints put down—"

"Or they'll keep coming," Iccadora said, finally. She was nothing but a child, really, grinning against the carpet, swallowing down her own barbed wickedness like it was a bonbon, liking how it caught in her throat. "They'll keep coming, and you won't be able to stop all of them."

"We will," said Hattie simply, and meant it. "I think you know this. Witches are Saints' natural predators, if only they brave the pain of honing their magic...."

"But they don't. Not in Petra." Icca's voice was cold, clinical. "Why invite such agonies, when one lives in the impenetrable capital?"

At that, Hattie sighed.

Well. The dark witch wasn't wrong.

The Petra population was comfortable. And the ignorance born of that comfort frustrated Hattie so, she who knew so acutely that the Walls didn't block out Wonderland, didn't render Petra a separate, untouchable world.

How often Petra chittered about the Red Queen's insanity for collecting her Culled Court, but now it was her Jabberwockies cleansing the streets. Her Jabberwockies, ripping the Labyrinth Saints off clusters of families pressed into the corners of their apartments, unable to lift a finger to defend themselves.

"Yes," Hattie murmured. "Yes, Iccadora. You are correct."

Too far away, to peer through the eyes of her created Saints she'd turned loose. But there were other flashes, coming up the threads she'd set taut between them and her.

"The sensation of slipping..."

"What?"

"My Saints. Tracking the carnage of *your* Saints, through the apartments; mine were slipping..." Her eyes were drawn low, now, unfocused as she recalled. "Bare feet against slick hardwood floors. Still warm. And, oh. The scent of those human lives still breathing in the air of their homes..." Hattie thumbed at her nose absently. "The people of Petra never wanted to touch their magic. That pain. But your Saints brought pain to them, anyway. So perhaps you'll inspire them—the ones who survive the slaughter, that is—to pursue their abilities. More than the holiday ever could."

"You're welcome," spat Iccadora, after a nearly imperceptible pause. And now Hattie did turn from the curtains. She lowered herself onto the stool of her vanity table, facing the dark witch. She knew Iccadora's calm expression was a mask. Hattie could feel the rise of her heartbeat, her teeth, pushing into the flesh of her tongue. . . .

"Could you taste their deaths, Iccadora? The ones your Saints ate alive?" whispered Hattie. "Can you taste them still?"

"How will you execute me?" Iccadora snapped, as if Hattie was boring her. "Wait, let me guess. Use me as practice for your mad arts, pluck some other heretic to sew me together with—"

Hattie stilled. "That's not an execution."

"No, no, of course, it's *art*."

Displeasure spiked through her. Hattie knew it did not register on her face.

"I do mean to execute you," she said, moving along. It was clear explanations would be wasted on the dark witch. "As, I suppose, you meant to do to me."

"I still mean to."

"Yes. I still don't quite understand why."

"Oh, there are so many reasons." Her voice was a growth of thorns.

"Well, I would like to hear them," said Hattie, though only because she was interested in what other people hated her for—not from a self-conscious desire to fix such things, but because how others viewed her told Hattie so very much about them.

Iccadora scoffed. "Oh, Your *Majesty*, I wouldn't want to *offend* you."

Hattie, having the thought that she didn't believe anyone had truly offended her in her entire life, forgot to wipe her nose, and her magic dripped from her chin into the skirt of her already-stained nightgown.

"Up until this morning, I was the only one who came out of the Labyrinth alive. Now I'm joined by both you and Carousel."

"Aw, did you want that title all for yourself?"

It was only that Hattie was choosing her words carefully. "It was just an observation. Any skilled witch without a death trace could survive the Labyrinth just as well as they could Wonderland. Which, of course, is not very well at all, to be fair. . . ."

Iccadora now did try to rise to her knees; Hattie fixed her with a look, which, as her nose bridge stung, was to fix her to the ground, where Iccadora grunted and seethed, "What would *you* know about surviving Wonderland?"

"Oh," Hattie said. "So that's it."

"What?"

"I think it's unfair, too. How you collected your death trace. Appeals can always be made to the Crown, of course, but most Wards are more concerned with getting Jabberwockies out past their Walls as soon as possible, before the Saints decide to come in. Wholly unfair and barbaric." Before Iccadora could spit at her again, Hattie continued on calmly, holding the witch's black gaze, hands folded in her lap. "It should have been me, correct, who was pushed out to Wonderland at a child's age? For killing Delcorta? Or is that rumor just convenient for you, Iccadora? Because if it wasn't for Delcorta, I should be put to death for something else. Sins of my great-uncle, perhaps, but that's a little flimsy. Making a spectacle of Saints, I suppose, since that must be what I'm doing, since it looks like that is what I'm doing, doesn't it, Iccadora? I am making a joke out of all of it; I see the seriousness and darkness of nothing of this world. Perhaps I should die for not doing enough for the other Wards; perhaps I should because I am in Petra and Petra is the safest place in Isanghan. Perhaps because Carousel Rabbit does what I tell her to do. Perhaps because I am alive and Tecca Moore is not—"

"Shut the fuck up." Iccadora's voice had transformed from the brambles;

now it was darkness touching down on a room when the candles were blown out. It meant Hattie was doing exactly what Hattie meant to do; of course, readers, this was always the case. Delcorta had had a mastery over her words, too, and the Thia Court had never been the wiser, the nobles never knowing just how much they'd exposed themselves with simple conversation.

"Well. Yes. That was a bit crass of me," Hattie said. "It's really none of my business or concern, anyway. . . ."

"Oh, do drop the acts. Drop all of them."

"What, exactly, do you think I'm pretending at?" She was genuinely interested.

And Iccadora Alice Sickle responded, "Are you Hattie November Kkul?"

Hattie was startled. It did not show on her face; perhaps the surprise would have a chance to form if it were not so easily overtaken by fascination a moment later. Iccadora was more attuned to the Saints than Hattie had expected, and Hattie delighted in finding her expectations were wrong—they hardly ever were.

"Yes," Hattie said.

"Were you always?"

"All my life." And a smile touched the corners of her lips again. On her cheeks, Hattie felt her dried magic, the color of blood, strain and then fissure.

FORTY-FIVE

Year Zero Zero Ninety, Autumn Season

There Are 1087 Remaining Saints

"'***EARLY YESTERDAY MORNING,*** *the Red Princess Hattie November Kkul emerged from the Labyrinth holding one shoe. The event was witnessed by the awaiting Thia Court, who watched on in struck silence as the young witch strode barefoot on the cobblestones, reportedly speaking to no one as the Labyrinth doors closed in her wake. Though it stood as a reasonable belief that the Red Princess would perish within the Labyrinth—as no living soul has survived its depths since its institution as quarantine for pre-transformation Saints following the end of the plague raids—it is with great humility that those at the* Petra Daily Paper *apologize for the publication of the assumption that Hattie November Kkul had met her demise. Murmurs in the general public regarding such a miraculous and peculiar re-emergence have generated a new moniker for Kkul—the High Priestess of Isanghan—*'"

"I think that's enough," said Hattie, which meant she'd grown bored.

She was making rounds at the palace, ensuring things were set for the coronation that night and the wedding to take place the next day, and Il-Hyun had found her, begun reading the day's issue to entertain her. Now they stood in the tearoom as Hattie checked the place settings. Pretending as if she cared about such things, as if anyone did. Still she straightened tablecloths and touched the edges of flowers to perk them up, because she could not seem to stop moving.

"Quite." He cleared his throat. "November..."

Here it was. Now, finally, Il-Hyun would ask her the grand question—had Hattie murdered Delcorta for the crown?

But Il-Hyun surprised her, wonderfully. "You want to go back, don't you? Back into the Labyrinth."

Hattie found herself so extremely pleased with this observation that she turned toward him with a small smile. He held the newspaper bunched up in one hand, and she felt his heartbeat speed up as she wiped her handkerchief against her wetted nostrils. "You know me so well."

She wondered if it could really be true, now.

"Is it because you... can? Go and survive?"

Oh, how glad she was, that she would be married to him soon. She was sure she did not love him, not in the way he did her. But Hattie could not have wanted for a better companion. Even with all of her gifts, the intelligence of another was something she cherished.

So she'd give him this piece of herself. See what that brilliant mind found in it, how it would react. Hattie did love to see others react to her. It was further proof that she was really here.

"It is because," Hattie said, "while I was in the Labyrinth, I found a new god for myself." She adjusted one of the black peonies in the crystal vases, watching her fingers around its delicate stem, knowing, somehow instinctively, how much pressure to wield to turn it and yet not have it snap. "It dwells there. Dwells everywhere, but it likes the Labyrinth especially."

"Oh? And what god would that be?"

Hattie, even as little Hattie, had always found Divinity in Quiet. She thought, perhaps, Quiet was the same god she'd felt watching her within that strange maze twisting within the Petra Walls, but simply wore a different name. "Death."

Hattie continued to press on the stalk of the peony as she waited, the glass dome of the tearoom rising around them, so anyone could look in.

Let them look, Hattie thought. *I doubt any of them will ever see.*

"Well. Even so," Il-Hyun returned, after a moment, but not a very long moment. Paper crinkling softly in his hand as his other rose to press over his heart. "Long live the High Priestess."

And the words were kind. And Hattie thought it was a very wise reaction indeed.

FORTY-SIX

Year Zero Zero Ninety-Four, Winter Season

There Are 987 Remaining Saints

MORDEKAI CHESHIRE HAD A HEADACHE. Her name was Carousel Rabbit, and she would not stop talking.

"... very, very confused by the both of you," she was saying now, as she drifted in and out of view—she was clinging to the unlocked cell door next over from his, swinging herself back and forth in steady beats. "Icca's not got much of a purpose with this—besides that she wanted to siege or just get attention or something—and you're apparently here without a purpose either—except wanting to see"—it *was* a purpose, to Kai, though one he was deeply regretting—"unless you're in love with her, of course."

Kai hadn't spoken up until this point; hadn't really gotten a chance to get a word in, actually—Carousel had come bouncing down the stairs and into an open cell, promptly vomited into the waste bucket, and hadn't stopped chattering since. But now he said—he *needed* to say—"I am not in love with Sickle."

Kai liked Icca. Well, at least, he was entertained by her, and she by him; that is what they offered one another—and wasn't that just as important as fondness? How could one keep fondness for another if one found the other boring? Maybe there had been something softer, a kind of affection that felt less greedy—no, no. It had been a long week. Kai was only fantasizing about kind things, kinder witches. Icca really did lose her gleam so quickly, in reality.

Carousel had caught him up on what the dark witch had been up to: being others. Spreading herself in the Saints like an ink blot stemming through water.

Damn. She still really was interesting.

"I am not in love with Sickle," Kai repeated, which pulled Caro out from whatever ramble she was on now. She let her train of thought go without ceremony, now swinging on the door to peer at Kai through the bars.

"How much has she told you about me?"

"That's a question of perspectives. I wouldn't know."

"My, you're such a philosopher!" Carousel exclaimed, like she was thrilled by the realization. She was much like the birds she sported, twitchy at her joints, with the wired fix of her eyes—or maybe it was a lack of sleep, or her nausea. "Do you think poorly of me?"

Yes, he should say, for the sake of his headache. But instead Kai went, "I don't know you."

"That's a no?"

"That's an inconclusion," he said, since she was clearly more interested in truth over appeasement. Kai was fresh out of appease.

"Do you think poorly of Icca?"

"No."

"Then she has been lying to you, about some of it."

"I truly don't think she would bother." Kai swallowed to flush his dry throat. "She's done bad things. I don't think badly of her."

Caro seemed to turn this over in her head, then, satisfied, she nodded. "Why not?"

He shrugged, knocked his temple to the cool metal of the runeworked bars. "I don't think I can justify it. I just don't. Aversion is simply not the trough that naturally fills when I muse about her."

The crow witch's black eyes blinked once, slowly, and then she was smiling.

"That's why she likes you," Carousel finally said, seemingly having wrestled the thought in her head, and the smile relaxed to something truer. Now—now it was cruel.

"Because I muse about her?" Kai didn't see a point to hiding this.

"Because you've a poet's tongue."

"How kind."

Carousel glanced at her nails, which were cragged, though her hands were long and elegant. Somewhere up the dungeon hall, water dripped on stone, the sound whole and small. "And what do you see of the Queen?"

He didn't have to think about it. "Unfathomable power with startling control. In a blank-faced shell that knows the extent of both."

Carousel shrieked her laughter. "That's very good indeed, Cheshire! But what is she hiding?"

The giggles abruptly stopped. Caro's hand jumped to her lips. Kai pulled it all together quickly, like the drawstring of an herb bag: Caro had told Kai—though it was very possible she'd been talking to herself—how Icca had attempted to tangle their agencies together.

The crow witch had seemed so sure of herself up until this point, too, which is why Kai answered, with a grin that he'd missed the feel of, hoping that she might be shaken a little more, "Is it *you* wanting me to answer that, Carousel?"

Now the laugh that bubbled up her throat was airy. "Ha! No. It's not. Don't mind me. Don't mind—Alice—oh." Her hands fluttered at her sides. "Oh! What. I don't want to be here at all, actually. There *are* chambers upstairs. What the hell am I doing here? Her delusion in my head . . ."

Caro stepped off the door and trotted up the hall. But Kai was leaning into it now, weight against the bars, feeling better than he had in days.

"Please. It's water in water, Carousel darling," he called after her lazily. And Carousel darling stopped. "We're all mad here, in a world like this, thank the refracted gods for it. I'm mad. You're—"

"I'm not mad," stated Carousel crossly, spine toward him. She had quite an array of nasty gashes in her cloak, and in the skin up her legs. Kai wished he'd seen the fight between them; the one in the courtyard had only whetted his interest.

"You must be," he purred. "Otherwise, why would you have come down here? It's not only Icca pushing you along, now. You're wanting an answer to that question; it's one you share. At least, it is now." This last portion was pure speculation, and Kai knew he had aimed it admirably, because now Caro was turning and drifting back.

She scratched the back of her head, a gesture that seemed bashful—a lie, Kai knew, his grin splintering wider; sheepishness didn't suit her at all. So when she said, "Well, I guess, since I'm already here. I do like to know what other people think they know," he knew she didn't mean it lightly, under the nonchalance she steeped her words in. Carousel full well knew she was treading on dangerous ground now.

"Hattie November Kkul believes you and Iccadora are in love." Caro blew out a laugh between her teeth. Kai smiled idly along with her. "Yes. I don't believe Iccadora is capable of it."

"Is that all? Really?"

"You would do well, to mind the obsessions of the High Priestess."

Caro rolled her eyes, then stuck out her bottom lip. "Come on, oppa, tell me something interesting."

Something interesting.

"I've heard her, you know," said Kai, his voice growing hushed. "I've heard her, while she works on her projects. How she murmurs to them."

Now Carousel had gone still, so absolutely still. "Yeah, well, she's a kooky one," she attempted.

But Kai only shook his head.

"She's looked out through my eyes." He closed them, now. Rested his temple against the bars. "I've felt her walk in the marrow of my bones. You couldn't understand. Your magic doesn't feel like mine does—how far she can dive. She moves through people like water. I thought the High Priestess title was propaganda, the public's fanaticism—their need for something greater. And I thought Icca was hotheaded and reckless, towing herself along on blind hatred. She squawked about the Queen being mad, but I don't think she really ever believed she was in danger. But Hattie November is not like you and she's not like me. Her body might be human, but I swear to the gods. Her head . . . her head is all Wonderland."

"I don't know what you mean." But Carousel did in fact look like she knew what he meant. She smoothed a hand down her paled face, then laughed, high and thin. "What would you know? You haven't even been!"

"I know what it feels like!" He was shouting suddenly. Screaming, really. The crow witch actually started from the outburst. Kai didn't want to scare her. Except he did want to really scare her. He added, the franticness uncontrollable in his voice, "Thanks to her. But you know the Forest as an old friend by now, don't you, Carousel? So why don't I tell you what it feels like. Why don't I try to put it into words, and you can tell me if you find something familiar in them? Poet's tongue, is that what you said? Perhaps the only way to convey it accurately is if I feed it to you like a fever dream. Ask me. Ask me what Wonderland feels like."

"You can't," Carousel murmured. "Put it into words."

"Ask me."

"I won't."

Kai slammed his hands against the bars. "Ask me! Ask me!" Carousel shrank away, the blacks of her eyes flashing in her whites. His palms were bruising, now. His magic frothing and stinging uselessly down his throat. "Ask me what Wonderland feels like! What Hattie feels like!" He was laughing, laughing. Hattie had turned him into something else without even realizing it. She was beyond comprehension, and perhaps now so was he. Carousel had turned and fled toward the stairs. Kai pressed his face between the bars and screamed after her, "Ask what it feels like—to be so *alive*! *Alive! Alive!*"

FORTY-SEVEN

Zero Zero Ninety-One, Autumn Season

There Are 1068 Remaining Saints

IN THE CHURCH OFF the Labyrinth, Hattie November Kkul stood over the unconscious yellow-haired girl and felt, in her fingertips, the death trace sitting quiet and still in her marrow, much like a fog. Around her bare feet were tumbled three rotted heads. They'd been four, of course, originally—one that had crumbled into black dust across the dais, the one from which Hattie had siphoned decay, and now wound this decay around the death trace, watched as it guttered and suffocated and faded.

Hattie pulled her mind and her magic back from the young Jabberwocky, and as she did, brushed against her age, her history, her strange cord of hatred and her strange name. Carousel Rabbit.

She watched the rune that repelled criminals from the Ward Walls pale into smoothed skin. Then she gathered the remaining three heads in her sack, and, leaving Carousel Rabbit to her sleep—to the rest of her life—stole quietly out the front doors.

It was early evening, and the sky blushed overhead—the section of it that Hattie could see when she tipped her head back, back, back, so her gaze could best the high Walls of the Labyrinth.

The square plot the Church sat upon was barely big enough to allow breathing space edgewise. It existed imprisoned in the stone confines of the four sides, save for the one Wall that contained the sliver of passage that allowed entrance from the sole pathway in and out of Petra. This is not where Hattie turned her feet.

If one happened to squeeze past where the side of the Church Off the Labyrinth met its stone outline, one would be bored, seeing nothing but a few overgrown thistles, the bottom of one of Petra's ginormous syllables—라. But shoved into the corner there was an invisible seam in the stone, and when Hattie pressed her palm above it, it gave. Now there was a tunnel through the Wall of the Labyrinth that extended into it, into darkness. Hattie gathered up the heads and hoisted herself up, and through.

She spilled out into the small clearing that only she herself—and now you, dear readers, but do keep respectfully Quiet about it—knew existed directly behind the Church. Though, Hattie supposed, every now and then, a Jabberwocky might end up here, if they indeed made it this far into the Labyrinth without something swallowing them up. Perhaps they would even come across Hattie herself, after she'd gone to her knees.

So many of her Courts whispered about what devious things the Red Queen—or, when they were feeling holy, she supposed, whatever pious things the High Priestess—might be up to, whenever Hattie wandered for the Labyrinth. What horrors must draw her within its depths over and over again; how, after she'd first stepped within its Walls to prove that she did not carry a death trace—and so proved she had not sent Delcorta tumbling to her demise—she could not seem to leave it well enough alone. Not for very long, that was.

Hattie would never bother to explain; she doubted they would understand, not truly.

How those first steps into the Labyrinth, trial though they may have been, had felt like coming home.

Though, if anyone could come close to understanding, it would be the Jabberwockies of the newly created Culled Court, so exposed to Wonderland as they were. Besides the desire to keep an eye on these volatile elements of society, Hattie was intrigued by such people. She'd never come across an absolved Jabberwocky who didn't wander back to the Forest at some point or another, telling themselves it was to follow a bounty or indulge themselves in the violence of butchering a Saint.

Hattie knew the truth.

She knew how the roots of Wonderland called to them, that dark, wicked place within which they had never been so terrified, never felt so alive. She knew because Wonderland called to her, too. In this way they were kin; though, shy of a century ago, such a connection would not have been so rare.

Before Saints, before the plague raids, when most provinces of Isanghan existed within Wonderland Forest, more of the population turned toward the practice of their magic. There existed the same cost, of course—that of pain. But the Forest soothed them, held them, whispered to them to be in their natures.

Arguably to a detrimental extent.

Glorious magic was seen in those days, but also glorious hubris.

The rampant epidemic of saltfever was said to have been balanced out by merciful Nature with an influx of witches born with abilities that could soothe sicknesses—but also, in turn, amplify them. Bolstered by Wonderland, some chose to lean into the darker side of their abilities—seeing disease as a kind of cleansing, a ritual to cull the weak—eventually starting the sect of plague raiders that would consume Isanghan and cause King Min Titus Kkul to take his drastic measures with the Saints. All acts of bold witches, and Hattie believed those were so few and far between nowadays, and that such rarity was a cause of a lack of Wonderland.

What would Hattie become, in the Forest?

Perhaps lesser witches did darker deeds. Perhaps senseless violence was uncreative, and so Hattie needn't worry about becoming some wicked creature. Hattie didn't need to worry about anything, really. She knew how to sate herself. Knew how to keep herself from wandering into Wonderland, where, most likely, she'd misplace any ideas of ever wandering back out. She simply needed to continue to come back here. Back into the Labyrinth.

And, of course, collect her absolved Jabberwockies, carrying around that invisible essence of the Forest. Because a person would always carry around a place where they had become someone else, the way the gleam of a porcelain vase remembers the furnace.

But even the Jabberwockies believed the Labyrinth to be a more terrifying place than Wonderland. First it had been a spectacle, then a quarantine, now a kill box. But to Hattie, it existed as a place partially Forest and partially Petra. Like how Hattie felt she was partially different things, and so the Labyrinth fit to her, whispered to her in a way she imagined Wonderland did the Jabberwockies. She was a Queen, a witch. A body that was physical, a mind that was not. A votary, of course; an artist, of course, or perhaps as consequence.

It was Delcorta who had taught little Hattie the trick of it, of course, in stripping the death trace off of someone's soul. She could follow the Logic of it down, and thus she understood this magic, and thus inclined her head to it, respected it, as the magic did her in turn, and came when called.

A death trace healed by decay—after all, didn't decay trail after death, anyway? Soothe it, and ultimately Quiet it, any angry marks the soul had thrashed upon the forgiving flesh, the delicate, proudly formed bones—marks, of course, that no one but those lucky few in Hattie's bloodline could even think to peer at. Such hidden, sacred sciences—how the elements of the mind affected elements of the body, and thus, the person inhabiting that body was able to affect the world. And threading it all together: magic, which was Divinity, which were the gods, which were, of course, the world, again, rendering everything and everyone, even herself, one grand smear; and Hattie found herself falling apart for the glorious ridiculousness of all of it.

Hattie found herself on her knees, in the Labyrinth, in the Quiet.

And sometimes she'd lie there for three days. Just breathing. Sometimes the Saints would come sniffing along, and Hattie would lift her head to make them go away; she'd show them the heads she brought along, would leave behind; she'd make them unravel, if they were being stubborn. And then she'd go back inward. And later she'd emerge from the Labyrinth a stronger witch, she was sure. A part of her sated, that desire to dissolve in Wonderland. At least for a time.

And all the while, she'd be Quiet.

Prayer was a strange magic indeed.

—

"Oh. Carousel Rabbit." Hattie folded her hands in front of her, studying the yellow-haired witch quietly. "You're still here."

Indeed, the young woman sat on the front step of the Church. Around her worn boots, there was gathered a small murder of crows. Hattie wasn't quite sure what they were doing; she was sure they didn't, either, lined up as neatly as they were. It seemed Carousel had been keeping herself entertained by poking at each of their bowed heads, one after another, and then back down the line. She continued to do this as she tilted her head up and smiled at Hattie. It was very sharp and not at all warm.

It was in this smile that Hattie knew Carousel Rabbit had been awaiting her return.

"So you're the famous Red Princess," Carousel mused. "Thank you for yanking away that nasty death trace off of my soul or whatnot. And removing that rune. I always thought it was ugly, ugly . . . though, of course, I pull it off. . . ."

It was not a genuine thank-you, Hattie knew. She sensed the dark resentment that simmered under the cheery exterior. Hattie simply said, "Queen. I'm the Red Queen."

"Right, right. Dear Delcorta is dead, then? She was still alive when we—when I went in." Carousel gestured vaguely in the direction of Wonderland. Perhaps also to someone within it. Hattie remembered that cord of hate. Had felt it shot off somewhere toward the Forest. One of the Wards that sat past it, maybe—though Hattie, for some reason, doubted it—one like the many in Isanghan that were separated from Petra by ribbons of Wonderland and effectively, slowly choking because of it. For decades Saints had been wary of the Walls and their protection runes, but it seemed that over the past few decades they'd grown bolder—Hattie preferred that to the thought that they'd grown smarter, realizing that the runes couldn't kill them. She was still figuring out what to do to bolster the Walls of these distant Wards. Transportation of the materials needed was enough of a conundrum, as not everywhere was connected by trolley tracks—and even if she could get an operation on its way, then the builders would have to worry about the noise of it, drawing Saints.

"My frien—*some* girls in my village were always talking about knocking her head off. Now we don't have to, apparently."

Carousel lifted her chin and grinned brazenly. A challenge, then, Hattie observed, without anger, and void of any desire to meet it.

"Some people think I killed my mother." A heartbeat later, Hattie realized she wasn't exactly sure why she'd said this, offered this. Perhaps to scare her.

But this didn't seem to be the effect. "Did you?" Genuine interest glittered in the words.

Hattie touched her dripping nose, contemplative, and suddenly quite tired.

And found Carousel Rabbit watching the gesture with widened, hungry eyes.

There was something genuine and wholly exposed in the look. Some piece of this young woman she was putting out into the open light for Hattie to see, so blatant and surprising for it, so much like a map unraveled—Hattie thought... yes, looking a little closer, she could see Carousel Rabbit's whole history laid out in those unsettling and blown-out black eyes. A childhood of tragedy, a broken heart somewhere between then and now, Wonderland, of course, which had been a nightmare incarnate and then a kind of companion. Perhaps born cradling a dangerously clear-eyed view of this world, and thus the habit of honing herself into the sharp thing she stood as before Hattie today, knowing the value of power so intimately that her awe of it was almost indistinguishable from affection.

So here was Carousel Rabbit, flayed open before her with that single expression, and such openness struck Hattie, and had her saying quietly, "I suppose."

Of course, she immediately undid it. It wasn't right. She shouldn't have said it; she hardly knew the girl, after all.

Hattie blurred the witch's hearing out briefly; the *I suppose* smeared from her ear drums, drowned out by some hum, or maybe a ringing. Carousel glanced over her shoulder, briefly disoriented. Then she looked back and said quizzingly, "What did you say?"

Hattie wiped her nose again. "Oh, nothing."

"Well, I'm sorry," Carousel said, even though Hattie saw nothing to be sorry about—it seemed, anyway, apologies were not the crow witch's strong suit, grinning as she was. "I don't have a mother anymore, either. Oh—your father is dead, too! Mine too! I didn't realize the rumors were true—you really do *bleed* magic constantly, don't you? Doesn't that hurt? How powerful *are* you, really?"

Hattie ignored this. "Miss Rabbit, there are accommodations in the city for absolved Jabberwockies such as yourself, if you like. If you do stay here, you'll be receiving a letter soon officially inviting you to join the Culled Court."

Suspicion shuttered over Carousel's black eyes. "Oh? And what would I have to do there?"

"I have certain Saints I have anatomical interests in that I'll ask you to collect. For compensation, of course."

Carousel flicked a bird's head, the last in the odd little line of them. "Can I say no?"

Hattie wasn't sure why she'd asked this, so she did not answer. She had already seen Caro's gaze dart briefly toward where she'd gestured—back toward Wonderland. It was a look Hattie had come to expect.

Hattie, again with the thought she'd never be able to leave Wonderland if she wandered in, let herself imagine it for a moment.

How her gods would whisper ever more clearly in the undergrowth. How her magic would sing and dance in her veins. What would she become, in Wonderland—that question again, one she'd been asking herself all her life. Less than a Queen, surely, and yet something more. A wild, yet certainly clear-eyed thing, with dirty hands and dirty feet, holder, at last, of all the truths she'd been seeking. And what then? Nothing then. With everything known, Hattie would lie down under some watching tree and not move again.

She smiled privately to herself.

Oh, but how Hattie wanted to *know* other people, dear readers.

How she wanted them to impress her, with their strange habits and strange, moving emotions; how she wanted to indulge in her arts. Wonderland would have to wait. And, of course, it would.

Carousel Rabbit was cocking her head. Her next words came shyer, and Hattie looked at the girl with more attention. And, because Carousel had noticed her doing so, she leaned in before asking, "Are there . . . parties, being in a Court and all?"

"Yes. There are some."

"I've never been to a party." The witch's eyes glittered once more. It was uncannily similar to the glint of a crow's gaze—when they weren't how they were now, of course, dulled out with the proximity to Carousel and her magic, which beaded blue across her eyelashes. "I think I'd like them a lot.

"Where did you just come from?" asked Carousel suddenly. It made a small smile branch across Hattie's face.

"The Labyrinth," said Hattie.

"Hm." The witch tilted her head in the other direction, but stayed unflinching under Hattie's gaze. People did flinch, so often, away from her. "I thought only Saints and bad, bad Jabberwockies went into the Labyrinth."

Hattie shrugged. "Some Queens, too."

"Why?"

Hattie restrained the urge to tip her head back and look into the dark pass from which she'd emerged. Instead she continued to meet Carousel Rabbit's gaze and tried to see if the crow witch would notice this, this extending of something significant in her metaphorical hand. She would not mention the praying, not now. Perhaps if the girl ever thought to ask again. "It's Quiet, in the Labyrinth."

Carousel shuddered visibly. "Well. Another reason not to go, then."

But even though her reply was brushed with apathy, Hattie thought Carousel might've clutched the words and pocketed them secretly.

Hattie turned over in her head the witch's clear desire to *see* her. Did Hattie like it? Did it matter? Carousel would see what she herself deemed important. This was, after all, how most people, all their lives, would observe the world around them, picking and choosing which of its aspects held weight, what could be overlooked; what Hattie saw of the world, saw of herself, would thus prove disparate from how others believed she existed. Hattie and Carousel and everyone else—they were all looking at different Hatties. They were all looking at different Carousels. They were all, even, looking at different Saints—things to be feared, things to slaughter, things to jeer at, things to—for gods' sake—leave the hell alone; don't bother or look at them; please gods; things that didn't exist, that couldn't exist, because how would one sleep at night if there *were* truly such things scuttling out in the world?

Things to make art of...

Carousel waved a dismissive hand. The birds stumbled out of line, and Carousel rose off the step, dusting her pants with stained hands. Saint's blood; Hattie could smell it.

The crow witch did not move away. She scuffed her boots in the dirt again.

She reminded Hattie of... little Hattie, perhaps. Time would tell.

"I can walk you back," Carousel said. "Back to whatever... D'you live in a palace? Like in fairy-tale books?"

Hattie smiled again. This one was softer. "Do you like fairy-tale books?"

"No. No!" Carousel said immediately. She fell into step behind Hattie as they made for the path out. Hattie could hear her kicking the thistles that leaned in the way. "Dreadful things, really."

FORTY-EIGHT

YEAR ZERO ZERO NINETY-FOUR, WINTER SEASON

THERE ARE 978 REMAINING SAINTS

AND ICCA COULD THINK herself, perhaps, tired.

Her Saints wore on. She turned to think of something and kept ending up in another head, another monster, spilt into their limbs, even though there were less of her, now—she was getting killed off, one by one. Shouldn't she be more whole, again, when they died—no, she'd been whole this entire time, of course. Shouldn't she be less stretched?

Hattie November had left her alone, bound up in the sitting area of the bedchamber, which didn't seem very ceremonial. But what was the use of a cell, really? She and Hattie both knew Icca wouldn't run. Knew Icca was still chewing on something, some query she wanted answered . . . it all seemed so distant now. She was nodding off.

And when she did fall asleep, she dreamed of feeling blank, and of eating bone.

Icca started awake when the last of the petals in Carousel's body were broken down. She felt the connection gone suddenly, sucked in a gasp at the absence, as this larger portion of her clarity *was* returned to her, that smeared edge restored. She felt her binds behind her back, and the blood it'd built in her fingertips. She felt the Dark a little more clearly as Carousel slipped away from her. The muddiness of her head had made her feel sick of her Saints, sick of her plan, had made her feel done and tired with it all.

Thankfully—else the story would end here, dear readers—now Icca was lucid enough to know how ridiculous she'd been being, thinking.

Of course she wanted more Saints.

Of course she was far from finished.

She dropped back her head to the wood of the chair she was bound to, flushed her dry throat with spit and the useless magic that had welled in her gums, and brought Hana and Dul to her focus. Looking to the darkened ceiling, the shades of the chambers still drawn low, she thought, *Come to me.*

And Carousel Rabbit strode into the chambers.

Posture obscenely confident for the state of her clothes and the gashes on all her limbs, the crow witch put a hand to her hip and looked about. "Oh, my, it's dreary in here! You're not even totally to blame for it, Alice."

Carousel drew the curtains away, leaving Icca to blink at the settling sunset, completely disoriented as she tried to piece together where the hell the day had gone. When her eyes adjusted, she saw Caro knelt before one of the bookshelves beside the windows, collecting its tomes in her arms.

"Have you eaten?" the crow witch inquired, turning with the stack balanced on her hip, using her free hand to smooth back the hair on one side of her head. It was a motion Icca used to witness her make often, one she'd watched carefully, the casual grace of it.

"I don't remember."

"Well, d'you feel like it?"

Icca suddenly recalled what she'd been dreaming about. Splintering bone, marrow on her tongue... She wasn't sure she'd been dreaming at all. She'd tried to pin back all their hunger, hadn't she? When had she misplaced that intent? She'd—they'd only been meant to eat the Queen.

"Not hungry," Icca murmured, nausea rising in her throat.

Don't cry, she scolded herself, mortified that it had to be thought at all, how fast it had all set in. *The petals are the reason you're out of the Labyrinth in the first place.*

Icca realized that Caro was staring her down. She lifted her chin a little, silently grateful to find that it did not tremble, that she could meet Caro's black eyes steadily, and certainly, readers, feel nothing at all but a bitterness so total it was like solid earth beneath her feet. Grounding, Icca had always found Carousel. She could be thankful for it now and still not have it mean anything affectionate.

"What?" Icca demanded finally.

"You can read, can't you?"

"What? Yes." Icca flicked her gaze again upon Caro's clutched tomes. "Same as you."

Caro's lip quirked irritably, showing off one of her canines. "Halsu eobseo." She flapped a hand. "Pretentious bitch."

"Can't do what?"

"Read."

Icca blinked. "I've seen you read."

Carousel had read to Icca before, in fact, Icca's head in her lap, there in the orphanage bedroom when her own voice had grown tired. The ridiculous airy lilt of her voice growing sweet against inked pages, the creation stories indulgently fantastical, playing out in Icca's head as the curtains fluttered, as the room arched around them, air smelling like dust and the wisteria of the fields beyond their walls. She would smile into Caro's thigh at the violent parts, though not because of the violence. A narrator would understand why that would be such the assumption about our horrible barb of a girl. It was because Icca recognized that she felt the same during those vicious parts as all the rest of the tale—Icca was fine, just fine, with all of it. The good and the bad parts, all just parts, all of it threaded through her head with Carousel's hand on her ribs the entire time.

Caro lifted a shoulder now, and said indifferently, "I picked up a curse off a Saint in Wonderland at some point. I wasn't sure if you had, too. If it had happened when we were together." Her laugh came harsh and quick. "I could picture you carrying around that book just for the university look of it."

A startling pang of sadness hit Icca in the throat. She promptly swallowed it down as a side effect of her existence as an academic.

"So," Caro said, breaking the sudden silence. She held out one of the tomes. "Read this to me."

Icca glanced at the blank cover and said, "No."

Without hesitating, Caro chose the next one and held it out. "What about this one?"

"It's not the choice of book I despise, you nit."

And Caro took a step closer, eyes glittering. She swept herself gracefully onto the arm of the chair Icca was bound to. Icca knew she could turn her head and have her nose glance the full curve of Caro's cheekbone, which is why she did not turn her head, just looked forward and felt as Caro's next breath brushed her temple, as Caro dropped the tome into her lap.

"Ah, Alice," Carousel said, moving the hairs dropped against Icca's brow. "Who said they were books?"

And Caro opened the front cover. Icca couldn't help it—her eyes latched upon the ink, heartbeat rising in her chest as she skimmed the words, dropped down and down, line by line, until they'd eaten up the page.

Reflexively, Icca went to turn over to the next one, and her wrists pulled against the back of the chair, unmoving within the binds.

Damn it. Icca seethed. Now she did turn her head, a little, just to find the corner of Carousel's grin. *That was a decent play.*

"Diaries," Icca breathed, careful, careful now. "Whose?"

The smile cracked deeper. "Unnie's, of course."

Icca scrubbed at this in her head. "Why?"

"Does it matter? You want answers."

"It matters. You want answers."

"Hm. Then that *is* your answer, isn't it?" Now Caro's smile seemed less sharp, though she was certainly very much still threatening Icca with her proximity, with the lean of her body over Icca's shoulder. With a light wrist, Caro traced her fingers upon the paper in Icca's lap. "So. You read aloud. I'll turn the pages."

Icca was fully studying her now, head tilted back slightly so their faces would not touch; Carousel, liking to be studied, of course, sat still and let her take her time with it. Something had happened, Icca knew, something had been unearthed in Caro's head about her precious Queen.

"What is it?" Her voice came out a hush where she'd expected a hiss. "You look . . ."

Caro met her eyes.

Then her hand tangled in the back of Icca's hair and drew it back, with a quickness that clattered Icca's next inhale down her throat, exposed now as Caro leaned forward, so her breath traced its line.

"I am not going to beg you, oh, Alice," Carousel said softly, fingertips rising from the diary to skim Icca's jaw, slow, slow, as if she was admiring its path, instead of thinking about the way her knife would split it apart. "Okay? Start reading or I'll just spill you out over your chair, onto the rug. Unnie won't mind, won't care about her floorboards one bit."

Icca rolled only her eyes at the display. She hadn't been expecting an answer anyway. "It would be much more terrifying if you weren't so blatantly enjoying yourself."

"Now, if anything, I think that should make it more terrifying."

Icca supposed this was true. But she tried to find her fear and came up empty.

Well, perhaps not empty, dear readers, but her horror of Carousel—of the easy way she went about indulging herself in her own violence, like she indulged herself in everything else—did not make Icca recoil. It felt strange, simply to have the idea of fearing Caro hover without particularly wanting her, or the thought of her, to move away. Perhaps it was the intrigue of it, the crow witch's odd and wholly uncommon personality, the fact that she liked her things and her luxuries and her own face, alongside butchering feral Saints in the Forest. Maybe it could also be this: Icca knew herself to be a scary thing, too. She knew Carousel thought she should fear her, too.

Knew that Caro would be fine carving Icca down in her next breath, but up until the moment Icca went slack, until all of it was done and over with, she wouldn't move away either.

And so Carousel turned the page, and Icca began to read aloud.

FORTY-NINE

Year Zero Zero Ninety-Four, Winter Season

There Are 978 Remaining Saints

5 Summer 0088

Umma says that she thought herself ancient by sixteen, and sometimes I see what she means. Maybe it's that this age is only a week new but recently I feel I flicker back and forth all the time. I'm sixteen, I'm arcane. I'm sixteen and this power still corrodes me when I summon it. I loathe it, I like it, I despise its inconvenience, I love it even more because if it didn't ache at all, I'd be numb to it, I think. I think when something doesn't demand attention one's bound to become indifferent to it. I don't want to be indifferent to this. I want to pay so much attention to all of it.

I want to see what happens to the world when I'm Queen, one day, and I haven't bothered to unstitch the distinction between what I could do and what I want to do.

10 Summer 0088

Il-Hyun had the thought today that I could leave the court dinner tonight whenever I wanted. Make them see me sitting in the chair, nice and quiet and still, at Umma's right hand. "Do you really believe I could fool Delcorta?" I asked him, which was unfair to pose as a question, there wasn't another answer he could give me besides "No." He doesn't know that Umma wouldn't really care if I did what he suggested, but I like that. That only I know she'd look at me out the corner of her eye while the Courts went along with their stitched sight, believing me still before them, and she'd smile, and let me do whatever I want to do, really. Sometimes I wish we were the only two people alive. Then I could really do whatever I wanted.

11 Summer 0088

I tried to make raspberry pancakes and fucked up the batter. I could tell the cook wanted to yell at me for being in the way, but she didn't.

—

Icca paused. Carousel was smiling.

"We could've all been friends," Caro said, really and truly believing it could be true. "You, me, Hattie, and Tecca."

"So?"

"So what I just said. A hypothetical that means nothing at all, like all hypotheticals. I thought you were the academic."

"This isn't where we want to be," Icca said, shaking her chin at the diary, Caro's fingertip braced on the edge of the page. "She's so young. I think we want to be closer to her age now."

"Why's that?"

Icca didn't say anything. Caro drew her hand from the page, delighted when she saw the dark witch begin to gnaw the inside of her own cheek, choosing her words carefully. That was fine. Carousel waited. She considered speaking to Hattie's furniture, but she didn't want to startle the tea table or the candle holders with her queries, since she was almost sure Hattie never spoke to them at all.

"She's so young, here," Icca repeated slowly, choosing, choosing. "She doesn't think like this now."

Caro thought this correct, but regardless said, "Do you know that?"

"I know I am far from who I was at sixteen." She paused briefly. "Aren't you?"

"Deities." Caro laughed. "Thank them, yes. I'm so much prettier now."

"That's a matter of opinion."

"Yes. My opinion. The only one that matters on that subject."

"We're working with heads, not faces. Hattie November changed. I want to see when she did, and how she did."

"Not why?" And Carousel felt something go still in herself. She might even have thought that Icca felt something similar, a shift in the air. Not exactly the weight of it, but maybe how it held their voices, like it wanted a hush. That made the hairs on Caro's neck prickle, just a little bit. Hattie never talked about the gods she'd found in her life, but Carousel thought she knew that Quiet was one of them, and now it seemed to be listening.

"I think I know why," Icca said, in a voice like knotting smoke, and met Caro's eyes.

Caro took the diary from Icca's lap. She squinted through the cover flaps of the others crowded at their feet until she found the date 0090.

Zero Zero Ninety, the year Delcorta October Kkul was found spread out at the center of the spiral stairs leading up to her study, like a tea leaf unraveled at the bottom of a cup.

FIFTY

Year Zero Zero Ninety, Autumn Season

There Are 1089 Remaining Saints

YOU MIGHT REMEMBER the year, dearest readers, but it still stands perfectly all right if you do not. A deeply repentant narrator has pulled you through a number of heads at this point, a number of years, and you'll excuse it, of course, seeing as how you have reached the end of this sentence.

So. Year Zero Zero Ninety, Autumn Season. Iccadora and Carousel find the heads stolen, find the worst of themselves, and of one another. At the same time, in the capital Petra Ward, eighteen-year-old Hattie November Kkul is found looking down onto the body of Delcorta October Kkul, who is determined to have been killed on impact after falling seven stories from the door of her tower study.

A few hours prior, Hattie and Delcorta, in the study rather than below it, discussed what remained of the Petra Saint Ledger—a record perhaps kept by the Crown for the benefit of future historians, to distinguish the caliber of Isanghan's piety and goodness as a country—in which, if you might remember again, dear readers, were four entries.

Little Hattie had always known there to be only four entries left, had thought it such a fine, mysterious number. It seemed so sparse that it became a delicate thing in her head, a number so frail someone could blow on it and all the entries might flit away before she finally, finally was deemed of appropriate age by her mother to learn what was written upon its pages. To learn how the world had ended.

A narrator supposes they have kept you from the cruel truth of it long enough, dearest, bravest readers, of how exactly Divinity was given in excess to the Saints.

It seemed the cleanest way to do it, with the enchanting of the Ledger, with each cherished Saint of the country of Isanghan all in one place, with their names already inked upon its pages. King Min Titus Kkul, Hattie's great-uncle, wielded a particularly unique form of the sense-magic of the Kkul bloodline, able to make his power and the power of others bleed excessively. Following the feraling of the Saints and his death—resulting in a few decades of unrest while the throne was rolled between greedy hands, eventually being restored to Delcorta's mother, Hattie's grandmother, who died from saltfever within weeks of her coronation—his madness would be attributed to his magic, that the King kept himself corroding down long after possessing an age that could sustain it.

The King also was known for a strong affinity for runework—though, it seems, championed not the logistics of the practice, that a rune aimed to affect a person often required a matching rune on said person, a bolt and a rendered conductor. Likely he knew exactly what he was doing, what he was doing wrong, and was simply desperate to move the process along. Receiving the consent of the Saints, scattered all over the country, for his plan to bestow upon them Divinity in profound amounts, giving them proper time to consider—it was going ever so slowly. Meanwhile the plague raids were reaching a critical point, and his people were dying. And Divinity was good, of course.

Hattie, tucked beside her mother on the floor of the study as Delcorta spoke this history, had looked up at this piece, startled cold.

"Good?" little Hattie repeated, feeling, surely, she must have missed something. It pained her to interrupt. This was sacred knowledge her mother was whispering to her, beside the ember-low breath of the fireplace—she'd waited for this, anxiously, her entire life. The specifics of how exactly Divinity had been overexposed in the Saints was generally unrevealed in Isanghan—letting the process be known, that such a thing as inked names could be utilized, would be risking a potential genocide, in the wrong hands.

"Good," Delcorta murmured. She ghosted her pretty fingers over the Ledger, opened on the rug before their legs, the torn-away pages leaving its spine irregular, but soft. Exactly two pages remained, four entries limp between the cover flaps with the runes drawn so small, hairbreadth strokes, that Hattie could not pick them out as anything but nicks in the black leather.

"But they knew Divinity to be everything, as well?"

"Yes, love. We know, now, that we cannot expect existence—the world—to adhere to human moralities. The world is not good or bad; everything is both and is everything else so completely, and constantly."

A mere eighteen years old, little Hattie turned this over in her mind, and had another instance of feeling like a child and feeling arcane all at once. Just like how she was, all at once, human and Divinity, an individual and, in her head, the entire thing.

She found herself shivering. Min Titus Kkul's negligence of the Saints' consent surrounding such a volatile spell . . . it was a disgrace. A horror. What else could have spilled from such an intent but the nastiest manner of creatures imaginable?

"Keep going," Hattie whispered. "I need to know how it ends."

Though really, she already knew.

King Min Titus Kkul, with the thought of saving his people—though who can really know for sure, readers—stole away with the Ledger to the very room Delcorta and Hattie now sat, and began his runework. Dripping his black magic, he runeworked into the night and into the dawn, when his servants would find him both slick with his power and with the blood from his gums, all of his teeth corroded out of his head and set in a neat line on the desk. He used runes to connect inked names to the Saints they belonged to, drew greater Divinity into their little Divinities, made the drops they held swell into profound oceans.

It seemed, for the first couple of weeks, that the King had been successful: Saints were reported fighting back with unimaginable ability, cleansing Wonderland of the plague raiders. Witches celebrated the intelligence of their King in the Petra streets; the High Cardinal Oh inked the King's accomplishment in the Ledger retroactively and pretended it was all carried out with due permission of the Saints—what was the harm of future generations believing it was all done properly, with success like this?

But Divinity kept building within the Saints, Delcorta explained to silent-and-still Hattie, and the magic burst their minds like dams. It changed their bodies; it drowned the souls within them.

It would have been different, if the Saints had had a choice, if they had been bestowed with matching runes on their bodies, had taken the power in properly, translating it to their forms. But instead they were lost in it, and soon they were nothing at all.

And the Ledger, like the Saints, seemed to keep swallowing down power. Cardinal Oh and a young chimneysweep named Cedar Kim—who'd scrawled predicted damnations on its pages—became sickly, and their magic turned black as it bled from them. The King, bedridden from what he thought had been the excess of his magic and the stress of the calamity, now knew it was because his name was inscribed upon the pages as well, and so practically crawled from his chambers to steal away the Ledger from the palace chapel, and then up to his tower-study. His Queen found him attempting to feed it page by page to his fireplace.

Hattie didn't need ask why he went along so slowly. How it must have pained him to let all of his work crumble into ash. It was, after all, a truly incredible feat of magic, and it did seem that adoration, that obsession for their arts, spun thickly in the Kkul bloodline.

"It gets a little lost from there," Delcorta admitted thoughtfully, still tracing upon the Ledger before them. "I've heard that Min Titus collapsed before he could finish it off, but his Queen was apparently the only other witnessing soul, and we both know how she was the first of a plethora of them to try and take his title."

Her mother was saying that the Queen might have plucked the Ledger from his hand before he burned away the last of his name on its pages, lest he truly be able to save himself by doing so—but, Hattie knew, it was a wasted effort on both their parts. The King would soon succumb to his mortal injuries, and his Queen would lose the throne to his heirs; the Saints stayed feral.

But his spell *had* worked.

It was a note that Hattie felt was important, that the plague raids did cease, raiders picked off in Wonderland as the rest of Isanghan was driven out into the moorlands, save for the stronghold of the Petra Ward. And what was left over? Saints in the Forest, drawn by anger, drawn by grief, chewing them down until the person who contained them couldn't hurt, and couldn't hurt others because of it. The Saints were still protecting humanity, in a way, in their own way.

Hattie lifted her head from the page, from the image of her mother's fingertips upon the time-thinned parchment, up to Delcorta's face, the Queen's brown cheeks tinted with her fever. She'd been ill for a while, now, the pale magic that shone on her upper lip of a watery consistency. Hattie knew this was why Delcorta was choosing to tell her about this history, today—such a dark past they'd inherited, one that she knew her mother would have preferred to keep from her for at least a few years more. Hattie was still nothing but a child now. She was nothing but a child, and soon she'd be all alone, crowned, on a throne cold to the touch under her mother's absence.

Delcorta reached to wipe away the tears on Hattie's cheeks. Hattie closed her eyes, her own magic dripping onto her lips, droplets swallowed up by her skirts and her rug—she'd been too fixated on the tale to wipe the trail away. She'd always felt her mother's magic so much more keenly than she did all the others', and all of their parts, outlined for her in her mind without her second thought. They were static until she focused, until she made them noise—but her mother always felt like noise, and Hattie liked it, even though Quiet was her favorite god.

"I don't want you to go," Hattie whispered. Her words shook out of her, hands in Delcorta's skirts. She tilted her brow to rest in the crook of her mother's neck as her shoulders began to tremble. "*Kajima*, Umma, *please*, I—I can't be alone in a world like this."

"Oh, my love," murmured Delcorta against her daughter's hair. "You are far from alone."

She was talking about Il-Hyun, and the Thia Court, and the country that feared and fawned over their bloodline. It wasn't enough; compared to Hattie's love for Delcorta, it hardly seemed like anything at all.

And Hattie was afraid of grieving.

She was afraid all the Saints would crawl up and out of the Labyrinth, when Delcorta was gone and Hattie was hurting, that they would come in from Wonderland in stampedes. It was ridiculous—but was it? Hattie was the most powerful witch of her age, of any age. Maybe her grief would carry further, make a hollow in their stomachs the shape of her body—it wouldn't matter.

She shouldn't be afraid of drawing the Saints. Hattie would fell them all, one by damned one.

So, then.

She was afraid of her grief killing her all on its own.

"I cannot keep Death away, sweet child," Delcorta said softly, one hand braced to the back of Hattie's head. "This is the cycle of existence. We live. We pass. I will still be here, in a way. I will still be everything else."

Hattie swallowed. She felt her magic against that of her mother's; she felt the lines of Delcorta's bones and the way they eased against her breath. She felt how she could make her mother's pieces unravel, joints tumbling loose, muscles going limp, organs slipping down. She felt how she could draw them all back together, and so much more—she'd done it before.

Pulled two heads into one.

"Would you stay, if you could, Umma?" Hattie asked, voice small, form small, in her mother's arms.

Delcorta kissed her on the top of her head. Hattie knew her eyes were closed, to keep her own tears in. "You know I would do anything for you, my love."

FIFTY-ONE

Year Zero Zero Ninety-Four, Winter Season

There Are 977 Remaining Saints

19 Autumn 0090

Umma's going to tell me, today, about how it all happened. It's because she's dying. It's not fair. I feel three years old writing it, but it's not fair. That I have to know the true darkness of this world and then be left to it. That she is going to be gone. No

NO

NO

I can save her. I just don't think I'm going to be able to save myself.

20 Autumn 0090

She's gone. She's gone.

I'm not sure where to put all of it. I am not sure where to put myself.

They do think I pushed her. Of course they were going to think I pushed her—I think I'd rather have it so, than to have them believe she stepped off the top of the stairs herself. Now Il-Hyun says I have to be locked away for a few days, to soothe them.

I would say it was her final gift to me: a cruelty to my image to begin my reign. Maybe it wasn't only the final one, but the first as well.

But no. That's not quite right either. First, of course, of course, Delcorta gave me myself.

I grieve, I think. It's strange to. She was right, after all. She is still here, in a way.

She was right about the Ledger, too. Keeping it to ourselves—to keep the knowledge of this horrid magic solely to our bloodline—is a kind of repentance, I think I must think. I've barely moved it from where it was before our knees, on the study rug. I'll let it get swallowed up by the mess. Because there might be repentance here, but I still want to punish him. She wasn't sure if the King Min Titus Kkul had let the Ledger burn down slow to try to wring a salvaging enchantment from its pages, or if he was sore to let his work disintegrate—but I am very different from her. I am entirely my own person. I know. He wanted his success preserved as long as possible, even if he thought it was killing himself, too. I won't feed his profound magic to a god as pure as Flame. I'll let its bindings go soft in obscurity; I will not show it to my heir. I'll let it be nothing at all.

—

Icca stopped reading, and Caro put a knife to her throat. Caro was drawing blood, now, just a little.

"Go back," she growled. Icca kept her features in a snarl.

"Deities. What are you—"

"Go *back*, Alice."

"To *where*, Rabbit?" Icca spat.

"To whatever you just glanced over. You always were a shitty liar."

Icca didn't necessarily think this was true, and she did want to argue about it, but she was also fairly positive it would result in something like Caro saying that she had known Icca well enough to know when she was lying about something—she *was* lying about something, after all—to which Icca would, of course, have to respond that Caro didn't know anything about her at all. Which would also be a lie.

"Fine." Icca swallowed against the edge at her throat. "Put the blade away before you hurt yourself."

Carousel put her other hand on the back of Icca's neck and leaned in as her grin sprouted. "Aw, but you'd like that."

"I'd adore it. But I'd rather do it myself."

"Tell me, what else would you like to do to me, Alice? You've thought about me a lot, I'm sure, when you were with Cheshire—it's hard not to think of past lovers, even when your current one is as pretty as he is." Caro hummed, musing. She was so close the sound buzzed against Icca's skin. "I am a hard act to follow, aren't I?"

"Is that *jealousy*?" Icca laughed. "Isn't your narcissism enough to cast it off?"

"Jealousy? Ha. Why would I be jealous, darling? I've got you all to myself, here."

"You haven't a single piece of me."

"I can always cut one off."

"Then do so, you insufferable bitch."

They were inches apart. Blood slipped quietly over Icca's collarbone, and she felt a drop of her magic break uselessly from the corner of her mouth. Caro's knife stayed fast and still in her hand, against Icca's throat, and Icca saw the flicker of her own silver glint in the crow witch's black eyes.

She watched the thought cross Caro's expression, and so knew what was going to happen before Caro even leaned in. Carousel always did whatever she wanted the moment she wanted to do it.

Icca expected a tongue, traced excessively against the bead of her magic. She did not expect the kiss, pressed lightly at the corner of her mouth, there, gone, Caro leaning back, touch and knife falling away so her thumb could brush the silver now staining her lips.

"What the hell was that for?" muttered Icca, every part of her stiff.

Caro's nail skimmed thoughtfully against her mouth. "I wanted to see if it would rouse anything in me."

"Well?" asked Icca irritably, and regretted it a beat later. Asking, and thus actually wanting an answer, was a tell in of itself, to herself, which mattered more to Icca than if Caro saw it as a tell, too.

"Nothing at all."

"You're lying, Rabbit." She didn't know why she said it, a moment later.

Caro's smile was easy, like all her others. "If you want me to do it again, all you need do is beg."

"I don't. I won't."

"Then *read*, and correct what you glanced over."

"Fine."

—

. . . I will not show it to my heir. I'll let it be nothing at all.

I find that perhaps it's a habit of the body, writing my thoughts. I like it less. I think I will be done, and keep everything in my head. Perhaps this is just a farewell. I'll miss her as much as I do Delcorta.

사랑해. 사랑해.

—

"Her." Caro's voice was distant. Icca glanced up to see her looking at the far wall. "Who is the 'her'?"

How peculiar. Icca traced over the print again with her eyes. They had the same handwriting. The same hands... how deliciously peculiar...

And Icca, momentarily pausing to seemingly shake the hair from her eyes, tilted her head back, and called upon her Saints to scale the palace's tower wall.

They'd made Petra their playground, left the city in terror and dashed the myth of its unwavering protection. All those who survived would never allow themselves to be so helpless again—they'd reach for their magic, realize the pain was a nothing price. Now it was time to knock down the final defense, the final delusion—the High Priestess of Isanghan.

"Isn't it obvious?" It was such ecstasy. Perhaps, tied to her chair with her most-loathed person breathing down her neck, Iccadora found herself a new god. Truth. Or, perhaps, just glorious, glorious Judgement. "Hattie November Kkul."

FIFTY-TWO

Year Zero Zero Ninety-Four, Winter Season

There Are 976 Remaining Saints

CAROUSEL GATHERED UP the diaries.

"What?" Icca was laughing her horrible, spiked laugh. "What are you doing?"

"We're done." Caro's expression was hidden from the dark witch by the tangled sheet of her hair. "It'd be rude of me not to clean up unnie's things."

"These aren't your *unnie's* things."

Caro lifted a shoulder. "We don't know. It's all rather vague. You're rather biased." A beat. Diaries towered from Caro's arms as she rose. "I'll ask."

"You'll *ask*?"

"Well, no, actually." Caro shrugged again. "Probably not."

This was answered by another barbed scoff, upon which Caro savagely kicked Icca's chair over, then stepped over the writhing dark witch to return the diaries to the shelves. When she turned back, Icca had bent her head, temple scraping the carpet as she peered up at Caro.

"You don't care," Icca breathed, and then her words came faster. "Whoever she might be. *Whatever* she might be—killing for the throne, and she—she might be wearing a skin suit of the Red Princess and you don't even *care*—"

"It's a very pretty skin suit. I'd understand wanting it." She pretended to think. "If I did want it. I've spent a lot of money on my tattoos. And I like—"

"Your face, your form, I know, I know, you're the prettiest, you're the vainest, and yet you still bow to her. Gladly." Icca's gaze slipped off of Caro's; Caro found she didn't like it, when Icca's words seemed spoken to the ceiling instead of her. "I just assumed you'd want to know her truly."

"I do know her truly," Carousel snapped, even as she thought to herself, *I know Hattie well enough to know I won't ever know all of her.*

"Oh, really? Would she leave you behind in Wonderland?"

"Would Cheshire?" Caro shot, just for the sake of arguing, because she was feeling like she'd like to argue instead of storming off and being alone.

"I wouldn't want him there, the coward."

"Right, right. That was an unfair comparison on my part. Anyway, yes. Hattie would leave me behind. I don't think the intent would be so sour though, not like ours, the one we shared, Icky." Caro winked. "She'd probably just get distracted, wandering off to find the deepest part of Wonderland."

"You don't have to sound so awestruck, being abandoned."

"Better than the alternative."

"What's the alternative?"

"What's the alternative! Wouldn't you—you'd know." Caro rolled her eyes and huffed a breath when Icca did not answer, and would not look at her. "Or not, right." Icca probably thought it was the best choice they'd ever made, separating.

A few heartbeats of silence. Then, "I know."

Even though there was some kind of admission in this that soothed that bruise in Carousel's heart that would never quite heal, Caro—of course, readers—couldn't leave well enough alone. "For gods' sake! Then why even *ask*?" But they were getting off topic. "Why do you care whether or not she killed the White Queen? Us and Te— We were always saying how we were going to do that, anyway. You're being prickly for no reason. You don't actually care. You just want to wreak havoc and can't admit it to yourself that it's just because you're a bad person, and this has nothing to do with Hattie at all—"

"Oh, Carousel Rabbit, such a *moralist*."

"Oh, Iccadora Alice Sickle, such a *bitch*."

"Don't act like you don't care, like it doesn't bother you. Like *she* doesn't bother you, all her lies. You're pretending everything is the same so you can keep your life just the way you like it." Icca bared her teeth. "I thought Wonderland would beat it out of you."

"Beat what out of me?"

The dark witch's voice was cutting. "The need for other people."

Carousel grabbed a diary and threw it at Icca's head.

It wasn't particularly because she was offended—Icca's claim was laughable, after all. She just wanted to throw something at Icca's head.

"I don't need other people, Icky. I *like* other people. I know you are so jarred by the concept, having kept Cheshire around for—what? A lover, yes, yes, it's clear. But that's a footnote. He's an audience. Perhaps a stage."

Caro expected some rise of expression, of voice—Caro realized this was her whole point, to get the dark witch to snap at her, but Icca only kept her gaze drifted on the ceiling and murmured, quite a bit quieter than Caro had sought after, "Perhaps."

Caro, wanting more, said, "You could have found just as interesting people here, too, you know."

"Here. In Petra." Icca's voice was flat.

"Yes. Lots of Jabberwockies. Lots of other witches to pin your incorrect assumptions to." She drummed a fingertip on her bottom lip, as if to ponder. Gods, was Icca so awful and still and dramatic, with her silky hair like an oil spot against the carpet. The length of it seemed the only vanity she allowed herself, besides the mushrooms ringing her wrist. Caro had marked it after Icca had knocked her to the earth in Yule. Faerie circles. What a vicious idea to press into one's skin. "But I understand the charm those damp little inns might have. A dreary setting to fit a dreary character, as you, specifically, would say."

"I like my inns. And I like being alone more than anything else."

Dear readers, a sidenote: Icca did not dare add that she didn't put weight in the concept of home anymore—she wouldn't just *give* that to Caro—much like she'd barely give it to herself. And so a narrator must step in and pry these pieces into the open Light. If our Icca did say anything like this to our Carousel, her frustration might be too obvious—that Caro did have a home, here, that she could manage a feat like that and adore it while Icca couldn't stand the thought of pushing a key into a lock at the end of the long day, dropping her shoes in some usual place and her coat on some usual hook, and cook dinner when it got Dark, and have the book she was reading on a nightstand and the ones she'd finished on a shelf at the end of a bed. Having a home meant having habits for herself, habits that were mundane and comfortable and even kind, and for some reason the notion of it made Icca feel so raw and exposed it was like her chest had ruptured; it made her feel like a child, and that made her want to cry, and she didn't know the why of that, either. Better to keep to the inns, to the picking, to the movement of it all. Maybe she'd come here to knock off Hattie's head just for some godsdamn variety; it was a vacation, and she'd be back to thinking, *Soon, soon, I must be someplace else. . . .*

After all, after all, dearest, darling readers, Icca knew she'd been the one to run away first. Perhaps she had never entertained the idea that she might stop. Surely, she must keep running and running, getting wickeder and wickeder—she must be the villain of this story, because with what she'd done to Caro, she had made clear she wasn't the hero, and to be a side character! A fate worse than death, certainly . . .

But back to Carousel's gorgeous head. She watched Icca's dark brown eyes slip a little down the wall; she watched a breath rise in her stomach. "I figured you were here, in Petra, too," the dark witch muttered.

Caro had the unmistakable urge to bite Icca's bottom lip. But this might be taken the wrong way, so instead she jeered, "But aren't we having so much fun? We could have been doing this for years, now. You trying to poison my tea at every soiree. Me ripping out all the pages of all the books in the Ward. We would have driven unnie mad!"

"She is mad."

"Alone, alone..." Caro hurried along—she needn't hear Icky Sickle's criticisms. "You said, once, that being with me was like being all alone... did you tell Cheshire that, too? Did you explain what it meant? It's rather hard to put into words, isn't it, and even then, I feel that understanding, not some sorry attempt at empathizing but understanding *truly*, would be impossible—unless you're you, unless you're me, or Tecca, or yes, if you were Tecca, I suppose, I suppose... she felt like she might be us, a skin over, like you could be me, and me, you... that's what you meant by it, isn't it, Alice?"

And Carousel knew that she herself would never have tried to split herself among Saints and siege the Petra Ward and kill Hattie, and that Icca would never have spent all of her Saints'-heads cash on a fresh dress, as Caro had done multiple times. They were different, had always been different from one another, but tucked into the corners of the orphanage, tucked hands and souls, it had felt like it couldn't be so. How strange it was, other people being other people, and familiar.

Wasn't there something still familiar, here?

It felt like it. The air between them electric, as it had always been.

Does it feel like you are alone now, Alice? Carousel wanted to ask. *Like we could talk for hours as we do to ourselves and never once feel* so tired *of it, as we do with other people...*

"Yes. It's what I meant," Icca said. "I was wrong."

You're boring me.

They'd each said it to the other witch, at some vicious point. What lies, Caro was sure. What laughably terrible lies.

"Ah, Icky," Caro sighed, something twisted up in her throat as she stood above the unmoving dark witch. "Don't be so harsh on yourself. We both thought to leave Wonderland, without the other."

And Caro wondered—*But don't*, she begged herself, but the thought continued to flutter through—she wondered if she herself was the cause. If she'd broken Icca in some way that now Icca had to go around breaking everything else. Because Caro knew—though she hadn't ever wanted to know—that Icca had toppled something over in her, too, scattered pieces of herself so Caro could never be home for too long, could not care about making friends in the Courts, could never even look at Hattie too far past the superficial, because on the surface level Carousel could marvel at Hattie and could even love Hattie, without it hurting that yes, yes of course, Hattie would leave her behind in Wonderland.

"Yes," Icca said, quietly. "We did."

Caro patted the diaries into a neater line on the shelf and smoothed over her expression, just in case it looked unsmoothed. She turned back to the candlelit chambers and Icca staining the soft look of the room in her inkblot-like way. Caro crossed the rug and untied her; Icca's eyes flicked to her, but Caro only chuckled. "Don't get so excited. You need to wash up before the trial."

It was after Carousel had herded Icca over to the washroom and she relieved herself and began to fill the sink with hot water, and noted that Caro was still in the open doorway—and she thus wouldn't have a chance to break the mirror for a shard of glass—that Icca finally spoke. "So there *is* to be a trial?"

"Of course," responded Caro, looking politely at the ceiling as Icca stripped. "It's for the sake of the Thia Court, primarily, those nervous nobles, but the Culled Court should see attendance, too—you know how Jabberwockies can't help themselves with a scandal. It's to be held in the

Church Off the Labyrinth, where we got that nasty death trace peeled away like a scab."

As if it were so superficial. As if Caro hadn't lain there on the dais afterward, finally ready to mourn Tecca, and found herself coming up with blanks. She was an entirely different girl than the one who'd left her Ward clutching Icca's hand. As if Carousel hadn't, then, realized she was mourning herself instead.

Some memory. A distant conversation, floating up . . . Icca-Caro-Tecca, sitting in this proper order in the classroom.

No. I don't think so.

You don't think so, Icca, that you'd mourn me? Ha! Tecca? Tecca, don't you have something to say about this? Now you're being very quiet indeed and it is deeply unnerving, as Alice is being kind of a bitch and that's something you usually comment on.

A weighted pause. *I don't want to talk about this anymore.*

Caro shook her head. Her words came up chipper, to beat the memory into dust. "Traffic should be fine, at least! Lockdown and all."

Water splashed around in the sink, drip, drip, dripped onto the stone floor, and Icca voiced, "A judge?"

"Hm?"

"Is there to be a judge?"

"Hattie unnie."

"A jury?"

Caro lifted a shoulder. "Hattie unnie."

"That doesn't seem very fair."

"It wouldn't, I suppose, but you're going to be proudly spitting every single horrid thing you've done as soon as you get your seat comfortable as it is, correct, Alice?"

"I mean," Icca said, "it doesn't seem very fair, seeing as she's not the Red Queen."

"She is." Carousel had no doubt. Caro had questions, certainly, but no doubt. Over the past three years, Caro had only ever known one Hattie November Kkul, and she was already an odder duck than the rest—so what if the Red Queen had killed the true heir, the Red Princess, stolen her body and station? Or something. This would all be fine with Carousel.

"She is the Red Queen, regardless of whoever she *actually* is, silly." She flapped a dismissive hand. "Besides. You'd die of spite anyway if a jury found you perfectly pleasant, and absolved you from any atrocity in the eyes of the great country of Isanghan."

"Yes."

"Yes. Then."

"An executioner?"

"What?"

"Are you my executioner?"

"Oh!" Caro did not know, and now delighted at the possibility. Executioner was a rare title, nowadays, what with the death trace and the like—but Hattie could peel that from her in record time, if there was a Saint's head around. "Well. Probably. I was due to butcher you anyway, in the Labyrinth." But then again, she had failed. Caro stood there in the doorway, eyes still trained on the rafters of the chamber, the way they filled with the haze of the candlelight, a little bothered by the thought. Was Hattie cross with her, for letting Icca get toiled up in her head?

Would Hattie be cross with her, now, if she'd found out what Caro had asked Icca to read aloud?

Before she'd swept into Hattie's chamber to spend the better part of the evening with the horrible little dark witch, she'd glimpsed Hattie unnie in the front yard, commanding the guards. It seemed that of Icca's thirteen Saints, seven had been put down by the Queen's forces or the Queen's own monsters, no doubt more by now—or maybe not. There were other Saints coming into the city, now, scalding themselves over the Labyrinth Wall, some of them dead on impact, Caro had heard, but some of them fine, just fine, just hungry.

Last Carousel had seen of her, Hattie had been murmuring to the head of the guards to bring them to the palace alive, if possible. In another world, with another Queen, it might have been viewed as a mercy for the sorry creatures.

Carousel knew better. Knew Hattie better than that.

Didn't she?

The diaries—it was a betrayal, yes. But maybe Caro had gone through with it anyway, besides the needing to know, because it was difficult to picture Hattie wanting to bury any part of herself. She might not speak a lot about the certainly great many thoughts in her head, but that didn't mean shame—Caro thought it couldn't mean secrecy, either. Hattie would answer her about anything, but only if her question was right. Caro just hadn't known what questions to ask.

With the thought, she opened her mouth to say it was far past Icca's bedtime, and Caro had better things to do than babysit her, when the sound of breaking glass cracked the quiet. Carousel stepped away from the doorjamb and Icca, clothes sticking to her wet skin, drove a shard of the mirror into the wood that had lined Caro's spine a moment prior. It cut into the dark witch's hand as she did so; blood streaked down her pale forearm.

Caro couldn't help but admire the look of it—after she'd wrapped her arms around Icca's neck and made her limp once more, there on the washroom floor among the glittering, sharp mess she'd made—the line of red Icca had pushed into her palm, the way she held the little growing pool in the natural way the tendons in her hand curled.

—

Carousel bound Icca's wound up with a washcloth and then lugged the unconscious dark witch down to the dungeons. She placed Icca in the cell opposite Cheshire's, for the potential drama of it.

"Play nice, you complete nutjob," she told him.

"And where are you off to, Miss Rabbit?" Cheshire cooed as she began to waltz away. His voice sprawling evenly again, as if she hadn't witnessed him, hours ago, practically frothing at the mouth. And Carousel, a chill clutching her spine, reminded herself that she didn't like talking to crazy people who weren't gorgeous girls, so she hurried on upstairs.

Caro paused in the hall before the corridor that fed into the tearoom. Arms looped around herself, she peered straight down the pass and between the long, blank tables to where the opened doors of the courtyard laid clear the maw of the trees. This serene, untouched center of Petra... being able to stare so far and see not a soul—even as she could sense that Hattie was drenched in magic just outside her line of sight—made Carousel feel very alone indeed.

Could it be true that she was done knowing other people, and the very last one had been Icca?

It was like staring up at the Forest for the first time, facing toward the palace courtyard, where somewhere within, Hattie was being so viciously Divine. Fear, and a want to know what lay within, twining, twining, twining...

"Oh, I don't like *contemplating* like this," Caro exclaimed irritably to the nearby wall. "Leave it *alone,* Carousel."

She stood there, twisting her hands and vaguely fuming.

"Well, but if anything, if I ask Hattie, it will be proof that Icky Sickle hasn't affected me so much that I no longer ask people what I'd like to ask them. Even though I suppose I simply haven't *felt* like knowing anything deep and dark about other people lately. I know this about myself, I do. And why would I do anything I don't *feel* like doing? Deep and dark is sticky—impossible to draw back from. I mean, to ask, to *know* unnie like that would—feel—it would *feel so*—gods damn it. You do actually *not* want to ask her anything, do you, Carousel! You're scared she might actually tell you! But I'm *sure* we used to not—oh, fuck you, Iccadora."

A musing narrator wonders if we should all live with a general terror in our hearts, that one day we might discover that other people are absolutely real, absolutely distinct from ourselves, and as a consequence, are wholly invulnerable to what we might desire from them once such realness and distinction is proven. Discovering what Hattie was hiding would serve as such proof to Caro—secrets being, of course, irrefutable evidence of a private world—and then Hattie would have distinction, and no longer be some glorious fiction come alive before Caro's eyes. And Caro knew what would happen to herself then, had already witnessed it before, what had happened after coming to know another girl, who was also a powerful witch. Hattie would be known by her and thus become real to her, and Caro knew with total clarity and total terror that this would be the end, because then, of course, of course, dearest readers, Carousel Rabbit would, after many years, desire to be loved.

And she wasn't sure if Hattie was capable.

"But I am," Caro said to the empty hall.

She felt sixteen again, wringing her hands with particular care, shuffling her feet.

"I love you very much, Carousel. So I would like you to be very courageous right now. Because we won't let Icca win like this, we won't. I refuse."

Caro, fidgeting, stomach in knots and surely pooling in the bottoms of her shoes, nodded to the wall.

And then began to move for the courtyard.

Walking through the unlit tearoom felt like being a faerie dropped in a glass jewelry box, placed on a high and dark shelf so the cat couldn't get to it. Caro pushed open the double doors at the back of the room and counted herself ever so lucky, to find Hattie in one of her rare circumstances twice now in the last fortnight: barefoot and kneeling on the grass, making a monster.

Caro waited until she was finished, until Hattie leaned back with a soft gasp as she severed her connection with the new beast. She looked over her shoulder, toward Caro but certainly not at Caro, slick from the eyes down and from the fingertips up, crimson magic streaking from her cuticles.

"Carousel," greeted Hattie in her murmuring way.

Caro, though still feeling nauseous, could just squeal with the look of it, the casualness and calm and the *gore* of the image before her, Hattie knelt on the grass with her distant expression smeared in red, the new Saint beginning to rouse and rise in a twist of limbs before her disinterest.

"I wouldn't want to distract you, unnie," said Caro.

The Queen's eyes moved momentarily back to her stitched Saint, who shuddered—she was obviously already plucking around its new seams, keeping it at bay. Then she gestured for Caro to come and sit beside her; the crow witch did eagerly, dropping to a seat on the dampened grass.

"You've digested all of Iccadora's petals, I see," Hattie noted, and seemed to pluck away the Saint's sense of balance. Like a building with weathered supports, it tumbled back into the water of the courtyard shore with a croak, drowning a few of the paper lanterns. "No longer tangled up, each other's gods..."

Caro didn't know exactly what that meant, but she said, proud and clear anyway, "I've high metabolisms. You've been busy as well, I see."

"It seems a stranger age lately, yes.... What have you done with your evening?"

"I gave Iccadora a bath. And unconsciousness." Caro fiddled with her hands in her lap, all those questions she had in her head. The practiced voice in her head said irritably, *Hattie is an enigma, and I enjoy her like that. I don't need truths. I don't. I tell you, Carousel, I* don't.

Caro had been afraid to know Wonderland, too.

She'd collected her Saints' heads, collected her gods, her heartbreak, her threads that would sew together a new self. Fled, when she was allowed, and returned, again and again. She'd asked it questions, in this way, with each foot she'd placed in front of the other; such queries had come naturally, when she recognized her terror and kept going on regardless.

And didn't she already know she was terrified of Hattie?

"Unnie, I was wondering..." Caro swallowed. "How *did* you come to be Queen?"

Hattie rubbed at her nose a little, licked her lips so the red at her mouth began to pink, which, Caro thought, was darling.

"My mother died," Hattie said. "I inherited the throne."

"Your mother? The White Queen?" Cold immediately clutched at her spine, with the way Hattie had stilled her hands. She knew exactly what Caro was digging for. Digging! Caro was being so disrespectful. But she couldn't stop, chilled and liking the bite of it. She wanted to know the truth. She held her breath and waited for Hattie to speak.

"Yes, Carousel. The White Queen was my mother."

"Yes. I mean. Well. I suppose that's the *how* I'm truly asking after . . . ?"

"Carousel."

"How did she die?"

Now Hattie turned to fully look at her. Somewhere off to the side, the Saint's movements were sluggish, rippling water softly at the courtyard grass. It seemed to Caro a very distant monster.

"I'll answer," said Hattie after a moment. "But you'll have to tell me why you want to know, and why at this moment in time."

The diaries were merely a tool, not the query; Caro did not hesitate in her answer, but she did not mention what she'd been doing all afternoon with Icca, either. Wouldn't Hattie want to know the core truth of it rather than the actions prompted by it, anyway? "Because I am infatuated with your magic and your face and your quiet, and how you hold it all. Because you're horrific, Hattie unnie, and I love you, and I want to know how you came to be like this. That's the truth of it, I swear it. I think I'd rather know the people I love over having the people I love know me, if I had to choose one. I think I'm more, that way."

Maybe Caro hadn't intended to say all of that. To reveal there, on the blood-and-magic-soaked grass, that she was a heretic, that she found Divinity in other people more than she found Divinity in natural forces—but then, Hattie was a natural force. She'd been wanting to read those diaries for years now, not to catch Hattie in a lie, but to draw back a past that had shared the same seasons as Caro's own. Why did it have to seem such a silly, childish thing, just wanting to *know*?

Caro felt off-center, suddenly, with the words that had bubbled up. The day had been so long; Carousel was so tired. She'd spent the hours remembering over and over again that she used to know Icca, had started again and again at the thought that she felt she knew Icca now, too, and that it didn't matter one bit. Nothing between them could ever be forgotten, or burned down, neither their love for one another in their girlhood nor all the hurt they'd inflicted in Wonderland. They couldn't go back; they could hardly move forward. They kept tripping over the memory of themselves pressed into the other.

Beneath all the magic on Hattie's lips, Caro found a smile that was small, and sweet. "That is a very different question, Carousel."

"What?" She felt like she could start weeping at the softness in Hattie's voice.

"How I came to be Queen—it's a very different question than how I came to be like this."

Caro realized that Hattie was inviting her to ask a question. But now, if Carousel squinted, it seemed that Hattie looked a little melancholy. Why was Caro rushing this? Because of Iccadora, certainly; that was the genuine sickly Sickle presence for you. Caro could wait, at least until Saints stopped eating witches alive in their Petra apartments. She'd have a long life by Hattie's side as it was. *I've come very far in my own head, as it is, today, and I'm tired. . . .*

"Ah, that's all right," sniffed Caro. "I don't have a good answer for why I need to know anything right now."

"Wanting to know right now is a good answer, Carousel, if it is the truth."

"It is. But I take back the query."

"Do you?"

Caro hesitated. Hattie laid her hand against one set of knuckles, covering the tattoos there with soft fingers.

"You gave me the pure truth, Carousel. I thank you humbly for it. So I will answer you." Caro looked up, startled, even more so to find Hattie's mudwater eyes locked on hers—*locked*, not like Hattie was somewhere else in her head, but like she emerged from her depths, had to remember herself as a physical thing, just to say to Carousel, "I killed my mother."

Caro's mouth went slack. Words from what seemed an age ago ran in her ears.

Some people believe I killed my mother.

Did you?

I suppose....

Hattie glanced past her, unhurried.

And then Saints came shrieking in from the Woods.

FIFTY-THREE

Year Zero Zero Ninety-Four, Winter Season

There Are 974 Remaining Saints

HATTIE TILTED HER HEAD.

The red threads of her magic rose from her cuticles and drifted through the air, shimmering and then gone. Her stitched Saint lifted its massive skull from the water. Three of them she'd spent the twilight binding into one—it was truly one of her most terrible pieces, one of her best. She felt its indifference as it turned toward the disturbance of the water, as two Saints came crashing over the palace wall. Hattie recognized them both. One she'd made herself, and the other . . . well. Iccadora had been keen enough to notice that it had been brought to life by a different witch. The other Hattie. The first Hattie.

She took her new Saint's indifference, and she twined it with its hunger. And sent it from her, slick as a water viper as it shot between the trunks of the trees.

"Unnie," Carousel croaked, as Hattie got to her feet. Hattie looked down; Carousel's fingers were on her stained sleeve, the full black circles of the crow witch's eyes exposed in their whites. "You killed—"

Hattie brought her sleeve away. It was not a sharp motion, but Carousel immediately swallowed her sentence, and rose as well. Hattie had wanted to tell Carousel about Delcorta, but explaining was another matter—she'd wanted to tell her in order to watch her reaction. To see if she'd demand something more. If she'd be disgusted.

Instead, the crow witch bowed below even Hattie's own height, came up with her fingers braced upon the white rose pin of Hattie's Courts.

It was a small gesture; Hattie felt it grandly.

And then the Jabberwocky turned on her heel and was gone, off to kill more monsters for her Queen.

Hattie tilted her head back, broke her hair away where it had fastened to the dried magic on her face, and saw that one of the Saints—the one she'd made herself—was beginning to scale the tower-study walls. The other was fighting her new Saint in the water; she knew the other would lose. It was Delcorta's first daughter's work, and Hattie was so much more of a witch than the Red Princess had ever been.

Than she'd ever given herself the chance to be, before dying.

Before creating Hattie as she existed now.

Hattie stood upright, watching the brawl. She tugged the threads; she separated the Saint's blank fury when it began to bleed into her own calm. She liked this bit, finding new enchantments, the new ways the world gave in to her insistence. Awe was perhaps a better word for it than arrogance.

—

Icca's eyes were rolling back in her head, but her sight was fairly clear.

She was down to two Saints, and they were her best, more horrifying bodies—no—one, now.

Fighting a new monster in the water ringing the palace, Icca's sight was suddenly black, and then nothing at all, and she choked, momentarily stuttering back into her body, twitching and cold on the stone floor of a cell. Kai blinked down at her from his own. Icca ignored him; she slipped away once again. She—Dul had been killed, by the Red Queen's most recent beast. Icca had one more left.

Which might be better, after all. She was very settled into this, as this one, Hana, without all the other consciousnesses pulling at her. She was climbing up white stone and wisteria-threaded perches, their perfumes like sulfur in the slits of her nostrils.

She smashed away a window at the very top of the tower and came reeling over a desk. Some part of her popped from the cramped entrance, and she marveled how the aftershock rang through her strange, sprawling body without pain trailing after it. She fell upon a book-strewn rug and began to rampage it. Time-weathered parchment took to the air upon under her scrambling limbs; ash from past fires lifted out of the hearth. What was she looking for again? A book, certainly. A Ledger.

The bookshelves pressed to the back of the study were foothilled by stacks of tomes; it took a few tries to get all her eyes to keep from spinning in different directions, to pause herself and look carefully. It would be thin, just two leather covers flattened by their surroundings, holding what must only be a few pages at most, if Hattie wrote true in her diary, that the King had tried to burn it all down. Icca couldn't help but respect Hattie's decision a little, damning Min Titus's greatest magic to obscurity, not even to flames, but to dust.

And there—a thin pad of leather jammed nearly at the bottom of a stack of tomes.

Getting over the momentary startlement of reaching forward and finding her hand massive, with ten fingers sprouting from the palm, she eased two of them around the Ledger's corner and pulled it free. Books tumbled; she barely heard them.

The eyes in this head were actually a beat better than the eyes in her own—there were fine, tiny runes edged into every part of the leather bindings. Icca turned and lumbered over to the desk, finding an ink pen, but all her fingers wouldn't fold right around its length. Damn it. She'd have to bring it down to the dungeons.

She turned. Carousel Rabbit was in the arched doorway of the study, leaned up against the frame with her arms crossed and smile full of mirth. Her cloak was casually brushed off of one hip, revealing knives strapped to her long thigh under the trim of her black skirt.

"Holiest shit, is that you, Alice?" she greeted, grinning, eyes clearly drawn to the pen in Icca's awkward hand rather than the Ledger, which Icca shifted to hide behind her back. "An academic, even like this!" Now she was shrieking laughter. "You look downright ridiculous!"

Forgetting her throat, which had long been absent of ability to create anything much more than shrieks, Icca tried to speak. But the sound that came from her was grating, and undeniably not hers, and the consciousness stuttered away. The thought she'd tried to voice carried alongside her as she came back into her body, down in the dungeons, rasping, "—ing *deities,* you are *insufferable.*"

"That's not very nice," said Kai.

"You—" croaked Icca. "You pathetic—"

She paused, peering up at him from the floor of the cell. He looked so tired, that bright, obnoxious personality still glittering in his eyes but hung with dark crows'-feet, and it was clear he was bracing most of his weight against the bars. No doubt the Queen had made use of him—that's what he got for running away. The cowardice of it made Icca broil momentarily, but then she simmered, leveled out as she remembered how there wasn't much use expecting anything of anyone besides herself. She'd never demanded anything of Kai, and nor had he of her. It was part of the reason why they liked one another's company, past the entertainment factor. They really never expected the other not to be a horrible person.

Which is why Icca said, with a growing smile, without an ounce of guilt, "Deities. You're a sight for sore eyes."

Kai grinned back just as sharply. "You as well, darling."

"M—" Icca winced, and saw a flash of Caro tumbling down the tower-study stairs. It was up to Hana, now. Icca flushed her dry throat and the foreign hunger seeded in it, and tried again. "Make me more rose draught."

Kai's grin split wider, but now his voice was harsh. "Shibal, Sickle, isn't it enough already?"

"I don't expect you to understand."

"Do *you* even understand? That's what I've been sitting down here wondering over, after the Queen t-took my eyes—I saw you too, in the Labyrinth. You're unraveling—you wanted to kill Hattie November, and where are your Saints now?"

"So *pious*, Cheshire." Icca spat out the word as if it were venom. "Your moralities mean nothing to me. Carnage is one of my gods."

Kai barked a laugh, the sound incredulous. "Is Fear? Is Grief? You're feeding those deities, too."

"I don't care!" Icca was shouting now, on her knees as she gripped the bars and leaned for him. She was flecking the path between them with silver spittle like a child. She could act a child. She could act a child and she would ruin it all regardless. "I don't care I don't care I don't *care*! Her bloodline threw me to the wolves, and I ate them *alive*—I'm the scariest thing the Kkuls ever created. And I am the only one of their monsters that's going to make them pay for it."

And then Icca went quiet. Somewhere far off, Kai was laughing, Kai was saying, "Oh, *please*, Sickle, marry me?" but she could barely hear him, because she realized that he'd been right.

She hadn't just been harming the Queen; she'd barely given Hattie November a scratch. Icca had been so twined up in her Saints that she'd fallen into their hungers; she'd let them chase it down, in the streets, in apartments hiding terrified witches in their corners.

She felt full, and then sick for it. She turned to relieve her stomach and found it already empty, and spat up only clear bile and magic.

I can still do it. On her hands and knees, Icca's head was swimming, still trying to push her into different depths, a different head. *I'm not done. I'm not done yet.*

"You are an empty, pathetic shell, same as the Saints," she spat to Kai, who was still laughing.

And Hana was clattering down the stairs.

Icca wanted to shriek when she saw the Ledger choked in its grip, almost completely hidden in its many-fingered fist, weight leaned upon it as it scrambled toward her on the curl of its knuckles. It flattened itself against the bars, near nine feet of bone and skin and braided torso, one arm so long it seemed ever-extending as it reached for her, and she caught the Ledger and the pen as they dropped from its grip.

Greedily, ignoring Kai's gagging, Icca peeled open its cover and found that of its two remaining pages, only one was still attached to its binding. She let the loose page flutter to the floor and took out the pen, arched over the Ledger as she pressed the tip to the final page.

But it startled her. Magic immediately rushed out of her gums and broke at the corners of her mouth; she had barely scratched out the first couple of syllables before a shockwave of sheer *power* radiated from the Ledger. Her breath tumbled down to the base of her lungs and she choked, and there was the fleeting thought that if she had not spent the last couple days splitting herself, she would have been smeared away by the sensation that overtook her, that she must be in two places at once. Beneath the palace, her knees cut by the frigid dungeon stones, but also, also, standing in the grassy knolls of the moorlands, head tipped back as she searched for sky, only to find, tipping, tipping, tipping, the colossal rise of Wonderland Forest. And from its gaping black maw with trunks slicing heavensward, there rumbled that same depth of power that flooded from the Ledger, but here it was quieter; there was no need to shriek, for such noise Wonderland liked to swallow down, just as it liked to swallow little girls and turn them inside out and outside in, so that they stumbled back out again believing they held the same blood and bones, but really, really, there, under their skin, grew roots. . . .

Icca gasped, the vision peeling away and the pen clattering from her hand, and like a plucked chord, she felt the conscious edge she shared with Hana shudder, and then snap.

The Saint flinched, and then it took a step back. Icca choked again, coughed, splattered the magic that burst from her bare molar beds against the wall.

That's when Carousel Rabbit came barreling through, and hit the jarred Saint with the weight of her entire form.

It collapsed in a fury of teeth and limbs, and Icca was choking on air as she found herself entirely herself again; such a complete and singular thing. She was panicking. It was so much. She was so much bigger than her body and now she had only one.

Somewhere to her left, Caro had sent the Saint to the ground, feet braced on its chest as her knives dug home, and again, and again, and Icca's hands were over her ears, and she was sobbing with her whole form. Curled over the Ledger now, she shook, and she breathed, and she found it all so much; she was *so much*, and she didn't know if she was crying with relief or despair at the thought.

Her neck was burning; she touched it and found lengths of skin raw and stinging, but no longer the ribbon of the suppressing brand—it seemed the gracing of Min Titus Kkul's magic upon her skin, the mere physical touch, had not only shocked away her connection to this last Saint, but also had disintegrated the rune keeping her power locked to the Labyrinth.

Icca's magic flowed at its broken restraints but still found opposition at the runes etched onto the cell bars. Now she was weeping at the barrier, and at the grief she hadn't realized she'd been carrying around for her power, how she'd only been separated from the touch of the Dark for little more than a day, and had missed it so much it ached. She'd missed herself; she hadn't been herself, and she grieved for that brief, black death.

Before her, the Saint she'd been turned toward the cell, sensing Icca's mourning and wanting to swallow it down even as it was being torn apart by Caro's blades. The line of its fingers closed around the bars just as Carousel drew away head from neck.

And Icca wanted to close her eyes, to shut it all out, and stumble upon herself in the Darkness.

"It's in us," she slurred, and unsure if she actually was saying any of it aloud. Roots, under her skin, surely, surely... "It's why she made the Culled Court. We can't ever leave Wonderland. We can't. We carry it everywhere."

She was laughing. She was sobbing.

What relief. What protection.

She'd survived Wonderland. She'd survived the Labyrinth. And so she was blessed, and chosen, and destined. Destined for what? Whatever she wanted... and Carousel was, too. An equal opponent. Icca wouldn't have it any other way.

Perhaps she was in delirium. Perhaps she was greedy. *I'm not done yet....*

Iccadora Alice Sickle wanted everything. Ruin, and Rabbit. To love and hate her and think of her and kill her. She wanted everything....

FIFTY-FOUR

YEAR ZERO ZERO NINETY-FOUR, WINTER SEASON

THERE ARE 972 REMAINING SAINTS

"WELL," SAID CAROUSEL TO the occupants of the general area: the watching Cheshire, the crying and trembling Icca, the slack body of the Saint, its head weighing in her hand, and, of course, herself. "That got a little messy."

She stood at the Saint's shoulder, which was collapsed against the bars of the cell, and knocked its skull against them. "*Ya*, Alice, give it over. Don't make me take it from you."

She didn't know why Icca had sent the Saint up to the tower just for a pen, but knew it couldn't be anything particularly good.

Under the slant of her brow and the messy ink of her hair, Icca looked at Carousel with one dark brown eye. An expression flickered there that Caro didn't care to catch.

"Now," Caro hummed.

Icca, keeping her other hand cradled to her chest, knocked the pen over to the edge of the bars. Caro plucked it up, a little surprised the dark witch had let it go so easily. Maybe it hadn't been Icca at all, in the Saint, in unnie's tower study. Maybe picking it up was just some remaining thread of its personality, from one of the witches it had once been, like the flower-picking or tea-making Saints Caro had encountered before.

"Get some sleep, you horrid little imp," Caro called back affectionately as she moved for the stairs. "Your trial is first thing tomorrow morning. Jal ja, Cheshire dear. Adore you."

Caro came out of the dungeons and into the low-lit hall. The bodies of the guards who hadn't dispersed quickly enough had been strewn here and there by Icca's barreling Saint, Caro's own Birds peppering the stone of the floor. She glanced out the courtyard-facing windows and found no sign of Hattie's new triple-stitched Saint or the one it had been brawling with in the water, or even Hattie herself.

She passed by medics and other guards helping to carry the bodies away as she reached the Queen's wing, nodded to by guards she'd never seen before—which did suggest that Aarnik oppa and Chun-Ho oppa were dead too. She hoped in a musing way that this wasn't the case, or, at least for Chun-Ho, because he'd complimented her hanbok every year she'd been at the Midwinter Tea and Aarnik was generally pricklier, so if she had to choose . . .

"Unnie?" Caro called carefully, announcing herself from the entryway of the unlit bedchamber. She took off her boots, and, finding her socks were also stained with blood, removed those too. "You're still kicking too, right?"

The silence beat forward. Caro dared another step into the room.

In the dark, the Red Queen was seated before her vanity, her face in its mirror hazy in the low light. She'd cleaned herself up, donned her sleeping gown. On the table's surface lay her diaries, some closed, some half opened.

Caro's mouth went completely dry.

She couldn't even revel in the fact that Hattie had such an ability to terrify her, as she usually did, as the Queen's head tilted over her shoulder.

"You missed putting one away, Carousel," said Hattie. "I found it discarded on the rug. Can you read, then, after all?"

Caro swallowed. "No. I made Alice read them aloud."

"That explains your sudden queries."

"I explained my queries, unnie. What I confessed to you in the courtyard was true. My intentions to you are true."

Caro bolted back the instinct to flee—one that was rare to rouse in her—as Hattie turned toward her fully.

"Would you light a few candles?" asked Hattie, surprising her.

"I—yes. Of course."

Caro found the matchbox and struck, bringing flame to the wicks standing on one side of the vanity table. The light shuddered before going steady and soft, and Caro, now only a couple of feet away from Hattie, looked down to find the Queen's expression to be much altered than how it'd seemed to Caro in the dark.

Hattie looked tired, and sad. The fear in Caro's chest did not flee but eased over for the swell of a heartache. *Oh*, she thought, *I am afraid. I am so afraid.*

She knelt on the rug before her Queen, and, carefully, took Hattie's small hands between hers.

"Unnie," whispered Carousel, "you don't have to be so alone in this, in the depths of your spectacular head. I—I wish to know your past, if you'll have me. I'll try my best to understand what it's like."

The corners of Hattie's fine eyes were cloaked by her hair, and it made her seem all the younger as she tilted her head down toward Caro's. She was a witch of indescribable magic, the greatest Queen that Isanghan had ever witnessed, would ever witness. Caro had initially been drawn to the Culled Court because of that profound power, juxtaposed in such a shell of a girl. But even that would have been boring, eventually. Carousel had stayed because Hattie, not as a witch but as a personality, had made Caro fall, a little, and then a lot, in love. It was not romantic, but it was love, and Caro would be a heretic just fine; if it was a choice between the love of the world and the ones she loved standing upon it, she'd abandon her gods easily.

The Red Queen drew in a breath.

"I am," Hattie began, her voice quiet, and the look in her eyes distant, "the Red Queen Hattie November Kkul. Second of my name."

FIFTY-FIVE

YEAR ZERO ZERO NINETY, AUTUMN SEASON

THERE ARE 1087 REMAINING SAINTS

DELCORTA OCTOBER KKUL birthed a single daughter: the Red Princess Hattie November Kkul, first of her name, a bright young witch who would clearly grow to be an extraordinary power.

Most would know her to be a quiet girl; those who truly knew her—the young noble Il-Hyun Hyo, and much more extensively, her mother, the White Queen—were aware that she was only quiet in public, and observed carefully all the while her mouth was shut, and otherwise was lively, and arrogant, and witty, and curious about the magic of the world around her, and the magic within herself.

Then Delcorta became ill. Delcorta was going to die.

So the White Queen summoned Hattie November Kkul to her tower study, to at last tell her heir about how the Saints turned feral. And eighteen-year-old Hattie November Kkul ascended the stairs with a plan already in her head.

The official debut of her magic had been this past Midwinter Tea, stitching together a new Saint before the transfixed Courts, but Hattie had been creating monsters for least a half decade by then. At thirteen, she saw the Saints as something like dolls she was making for herself—certainly they were more trinketlike than anything else, empty shells as they were.

But over the years, she became more aware of sentience, its implications; she grew to notice consciousness, to admire and be in awe of the strange feat of it, and now knew what it meant in full to draw it all together, two into one.

But the Saints *were* still empty shells, their sentience a delicate layer above the depths of their Divinity, of their hollowness, thin ice sleeking over a bottomless lake. Hattie knew her ability to stitch them together relied on such a superficial structure, that the Saints' minds gave when she pressed them together, like brown sugar under the curve of a spoon. She had no idea whether the same magic would work for human beings.

But she was still going to try.

Because she was scared of being all alone without Delcorta, at the head of a country infested with monsters.

And because, perhaps, she could.

So it was okay, that Hattie wanted to stitch herself together with Delcorta, and that she, in a way, would be dead for it.

It was okay. It was going to be okay.

She was going to tuck herself into her own magic, fall head over heels over mind over thought into her own veins, and it would be euphoria.

Hattie was still scared, of this kind of end. It was an end. But her mind was made up.

So her mother, after agreeing—of course she agreed, after a set line in her brow, after Hattie trembled with her words but did not look away; Delcorta, after all, would do anything her daughter truly wanted—held Hattie in the tower study while she cried, and shook, and braced herself.

Little Hattie was going to be gone. She wondered—would whoever she was about to become grieve her?

"Now, my love," Delcorta murmured into the soft of her hair. "My brave, brave girl. There's no rush on it; we'll sit here as long as you like."

Outside, the dusk was soon swallowed up by the very shadows it'd primed. Delcorta opened the window to let the night air in; she called for tea, and placed the cup in her daughter's hand. Hattie drank, and wept more at the feeling of the drink warming her throat, and then her stomach, the spiced, sweet scent of its steam; she was going to miss this, so much, too.

Then, with her cup drained, it felt like time.

Delcorta kissed Hattie on the brow, one hand on the back of her daughter's head. And Hattie closed her eyes and found her magic, the Divinity threaded into the fabric of her soul, and then she leaned, and she found how it shone in her mother. It felt the same as hers; she was sure, for a beat, it was hers, until she remembered it was Delcorta's magic she was outlining in her head, and thought to herself, her last thought to herself, *We really are just ourselves, and one another, over and over again. What bliss. What bliss.*

And then Hattie November Kkul, first of her name, bleeding her magic, opened up the seams of her soul, and opened up those of her mother, and stitched them together.

It did not feel like dying. It felt like a lot of things. Like she was a lake drinking down a storm, like she was the glow of a candleflame against wallpaper, in a massive room where the sunlight was just beginning to come in. It felt like worship, and dreaming, and falling asleep, and then it felt like nothing at all.

—

And then, dearest readers, the Hattie November Kkul we've come to know in her depths, second of her name, came to in her mother's arms, which were cold, and still.

Hattie would remember it as an important note, that stillness, the stillness of the room arched around her. Because she did not feel still at all. She felt so achingly alive.

I am awake, she had thought to a self, then realized it herself. *It is so strange to be awake.*

Having come into existing with a fully formed head, for a time, in the dark, Hattie just lay there, her spine to her mother's stomach. She took inventory. Her age, her body, her magic, her memories—before she realized that the room was Quiet, and through the Quiet Wonderland was speaking to her, was whispering without words *Be here, be here now*, and Hattie thought, *Yes, yes, I promise I'll try. . . .*

And she took comfort in her thoughts, because those were all her own—everything was all her own. She was not the layered personalities and consciousnesses of Delcorta and Hattie the First. She was singular. Someone entirely new.

And then Hattie dragged her mother's slack body over to the top of the tower stairs and sent it tumbling down.

She grieved Delcorta. She grieved Hattie the First, little Hattie.

She's gone. She's gone.

That night, Hattie used her magic for the first time, weakening the balance of a servant bringing her a root tea, the tray trembling on his palm before clattering onto the bedroom carpet. She wept again as she crawled hands-and-knees to retrieve the cup, waving back the frightened servant with as much comfort as she could manage, which was little. He retreated, thinking she was crying over Delcorta, or perhaps her temporary arrest in the tower study. She was not. Hattie sat back onto her heels when he was gone, chin tilted up to the darkened rafters as her magic stung over her lips, eventually covered by her palms as she shook, as she spoke through them. "My gods. My gods."

I'm not sure where to put all of it. I am not sure where to put myself.

She was not only someone. She was someone powerful, and in a world like the one she happened to exist in, it rendered her Divine.

FIFTY-SIX

YEAR ZERO ZERO NINETY-FOUR, WINTER SEASON

THERE ARE 972 REMAINING SAINTS

IT WAS ALREADY SO DAMN DARK in the dungeons, but Icca wanted to wait for her god to really settle. So it was only when the candles in the wall alcoves sputtered out, when she felt the lightlessness click so cleanly into place that she opened her eyes, that she pulled the Ledger out from beneath her cloak.

Hana's massive palm had hidden it from Caro's sight; the fool witch had thought Icca wanted only a pen. Though Icca had been too hasty with all of it before, and was almost grateful to Caro for the interruption. This was an act of worship, after all. Icca wanted to do it right.

She opened her mouth, silver connecting the corners of her lips, glinting, not glowing, servile to the Darkness. Icca dashed a fingertip against the strands, the action quick, and, skin stinging, brought her magic to the page.

Icca could have everything. She'd be the most powerful witch in existence. It all came down to such a simple exchange. Sanity for Sainthood.

For safety.

But who needed safety? Tecca had been gone for almost five years. Even if Icca deemed Caro worthy of it, of protection from harm, the crow witch would consider it the dullest gift.

So—who was there left to save?

Just herself. Ha. Ha.

It was funny to Icca, you see, dear readers, the waste of it.

Icca didn't want saving. Wonderland Forest had killed the girl who had wanted saving, saving from the boredom of her Ward, the smallness of her world.

How petty it seemed now. Once Icca had seen what there was truly to fear, it wasn't the Forest. It wasn't the Saints that teemed within.

She knew what Hattie was. The Red Princess and the White Queen, drawn into one. Sewing together her monsters, craving that kind of companionship, that kind of mirror. She'd sought it from Caro and Icca, too. *You would've never been lonely again....*

"*I* was never the villain." Icca's grin cleaved apart her features. "Not yet... not just yet..."

With her magic staining her fingertip, Icca drew her touch to the delicate page of the Ledger. And began to write.

꿀 하티 노뱀쁘르.

Hattie November Kkul.

—

On a chair pulled to the side of the Queen's bed, Carousel started awake, and a moment later, recognized she didn't know why.

She didn't know how she could have possibly fallen asleep after Hattie had told her, told her everything, her quiet voice breaking several times as the candles burned down, eventually sending them into darkness. Caro had squeezed Hattie's hand, tears in her own eyes, which had stayed wide to find the Queen's features in the night. Later, she knew she'd revel in being Hattie's confidant, in her newfound awe; for now, all she felt was an empathy so carved that it ached. Caro had loved like that, once. Loved so fully that she thought she wouldn't be anything at all if Icca were gone.

But a narrator digresses, dear readers—Caro started awake. Her fingers found the rests of the chair as she pulled herself up, blinking back her confusion. The room was completely quiet.

Hattie was upright in bed. Her spine stark straight, unmoving. Her form was a slight outline in the dark, and Caro could not see her face.

"Unnie?" Caro mumbled. "Gwaenchanhayoh?"

"You love her."

The words startled her. Caro didn't know what was happening, exactly, but she did know Hattie was talking about Icca. Caro tilted her chin up, and her voice was simmering. The burst of anger did wonders for her disorientation. "I hate her."

"All of your cravings, Carousel. For rich things and violent things and storms—how close does all of it compare to Iccadora, in your head? Are you sated with the gap of it? You hate her—do you think you could ever hate anything else, as much?" Hattie's voice was light, slightly hoarse. She sounded, a little, like she was smiling. "Well. My mistake. It's just you romanticize one another's deaths so much that 'love' seemed a steady guess. What about Tecca Moore?"

Cold shot down Caro's spine. "What about Tecca?" she croaked, forgetting she wasn't supposed to mention Tecca.

"Oh," Hattie said, her voice distant. She turned her chin briefly to the left, like a spasm, before being still again, the action so quick Caro questioned whether she'd seen it at all. "Oh... what you all could've made. Who I could've made you into... She would've been glorious."

That's when Caro felt it. Felt Hattie leaning in her head.

But Hattie was just supposed to be able to loosen Caro's brain from her skull, or make her blind, perhaps identify an emotion—these pieces Caro would give gladly. But Hattie wasn't supposed to be able to sift. Caro felt her sifting, thoughts, memories, knew this was, impossibly, what Hattie was doing, because now Caro was thinking of Tecca. And Caro was not supposed to mention Tecca.

"What—" Caro started, and where she thought her palm lay on the wood rest of the chair she found it instead

upon the cool, soft flesh of a cheek, so then she was looking at

Tecca's

empty eyes, half opened, and the bedroom black and alive with smoke—

Caro snatched her hand to her chest, its rapid rise and fall, and looked about the unlit room in a panic she was unused to. Her mouth bone-dry, the corners of her eyes stung as her magic roused in time with the thudding of her heartbeat. Hattie was still in her head, sending the memories bubbling out from the walls, and it was as if Carousel were dreaming, when one is so sure that the world is so strange, and dear readers, so sure was Caro that the memories were screaming out of the dark of the room instead of out of her own head. Yes, it all must be coming out of the shadows—the skin weaving the rafters with the hazy morning light filtering through, the slack face of Pillar peering down at them from the ceiling, Tecca's body weighing the floor under their feet—it was all too much for Carousel to have possibly contained in her head.

"Stop," Caro gasped, her heels kicking at the rug in her franticness. Blue ran down her cheeks, the magic thinned with her tears. "Not Tecca. Not T—Tecca— Whatever you're doing, unnie, please, *stop*!"

"What about Tecca Moore?" Hattie asked again, her voice so calm compared to Caro's sobs that she nearly missed it.

What about Tecca Moore? Nothing about Tecca. There could be nothing about Tecca—she wasn't supposed to think about it. Standing beside her, Tecca shrouded by the smoke of her stolen cigarettes in the bell tower, and Caro couldn't think about it. Couldn't grieve, not with Saints in the Ward, not with it all already done and past and Caro, present and alive with all of her things pressing her into something bright and secure. She was real, and Tecca was not.

"I loved her." It broke from Carousel. "I loved her, and what does it matter, please, please, what does it matter now?"

The room seemed to breathe in, the memories gone, the space quiet and still once more.

"I think it could matter," said Hattie thoughtfully. "Doesn't it feel like it could matter... apologies, if it was cruel, it's just—she was buried, in your head, and I didn't expect it to be so easy to pry her out, but... something's changed. Something's changed and I wanted to try it."

Now the Queen's hands were rising to her own face. Caro, sweat clinging to her temples, pitched forward and fumbled for the matchbook at the bedside table.

She struck a flame but never made it to the candle wick.

The single match burning down in her fingers, Carousel could only stare at Hattie's face, which was tilted toward her, which was flooded, eyes and nostrils and lips, with—no, not crimson, but black—

"Okay." Hattie spoke softly, fingers tracing down her slick cheeks. "I suppose I could admit it. Now I'm a little mad."

The flame hissed against Caro's fingertips. She could barely feel it. And then it went out.

The dark swallowed them back down, and the moment it did, Hattie November Kkul twitched, and then she was upon Caro, hands on the crow witch's throat as Carousel screamed, and screamed, and then went slack, and quiet, and smiled up at her Queen.

FIFTY-SEVEN

Year Zero Zero Ninety-Four, Winter Season

There Are 972 Remaining Saints

ICCA WAS

Oh.

A grave mistake has been made, dearest readers.

Humor me, again, again, allow an embarrassed and grinning narrator to start this chapter over.

FIFTY-SEVEN

YEAR ZERO ZERO NINETY-FOUR, WINTER SEASON

THERE ARE 973 REMAINING SAINTS

ICCA WAS, APPARENTLY, UNASSUMING; she'd thought the guards would attempt to subdue her first, before they unlocked her cell—then again, they believed the Labyrinth brand was still locking her powers away. They believed themselves safe.

She didn't need to be so decadent with it, but had missed her magic and so she was *so decadent.* She spun shadows like silk clothes, when the guards opened the door, breaking the line of suppression runes; she indulged in a Dark as deep and rich as Wonderland earth. She drowned the guards in their own lightless spots, and left them half things on the stone floor. For a moment, Icca traced back and forth before Kai's cell. He'd been reduced to a grinning thing, sat nicely on the floor of his cell. Half-glazed eyes watching her thumb the key she'd taken from the guard's waist.

Icca lifted it toward the lock, and Kai shook his head.

"Oh, Sickle..." he murmured. "Don't you see that I'm hers, now?"

She couldn't keep the look of disgust off her face. He'd had such a weak will, to be reduced so.

"Yes. Look at me, just like that. Aren't I so lucky, to be in the attention of one of the greats?"

"You could've been one of the greats."

"I don't want to be," said Kai, folding his hands in his lap and smiling beatifically at Icca, or maybe the space of air next to her head. "I don't want to be."

Icca didn't have time to parse that. She was too excited to feed Hattie.

She thumbed in her pocket, where one single silver petal remained, shimmering with black Saint blood.

Icca cast a last glance over the fallen guards. No, she really hadn't needed to be so decadent with it—she was planning on going to the exact place they'd been instructed to bring her. Cast one more glance toward the pitiful witch grinning up at her.

"Goodbye, Cheshire."

"Go peacefully, Sickle," said Kai. And fell onto his side, laughing, laughing.

Magic stinging her throat, Icca slipped herself into a shadow, and wading through that familiar Dark, spilled out into the area of Petra Woods she'd tucked away in her head the night of the Midwinter Tea. She moved into the Light, pulling her cloak tighter around herself, keeping off the morning-lit path until she reached the back edge of the University campus. Her feet moved onto a deserted brick plaza, the school buildings rising up to thick pine foliage, the air sharp and clean in her lungs. In another life, the paths would be full of witches hurrying to classes, and Icca would be among them, hauling around her books and her parchments. Caro would either be at her side, arm looped around her waist, or else back at their apartment, her lipstick still warm on the underside of Icca's jaw, and Icca wouldn't have noticed it until the end of the day—*but stop that, now.* It was a scenario that Carousel had mused about to her, once, and one that Icca had thus thought about, to herself, now and again, and again.

It was a past dead and done.

They might remember, with vicious clarity, what they'd once been to one another, but it didn't matter if they'd thought that what they felt had been the closest thing to Divinity, more than any other force in the world, more than the magic in their own veins. Because Icca and Caro—and Icca truly thought Caro must think so, too—didn't want to be who they once were: lovesick girls, scared girls.

Icca had seen the truth, in touching the Ledger: they would never leave Wonderland, really. That was the revered madness that it inflicted. It's why Hattie had created the Culled Court—she was obsessed with Wonderland. But the coward would not venture into the Forest, and instead, collected some stranger form of its roots in her Jabberwockies, soaking in their magic, their heightened Divinity.

Because Wonderland grew in their heads the same way it grew outside of them; they, in turn, had grown into stranger beings.

And Icca liked that.

How she moved like a phantom through the Petra streets, blotting herself from one shadow to the next. Glimpsing blood flashing on the cobblestones, there before she was gone again.

Could she make up for all of it, with exposing Hattie for the monstrous being she truly was—could she make up for the way she'd lost her head, the bodies strewn throughout the Petra Ward? Torn apart by the hands of her monsters, by her own hands—

Icca pushed everything else away except the direction she was headed; she relished the shock of her weight against the ground. There was no stopping now.

She couldn't bring back those she'd killed.

She couldn't bring back Tecca.

But above them all, Icca couldn't bring back who she'd once been, the cruel and callous and oblivious orphan of her Ward. That girl hadn't survived Wonderland; she would have never been able to survive Wonderland. To pretend to have her morals now would be to waste her death, a strange, moving death that had taken her into its cold, blank grip and simply turned her inside out, wrung out the innocence of the child and the remaining ignorance of the nature of the world.

Power was the only thing that mattered, and so forward was the only direction she could go.

Hood over her ears, Icca stole into the massive, cool shadow sloughing from the rise of the Labyrinth Wall in the cast of the rising sun. Here she did not fall into the Darkness, making the trip in the blink of an eye; she walked luxuriously alongside the trolley tracks. On her either side, the Wall stretched under a clouded sky, dusted by the tips of the pines rising from within the Labyrinth. The path curved gradually so she could not see the Forest that awaited outside the perimeter, but she felt Wonderland in the breeze that came licking in, smelling like dew and undergrowth.

She breathed out. She breathed in the Dark.

The Church Off the Labyrinth rose before her in unassuming stone, bordered by the lengthening Light tipping off the edge of the Wall, the area quiet and empty. Yet one of the half-moon doors of the front entrance was cracked open, and Icca could just hear someone's voice, hissing and low enough that it sounded like a far-off creek.

Icca did not know what she had come to face, whether it was a Queen, or a Saint, or something worse. But if there was a monster to be found within, she was either going to feed it, be it, or kill it. Perhaps in that order.

Or she was going to die. And either way this whole mess would be over and done with.

Icca slipped between the crack of the door, where the air inside was cool and brushed with the scent of cold stone. There were no Courts to be found inside, either; for a creeping moment, Icca had pictured all of them sitting dead-quiet in the rows of rosewood pews under the modest height of the ceiling with its simple patchwork of rafters, all turning to look at her deadpan as she moved up the aisle. The only Light filtering in from the stained-glass windows was weak enough that the rays lost all color as they streaked against the gray walls. Icca could feel the magic in the air, like the thrum of a plucked string in her chest that carried without sound, hovered, unfading, through her veins.

On the dais where Icca had lain limp years ago, the Red Queen was kneeling.

Her curved spine faced Icca, her brow against the ground. Her palms lay flat beside her temples; she wore a hanbok that was black except for the trim of the sleeves, which were red. She was wearing that bullshit High Priestess veil. Hattie's form still looked like her—it might take a few weeks for a physical change to kick in, if the stories were true—but Icca knew she'd done something that stuck when she'd written the name upon the Ledger. Because the Queen was murmuring aloud to herself.

Icca did not listen to Hattie's rasping; she didn't care. She stopped before the dais and spoke, magic beading at the corners of her mouth and beginning to fleck her lashes. "I knew you weren't who you pretended you were."

The murmuring stopped.

The Queen pressed herself upright, slowly, slowly. Veil dropping from her head. Her full brown hair shimmered down to the small of her back.

"I have only ever been exactly what I am," Hattie spoke, her voice soft, but Icca heard the smile in it. And then the Queen turned her head, and looked at Icca over her shoulder. And Icca took a step back. "Until this. Until you did this."

Icca would have run. She would have run from that horrible, beautiful, dripping face with its black-flooded eyes, if she wasn't so absolutely sure that the Red Queen was going to catch her.

"Why?" Hattie whispered, her expression was blank and watching. "Why did you do this?"

It came so quickly. Icca was so terrified, she felt as if her age was unraveling within her; she hadn't grown up at all. She was still scared. She still had absolutely no idea what she was doing.

And then: anger.

Anger like an antidote, anger like the ground shot beneath her feet. Hattie didn't get to keep reaping the benefits of her bloodline when it had only brought Icca pain, when it would bring the world so much *pain* for decades to come. Hattie was pissed; Icca had cracked her like that, split open that shell-like calm water and found exactly what she knew had been hiding all along. The Red Queen was a monster.

And Iccadora Alice Sickle was a very good hunter.

And she began to laugh.

Why *was* she doing any of this? She had been perfectly fine. Perfectly content in her life—and then she'd seen Carousel, and remembered. Remembered she shouldn't be content, shouldn't be stable. She wanted revenge, or else she wanted closure, or else she just wanted to be fucking *loud*, and she wanted Hattie destroyed and Caro—gone, all of it gone, because this world was shot and someone should come along and remind everyone who wanted to cover their eyes and ears to the horrors of it, don't you see that we can't do anything that matters at all, don't you see none of us can be in love, here, you'd run away in Wonderland, too. . . .

"Because, because!" Icca threw her arms wide; here she was, grand and terrible, the senseless villain, everything and exactly what she wanted to be, with nothing to be scared of any longer. She was the thing in the Dark, and she deserved nothing but ruin, so why not *love it?* "I dreamed of destroying you ever since I was a little girl!"

And she stepped sideways into the shadows, and came out of the Red Queen's silhouette, pressed faintly on the dais beside her.

Icca snapped her boot to Hattie's shoulder and *hated* how limply the Queen dropped to the earth, how easily Icca was able to press her hands around her slick black throat. The Queen was twitching underneath Icca, and Icca's mind was reeling, too scattered with her terror and her fury and her confusion that she did not even think to reach for the last petal—why in hell wasn't Hattie doing anything else? And where in hell was C—

Icca felt something Dark move above her, in the rafters, and it was massive.

She glanced; the moment she broke her concentration, Hattie, with a startling burst of strength, shoved her away. Icca was airborne before clattering against the dais, rolling to a stop on her spine with her breath snapping against the back of her throat, and then, felt it leave her all at once.

Carousel landed.

One boot planted on either side of Icca's cloak, pinning her down, Caro leaned over with a glinting grin, and said, her voice strange, the murmur of gravel underfoot, "Oh, Alice. Why so pale? I used to make you blush when I learned a new trick."

Carousel was grinning. Carousel had wings so massive they blotted out the stomach of the church, and instead of feathers there were crows, and they were blinking, and moving, and shrieking, and Icca knew who had sewn them together into that horrible moving tapestry and who had sewn them to Carousel's back.

Hattie was murmuring, "Yes, I suppose I didn't need you after all. Oh, I made her so beautiful. . . ."

FIFTY-EIGHT

YEAR ZERO ZERO NINETY-FOUR, WINTER SEASON

THERE ARE 973 REMAINING SAINTS

CAROUSEL HAD UNDERSTOOD, after a moment, Hattie's hands on her neck, that the Red Queen was digging for something. Unearthing in Caro's soul the drop of Divinity like a seed, Hattie breathed her greater power into it, sent it cracking apart with new life.

And Caro had never felt so like herself before.

She called down the crows, and they had come screaming out of the night and into the bedchamber, and Hattie had been... glorious with them, drawing the little beasts together, drawing them to Caro's form. Caro had hundreds of eyes now; she felt a hundred times more herself, now.

Hattie could feel she felt a hundred times more, now.

Apologies, readers—did you think you were in Carousel's head?

You could be, a smidge over; it was quite close to Hattie's own. Hattie could feel, still quite still against the dais, bruises blooming on her neck. Hattie did not feel like herself at all.

She felt so angry.

Hattie November the First had rarely ever been mad; Delcorta herself had grown into a woman of even temper, knowing the control it lent her, in turn, over her own magic. It was one of the first things Hattie had found about herself, when she came to be on the floor of the tower study, folded in Delcorta's arms—her calm.

But now, Hattie couldn't help it, her frustration that Icca had inked her name in the Ledger—she knew what had happened as soon as she awoke with her magic boiling out of her. She knew that she had been transformed, but into something never seen before, not quite Saint and not quite human, a stranger consequence. Because her existence was of a stranger consequence.

It had taken weeks for the change to settle in the other Saints, the influx of Divinity, but Hattie felt she had become something else all at once. There had never been another witch quite like her, not even Delcorta's first daughter—no, Hattie had cultivated an aptitude that was all her own; she had a connection to her magic that little Hattie would have never grown to forge. Hattie was better at her Divinity; it hadn't needed time to stretch when her name was written upon the Ledger. It was already a tilled field in her soul.

Or maybe it was early on in the transition. Perhaps she would wake up tomorrow, her body changed and her mind gone.

But for now.

Now, she got to try something new.

Rolling her temple on the stone of the dais, she looked up at Carousel—glorious Carousel Rabbit—arched in her teeming mass over the dark witch. She thought about the insignificant life Iccadora had led, until her own arrogance had built up enough to burst forth, to begin this whole mess, with such sloppy fucking planning, with all the Saints she'd let run circles around her head. A child practicing such excess that it seemed frantic, and it made Hattie pity, and it made Hattie despise the desperation of it. And Hattie wouldn't have, before.

But Iccadora was just being in her nature, the one Wonderland had pressed into her like a stone in sand.

And Hattie, too, now, was just being herself.

The self that Iccadora had tried to rip out, and failed, and made into something quite terrible, quite horrifying indeed.

"The trial is concluded," Hattie said, fingertips curling lightly on the dais.

Iccadora let out a little shriek of laughter. "The fuck it is!"

The weak light streaming into the windows shuddered and scattered. The darkness collapsed, and Hattie would have been blind if Hattie only used her eyes to see, and if Carousel's features weren't smeared and dripping with the electric blue of her magic. So Hattie did see, when Carousel's wings rose with terrifying poise, and when she spoke, Hattie wasn't sure if it was Carousel's lips that moved or if it was just Carousel's voice in her head.

"Off with her head, unnie?" The words had none of Carousel's usual delight, that excited gleam of her personality. They were murmured in the tone of a sleep-walker. Hattie had tucked Carousel's power within her own, to make it stronger, to make it more Divine, and so it was so, and so it was suffocating Carousel until she would soon be nothing but magic, be no one at all.

So the Red Queen was doing what she'd always done—she was making Saints.

And she liked this way of doing it a whole lot more. She wouldn't even have to ruin her hanbok.

"Yes, Carousel," Hattie whispered into the black. "Off with her head."

—

And Icca heard this. Icca was going to make Hattie pay for it.

So in that glorious Dark she'd summoned over them all, she arched her back against the dais, and, as Caro went to tear out her throat with clawed fingertips, she made the shadows swallow them down.

Icca had never brought this much with her, down into the black place, into what might truly be the stomach of her god. But she felt herself succeed, felt Caro and Hattie and half the church being pulled alongside her, clattering out of sight into the strange, blank space, and the pain that cracked through her veins was a bright and alive thing.

Icca coughed, felt both the sting of magic on her lips and the lash of blood on her tongue, but Caro was no longer pinning her down, so she reached out into the Darkness to look. She could only see what she touched, what she crawled against, a fragmented chunk of the dais beneath her feet and void past its jagged edge, but far above, she heard the flap of wings.

I could just leave them here, Icca thought, her voice in her head frayed with a dry, pealing giggle, blood singing with the gravity of the decision. Icca thought as she listened, as her ache grew inside her, magic corroding her with every second she spent in this place. But there wasn't a day that went by where she didn't have that pain, inviting it in so often that her body was home to it. She knew what halls it liked to walk, what parts of the wallpaper it liked to peel away, strip by agonizing strip; knew what parts of herself to brace for it. *Iccadora Alice Sickle, host of agonies, eater of churches. I could just slip away and leave them to starve. . . .*

She wouldn't. She wouldn't taint this place like that—she wouldn't let this end so easily, not even for herself. This was going to be grand.

"Can you find me, here?" Icca called, her voice sounding hollow in the near emptiness. "You don't want to find me here. . . ."

Icca made it to the edge of the dais, and it seemed to vanish as soon as she took her weight off of it. Nearing the sound of faint, fluttering breath.

She reached out and touched skin, and then the Red Queen was before her, one of her slippers lost, a delicate ankle under Icca's fingertips. Features reduced to nothing under the black mess of her own magic.

Here, in this painful, not-quite place, Icca could outline Hattie with a clarity that she doubted the Queen thought would ever be attempted against her. Icca could feel the Dark in Hattie's lungs, in Hattie's veins, pressed in the lines where her organs met. The Dark buried under the roots of her molars, worked into the folds of her brain.

This was Icca's realm, and it would be Hattie November Kkul's grave.

And yet, when Hattie's lips parted to speak, "Oh, what miraculous place is this?" there was godsdamn *awe*.

Icca growled and pulled at the patchwork of Hattie's Darkness, and here was her power, making that simple element move as she liked, sink and twist and burn like it was a physical thing. Hattie spasmed beneath her and *damn it*—why was she still not fighting? Why was she—

Icca detached from Hattie and threw herself to the side, and for that one moment where a wing scraped her hip, she could see Caro in full, down to the dirt flecks on her boots and the talons of her crows. She could see that Carousel was hardly there at all. Hattie had known where Icca was, and so Caro had known, too, but Icca knew that didn't mean they were sharing a head. It meant that Caro didn't have hers at all.

It meant Caro was gone.

And Icca had won.

So, here, here was the glorious new world.

Icca flinched. Quietly startled, she put her hand to her chest, thinking that some massive, sharp thing had cleaved her through. Her palm came away without Carnage.

And then Icca, now knowing, knowing, tried to get to her feet, to outrun the priming tightness of her throat.

She collapsed under the rake of her sob. The Darkness shuddered in rasping tandem.

"I won't fight you, Iccadora," Hattie spoke, her voice thin and sounding as if it were unspooling from a far distance, though Icca knew her to be only feet away. "I won't take that away from her."

"You've already taken *her* away from her," spat Icca, but it wasn't vicious enough. She curled her fingertips into the ground and *shrieked*, "You've already taken her away!"

"She likes it," Hattie responded, as Carousel laughed somewhere in the black, the sound a dry rattle, void of emotion like it was nothing but a physical reaction, the rustle of crows against the ground as she searched for Icca.

And Icca had been scared, before, of dying. It was a fear that came in waves.

But when she thought of killing Caro, she also had thought, perhaps inevitably, of Caro killing her.

And of that, Icca had never been afraid.

In her daydreams, in the sickly little fantasies she played with like candies stuck to the roof of her mouth, Icca had always been snarling, or grinning, or laughing when she died, when Caro finally caught her. Never scared—she'd never give the crow witch that satisfaction, but besides that, Icca knew that as terrifying as Carousel Rabbit seemed, she was actually just ridiculous, and eccentric, and that she could be scared, too.

Icca had seen her scared; she'd seen tears on Caro's cheeks and heard her screams ricochet off the walls of the Moore home, and Icca had been sure it must be the worst sound in the world, cracking from her throat, and it had matched the terror in Icca's own chest so profoundly perfectly. . . .

And then, and then, they had lived.

Now Icca realized, trying to pull her ribs up from the ground just to have her magic pinch her back into place, that whenever she'd thought about death, and how she'd wanted to die—if she could choose—she'd fight to choose—Carousel had always been there. Whether Caro was next to her, both of them ancient and weathered, her arms looped around Icca's waist with the pale skin long softened, those poet's words in her ears the last thing Icca heard before it all drifted away; whether it was Carousel cutting her throat.

Icca still wanted that. Still wanted Carousel there for it, for her end.

She didn't know what that meant. Didn't know what it meant when she wanted everything from Caro, to love her and hate her and kill her all the same. She just knew that Hattie had made it so Caro wasn't here at all.

So by the time Caro—Caro's body, Hattie's puppet—caught her, Icca was ready. Icca was so angry that she had magic bleeding out of everywhere it could; she could barely see it past its flood in her eyes, feel past the sting in her cuticles. Caro had a hand around her ankle and Icca was being pulled under the twitching, shrieking canopy of her wings, the black bodies of the birds teeming under the glow of Caro's power. Icca sloughed them all off, pressing on each teeny set of lungs to send the Darkness flourishing, corroding, and Caro's teeth flashed blue in her own pain as crows came unraveled, raining down around them both as Caro curled a taloned hand around Icca's shoulders, pinning her.

"There was so much grief in her," came Hattie's voice, out of Caro's mouth. Icca could see nothing of her eyes past the magic in them. "I took that away. I could take it away from you, too, Iccadora. I feel it. I feel the cord, again, stringing you together. I know what it is now. I thought it hatred, but it was Mourning. Such a parasitic god, holding so fast and tight. Kinder people wouldn't have survived its bind. How much you must have sensed it in her, and her in you. How scared you must have been, in Wonderland, should either end snap. You only have to ask for me to take it away. You won't have to grieve, snip the cord, and face any of it. It'll be just as Carousel said. That it doesn't matter at all in the present, to have loved someone in the past."

Icca could drop away at any point; she'd roll out into the real world bruised and alive and no one would ever see her again. She could fight harder, kill this near blank shell of Caro's, a flowering Saint. But that hadn't been the purpose of any of this.

"Caro—" she gasped, clawing, "Carousel—"

Icca had wanted damage; to end a bloodline for how they had ended the world, for how they told Tecca she'd be safe in her home. But now a witch who was not quite Carousel Rabbit anymore was going to kill her, and Icca knew the truth. She wouldn't have given a damn about Hattie if she hadn't found out Carousel served at her side. Not enough to come here. Not enough to have come this far. It was not jealousy; it had been closer to a want for revenge.

And, even closer—a want for closeness.

Any single excuse to be back in Carousel's proximity without having to say that was exactly what Icca wanted.

Good deities. Icca's vision flushed slightly—she was crying. *That's just fucking ridiculous.*

After everything she'd done—she didn't deserve Carousel.

But neither did Hattie. Not like this.

"You know nothing about my deities," Icca screamed, at Caro, at Hattie, screamed so loudly she was barely even a person under it, just a bright, raw smear of hurt and guilt and anger. *"You know nothing about Wonderland!"*

As Caro's hands moved to crush down her throat, Icca's magic surged, and she tasted first its sting and then her own blood, before she took her last breath and, over them all, sent the Dark to its knees.

—

Above, past Carousel's head: tall, watching trees.

Icca's feet kicked undergrowth; her vision was blurring with the press of the cold hands around her throat. A breeze caressed her purpling face; she thought to the Forest, *Oh, I know, I* know, *you're liking this. . . .*

Indeed, readers, Icca didn't know exactly where in Wonderland she'd brought them, tucking that black realm into her own form and sending them all tumbling out with such force that Caro was currently killing her between the two stone slabs of fractured dais. But Wonderland was attentive everywhere, really, a curious force. Curious about that which resides in the most private depths of a person, their most volatile and most wicked potential, the sprawl of their daydreams, how distinctly and exactly they loved, and hated. How vivid the little humans were, in defiance of a collective fate Wonderland itself would never know. . . . Yes, yes it did like watching Iccadora Alice Sickle die at the hands of her former lover, just as it had liked watching her live, twining those hands with her own.

"I never thought you would w—in," Icca said, Icca lied, as Carousel, blank-eyed, crushed the fiction down. "N—not for a mo—ment, Rabbit. . . ."

They were nearly cheek to cheek, and Icca's eyes burned with the luminescence of the crow witch's magic. At least she'd die here, where she'd died before, certainly. It felt right. Icca would have done something right.

Carousel's talons slipped under her skin. She was going to rip off Icca's head, just as commanded. It was all going to be all right. It was all going to work out in the end, at her end.

The world went Dark, truly, truly Dark.

And then there was no longer a hand around Icca's throat.

Icca gasped in a breath, rolled to her side over shrapnel from the broken dais, stones working into her ribs. She gagged around her bruises. Her hands rose, searching for the puncture holes in the sides of her throat. She found them shallow.

Stunned, Icca glanced back up, where Caro was on her hands and knees above her, her hair a blond tangle that cloaked her eyes.

Caro was breathing hard—with her spine arched, Icca could see that her back was bloody but clear, crows littered all around them.

A dozen paces away, Hattie November Kkul was still, and standing.

Her hands were cradled to her chest, all of it soaked in black. Where her hair wasn't sticking to her magic it fell down the length of her spine; her head was tilted back. Icca couldn't help but stare at those wide, wide eyes, dripping black, dripping tears. Had she ever seen Hattie look so . . . *there*, before?

It made her seem so young, and small, the Forest arched around her, her gaze fixed to the foliage, where a higher breeze was lashing through. The leaves danced and chattered, washed the Light against the ground, and Icca gritted her teeth, preparing to haul herself over the edge of the dais, to . . .

And then Hattie breathed in.

Icca's vision churned.

It wasn't possible.

Wonderland was—folding in around Hattie, toward Hattie. As she inhaled, the lines of trunks reached for her just as shadows did for Icca, and the sky, certainly, was leaning down. The wind picked up, and the Forest sounds rose and smeared, like they were standing before a gaping maw that was also breathing in, taking in, taking apart the world, and it was all Icca could do to not throw her hands over her ears, but she knew that wouldn't keep this out, wouldn't keep out the raw nerve of Divinity and insanity that was the mixture of Hattie in Wonderland. Birds shrieked, and Icca, instinctively, looked at Carousel, and was startled to find that Caro—who must be *truly* Caro—was also looking about wildly, one hand braced on the dais as if to hold on. . . .

Then Hattie exhaled, and Icca blinked, and everything was righted again. Icca was looking at what should be there: a young woman standing quietly in the Forest. All, suddenly, was quite quiet.

Hattie's head tilted slowly to the side as she peered toward them both.

"Well," Hattie said finally, drawing her fingertips under her eyes. Icca could see her whites had cleared slightly. "I guess I was right, after all, Carousel."

The crow witch tucked her hair behind her ears and sat back on her heels. She rolled her eyes; she gave a little laugh that was half-disgusted, half-disbelieving, and all her own.

"All right, all right, unnie," Carousel murmured. "But look. Alice couldn't kill me, either."

FIFTY-NINE

YEAR ZERO ZERO NINETY-FOUR, WINTER SEASON

THERE ARE 973 REMAINING SAINTS

NAILS JUST BEGINNING TO fill with Icca's blood, Carousel had remembered herself.

She felt herself unwind from Hattie's head; she felt Hattie let her go without opposition.

It's just I don't need her help, Caro had thought to herself, when she could think to herself again. *It's just that I want to be me in full when I take your head, Alice.*

But then Caro was fully returned to her own head, above her Divinity and instead of where Hattie had placed her, pressed down under the swell of it. And she still was not killing Icca. And she had taken her weight away from Icca's throat.

Then it was light again. Caro, on hands and knees, hair in her eyes, closed them tight, a little sick with her regained individualism, and confused and disgusted with her hesitation.

"Well," came Hattie's voice, soft behind her.

Hattie, who had become something worse, who had—of *course*—retained herself through it. At least, at least, for now.

Hattie had barely lifted a finger to kill Icca, because she knew, like Carousel now knew, that if Hattie truly wished to kill anyone, she wouldn't have to lift a finger at all.

"I guess I was right, after all, Carousel."

You love her.

Icca was turning her head back now and meeting her eyes.

Carousel got off her hands, sat back on her heels as she brought the hair away from her face. She laughed; it was not a kind sound. But that was cruelty to herself, *judgement* of herself—*stop it*—she would not do that.

I'm sorry. I didn't mean it, darling, Caro told herself, face lifted in the soft light coming down from the trees. Her own voice was always so much clearer, in Wonderland. *Did I mean it, darling?*

This she was asking Icca; this, she would not ask aloud.

Had Caro meant her threats, meant all the hatred she'd cradled in her head, waiting for Icca to show up again?

Yes. She'd meant all of it.

She'd liked all of it, the violent fantasies, drawn out in her thoughts, beginning, middle, and end—well.

Well, dear readers, they'd reached the end, nearly. They'd both paused, before the close, the final blow, before the pages ran out.

And Carousel knew what it was, that pause. The difference between their hatred for one another and their love for one another. Disparate lifespans. Or, perhaps, simply shallower roots.

"All right, all right, unnie," Carousel murmured. "But look. Alice couldn't kill me, either."

Beginning, middle . . . they were both so young.

"Are you alive?" Icca rasped. "Are you in your own head now? Because then I could. Then I will."

"I'm alive," Carousel said. "So. Proceed, Alice."

And Caro made herself still, for once in her life.

But Icca only gave her a scowl that shone beneath the silver slicking her features. She turned this scowl to Hattie and spat, "I know your purpose, with the Culled Court. You've been attempting to bring the Forest to you."

"Perhaps," responded Hattie contemplatively, unruffled by both tone and accusation. "I thought... I could be sated like that. With my Court and my Labyrinth and the Saints' Races." She slid her calm eyes over to Caro, which somehow still held the same effect as a static shock. "But, now..."

Hattie's hands clutched tighter to her chest. There was so much in that gesture, holding herself so, trying to retain that Wonderland sensation that was so vast and uncontrollable and unnamable that it seemed prone to flee from her; of course she did not want to let it go. Caro knew this because she'd felt the same, here, at once so herself and so endless that at any moment she might spill over her edges and splatter the Forest quite gruesomely; she wasn't particularly sure if she'd mind, either.

"Oh, just go run free already, you lunatic," said Caro, not without affection. "Make yourself happy—go and converse with the trees...."

Her words trailed off into several beats of silence.

Black trickled down from the Red Queen's nose. Dripped off of her chin, onto the Wonderland floor, a silent metronome as she beheld the two witches.

"There is so much to do," Hattie said at last, quietly, reverently. "Iccadora has made it so I can hear Wonderland just fine, now, and it's telling me... everything... yes. I understand in full. I was right. I'll never truly leave this place." And Hattie smiled. There were *teeth* in that smile—black as they were—but had there ever been teeth in Hattie's smile? "Wherever I am."

Caro glanced at Icca the same moment Icca glanced at her.

She knew they both felt it. That being next to Hattie felt the same as standing at the edge of the Forest that very first day, peering in. The wind at their backs, nudging their spines. Within: the promise of absolute beauty, the promise of astonishing horror...

When Hattie breathed in, did Icca and Caro lean for her without realizing it?

"Oh, well, fuck this, then," Icca half laughed, half scoffed, and then she was gone from beneath Caro's hovering, vanished right into her shadow.

Caro massaged her temples as she rose to her feet.

"I'm sorry, unnie," she said, turning toward the Red Queen, knelt quietly on her piece of dais. "I thought—I mean, I *really* thought—"

"I've known love like this, before," said Hattie quietly. "It did not grow so twisted but... I know the caliber. Part of me once knew the caliber. Perhaps. Perhaps past lives... is the best way to put it...."

Carousel knew Hattie had changed—*Icca* had changed Hattie. She was speaking words, but she hardly seemed to intend them for Caro at all; she had done great magic, but standing there, watching Hattie's chin drop down, and down, in beats, nodding to herself, her own thoughts—Caro got the sense that all of this, her terrible wings, luring Icca here, expecting a fight... it wasn't all as dramatic in Hattie's head. Hattie had just wanted to test the waters. She'd just wanted to play.

And so Carousel neared, and kneeled before her Queen.

Hattie November Kkul deserved this, deserved Caro's brow bent to the Wonderland earth, deserved the chill that clutched Caro's spine when she felt those mudwater eyes level upon her. Because Hattie November Kkul could have kept Carousel as long as she liked, kept her body churning Divinity until it ate her down like it did for the Saints—Caro had jumped at the chance to become something worse, because something worse had power.

But she'd hesitated; she'd regretted when she felt herself becoming less and less focused, like falling asleep... she was losing all of it, her bird tattoos and her pretty hair and pretty thoughts, and Hattie had felt that panic; Hattie had let her go free without complaint.

So now Carousel bowed. She knew one must take grace with a more merciful god.

"This was my blunder, unnie," Caro murmured against the stone. "There are still Saints coming in from the Labyrinth, and to you... Alice's damage will linger. I will go after her, if you command it. I'll finish the job this time, I swear it."

She looked up when Hattie began to laugh.

The Red Queen looked so pretty, just like a little doll—save for the slicked black from her eyes down—lithe fingers up to her mouth as she tried to contain it.

"Now, now, Carousel!" Hattie exclaimed, fingers interlaced, now; she pressed them lightly to her lips, pressed into them her words and her smile, the high, quiet silk of her voice. "Are you really attempting to lie to me?"

Had Caro been lying? She truly didn't know. The fear was blocking out her memory, her introspection, and now the Queen had toppled forward, Caro's chin taken into the palms of her hands.

Was this it? Had Caro been wrong—Hattie had only let her go to devour her all over again. Caro was going to blink away from herself, from her place on her knees. She would even like it at first. She'd forget everything, all she liked about herself, her world. She'd forget Wonderland. She'd forget Icca. She'd remember nothing but the rush of the power as it swallowed her down, and then, and then—because she didn't think she could pull herself away from it, a second time—she'd be nothing at all.

"Unnie—" she gasped, but did not know what else to say, was no longer a person who could beg for her life. But Hattie smiled down upon her, and even in her terror, awe fastened itself at the back of Caro's throat.

"Carousel Rabbit, I don't want Iccadora's head!" Hattie was eager; Caro knew that to be a new trait, at least, in what she conveyed aloud. Who could say what truly went on in that strange head? If Caro could imagine it—and she did try, now, for creativity often twined with a desire to understand—perhaps in the Red Queen's mind, there was nothing but a looking-glass . . . what else could survive such a place but Hattie herself? "Not specifically, that is."

"Wonderland's told you something, hasn't it?" Carousel breathed. "What is it, unnie?"

"Oh, oh, my glorious champion. Only how to end the Saints," said Hattie, and slid a fingertip below Caro's chin. And now Caro was meeting her eyes, all done up in black, and behind her head, the golden light through the foliage was a crown. Caro's heart drummed on in her chest—how deliciously terrifying it was, to worship someone. "I want you to bring me more Jabberwockies."

SIXTY

YEAR ZERO ZERO NINETY-FOUR, WINTER SEASON

THERE ARE 961 REMAINING SAINTS

AND THIS MIGHT FEEL familiar, most cherished readers, from this story, from another: night pressing the Light out of the sky, and Alice following Rabbit into Wonderland—mind, a distance away, soaking out of sight, in her shadows, as she watched Carousel pull up her hood.

She had known that Caro would return to the Forest at some point, had kicked around Petra watching, waiting. They always returned to the Forest.

Nestled in Icca's pocket was her last petal. Icca had taken to patting the fabric that enclosed the flower-piece, the vicious little alchemy. It was a better habit than poking at her face—though she might return to that nasty practice, once she fed the petal to something. She knew, almost certainly, that she would.

Icca did not know what she was going to say to Caro. Do, to Caro. There was still disgust, still betrayal. Icca still might kill her.

Or maybe she would just say something. Maybe Caro would say something back.

What then?

A then.

Again.

Icca watched, pressed into the long shadow cast off the Labyrinth Wall, as Carousel stopped before the closest bit of tree line. Briefly, she turned her head over her shoulder and Icca saw the black eyes, lashes flecked in blue, and, feeling someone watching her, the quirk to the painted mouth, an excited query of a fight.

But she didn't see Icca, and so shrugged easily and to herself, and turned back to the Forest with her hands braced on her hips. Her head tilted back, following the pines up to where they serrated the sky, far, far above. Taking it in.

Icca liked Carousel's devoutness, really. Their Religion was so simple, the world hewn from gods, gods hewn from the world—Icca found comfort in it, but really, their existence could happen to be anything else at all. They could be anything at all. A dream of a girl, lying in a flower field. A story in a book—forgive a delighted narrator, readers, who couldn't help themselves...

And still Carousel dropped her chin, in a quiet, reverent bow to Wonderland.

Everything Icca had done—it proved that she was one of the greatest witches of her age. But she'd known that before she'd walked into that stupid Tea Party.

If this were one of her storybooks, she'd been the villain, her defeat marked from the beginning.

She didn't care.

Because Icca was devout, too. She was reveling in her gods. Wasn't she dangerous, wasn't she Dark... she smiled to herself, half-drowned in the ink of her shadows.

I'm not smiling.

You are! I saw it. I didn't know you could, Icky.

I saw it too, Caro. Say something else, something odd. Maybe she'll do it again.

The Red Queen was still on her throne, and she was Icca's own creation, Icca's aftershock. Icca had changed the world—though it certainly wasn't for the better, perhaps, it was something needed. There were quite a lot of Saints left, after all.

Carousel took the first step into the Forest. And then, right before she slipped out of sight, she turned her head again, and smiled. She couldn't find Icca's eyes, but Icca had been mistaken—Caro knew she was near.

Or maybe she was just smiling at Petra, a flirting goodbye to safety, the ridiculous creature.

Either way, Icca scowled. Either way, Icca began to move.

Following Rabbit in, down, down into Wonderland.

EPILOGUE

WHEN HATTIE MISREMEMBERED, and believed her obliteration was near, she would sit down and attempt to write the letter again:

~~Dear Hattie~~ Dear Iccadora,

Hattie is going to go away soon. She requests your curt return to the capital city, as you carry around that dark place where you attempted to end her, and she has never been somewhere Quieter. Hattie hadn't realized how much she could feel everyone else until she was in that dark, other place, nearly completely alone. And now Hattie would like to be left alone there, when you allow her to go, Iccadora Alice Sickle, so she may die in the stomach of her god.

Hattie reminds you this is all your fault, after all, writing her name in the Parish Saint Ledger this now half year ago. She reminds you that you flooded her body with Divinity in an attempt to destroy her, and it failed, and what does she do instead? Hattie makes wonderful things. Hattie feeds Wonderland her monsters, her treasured, beautiful Jabberwockies. Fewer Saints running around, now, and so Hattie still hasn't killed Iccadora. It is requested tha–

But something she couldn't place would always feel off with the letter, and her pen would pause and be abandoned.

Yes.

Yes, she would recall, correctly this time—she was, in fact, *not* being obliterated by the excess of Divinity that now beaded at the seams of her soul. Because Hattie was still right here, wasn't she? Hattie was perfectly fine. She was going to stay right here, perfectly fine. . . .

When the Culled Court flocked to her halls at her invitation, Hattie only asked if they wanted power; they only ever said yes. They came out on the other side of it certainly disparate from the flesh-creatures skittering around in the Wonderland Forest, or the Labyrinth—which had been fortified and was, currently, secure—because of the care Hattie took in her work. She made them so beautiful.

They all stayed close, close in her head, close to her Divinity, while she bent their magic into new shapes, while she sent it tumbling into her bodies.

And so Hattie was eating them all, in a way, when they eventually blinked away.

Then she was left with their shells, the ones she'd changed, like she'd done for Carousel Rabbit. Such pretty shells.

Such a way to end the Saints.

She thought her mother would be proud. She thought little Hattie would be, too.

How delighted they would be for her, that now Hattie needn't gaze longingly outside the window of the tower study, wanting to run her fingertips over the distant peaks of Wonderland. Needn't fear one day her feet would move her within its depths to where she could not return.

What a glorious realization it was, standing on the Forest floor, those whispering syllables had solidified in her head, and Hattie had recognized her own voice.

And now, whenever she found herself misplacing—or else wanting for—the Forest, or desired to pray, there was no longer a need to move to the Labyrinth. Whenever she craved to feel absolutely real, all Hattie had to do was sit in front of her looking-glass.

Or maybe she'd just gone mad.

Whichever.

It all made such glorious sense to her.

Once upon a time, Hattie November Kkul, second of her name, felt completely herself, starting awake in the dead of night, woken by one of the Jabberwockies' bad dreams. She smoothed her hands over her sheets, grounded herself in the feel of the silk, the feel of the Quiet in the dark, which was different from the Quiet in the light.

"I am completely myself," Hattie whispered, and smiled. "And completely everything else."

Black dripped over the curve of her lip and splintered through the lines of her teeth. Now she was laughing, small and shrill, spine arching on the mattress as she tilted back into this feeling, such a wonderful feeling; it was such a celebration all the time, now.

"Hattie November Kkul…" Her words giddy and stinging, sung all to herself. "The High Priestess of Isanghan. The Red Queen. Queen of the Saints."

THE END

ACKNOWLEDGMENTS

I have so many people in my life I would like to thank for their unwavering support—so many wonderful souls always encouraging me to be my deepest creative self, who, in exchange, I have attempted to creep out a little. For fun!

To Kiva and Mira, my Hex Girls, my solid ground no matter how far apart we are. I adore you both so very much. The friendships are very toxic in the story, but if I took inspiration from ours, you know they would be all lovey-dovey gooey.

To Dad and to Mom. Someday I'll write books that have parents who are alive. But not yet.

To Titan, who I hope I especially managed to freak out.

To the DACU lovelies: Tashie, Rocky, Chloe, and Christina.

To Roundtable: Nicki, Daniel, Eric, Molly, and Spencer. I am so grateful for our little literary community, our friendship, and, of course, your writing. Your bizarre, gorgeous writing.

To Laura, my wonderful agent, who saw my potential even when I initially came to her with a half-finished draft. Thank you for always encouraging me to write as gruesomely as I like.

To Rebecca, my editor extraordinaire, for bringing out the best in this story, and to the incredible team at Hyperion.

To Zareen Johnson for making this book absolutely gorgeous inside and out, and to Tran Nguyen for the incredibly unnerving cover art.

And to the readers who read my debut and stuck around for this one, too. Thank you so, so much.